runt

Enjoy

KERRY CASEY

ISBN-13: 978-0-9769765-5-4

Library of Congress Catalog Number: 2019902184

Printed in the United States of America

First Printing: March 2019

24 23 22 21 20   6 5 4 3 2

Published by:
five friends books™

fivefriendsbooks.com

The best books come from friends. That's why Five Friends Books™ puts the destiny of a book in the hands of readers. Please pass along your bookmarks to five book-loving friends. How far this novel spreads depends on you. Find out more by visiting **fivefriendsbooks.com**.

five friends books™

ALSO BY KERRY CASEY

The *Fall to Grace* trilogy:

Fall to Grace
Singer
Slender Wish

For those who silence the naysayers with their actions.

A mighty wind rocked the tree, but it came back into balance.

Dannaka
12U AAA All-Stars

Coach: Leo Hamill
Assistant Coach: Tom Tink

1) No. 1 Runt .2B
2) No. 8 Rabbit . . . . .LF
3) No. 3 Havoc 3B
4) No. 13 Rip . . . . CF
5) No. 4 Money. . . . . .SS
6) No. 11 Pot Roast. C
7) No. 12 Math 1B
8) No. 2 Seeds . . . . RF
9) No. 6 Walter . . . . .P
10) No. 15 Q-tip. . . . . .P
11) No. 5 Gramps 2B
12) No. 14 Bale. . . . . (IR)

Book

ONE

Arriving, Saturday, March 25, 1990

"If baseball was fair there wouldn't be foul lines."
—*Tom Tink, Dannaka assistant coach*

LEO

The rain was impossibly light. So much so it was imperceptible to the eye. No breeze stirred as dampness surrounded Leo. Similarly, his life hung suspended—an anxious mist—ready to transform meaningfully, or vanish into nothing.

Leo favored vanishing. He yanked down the bill of his cap and looked at his one-story ranch-style house, a place he once loved but had come to hate. The SOLD sign stood crooked in the matted front yard.

Leo was 29 years old—today, as a matter of fact. A birthday alone. He scratched his ungroomed beard. Everywhere, reminders of how far he'd slid.

Leo's fiancée had moved out months ago. His friends were done stopping by, only to wear out the unanswered doorbell. When his parents called, Leo said now wasn't a good time. Maybe they could visit next month. We'll see.

Distant church bells rang 10 times, telling the neighborhood it was 10 a.m. The rain started to pick up. The sky was like a soggy wool sock. The temperature wouldn't make 40 degrees.

Shitty day for baseball, Leo thought. *It will be BP and grounders in the gym.*

But not with him. Leo was minutes away from putting his truck in drive. He wasn't coming back.

When his house sold he hired an auction company to liquidate the furniture. What was left, he organized into a garage sale, which attracted more curiosity seekers than bargain hunters. It was amazing—actually it was pathetic—how people clamored for the old baseball trophies, game balls and scorebooks from his championship seasons. Two men wrestled for the framed jersey Leo wore during his one-week call-up with the Cubs. Vultures, all of them.

He had put aside a few items, which now he loaded into his pickup. Because of the rain, he stowed them in the cab's small back seat. A Rawlings five-gallon plastic bucket of baseballs. His infield glove. His fungo bat. There were three cardboard boxes. Two packed with clothes, towels and bedding. The other held his baseball card collection, a pillow, a Cubs jacket and a bathroom scale. The scale came along for sport. Leo enjoyed beating himself up over the 35 pounds he'd gained in the last eight months.

To say there was room to spare inside the truck was an understatement. The item that mattered most was on the floor, leaning against the back seat, wrapped in a Chicago Bears stadium blanket: Leo's framed poster of last season's varsity baseball team. His boys. His team. The team he coached to a record fourth consecutive state AA baseball title. No other high school in the nation had accomplished this feat. Leo's team won it all in 1986, 1987, 1988 and last season in 1989.

But that extraordinary achievement was not why the '89 team poster went with him.

A windbreaker kept Leo dry. Red with blue piping, his pullover had the words Coach Leo stitched above the Naperville Redskins team logo featuring a profile of an Indian chief in full headdress. The school board was currently split on the inappropriateness of the Redskins name and logo; there was no such division on whether Leo should remain on staff as a social studies teacher and head baseball coach. They voted unanimously not to renew his contract.

Leo dropped his head as he turned away from the simple three-bedroom house. A modest fiberglass awning hung over the front door. Cute green shutters framed the bay window. Three overgrown arborvitaes rose up along the pitched walkway leading to the garage around back.

He closed his eyes and pictured the backyard: a green space large enough to encourage dreams of playing endless wiffle ball games with his boisterous children. He had imagined a family so large it would leave their little home bursting at the joists. They'd have no choice but to add on. The remodel, though, would bump up, not out, keeping the spacious backyard intact.

None of this was to be.

Just off the front sidewalk, a dented silver trash can sat curbside, ready for the garbage truck. Leo walked to it, his long-legged gait encumbered by pounds his frame was unfamiliar with. The can was overstuffed, lid ajar, propped up by takeout pizza boxes and an empty two-liter bottle of Coke. He dropped the lid onto the dormant boulevard grass and looked at the remnants of his life crammed into that cylinder. Leo slipped off his baseball pullover and tossed it atop the heap. Rain nipped his bare arms. He had intended to turn and walk away from the can, but found himself instead repeatedly pounding the lid down on the overflowing contents. Slamming. Violent. Useless. The neighbors' dogs got to barking. From across the street someone separated the drapes only enough to peek through.

On the tree-lined street, Leo stood in the light rain, unmoored.

JESS

ess's new outdoor thermometer hung on a screw in the porch
post. The face was the size of a hubcap, fully visible from her
front door.

On principle, Jess refused to pay full retail. But she broke down
and made the purchase last week at the local Feed & Seed. She was
done squinting at the sun-bleached thermometer that had been
suction cupped to the exterior of the kitchen window since she was
a little girl. It astonished her how far she had strayed since then. Yet
here she was, in the farmhouse where she began.

Yawning, Jess went barefoot down the hardwood hallway. The
front entry had a sidelight window adjacent to the door. She glanced
out, blinking, still foggy with sleep. *Could it be?* She rechecked the
new thermometer. There was no mistaking the oversized numbers
on its face. Sixty-seven degrees! Two days ago it was spitting snow.
A smile appeared, starting at the right corner of Jess's mouth, reluctantly at first, before becoming a half smile that was cautiously
charming.

Saturday was sleep-in day, the only such day in the week for Jess
and her 12-year-old son. But today was an extra special Saturday.
It was her birthday. Twenty-nine. The final year of her twenties—a
decade she wanted to forgive and forget.

Outside, the novelty of the warm air was an elixir. Just as she was
sinking into it, a red Firebird roared past on the blacktop road in
front of her farmhouse. The intrusion was ironic. Jess remembered
the empty quiet of that road when it was gravel. As a teenager she
complained endlessly about living on the boring, dusty edge of civi-
lization. So far from town. So far from school. So far from friends.
What drama.

Now she missed those hushed days when there wasn't a neighbor within earshot, unless the wind was blowing in the right direction. Then, she could hear the screen door slapping shut a half mile away at the Smoak place. She'd hear Mrs. Smoak and her youngest learning a duet at the piano, and the thwump of a baseball smacking leather as the Smoak brothers played catch. And at twilight, while Jess was sneaking a cigarette behind the barn, she'd hear Mr. Smoak whistling the cows into the hay corral, saying, "Come now, beauties. Bedtime for you."

That quiet was forever gone. A development company bought up the Smoak farmstead and the neighboring place. Now cookie-cutter houses stood where once there were row crops. She never dreamed the day would come when a development in a place she called Dinkyville would make her nostalgic.

Jess sat at her regular place on the porch stoop: second step from the ground. She called this her listening step because she would talk and the step would never interrupt.

"Good morning, step. What a morning it is." Jess pressed her palm on the sun-warmed wood next to her. "I forbid a single gloomy thought. We have a bright sunny day and nowhere to be until I decide there's somewhere to be. And—" Just then Jess's mind flashed on a week's worth of dirty clothes heaped in two piles on the basement floor. "Crap. Laundry." She shrugged. "At least today we can dry on the clothesline. It's been a long winter."

As a teen, Jess cringed at the sight of a full clothesline. Like most things around her home, it embarrassed her. To have clothes hung out to dry announced to the world: We're hicks. We're poor. Or worse: My dad's clothes reek so bad they have to be washed twice and air-dried. That part happened to be true.

Jess's father owned a septic pumping business. He didn't duck from that fact. In his opinion the only thing worse than doing his job was doing it unsuccessfully. His motto: Plug your nose and go like hell.

He wasn't always in the septic business; chance was the instigator. Jess's father farmed for years before the uncertainty of the occupation blanched all joy from the man. He decided to rent his fields and went to work for an excavating company installing wells and holding tanks on area farms. It was a grunt job overseen by a family who got rich while those who worked for them got reminded how lucky they were to be employed. But it was a steady paycheck unbeholden to the whims of Mother Nature.

One day Jess's dad ended up on a farm with an old-timer who was there to pump the farmhouse septic tank. There had been heavy rains and the rear end of the old-timer's pumper was bogged down in the mud. Jess's father offered to pull him out with his backhoe.

Afterward the old-timer got to talking. He wasn't normally inclined to chitchat but he was comfortable in the company of Jess's dad so he asked him if he liked the excavating work he did. Jess's father said he most certainly did not. Said the work was backbreaking and the pay was lacking.

The old-timer offered a piece of advice. He said there's only one thing worse than a lousy job. That's a lousy job with lousy pay. Then he went into a pocket of his overalls for a roll of bills and stripped off two twenties, for the tow service. Jess's dad wouldn't have it. There are some things a person does where money has no place.

Slowly hauling himself up into the cab of his pumper truck, the old-timer fired up the diesel engine and raised his voice so he wouldn't have to repeat himself. I don't know why I'm telling you this, he said, but I'm looking at turning 75. I got aches and pains older than you and I can't keep running this truck much longer. If you ever decide you want a lousy job that pays well, look me up.

A month later, Jess's dad was driving that very truck while the old-timer handled the business end of things. After six months he officially turned over the keys to his truck, and his book of business. The old-timer had no family. He'd made more money than he could ever spend in the years he had left. He was worn ragged. I'm going home, he told Jess's dad. I'm going to open a beer, start a fire in the barrel and burn every stitch of clothes I own. I'll buy me some new duds, take berth on a cruise ship and swim in the salt water till I smell sweet as a powdered baby.

Jess stood up, stretched her back and touched her bare toes. "Time to get moving," she said to the step. "Summer's just around the corner, when days won't want to end and I'll be hitting grounders till dark."

Two cobalt blue streaks raced low across the open farmyard in the direction of the pole shed. Jess's father had set that outbuilding on a slab downwind of the house for his septic trucks. The nesting pair of barn swallows flew dangerously fast and curled inside the open doorway. Jess thought about her son's father. They, too, once flew dangerously fast together—on the back of a motorcycle—as close as two can get. He was out of the picture now. Good riddance.

She put her hands on her hips and looked at the long, vacant pole shed, sunlight slanting off its red metal roof. There, one septic truck became two, then four, eventually five. As the business grew, the outbuilding grew. Jess's dad didn't measure business growth with a bar chart. His measuring stick was a pole shed.

"I should have treated my Pops better," Jess told the listening step. She turned and looked up at the second-story bedroom window. Her brow creased. "That was my old bedroom." She pictured her son, who was sleeping there now. "Shouldn't have left the way I did."

Breakfast

Squeaking, smearing the rain more than removing it, the old windshield wipers had Leo leaning forward. The road was mostly empty. It was a dispiriting kind of morning that made people roll over in bed and pull the covers up to their ears.

Leo took two lefts, like always. He would miss his Tom Thumb, a regular stop on the way to school every morning. Today a much longer drive awaited.

He swung his pickup into the parking lot in search of the three essential food groups of a baseball coach: sunflower seeds, Gatorade, gum. Then his route would take him past the high school to the interstate . Leo would set the cruise control. He would not look back.

"Hey, Coach," the store manager said from behind the cash register. The young man had played ball for Leo. A first baseman with more natural talent than ambition, he was a likable kid. "Hardly recognized you with that beard. You look badass."

"Hey, Swede," Leo said, going to the cooler. Swede got the nickname because once in social studies when asked the capital of Norway, the boy answered, Sweden. Hard to live that down. Leo was his teacher. From that day forward, in the classroom, Leo addressed the boy by his given name. But on the baseball diamond he was Swede.

Swede wanted to say something more as Leo shopped but he didn't know how to approach it. An awkward silence mixed with the overhead Muzak. At the counter, Leo balanced a Gatorade, Trident spearmint gum, a large bag of sunflower seeds, a chocolate-covered donut and a banana. The banana was an attempt to distract from the poor nutritional value in his other choices.

"Been a while," Leo said to Swede. "What's new with you?"

"Working. All the time. They moved me up from assistant manager to manager. Ain't much, but it ain't nothin' neither." Swede started ringing up the items. Then he stopped.

"Coach. Just want you to know, what people are saying, we know it ain't true. Anybody who played for you knows it. Not my business, but I want you to know we think you got screwed. Big time."

Leo nodded. "Thanks." He switched gears. "That's cool, about your promotion."

Swede stood a little straighter. "Did you hear about what else is going on with me?"

"No. Haven't been around much lately."

"I'm gonna be a dad. No shit. Gonna have me a little first baseman!" Swede smiled the same unshackled grin he flashed after ripping a triple down the line, out of breath, standing on third, pointing at his teammates in the dugout. "Pretty rowdy, huh?"

Leo nodded. "Yeah. Congrats."

"It's with Becky," Swede said. "You remember her, right?"

Leo went back through the years, landing on a trace memory of Swede, after a game, his jersey unbuttoned and untucked, arm tossed around the shoulder of a girl who wore his cap backward. "Becky Till?"

"Yes sir," Swede said proudly. "She's studying to be a dental hygienist. Real reliable work. Everybody gets on average eight cavities, she says."

"Didn't know that," Leo said. "That's great." They looked at each other. Windblown rain tapped the front window, sounding like the start of sleet. "So, what do I owe you for this breakfast of champions?"

Leo sat behind the wheel, listening to the whipping rain and wind. Keys hung in the ignition switch, but he hadn't yet turned over the engine. That act was, in his mind, irreversible.

Rain covered the windshield, closing him in the cab. He put a tooth to the corner of a bag of sunflower seeds; trying to tear them open while driving is a rookie mistake that can get messy fast. His

Gatorade was holstered in a cupholder.

Swede, a dad. Leo shook his head. *He'll be tossing wiffle balls to his kid before I will.* A shiver thrummed through him. *How is that remotely possible?*

An envelope rested on Leo's lap. The return address read Dannaka, Iowa. He unfolded a letter that explained how the town, although lovely, wasn't big enough to always be included on road maps. To be safe, there was a hand-drawn map showing the interstate and a few landmarks, including the intersection where the highway met a county road north of Dannaka. The letter writer had quipped: Don't want to lose you before you get here.

Leo double-checked his route using a map of Iowa he bought from a gas station when he had the oil changed and tires rotated. Had he planned better, he would have had the wipers replaced, too.

He'd take a straight shot across Illinois on 88. Then I-80 across most of Iowa. Then south. The letter's map showed Dannaka in the southwest corner of Iowa. In all, a seven-hour drive. He took a deep breath and started the truck, cranking on the heat. Under his breath he muttered, "Not even on a real map."

The truck almost drove itself to the high school where Leo had taught and coached. He slowed, looking at the sodden baseball field. Circular green tarps held down with old tires covered the pitcher's mound and home plate. Rain was beginning to pool in the low spot at third base. Leo shook his head. *Wouldn't happen on my watch.*

Beyond the left field fence was a scoreboard with a steel banner extending above it. The banner read NAPERVILLE REDSKINS BASE-BALL. HOME OF 1986, 1987, 1988, 1989 STATE AA CHAMPIONS!

Leo took a right and headed for the interstate. He didn't look in the rearview mirror. Springsteen's *Nebraska* went into the cassette player. Leo wasn't driving to Nebraska, but damn close. He cranked up the volume and stepped on the gas. As his red pickup accelerated down the on-ramp, the passenger-side window lowered. A second later his uneaten banana flew out, cartwheeling for the ditch.

Truman

It was a matter of habit. Jess tiptoed into her sleeping son's room and studied the rise and fall of his blankets before touching his forehead with the back of her hand. Her face relaxed. No fever. Standing there, she fully understood that Truman's near death was her resurrection.

Her story, while not incomprehensible, still baffled her. *How could I have been so stupid?* To be 17, parked on the back of a Harley owned by a man five years older, her hair freed by the wind—not a good idea on its face. But to do it well into the second trimester of her pregnancy, this was not a memory Jess welcomed. Oftentimes, this recollection would ambush her as she stood next to her sleeping son, making him seem completely vulnerable. Her fists would ball.

Jess learned how fast joy can plummet. From apogee: the birth of Truman. To rock bottom: leaving her fever-stricken eight-year-old in front of the television so she and her boyfriend could party at a local dive with coke skimmed from what he was dealing. Their life had become one dingy single-bedroom apartment after another. In Nebraska. In Colorado. In Arizona. They scraped a diagonal line southwest across the map, leaving behind a wreckage of unpaid bills and shorted drug deals. She was stuck with a man who never lived up to his promises, including marriage.

"Ma," Truman said, still half asleep, "you gotta stop doing that." The boy sat up in bed. His hair was pushed up like a sprout of weeds. His thin arms stretched toward the ceiling as he yawned.

"Don't call me Ma. Makes me feel ancient."

"Mom," Truman said with more clarity now, "it's creepy waking up with someone standing there."

"I'm not just someone."

"Don't be a smother mother." Truman scratched his narrow, bare shoulders.

Try as she did, Jess couldn't put meat on the boy. But she would never say that aloud. He was plenty self-conscious about his height and weight already.

The fog of sleep lifted. Truman's eyes sparked. "You're not going to tell me the *'Fever Story'* again." Truman made miniature air quotes. "For the billionth time."

Jess shifted her sightline, just to the left of her child. "I tell you that story because I want zero secrets between us."

"A few can't hurt," Truman said.

Jess frowned.

"Ma—Mom, I get it. All right? You made some crap decisions. I got sick. But that was forever ago."

Jess thought about the viral pneumonia that almost killed her son. He was eight. She planned to leave him for just a few hours, on the couch, under a blanket, in front of the TV.

According to later reports, child services estimated she was gone between 10 and 12 hours. Truman's condition had deteriorated from being feverish and wheezing to where he could hardly lift his head. His breathing became so labored his lips were blue. Jess freaked. She called an ambulance, which triggered a cascade of events that were, ultimately, for the best. But at that moment, reality came down like a shit shovel.

The police were notified. As were child services. Three pounds of cocaine were seized. Jess's boyfriend left the apartment in handcuffs.

Truman interrupted her thoughts. "Hello? Mom. Okay?"

"Okay what?"

"I said that was a million years ago. We're good. Okay?"

"Yeah. Okay." Jess took a catching breath. She remembered staring at a chest X-ray a week into Truman's recovery. A doctor pointed out how the once clear lung tissue was abnormally clouded, air sacs filled with fluids and pus. He emphasized the seriousness of her son's condition. Best case, he said, it would take four weeks for the lungs to clear. Chances are—and he looked at her roughly now—because the pneumonia was allowed to linger untreated, the effects of his illness would manifest considerably longer. The boy would be weakened. He would lose weight. His growth could be stunted. She alone lived with this conversation. *So much for zero secrets.*

"What time is it?" Truman asked, kicking off the covers.

Jess went to the window. "You almost slept your age."

"It's noon?"

"Just about." Jess let up the shade.

Truman squinted. "Nooo," he lowered his voice as deep as it would go, which wasn't much. Holding his index fingers in front of his face in the shape of a cross he uttered, "Too. Much. Light." He rolled off the bed and fell to the floor.

Jess shook her head. "Come on, Count. Time to face the day."

"Can't. Move." Truman remained on the floor.

"I see you smiling." Jess toed the heap.

Truman sat up suddenly. "Hey. Speaking of sleeping your age, happy birthday."

Jess folded her arms. "I was wondering if you forgot."

"Forgot? We have birthday Pop-Tarts. Duh?"

Their birthday tradition was borderline sinful. Strawberry Pop-Tarts for breakfast, Ho Hos for lunch and cake and ice cream for dinner. Jess didn't allow sugary treats into the house, but birthdays were the exception. The rest of the year she was a nutrition task-master—an overcorrection for earlier lapses.

Truman wasn't of an age where *shower* was his first thought of the day. In his mind, it wasn't a daily necessity. If not for his mother's persistence, he'd make showering more of a weekly option.

"Take a shower," his mother commanded over her shoulder. She headed downstairs to start the laundry, but didn't mention it. Running the washing machine sapped water pressure, which was just the daylight Truman needed to wriggle out of showering.

He kept a neat bedroom. It was Truman's way of controlling the few things he could. Clothes folded in drawers. Shoes paired in his closet. A well-made bed. He kept his baseball trophies lined up, tallest to shortest. And the few game balls he was awarded were arranged by season, beginning with the most recent.

Truman had managed to win some in-house baseball trophies, but he never made the cut for the traveling team. He would have traded all his hardware in an instant for just one traveling team cap or team picture, but the coach only took the top 12 players. Every year it was pretty much the same group, many deserving, but some chosen more for "their name than their game," as was whispered by parents outside of the elite circle.

Baseball posters filled one wall of Truman's bedroom. There was Robin Yount, Kirby Puckett, and his all-time favorite, the Kid Natural, Ryno, number 23, Ryne Sandberg of the Chicago Cubs. A 1987 Homer Hanky draped over his bedpost, the year the underdog Minnesota Twins won the World Series in seven games. Truman and his mom had watched those games in their living room, joyfully whipping the mini-towel like they were among the 60,000 thunderous fans in the Metrodome.

Truman was more of a National League guy, though. He liked pitchers that had to hit, and respected the strategy behind a double switch. He was a self-proclaimed Cubs man, despite their horrendous record every year.

Stripping down to shower, Truman locked the bathroom door. It was a subconscious act. There was no danger of his mother walking in, but he was ashamed of his small, skinny body. So much so, he avoided full-length mirrors. Steered clear of cameras, too. Who wants to be reminded that he's a head shorter than everyone his age?

Back in his bedroom he pulled on last year's jersey and a pair of Nike shorts. Maybe Mom would hit him grounders or he'd hit wiffle balls off his batting tee. It looked like a great day to be outside. Truman was sick of winter. Boots. Jacket. Stupid wool hat. He wanted the freedom that came with a baseball cap.

Last season's team picture caught his eye. His in-house team was divided with six boys standing and six kneeling. Truman wondered what it would be like to be in the back row, standing with the big kids. To grow, that's what he prayed for every night. But chances were, God was a hoax like Santa Claus and the Easter Bunny. One day, most likely, his mom would stop dragging him to church. She'd sit him down and explain that God was make-believe, too.

Truman looked closely. In the photograph, the bill of his cap was pushed up, in the fashion of his hero Ryne Sandberg. Truman picked up the picture and studied his smile. He liked it because it wasn't a camera smile. It was a baseball smile. There's a difference. He could never smile like that for school pictures. As for his face full of freckles, Truman was not a fan. Freckles were dorky and he had too many of them. And his ears, jeez. Mom said they were cute but everyone else called them jug handles.

Yet as much as Truman hated pictures, this one was a keeper. Near the bottom of the cardboard frame, inked on white tape, it read: In-house Champs. Beat the Cards 7-5. Went 3 for 4!

"Maybe this year," Truman whispered as he set the photo back on his desk. He knew that the traveling team's coach and players had come to watch last year's in-house championship game. They sat in the stands in a cluster with their tournament caps and pull-overs. What Truman wouldn't do for one of those pullovers. To wear the traveling team uniform. Button-down jerseys. Stitched patches. Name on the back. Glorious.

Truman thought, *They saw the squeeze bunt I laid down that scored the winning run. They saw the plays I made in the field.* Truman allowed himself a moment of hope. It was the cusp of spring, when irrational baseball dreams are ready to bloom, like: "Hey, the Cubs might do it this year."

You never know. Truman smiled a baseball smile. Then he walked to the pull-up bar in his doorway and went to work.

DANNAKA

Cutting through the gloom, making decent time, Leo crossed the Iowa border in just over two hours. The combination of Springsteen's plaintive ballads and the back and forth of windshield wipers made his eyelids heavy. Rain clouds bunched on the horizon. He drove straight into the gusty westerlies, looking for a place to take a break.

Just off the highway, Leo pulled into a Shell station. He needed to fill the tank, empty the bladder and get another Gatorade. Five hours left to go through Iowa to Dannaka. For that leg of the journey he'd line up Jethro Tull and Led Zeppelin. That plus the Gatorade should keep him sitting up straight.

At the pump, Leo set the latch on the handle and shoved his hands into his pockets. He had a traveling heart, wavering between sadness and excitement. The tick of the fuel dial on the pump was mesmerizing. *How much does it take? How many gallons to leave all of it behind?*

The Shell station was stocked with Gatorade and sunflower seeds. Leo substituted a Salted Nut Roll for gum. Considering the amount of salt he was ingesting, he grabbed a few bottles of water, too. Being a competitive athlete his entire life made him alert to staving off dehydration. Cramps, headaches, dizziness—so much can be avoided with simple water.

As he pulled out his wallet to pay, Leo saw tins of Copenhagen behind the counter, next to the cigarettes. He quit dipping when he started teaching and coaching high school ball. After years of tobacco, he was ecstatic to be rid of the nasty habit. But in the last months, surprisingly, the urge had rebounded. When the cashier asked if there would be anything else, Leo hesitated. He said no.

Back on the highway, there was little visual interest. Leo's mind returned to an endless loop concerning his future: school, baseball, fitting in. *School: Continue prep workbook. Take the Praxis Test for Social Studies. Get Iowa teaching license so I'm good to go next fall. Baseball: Organize drills, practice schedules. Research Little League tournaments in Iowa and Nebraska. Build a calendar that gets us two tourneys a month. State tourney in August. Fitting in: That used to be easy. Rental house is set up. Get out and about like before. New start. If it doesn't work out—coin flip—no big deal. No mortgage, no anchor.*

Davenport, Lime City, Oxford, cities with no connection or relevance to Leo came and went. Eighteen-wheelers bellowed by as miles of flat, open highway were followed by miles of flat, open highway. Such terrain gives a person plenty of time to think. Maybe too much.

Leo squeezed the steering wheel, questioned the wisdom of his decision. He'd been driving three and a half hours, which he guesstimated put him about halfway to Dannaka. Every mile traveled, from this point, left him closer to his new home than his old one.

He spoke to the rainy road. "Future ahead, past behind." Puddling dormant fields and bare stands of hardwoods huddled around neatly maintained farmsteads and outbuildings. Windmills and silos rose out of the landscape as his truck gained on them and left them behind. With little better to do, his mind wandered to the encounter that put this unlikely journey in motion.

It was June third, almost a year ago. Leo had his boys dialed in. It was the last day of the state high school baseball tournament. His Naperville squad had marched to the finals as the top seed in Illinois. Not surprising. Leo had coached his teams to three consecutive state AA tournament victories over the previous three years. That was unprecedented in Illinois high school baseball.

On this blustery June afternoon, the quest for a fourth championship looked bleak. Leo's team had given up five runs in the top of the first, without recording a single out. Leo asked for a timeout and called the entire starting nine to the mound. What happened next became legendary.

All the players—and Leo, too—gathered around the pitching mound, removed their ball caps, lay on their backs and proceeded to roll around on the grass like sausages on a hot griddle. They rolled right. They rolled left. The rolled over one another. The umpire was struck speechless. The other coach protested. The fans, first incredulous, either cheered or jeered depending on their alliances. The sight of 10 uniforms rolling around a baseball infield ... it was up there with the strangest things you'll ever see in baseball.

The umpire threatened loss by forfeit. Shape up, he commanded, respect the game. Get to playing baseball. Leo clapped the ump on the back, apologized and sent his boys sprinting back to their positions. The smiles on their faces made a person think *they* were the team ahead by five runs. The next three batters went down in order: strikeout, pop out, groundout.

Leo's boys got two runs back in their half of the first inning. They tied it in the second. And allowed just one run the rest of the game. In no-doubt fashion, Naperville claimed their fourth straight high school title, winning 11-6.

After the postgame dogpile, pictures were snapped, hugs were exchanged and the stadium slowly emptied. Except for three older men sitting in the bleachers. One got up and stiffly made his way to the gate by the home team's dugout. Leo untucked his jersey as he approached.

The man introduced himself. "Hey there, Coach. My name's Gifford. Doc Gifford."

"Nice to meet you sir. I'm Leo."

Leo, 28 at the time, guessed the man was in his mid-sixties.

"Call me Doc," he said, extending a hand. Leo shook it.

Doc continued, "Whale of a game. Your boys played with plenty of starch. Must be proud." There was a charming calm in the man's voice and demeanor. Leo instantly liked him.

"Yessir." Leo tipped back the bill of his cap.

Doc's blue eyes twinkled. "Don't know I've ever seen ballplayers rolling around on the field like mares about to deliver breech." He let out a chortle. "By the way, that's the kind of doctor I am. Veterinarian."

Leo nodded.

"What was all that about?" Doc asked.

Leo shook his head and grinned. "The boys were wound up tight. When they came to the mound it looked like a wake. That's not us. We're a loose bunch. So I pulled out a move I saw in the minor leagues. Had a teammate there who was, to say the least, a character."

"Seemed to do the trick," Doc commented.

Leo agreed. "Took their minds off things for a minute. Let them reset. Baseball is a lot easier to play when you're relaxed and having fun." The two men looked at one another. "Well, I better get moving," Leo said. "Gonna be a get-together at one of the coaches' houses."

Doc kept eye contact. "Can you spare me five minutes? I have a proposition for you. I'll bet dollars to dimes it's like nothing you've ever heard before."

Leo was in high spirits, and he liked Doc. *What the hell*, he thought, *five minutes*.

Leo followed Doc over to the bleachers where two other men were sitting. "Coach," Doc said, "I'd like to introduce you to a couple of the most washed-up ballplayers you'll ever lay eyes on. This is Jerome and that's Frank."

Shaking hands with them, Leo guessed they were about the same age as Doc. All three men wore old, woolen baseball caps with bent, faded brims and a large brown D stitched on the sunken crown.

"I played ball with these old farts in high school and afterward, town ball. We've come all the way from the other side of Iowa to watch this game, and I'll tell you why. When we were in high school, our team won three state championships in a row. 1941, '42 and '43. Didn't get a chance after that. Can you guess what team got in our way?"

Leo said he could not.

"The Third Reich. We enlisted to go fight Nazis. It was boot camp, then shipped out for Sicily before the dust could settle on our '43 trophy."

Leo interrupted. "The country owes you gentlemen a debt of gratitude. Thank you."

The men nodded.

Doc continued. "As far as we can tell, no other high school team has ever won more than three in a row. At least according to

20

Jerome here. He's the editor and publisher of our local newspaper. He hounds the newswire for that kind of stuff."

Jerome gave Leo a crisp nod. "Our little town is mighty proud of that record."

His friend Frank stage whispered. "He slips it into the paper every chance he gets."

Jerome objected. "That is patently false."

"I saw it again just last week in Mrs. Deckerscheid's obit," Frank countered.

"She was a big fan." Jerome hesitated. "Back in the day."

Doc interrupted. "Guys. Please. Leo's a busy man." The men restrained themselves. "So, as you may have gathered, the three of us hold that record dear, and our little town, which has always been a baseball town, well, it means a lot to our community, too. Heck, we have a sign coming into Dannaka—"

"Dannaka is our town," Jerome interrupted.

"—that reads we were the winner of three consecutive state high school baseball titles, and lists the years."

"Never get tired of looking at that sign," Jerome said.

"They even got our uniform jerseys in glass at the Legion Hall," Frank added. "And a few of our bats. Including Doc's from a grand slam in '42 when we came ba—"

Doc nipped that story in the bud. "Can I finish? We haven't even got to the good stuff yet."

Leo, who had remained standing next to the bleachers, took a seat. "Three titles in a row. No easy task," he complimented.

"So when Jerome pulled an article that said you were playing for your fourth, hell's bells, we just had to make a road trip."

Frank piped in. "Seven hours. Not accounting for breakfast."

"Had to see for ourselves," Jerome said solemnly. "Would you break our record? Against all odds, you've done just that."

"But that ain't the half of why we're here," Frank said.

Doc had an impish grin. "Frank's right. Now stick with me Leo 'cause this is quite a curve I'm gonna throw at you."

"Let me guess," Leo said. "You want me to come to Dannaka and coach your high school baseball team."

Doc's eyes widened. He pulled off his baseball cap, let it hang in the air for a moment and stuck it back on, a bit off-center.

"Looks like you were sitting on that curve," Doc said, impressed.

"I've had some offers over the years," Leo admitted.

"Well Coach, not so fast. You got a piece of what I was going to ask, but it was more of a foul tip."

"True," Jerome said with a chuckle. "Not a complete swing and miss."

Leo frowned. "So you're not here to ask me to coach your high school team?"

"No I am not," Doc told him.

"Foul tip, you say?" Leo was puzzled but enjoyed the challenge. "You want me to coach your town ball team?"

"Strike two," Doc replied.

"All right," Leo said. "What then?"

"We want you to come to Dannaka to coach our Little League team," Doc told him.

"Twelve-year-olds," Jerome added.

Leo couldn't mask his you've-gotta-be-kidding-me face. "Well guys, that is a first," he said. "Doc, you threw me a knuckleball there." Leo enjoyed a laugh with the old ballplayers. But that didn't alter his thinking. *No way am I going to some podunk town out of a John Mellencamp song to coach Little League.*

Rumors

"**H**ell yeah. It's great out!" The screen door banged shut behind Truman. He spread his arms, feeling the warmth. Jess gave her son a scolding look. "No need to swear. Certainly not on my birthday."

"And you thought I'd forget." The boy nearly levitated in the newfound warmth and sunshine. "Dang glad I put on shorts." He noticed puddles in the driveway. "Did it rain last night?"

Jess considered saying it might be too cool for shorts … he could catch cold, but Truman was already calling her a smother mother. She looked at his skinny legs. He could kite off under a strong wind.

"It poured last night. And I knew you'd remember my birthday."

The air was scrubbed clean and she was grateful for that birthday present. Her eyes closed and she let the warmth soak into her bones.

"I made you a card." Truman was in front of her when she opened her eyes. He handed her a folded piece of paper with Happy Birthday Mom written on the front using a pageant of colored pencils. It opened to a note inside.

Mom, I hope you have a great day. Maybe we can play catch or hit some grounders. Mostly you should do nothing. Just hang out. You deserve it. You work so hard. And you are always there when I need you. Sometimes you say you weren't the best mom but you're wrong. You are always the best!!! And you deserve the happiest birthday ever!!!

Love, Truman

"Ah, thanks Tru. I think I'm going to cry."

"Mom. Please."

"I'll trade crying for a birthday hug."

He squinted through the sun, looking at his mother. Truman was not big on eye contact, but he made an exception.

Jess's heart swelled. "You are my gift. My forever birthday gift."

Truman gave her a birthday hug. It was full and honest and without the usual reservations. She was warm and smelled nice. Part of him wanted to remain in her embrace, part of him wanted to push away. This is life when you're on the fault line of becoming a teenager.

Jess held on. She thought about herself at his age. When popularity became all she cared about. That's when she began pulling away from her parents. From then on, for young Jess, all bets were off.

The phone rang in the kitchen. Truman wiggled out and bolted up the porch steps. Again, a flood of memories for Jess. When the phone rang, you needed to get there now. God forbid you miss anything.

When Truman returned outside he wore his baseball cap and had his glove and bat. "I'm going to bike to Bale's house. Then we're going to ride to school. Play catch and take turns pitching tennis balls." He looked at the thermometer. "Can't believe it's 70 out!"

"I thought we were going to play catch."

"Ma, we can. Later. Bale said some other kids might be showing up."

Jess was disappointed to be left alone on her birthday, but she understood the pull of friends and freedom on the first summer-like Saturday of the year. She'd get the clothes up on the line and maybe crack open that birthday novel she got herself. "Okay. But check the air in your tires. That bike's been in the barn all winter. I don't want you riding on rims."

"Can *you*, Mom?"

"No. You can. If you have trouble, let me know. I'm going to finish the laundry."

Truman felt a jolt of guilt. "Want me to help? I can sort and you can pin."

"Nah. Just get those tires filled."

"Will do," he said, jumping off the porch, nearly losing his cap.

"Can't believe it's baseball weather." Joy gushed from him, enough for both of them.

Truman's best friend lived a quarter-mile down Ranch Road on a good-sized farm. He was Truman's age and went by the unusual name of Bale.

As the story goes, when he was four years old, he lifted a 45-pound bale of hay off the ground, so his brothers started calling him Bale. And his solid, rather rectangular shape made the name stick.

There was never a dull moment at Bale's house. His oldest sibling, his sister, still came first in his world. She had always been there to dry his tears, clean him up and apply Band-Aids. Next came his three older brothers. They grew up tossing Bale around like he truly was made of hay. The brothers got away with it for a while, only facing rebukes from Bale's sister. But when Bale was nine he got tired of being pushed around by his brother, who was two up in the pecking order at age 13. They were about the same size, but Bale was stronger. The teasing escalated to wrestling and came to an abrupt end when Bale put his brother through the wall of the milking shed. His dad left the gaping hole there for months. He called it the "Beware of Bale" sign.

Now 12 years old, Bale stood five foot seven, 160 pounds. He was the biggest, strongest kid in seventh grade. Bale was athletic. Bale was funny. Bale was popular. Truman liked to be seen with him, hoping to be cool by association. But standing next to Bale only accentuated Truman's size. At four foot seven, he weighed only 75 pounds with his shoes and clothes on. Truman often wondered why God gave Bale so much and him so little.

Bale played all sports, but baseball was his favorite. Every spring he'd work with Truman, hoping to help him make the traveling team. But every year Truman wasn't among the final 12—the 12 apostles, as the coach called them—selected for the team.

Truman skid-stopped his bike in Bale's farmyard. Last night's pounding rain had shined up the outbuildings, making them appear a little less ragged in the bright sunlight. Their farming operation left little margin for error, and even less for new paint or shingles.

On the barn's facade, rising upward toward the hayloft door, there were three basketball hoops. The first rim was set at five feet. The second at seven. The last at 10. Each of the kids learned to shoot baskets there, graduating from the shortest hoop to the regulation hoop.

With his back to Truman, Bale stood in the shadow of the barn, a wooden baseball bat resting on his shoulder. He focused on an old tractor tire leaning against the side of the building. Unrushed, he eyed three baseball-size circles painted on the giant tire. Selecting one, he cocked the bat, lifting it slightly off his shoulder, keeping his weight properly distributed on the balls of both feet. WHOP! In a split second, Bale's hips torqued as his hands and bat exploded to the target. WHOP! The blurring bat struck the tractor tire again, finding the center circle. He paused to reload, rebalance and uncoiled again. WHOP! The lower circle. Powerful swings, one after another, smashing the circles, which were spread out in a strike zone, high, center and low. This trained Bale to attack certain pitch locations, while building thicker wrists and stronger forearms.

Truman brought his bat over. "Can I take a couple cuts?"

Bale stood back, perspiring. "What? You don't even say hi?"

Truman offered a compulsory hey as he approached the tractor tire. Getting situated, with the bat head resting on the ground, handle pinched between his knees, Truman spat into his hands. "First swing of the season." A wicked grin spread across his face.

"Oh no no no," Bale interrupted. "You have to use Babe Ruth." He held up the giant wooden bat he'd been swinging.

"That thing weighs as much as I do," Truman objected.

"More," Bale said.

"Bullshit," Truman said, grabbing the old club.

Bale did his best impersonation of the Russian boxer in Rocky IV. "You want to make team, you need to make strong."

Babe Ruth was the name of the bat that, according to family

legend, Bale's grandfather swung playing town ball. He allegedly used it to poleax cattle before butchering them, too.

"This thing swings like a telephone pole."

Bale laughed. "Quit being such a wuss and give me twenty good cuts." Truman, despite his size, did exactly that.

Afterward, they rode to the schoolyard, which was overstuffed with swing sets, monkey bars, slides, a merry-go-round and seesaws. Ignoring the bike rack they rode to the chain link fence—the home run fence—that encased a perfect square of blacktopped playground and abutted the brick wall of their school. What Wrigley Field is to baseball, this venue is to wall ball. They let their bikes drop to the ground.

"Did you bring chalk?" Bale looked panicky.

Truman's baseball glove hung from one end of his handlebars. A plastic bag from the hardware store was on the other. Inside the bag there were two tennis balls, two beaten-up baseballs and a thick piece of sidewalk chalk. Truman held the chalk up like it was a gold coin. Actually, it was more valuable than a gold coin. You can't draw a strike zone on a schoolyard wall with a gold coin. You can't mark the foul lines with a gold coin. You can't keep score of wall ball with a gold coin.

They played catch with a baseball to warm up their arms before pitching any tennis balls. "I heard a rumor this morning from my sister who babysits for Doc Gifford's daughter." Bale spoke as he made an effortless one-handed catch. "Back up a little." He made a longer, arcing throw with the baseball. Truman caught it. His return throw was more on a line. "Nothing hard and straight from this distance for a couple days," Bale instructed.

Truman watched the ball go into his glove, squeezing it. "I'm listening. What did you hear?"

"I swore not to repeat it."

"Then maybe you shouldn't." Truman threw the ball back.

"Yeah. But this is too much for one guy to keep in. If I tell you and only you then it will be twice as easy to keep secret."

Truman didn't trifle with Bale's calculations. "So let's hear it."

"You're not going to believe it."

"What if I do?"

"You still aren't going to, even if you do."

"Stop stalling."

Bale's eyes were deep-set and usually hard to read. But now they radiated mischief. He threw the ball. "We're getting a new Little League coach. He's moving to town."

The baseball hit Truman's glove and dropped out. "Like hell."

Bale smiled fully and nodded.

Truman stared at his friend. "Like hell," he repeated, with a twinge of hope.

"My sister overheard a conversation when Doc came to see his granddaughter. I guess he told his daughter the shit was going to hit the fan. New coach and all."

Truman's skin tingled. "What are they going to do with Coach Dickweed? I mean Dixon."

"Dunno. Maybe he's getting the ax. I'm thinking they'll announce it at the baseball meeting tomorrow."

"Truth?" Truman said, seriously.

"Truth," Bale assured him. "You know what this means?"

Truman dared not utter it.

Bale nodded. "You finally have a legit shot at making the team."

The first load of laundry was pinned to the line. Whites. Jess was left with countervailing emotions. Standing back, seeing clean white shapes clipped out of a stunning blue sky, she connected peacefulness with home in a way she was growing more accustomed to. But the sight left her sad as well. Those undersized socks and T-shirts and underwear. Truman was so small. Her neglect, to her reckoning, was to blame.

Jess was aware of the religious ritual of self-flagellation and considered the act ridiculous. She knew flogging herself with past mistakes would serve no good. But her life was connected in complicated ways to her little boy, her Truman, which means "loyal one." He made her heart whole, and ache.

Please let him grow, God. Please let him have normal experiences. She paused. *Normal experiences? Is that what's best for him or is that what's best for me? I didn't have normal experiences. Ultimately I'm better for it.*

She thought about the Harley that burned donuts in the muddy farmyard on a day much like today. Where she now stood, at 29, was not far, physically, from where her 17-year-old self rode on the back of a motorcycle, screaming at her life, one arm around her new man and the other raising a hand to the sky, her middle finger flipping off her current existence. When the Harley roared out of the driveway, all ties with her parents were severed.

Jess walked deeper into the yard, across the path the motorcycle would have taken. A path that led to Truman and to now.

She looked back at her child's white undershirt on the line. *Please God, let him grow. And let his experiences be a titch more normal than mine.*

POODLE LADY

I-80 west across Iowa is a highway of remarkable nothingness. It's like traveling through an endless sink factory, mile after mile after mile, with every faucet dripping. This abundance of windshield time gave Leo's mind another opportunity to wander back to the conversation with Doc Gifford and his old high school teammates, Jerome and Frank.

They sat on the old wooden bleachers trying not to pick up a splinter. Doc, the group's natural leader, made his pitch while Jerome and Frank chimed in now and again.

"I know it's an unusual proposition—you might say preposterous—asking a young man with your pedigree to come to our speck of a town and coach 12-year-olds."

Leo was too polite to disagree. "I appreciate your invitation."

Doc gave him a knowing glance. "I'm not sure you do, Coach. Heck, I'm not sure I would appreciate it either, if I were you. But let me tell you what it entails. It's a doozy."

Leo glanced at his watch. Then he looked up at the American flag rippling over the dugout. He was reminded of how Doc and his teammates shipped out for the European theater only weeks after they won their third state title. The least he could do was give these men a few more minutes. They had come a long way to say what they had to say.

"Let's hear it," Leo said.

Doc asked, "Are you fond of poodles, Coach?" Not the opening Leo expected.

"Not particularly," Leo said.

"We had a woman in our town, quite well-to-do. She adored poodles. Was known as Poodle Lady Thomson. Her husband was a vice president at John Deere. When he passed, she moved back to her hometown, our Dannaka, with five poodles and a pile of

John Deere stock the size of a haystack. She commissioned the construction of a large house on the outskirts of town. Each dog got its own bedroom. Granted, a little strange. She kept mostly to herself and her dogs.

"Now, her poodles weren't young and they had ailments. That's where I came in. She'd visit my clinic and over time we became acquaintances—even friends. She cherished her poodles like the children she never had. She was also quite fond of baseball, a game she grew up with and, more importantly, a game her deceased husband loved as a boy. He had told her that youth baseball kept him out of trouble and gave him the confidence to believe great things were possible for himself."

Jerome spoke up. "She would walk those poodles to the baseball fields spring through the end of summer, even if teams were only practicing. Stand by the outfield fence and watch the kids run and laugh and play."

Doc nodded. "Turns out, she paid close attention to the goings-on, and was an astute baseball person in her own right. When she'd bring one of her dogs to my clinic, she'd tell me that so-and-so was a whiz with the glove and that number fill-in-the-blank was a tough out with two strikes—that kind of stuff. She was generally a positive person, but she had two complaints every time we spoke: the poor condition of the Little League fields. And the temperament of one of the coaches.

"One by one, her old poodles died until only a single dog was left. Then one day, Mrs. Thomson was found dead by her cleaning woman. The last living poodle was sitting beside its owner. When the EMTs arrived, that dog wouldn't let them near her. I had to come over and sedate the animal."

Leo took off his ball cap and pulled his hand though his thick black hair.

"I appreciate your patience," Doc said. "Stick with me. We're rounding third and heading for home."

Leo nodded.

"Couple days later, out of the blue, I get a call from Cooper Lees. Says he has something I have to see. How soon can I get there?"

Frank interrupted. "He's the town's go-to attorney."

"Only attorney," Jerome corrected.

"Yeah," Doc continued. "So I zipped over to his office and he reads me Poodle Lady Thomson's will. She put three million dollars into a Dannaka Little League baseball trust."

Leo was doing his best to pay attention but he was sure he'd heard that number wrong. "Did you say three million?"

"Three million," Doc raised his eyebrows. "Her will stated that it was up to me and the attorney to budget that money properly, but she wanted Dannaka to have a state-of-the-art Little League complex. Three fields. In-ground dugouts. Clay infields. Lights. Electric scoreboards. The works. Make it a place every team in Iowa would want to come and play tournament baseball. Her first stipulation: It was to be called Poodle Park."

Leo grimaced.

Doc shrugged. "You get used to it."

"Her other condition was to appoint a new coach for the 12-year-old traveling team. She called the current coach … now what was her word? … ah, it's hell getting old. A lout. Yeah. She said the lout had to go. From my years of caring for her dogs, she knew I was the president of our youth baseball association. That gives me final say on coaching matters."

"Which brings us to you," Jerome said.

"Finally," Frank added.

"The fields will be ready next spring," Doc said. "And I need a new coach for those top-end 12-year-olds. I'm guessing I can pay you better than double what the high school pays you to coach."

"Maybe," Leo said, frankly stunned. "But I teach there, too."

"I get that. We have a few teachers who are itchin' for the right opportunity to retire." Doc nodded at Leo. "We can find you a classroom."

Silence ensued.

"Take a few days. Mull it over. Here's my card. Give me a call once you've had time for it to soak in."

Leo took Doc's card and shook the hand of each man. "I appreciate the offer. And it sounds like a heckuva good one, just like you said. I'll think about it. But to be honest and set realistic expectations, something would have to change pretty drastically here for me to take you up on it."

Exiting I-80, Leo went south on 59. The lion's share of the drive was behind him now. The way he figured it, if he stayed on the two-lane highway for about an hour, he'd make Dannaka.

The day got steamier as the rain pounded on. But since turning south, Leo could see a strip of clearing sky behind the thunderheads. He was deep into farm country. The black soil was pooling water. Around every bend, one farm ended and another began.

"Holy shit!" Leo stomped on the brake pedal. Adrenaline bombarded his system. His truck hydroplaned, the rear end drifting right. Quickly, Leo counter-steered and the truck came straight again. Gritting his teeth, Leo mashed down the brake with all he had.

The pickup slid to a stop. "What in hell?" Leo exhaled deeply and unpeeled his fingers from the steering wheel. Two feet from the front bumper, on the centerline of the road, drenched to the bone, sat a puppy. A flash of lightning was closely followed by an explosive clap of thunder. Both Leo and the pup jumped.

Leo quickly assessed the situation. The middle of the road was no place for either of them. Behind him was a blind curve. In front of him he could see no oncoming vehicles.

Maneuvering his truck around the pup, Leo rolled down his window to blowing rain. "Get going!" he shouted. The pup and he made eye contact. Leo noticed the dog's collar was nothing but baling twine. A torn plastic bag was caught up in it.

"Out of the road! GET!" The pup's butt remained fast. *Just keep driving,* Leo's inner voice urged. He swung the truck to the side of the road, looking back. The pup hadn't budged. "For chrissakes." Leo steered onto the shoulder, snapped on his hazard lights and prayed the lightning had passed.

Hunched, soaked, droopy-eared, the chestnut-colored pup sat facing the other direction as Leo jogged toward him. As for what happened next, it was surreal. Despite facing away from Leo, the pup's bobbed tail began to wag. The pouring rain stopped as abruptly as someone turning off a faucet. The sun broke out from behind a fist of dark clouds. And a double rainbow arced across the county highway.

"You got to be kidding me," Leo said.

Back in the truck, Leo reached behind him and pulled a towel out of one of the boxes. He wrapped the shivering pup and set him near his hip on the front seat. The pup looked Leo in the eye. Then he wiggled out of the towel, shook the rainwater off his fur and climbed in Leo's lap. He instantly fell asleep.

"Great," Leo muttered, soaked to the skin. "Make yourself at home." Leo wiped his face with the towel, turned off the hazards and pulled back onto the highway. "I guess you're coming with."

Of course Leo's sunglasses were packed away. Six hours ago when he left Illinois, sunglasses were the last thing he thought he'd need. Leo looked at the plastic baggie caught in the pup's twine collar. Then it struck him: It wasn't litter; it was a note wrapped in plastic.

The pup hardly moved as Leo drove with one hand and removed the baggie with the other. The note inside was written in ink and was mostly dry and legible. A few words were soaked beyond recognition, but the message was easy enough to decipher.

If you found this runt you (unrecognizable) two choices.
(unrecognizable) him to the coyotes. They have to eat too.
Or take him with you. I recommend coyotes.

Leo balled up the note and threw it on the back seat. He let his hand settle on the pup's head and stroked the small length of his warm, curled body. "Sounds like a peach of an owner you had," Leo whispered. The pup opened one eye, looked at Leo, and then closed it. "Well little guy, I know a man named Doc Gifford who's a vet. He'll know what to do with you." Leo continued stroking the pup.

The landscape was beginning to lift and roll. What had been flat and homogenous now developed character. Bluffs and swales played with light and shadow. The road wound over streams and around small woodlots. The sun was high and the blacktop was dry and it struck Leo that he had crossed from one world into another.

As he passed a farmstead, Leo glanced out at a man who stood stooped over an old gas tiller. He was preparing the soil for a large garden, which was surrounded by a deer fence. Just ahead, a barn caught Leo's eye—specifically the roof. Woven into the gray shingles was a pattern of darker ones that spelled out the word IKE. Leo wondered who belonged to that name. Was it a tribute from the man in the garden who loved a son or lost a son or both?

"Ike," Leo said out loud.

And the pup's head lifted off his lap.

Coach Dixon

In Dannaka, the sun was resplendent. It not only looked and felt like baseball weather, it smelled of it. The ground frost had succumbed and the earth was opening up like a bottle of excellent wine. Just like that, the last traces of winter were herded up by a southern wind and driven north.

Coming across his clinic's parking lot, Doc smiled to himself about the double meaning of having a spring in one's step. Yet despite the sunny afternoon's capacity to warm his soul, the pit of his stomach churned. He had put off this meeting for as long as possible but with a new coach due to arrive today and the Little League parents and players meeting tomorrow, his procrastinating had to end. Coach Dixon needed to know the lay of the land.

"Well, Doc," he said to himself. "Time to put your foot down. Directly onto a hornet's nest, that is."

Doc's Saturday hours were 10 to two. Usually something came up to extend them. Today he locked up at 2:15. Looking younger than his 65 years, Doc was tall and lean and maintained a professional appearance. Bald on top, he kept the hair on the sides neatly trimmed. Every two weeks he'd step up into the barber chair where Bert would snap a number two guard on the clippers, leaving the sides a uniform quarter inch—just a bit longer than the high and tight he wore in the army.

Wincing as he pushed off the running board, Doc swung himself up into his brand-new 1990 Ford F-150. His right hip was giving him fits. A horse kicked him there years ago and just when he thought the injury was behind him, he'd step funny on some ice or try to stretch a single into a double in church softball. That would send him looking for the stretching exercises he got from his physical therapist

36

in Iowa City. The printouts had inevitably been tucked away some-place by his wife.

Burgundy red with white accents on the door panels and hood, a new truck was one pleasure that Doc afforded himself every five years. A completely reliable vehicle was essential to his job. He spent better than half his working days making farm visits.

As he eased down First Street, lowering the driver's side window, Doc shoved his elbow into the fresh air making the arrival of spring official. He double-beeped at Bert sitting on a bench in front of his barbershop playing a harmonica. Bert lifted a finger and went on playing.

Doc's stomach roiled. Jerome and Frank would be at the hot stove meeting to further represent the association's board—they had full knowledge of what was about to transpire. Cooper Lees, the attorney who had drawn up Poodle Lady Thomson's will, would be in atten-dance so no surprises there. The only attendees getting blindsided at the meeting would be Dixon and his assistant coach. Doc didn't like blindsiding anyone, even if the head coach was a deserving idiot. His assistant coach was cut from the same cloth.

The agreed meeting place was the Legion Hall at 2:30. They'd use the banquet room in back for privacy. Downstairs there was a dance hall with long folding tables that the coaches used when drafting teams, but that was more space than the six men needed.

Parking his truck in front, Doc noticed a sparkling new black Ram pickup from Dixon Dodge. The vanity plate read Ru$$. "Subtle," Doc said.

Russ Dixon owned the largest Dodge dealership in Iowa, west of Des Moines. What began as his daddy's community dealership—selling new and used cars as well as farm equipment—changed drastically when a stroke took his father's life. The ground hadn't settled around the grave before his son got to changing things.

Dixon sold off all tractor and implement inventory, and instead of selling Fords, Chevys and the other big brands, he inked an exclusive deal with Dodge, whose truck business was on the rise. Russ always had a what-the-hell mentality. He went all-in with Dodge.

The man was mostly vainglorious but he had some business sense, too. He changed the company name to Dixon Dodge and tripled the truck inventory to advantage his pricing. He rented a network of billboards within a 60-mile radius of his dealership with the catch phrase: A SMALL TOWN DEALERSHIP WITH BIG TOWN DEALS. And he set his mind not to be beaten on price, or anything else for that matter. To that end, he hired two young women of questionable reputation and dim prospects, paid the medical bills for each to have breast implant surgery and put them to work on his showroom floor. Dixon Dodge became famous for some of the most unforgettable test drives in the five-county area.

Doc's eyes needed a few seconds to adjust, coming in from the bright sunshine to the darkened Legion Hall. But he didn't require perfect vision to know where he was heading; just follow the trail of blaring Dixon laughs reverberating from the banquet room. He stiffened his constitution and got on with it.

"Well, well," Dixon chortled. "Look who decided to show up."

The rest of the group was there. Jerome, Frank and the attorney. They sat on one side of a long table, Dixon on the other. A chair at the head of the table waited empty for Doc.

The waitress stepped in to see if Doc needed something to drink. Dixon beat him to the punch. "Stewardess," he said. "Another one of these before we land." He held up an empty, red-tinged Bloody Mary glass and rattled the ice. She playfully shook her head and took Doc's order for a Diet Coke.

Doc had expected to see Dixon's assistant coach. "Is Chad coming?" he asked.

"He couldn't make it," Dixon said. "Plus I'm not sure I'm coaching with him this season. His kid is getting fatter by the second. Not sure he'll be among my 12 apostles this year."

Just as well, Doc thought. "Okay, Jerome will you keep the minutes?"

Dixon sat up straighter. "Minutes? I thought we were going to shoot the breeze about this season's plans and other B.S."

Doc's eyes had adjusted well enough to see concern swipe across Dixon's face. An easy read—large-featured and mercurial—Dixon had once kept himself in decent shape. But now at 45, he was soft in the face, carrying more weight in his neck, a bit bouncy in the chest and had a beer belly that required a steering wheel adjustment as he climbed out of his Dodge.

Doc pushed ahead. "Dixon, on behalf of our board of directors I'm here to offer you a proposition. But first, I want to make you aware of two provisions directing our newly established Dannaka youth baseball trust fund, whose stewardship was commended to me and the board to manage." Doc's mouth was dry. He was off to a rambling start. "Since Cooper drew up said trust and its provisions, I will turn the floor over to him."

Dixon's voice was forceful. "Wait a damn second." The waitress bringing in the Bloody Mary and Diet Coke stopped cold. "Not you," he barked. "For shit sake, bring that tray over here." She delivered the drinks and exited quickly. "What's all this about boards and provisions?"

Cooper Lees wiped his reading glasses with a napkin. "As you know, our association was left a generous trust fund to build and maintain a new baseball complex, which we completed last fall. I'm not going to get into the legal jargon, but the trust also carries two stipulations. Failure to adhere to them dissolves the fund."

"Dissolves?" Dixon asked. "Like poof." His meaty hands made a small exploding gesture.

"In so many words, yes, like poof." The attorney licked a finger and flipped three-quarters through a multi-page document. "Stipulation one: The new baseball complex is to be named Poodle Park. You'll recall, we complied with this provision."

Dixon muttered something about dog shit under his breath.

"Stipulation two: A new head coach is to be secured for our incoming 12U AAA Little League traveling team." The attorney glanced up and removed his glasses.

Dixon paused. Then he broke into laughter. "You hound dogs. Who put you up to this? Are a bunch of coaches going to jump out and holler surprise?"

The room was silent.

Dixon stopped laughing. He looked at the faces of the board members. It was apparent this was no practical joke with a happy ending.

"You gotta be kidding me." Dixon squirmed in his chair. The stale carpet. The lingering dinge of tobacco smoke. The jagged cracks in the ceiling of the banquet hall, all of it agitated Dixon like never before. "You really pulled me in here on a beautiful Saturday to what, fire me?" He yanked off his baseball cap, which sent the sunglasses that were resting on the brim sailing over the back of his chair. He brought the cap down on the table with enough force to send the top button flying, ricocheting off Doc's glass of Diet Coke.

"We brought you into this room," Doc proceeded calmly, "to introduce you to the conditions of the trust, which we are all bound to, *and* to make you a proposition, as I mentioned at the start."

With his baseball cap hanging in the air, Dixon looked at the men in the room. When he put it back on, it had become a negotiating hat. "Fellas, listen," his voice coaxed. "We've got a pretty good thing going here. I've been coaching this bunch, what, three years, right? I know their strengths and weaknesses. We've won some good tournaments."

Frank spoke up. "You got creamed three years in a row in districts. You didn't even advance to regions."

"Shut up, Frank." Dixon took a moment to recompose. "My kid and a few others have really shot up this past year. I have some boys, some gamers. They're coming together, jelling. Getting more mature. I can take 'em on a run. We could make state this year. It's a process. Takes time."

Doc raised open palms. "It's not our money, only ours to manage. We have to abide by her stipulations."

Dixon's eyes fired as he started to interrupt.

Doc's voice was firm. "Here's the proposition. Just listen for a minute." He took a sip of Diet Coke. "Nowhere in the document is it stated you have to be out as a coach. What is stated is we have to get a new head coach. You can be on the field. Just not the head guy."

Dixon smirked. "You want me to be an assistant?"

"I don't," Frank said.

Dixon ignored him. "Assistant coach of the 12 AAAs is your … *proposition*?" He said the word the way someone would hold a dead mouse by the tip of its tail.

Frank couldn't help himself. "It's not my proposition. I don't think you belong on the field with our kids, period."

Doc's words were clipped. "Frank. Zip it!"

"I'm just saying it for the record," Frank said. "Jerome is over there taking the minutes. Dixon is not a standard-bearer of Dannaka baseball and I'm against him as a role model for our 12-year-olds in any capacity."

Dixon adjusted his baseball cap and stuck out his sizable lower lip to ponder. He reclined in his chair. He locked his fingers behind the meat of his neck. Then, summoning his inner car dealer, he played the pity card.

"C'mon. I've committed countless hours to this association. Hours of practices. Hours of phone time lining up tournaments and scrimmages. My company even shells out for the uniforms. This is the thanks I get? Really? Does that seem fair to you? Do we really need some crazy old dead lady telling us how to run our baseball program?"

The attorney spoke. "This legal document is a contract. We can't pick and choose which provisions we're in compliance with."

"Doc?" Dixon urged. "Really?"

"'Fraid so."

Dixon knew he'd lost. *What the hell,* he thought. *Torch a few bridges.* "You put her up to this, Doc." Dixon's face was hostile, scowling. "You can skip the high-and-mighty legal excuse. I know you've always had it in for me."

Doc shook his head. "Not true."

"Bullshit. You were always in my ear with one complaint or another."

Doc stiffened, his words pointed. "Parents come to me. They have kids crying on the way home from the field. My job is to make it clear to you that's not our brand of youth baseball."

"Boo hoo hoo," Dixon mocked. "Run to mommy and daddy. Where they're told that they're the second coming of DiMaggio. Too many soft kids."

Doc had a cannon load of things to fire back with, but he kept his cool. "I wouldn't call the Rippen boy a crybaby, would you?"

Dixon was momentarily staggered. "What? I'm not talking about Rippen."

Doc's voice remained flat. "To lose him to Des Moines last year was a blow. His parents told me they were looking for a more positive baseball program. We can't afford to have our best kid skimmed off by the competition."

"My kid can play with him," Dixon said. "Bale can play with him."

"Maybe Bale," Doc said. "I'm not going to get tangled in the underbrush. We've got a very capable new head coach identified. We'll introduce him at the parents and players meeting in the gym tomorrow afternoon."

A big eye roll from Dixon. "Really? Who's gonna replace me? I'm the last time this town had a high school kid that went on to play college ball. Now what? Someone's first rodeo?"

Frank, again, couldn't help himself. "The three of us won state in '41—"

"Yeah, blah, blah, blah. If I heard it once I heard it 40 million times. For chrissakes, can we move outta the dark ages of baseball and get with the new program?"

Frank locked eyes with Dixon and smiled, long and wide. "That is exactly what we're doing."

Dixon blew a gasket. He launched his Bloody Mary across the room where it shattered against the wall. The same temper that often erupted on the baseball diamond was now on full display under a Les Kouba Ducks Unlimited painting.

"Your fastball needs work," Frank told him.

Dixon stormed past him on his way out. "You watch yourself, old man."

NANCY

Not everyone was so lucky to have a real friend—especially
one as unflinching as Nancy. Or as people nicknamed her:
Raunchy. She didn't care. Hell, sometimes she referred to
herself as such.

"Hey, bony ass," Nancy called out, pulling open Jess's screen door.
"You in here?" She stepped through the entryway. "I ain't gonna
catch you in the bedroom needing a man even less than you already
do, am I?"

Nancy had a small present clutched against her untucked flannel
shirt. She owned three favorite flannels, which she wore almost
exclusively into early summer. She loved the touch of that particular
well-worn fabric on her skin.

Jess came up from the basement with a load of laundry.

"Should've known," Nancy said, looking at the basket of damp
clothes. "Birthday chores. Yippee."

Jess put the basket down and went in for a Nancy hug. Nancy hugs
were swallowing and strong. More so, they were genuine, versus the
little sideways embraces most people were good for.

"Happy birthday, girlfriend," she said. Nancy was almost a head
taller than Jess. Her shoulder-length strawberry blonde hair, parted
in the middle, swept down both sides of her prominent cheekbones,
revealing her broad forehead and face. Nancy was a low-maintenance
gal, so her hair often looked like she'd just been camping. She didn't
fuss much with makeup.

Where Jess would be described as cute, the word handsome better
suited Nancy, who became less plain the longer you looked at her.
She wasn't overly self-conscious of her prominent nose, full lips and
long wide mouth. In fact, a bar trick Nancy would trot out if she'd

had a couple too many drinks was to stick a pool ball in her mouth.

Jess stepped back. "A present? For *moi*?" She flashed her cute angled grin.

Nancy handed her the gift. "No fair you got dimples. As if you're not adorable enough."

"Ah. Thank you." Jess looked at the wrapped present with its pretty robin's egg blue ribbon. "What could it be?"

Jess and Nancy were friends in high school, even grade school, though not best friends. Jess hung with the cool kids, became a cheerleader and was a puppet of popularity. Nancy worked on cars with her dad, liked to draw and paint and was bigger and stronger than most boys well into high school. Those qualities got her ridiculed.

But Jess came to admire Nancy's independence and self-confidence. The fact that Nancy didn't give a damn what anyone thought about her—and said so out loud—made her intriguingly different from Jess. By junior year, the year Jess got pregnant, they were getting closer. Nancy, in fact, was the first person to learn Jess was going to have a baby. She didn't try to load Jess down with advice like everyone else. All she said was, "Oops."

The wrapped box was square, neither light nor heavy. When Jess gave it a shake, she felt something move inside—slide, actually—from one end to the other. It created no sharp sound. "A giant marshmallow," Jess said.

Nancy looked on, smiling.

Jess tore open the wrapping paper and lifted the lid off the box. Inside, under tissue, was a tie-dyed cotton T-shirt featuring a mesmerizing explosion of neon pink, yellow, blue and orange that splashed, dripped and swirled like Peter Max's artwork. There was a similar wild flourish on the back where the words, I Miss The 70s, swirled with the design. Jess looked closely at the hand-lettered type and the outrageously beautiful color combinations.

"Did you make this?"

"That depends on if you like it or not," Nancy said.

"I love it." Jess beamed.

"Then of course I made it."

"Really?"

"Yes, really." Nancy grew a bit self-conscious. "D'you think my only talent is rail drinks?"

"No. No!" Jess waggled her index finger with a twinge of sala-ciousness. "I know you have maaany talents."

"You bet your leopard skin panties I do." Nancy laughed. "You'll like how that shirt feels on your skin. I washed and dried it a ton before painting it. And some after too. Should be super soft."

Jess held the shirt to her cheek. "Mmmm." She looked away from the gift and into her friend's eyes. "Thank you so much. I don't know whether to wear it or frame it."

"You sure as hell better wear it. Now, let's get this laundry hung so you can get birthdaying." Nancy picked up the basket of clothes and the two of them headed for sunshine.

"You working tonight?" Wind tossed a single, long curl of Jess's hair across her cheekbone.

"Yep. Four o'clock." Nancy had spare clothespins clipped down the front of her flannel shirt.

"What time does the music start?"

"Eight-ish, I guess." Nancy's eyes suddenly sparked. "You coming out while you're still in your twenties?"

Jess thought about it, but only for a moment. "Those days are behind me." She shook her head, happy-sad.

Nancy worked at a roadhouse just off the highway northeast of town. Officially named The Sundown Saloon, it was better known as the Rundown Saloon. The owner was an unabashed cheapskate who would rather buy a dozen pails than patch a roof. He promised Nancy a pay raise and the position of manager—since she was the manager in everything but title—but that was before the calendar turned from Christmastime to wintertime. The doldrums. Just the hardcore regulars. Summer always brought the roadhouse back to life, with more tourists passing through, and biker clubs. More revenue—hopefully, for Nancy, too.

With laundry swaying on the line, Jess and Nancy sat on the porch steps, faced directly into the sun and soaked it in. Nancy opened the collar of her flannel shirt three buttons down to cool off and get some color on her chest. She wasn't against flashing a little skin at work. The good Lord put her on Earth with above-average-sized features. The way she figured it, play the cards He dealt ya.

"I am a sun sponge," Nancy said. "I don't care what it does to my skin when I'm 70."

Jess listened to the birds. A chickadee sang out for a spring mate. "So what's the latest with Dan? Any big decisions?"

Nancy smiled just a pinch. "He moved on, old Danny boy. After some encouragement on my part."

"I guess he just wasn't your type."

"A lot of 'em are my type. Until they're not." Nancy began rolling up her soft shirtsleeves. "About six months is my expiration date on relationships."

Jess looked at her friend. "We're not getting any younger. After 30, maybe the expiration date will be up on us."

"Not me, sweet pea." Nancy thought aloud about Dan. "He was fine and all. Laid around on the couch most days and slept. Like having a big friendly dog. Always glad to see me when I got home. Only he ate and drank a hell of a lot more. And was eternally hopeful for a belly scratch."

"Empty houses can get lonely," Jess said.

Nancy exhaled. "It was time. I need some quiet for myself after the racket of the bar."

"To make T-shirts?" Jess smiled.

"Yeah. Back doing some painting, too."

"Finally. That's great. When can I see?"

"Slow down, sister. I'm rusty right now."

"I bet they're great."

Nancy redirected. "And you? How are you and your insurance policy doing?"

Jess frowned. "You said you'd stop calling him that."

"Okay. How's our Wade?"

"Pretty excited, at the moment. He was named a Silver Status agent. Not sure what all that means. State Farm did send out a new awning for his office. It's red, on steroids."

"Yeah. Nearly blinded me on my way to the bank. So the insurance business is good?"

"Yeah. I guess. Steady. Secure."

Nancy's face softened. "Honey, is that what you're really looking for? Steady? Secure?"

"I've walked on the wild side. It's overrated. Like living on a steep hill." Jess shook her head. "Nope. Nothing wrong with security."

"Well, maybe. Maybe not." Nancy searched for the right words. "Security—just my opinion now—is an illusion. You're betting the present on the future."

Jess looked off. "Might be. What's so bad about that?"

"The future you're planning on might never get here. You can live one day at a time. Or you can die one day at a time. Pick."

Jess closed her eyes to the sun. She had come to love the sound of laundry billowing on the line. She said softly, "Truman will be college-age in six years. I can't afford to send him."

Nancy looked on as Jess snuck a moment for herself, her face raised to the sun, trying to keep the clouds of worry at bay. Stroking Jess's back she said, "You'll figure it out, smart girl. But remember that bread and roses lyric from your main man, John Denver."

Jess's eyes remained closed. "Hearts starve as well as bodies. Give me bread but give me roses." She exhaled wistfully.

Nancy sensed she'd said enough on that topic. Changing gears, she said, "Heard an interesting rumor yesterday at the bar."

Jess opened her eyes. "I'm not above interesting rumors."

"Might pertain to Truman—he's 12, right?"

"Twelve one day. Eight the next. Eighteen the following."

Nancy smiled. "I heard we've got a new baseball coach coming our way. He's taking over the traveling team for the 12-year-olds. Going to teach at the school, too. Social studies, is what I was told."

Jess covered her mouth. Her eyes twinkled with possibility. "No shit?" Her hand muffled her words but not her excitement.

"The powers that be are ousting Dixon. Finally."

Jess said, "Wow. I thought I heard some whisperings, but I didn't dare believe it. Really?"

"Really," Nancy confirmed.

"He'll never go," Jess said, the wind dying in her sails. "Parents have been complaining about him for the last three years. He's in deep as a stump. Not even chains will get him out."

"Cheer up, birthday girl. Have some faith." Nancy gave Jess a little shove on the shoulder. "From what I hear, when all that money was left for the baseball fields, it came with a catch. And that rotten coach was it."

Jess's spirits rebounded. "Really? Holy crap. Maybe." She nodded hopefully. "If it's true it's the best birthday present I've ever gotten—except for my shirt." Jess winked. Then the bad taste of Dixon returned. "That jackass won't even look twice at Truman in his so-called tryouts. I know I'm biased, but I think Truman is at least as good as a couple of kids Dixon picks every year."

"Maybe this'll be his year," Nancy said.

Jess stood up, resolute. "I'm going to work with him more than ever. If Dixon is out, he's got a chance."

Nancy left for her shift and Jess stood in her kitchen making a chocolate birthday cake. How different their two lives were. And yet—Jess thought about them side by side putting laundry on the line—they were much the same. "It could easily be me at that bar and Nancy here with a mixing bowl." She felt fortunate. Jess was where she was meant to be.

Truman had called around 3:00 to say he was eating peanut butter sandwiches at Bale's house and would be home and game for playing catch around five. Relieved he was eating more than birthday Pop-Tarts and the bowl of Rice Krispies she insisted he finish before leaving on his bike, Jess redoubled her vow to get more protein in Truman's diet. That shouldn't be too difficult tonight. They were invited to Wade's house for birthday dinner. He was grilling Kansas City strips, his specialty. Jess would bring dessert.

Truman's bike rattled into the yard just as Jess was frosting the cake. The back fender sounded ready to fall off as he coasted across the brown, uneven lawn to the front porch. She heard his bike hit the ground.

"Don't leave your bike in a heap."

"How 'bout leaning on the porch?" came shouting back.

"Why don't you just put it in the barn where it belongs?"

"Too far. I'll put it leaning very neatly and perfectly against the porch careful not to scrape the paint?"

No response.

"Ma?"

"Don't call me that."

"Mom?"

"Okay."

Truman bounded into the kitchen out of breath. "I got friggin' amazing news."

Jess didn't spoil the moment by reminding him about the ban on partial cuss words.

"Let me guess," she said. "They're shutting down school early for summer this year."

"You'll never, ever guess!" Truman was almost bursting.

Jess was pretty sure the rumor Nancy had just shared had also made it to Truman.

"What is it?" she asked, trying to sound genuinely in the dark.

Truman spent two ecstatic minutes explaining the greatest baseball news he had ever heard and why it was probably the best thing to ever happen in his life. He paused once for a breath.

"Tryouts will be in a few weeks," Truman said.

"We'll have to work harder than ever now."

"For sure. And Bale said he's going to really push me right up to tryouts." Truman caught his breath. "What do you think he'll be like,

Mom?" He hoped she'd have a clue about the mystery coach. "Do you think he'll be great?"

Jess was intrigued by the idea of a new coach and teacher coming to town. "I don't know, Tru. But he's gotta be an improvement."

Her mind drifted to random visualizations of the new coach. Younger? Older? Tall? Squat? Then she clapped her hands like a quarterback breaking huddle. "Okay. We got places to be. Is your baseball stuff already outside?"

"Yep."

Jess pointed at Truman's wardrobe, her finger making a little circle. "Clean shorts, clean undershirt, clean shirt. I have to put on a little makeup."

Truman frowned. "For baseball?"

"Remember?" Jess said. "We're going to Wade's at six. He's grilling birthday steaks. We have just enough time to stop at the field to work on grounders."

IKE

Snuggled, Ike slept in Leo's lap. The ribs of the scrawny pup were visible as his chest rose and fell in rapid, tiny increments. Leo was no expert, but the pup looked malnourished. He couldn't help but wonder how long the little guy had been wandering in the elements.

So as not to disturb his passenger, Leo avoided shifting his body as he drove. Consequently his left leg was long asleep and his accelerator foot felt like it was on fire. Finally Leo scooped the pup and carefully set him at his hip. The pup's big eyes opened fearfully, locked onto Leo, begging not to be put out on his own again.

"Don't worry, Ike." Leo's voice was reassuring. "Where we're going, there's a guy named Doc. Good man. He'll look you over." Leo stroked the pup, who immediately fell back to sleep. "Probably didn't get much rest out there, did you?" Ike leaned into Leo's soothing voice.

The pup's coat was cinnamon colored, a smooth-wiry mix. He had oversized paws and a bobbed five-inch tail. His big floppy ears and long muzzle were features he'd grow into. There was a fuzzy trace of future eyebrows and the first stray whiskers of a beard. Leo whispered, "Not sure what breed you are, but you seem like a good one." His truck passed a sign that read: Dannaka 10 miles.

Jess pulled her ponytail through the opening in the back of her adjustable baseball cap. Not accounting for the cap, she looked very unbaseball-like. Her pleated mint-colored skirt with a flowered print fell just below the knees. She matched that with a pressed blue chambray shirt, cuffs turned up one fold so she could wield the bat more freely.

Most women in Dannaka, regarding cosmetics, believed anything worth doing was worth overdoing. Jess's use of makeup was more discreet. Her eyeliner thinly traced the top of her lash, winging up slightly at the outside corners of her eyes. This nicely complemented a small touch of mascara, setting off her green eyes.

"Charge those slow ones." Jess studied Truman's technique as he vacuumed up ground balls. They were practicing in the warmup area adjacent to the new fields, which were too wet from the spring thaw to use. Each field had a Stay Off Until Further Notice sign on the padlocked entrance gate. Truman couldn't wait to set foot on those diamonds. He'd been staring at them all winter.

"Step and throw," Jess said. "You're not getting your legs behind it."

"I don't want to overdo it, Ma." Truman wore a clean white undershirt. His checked dress shirt was carefully hung on the nearby fence. His routine after fielding each baseball was to spin and throw into the net of the batting cages. Balls gathered there on the ground.

"Let's take a break," Jess said. "Ah shit," she uttered, just loud enough to be heard.

"What?" Truman asked.

Jess shook her head. "Got mud on my skirt."

Leo slowed his truck down to read a large wooden sign standing at the town limits. Welcome to Dannaka. Home of the 1941, 1942 & 1943 State High School Baseball Champions.

"Hey Ike," Leo whispered to the sleeping pup as he powered down the front windows. "We're here." He looked at bare farm fields stretching in all directions. "I guess." The pup managed a big yawn.

Leo pointed out the window. "There's the championship sign Doc told me about. Long drought since 1943." A breeze swirled through the cab, lifting Ike's nose. He climbed on Leo's lap and thrust his snout toward the window. "Careful now. You probably don't understand how open truck windows work."

Ike knew all too well about open truck windows. He was pitched out of one into the ditch by the farmer who decided his runt of a dog wasn't worth the kibble he was eating. Ike was scrawny and meek. He had a left ear that folded back on itself and the nose on the end of his muzzle was slightly crooked. Other pups in the litter were quickly snatched up; the farmer had a reputation for breeding smart, athletic field hunting dogs. No one wanted the runt. So the farmer did what he had to do. The pup reflected poorly on himself and his breeding stock.

Ike let out a whimper and looked intently at Leo.

"What is it, boy?"

The dog cocked his head, waiting. He gave another whimper. Leo, being dog illiterate, didn't get the message immediately.

"Oooh. I bet I know. You need a potty break."

As they approached town, the expansive, empty farm fields gave way to a few outlying businesses. There was a fabrication and welding shop. A two-stall car wash. A lumberyard. A meat market, fire station and medical clinic. They bumped over the train tracks as the late-afternoon sunlight polished the silver bins next to the grain elevator. Leo checked the dashboard clock. 5:45. The speed limit dropped to 25 MPH as Leo passed an ice cream shop with a sign out front that read: See You May 1!!!

"Let's find those baseball fields. Should be plenty of open space around there for a pup to relieve himself. I might have to join you." Ike looked at him like, *you better step on it.*

Downtown was quiet and closed up for the day. Leo instantly liked the vibe. Maybe it was the permanence of the stately red brick buildings. Or how street intersections had glass-windowed shops that faced one another. Or how this town just magically appeared out of nothing but farmland. Evening light began to insert itself into the color palette.

Having the windows open and driving with an elbow out the window didn't hurt Leo's first impression, either. The bank sign said the temperature was 68.

"Take a whiff of that," Leo told the pup. "That's what home smells like now." Just then they passed Eilleen's bakery, the aroma of bread and donuts lingering. The two looked at each other like they didn't need to travel an inch farther.

A small public park with a covered picnic area was squeezed between Dannaka's downtown district and residential neighborhood. In the distance Leo saw one of the landmarks every coach looks for when trying to locate ballfields: towering, silver light poles rising above the tree line. "I think we found our diamonds." Leo's tone set Ike's tail in motion. They took a right and headed for the stanchions. "Let's find you a private pine tree."

The pickup pulled into a three-field complex. Leo parked and closed his eyes but the sensation of a vehicle in motion remained. When he opened them, he found himself staring at the giant sign. The words POODLE PARK were arched in large, white type on a green background. Below that, sporting a baseball cap with the Dannaka D logo on it, sat a respectable likeness of a poodle with one fluffy paw perched on a baseball.

"Come here. You got to see this." Leo stood Ike on his lap, putting the pup's big front paws on the steering wheel. Ike looked through the windshield. "What do you think of that?" The pup cocked his head. And cocked it again, looking up at the sign. "Yeah, I agree. Not something you want to judge too quickly." Leo continued to take it in. "Hey, look at that." Printed smaller along the bottom it read: Dogs Welcome! "Looks like you've come to the right place. If that isn't the definition of coincidence, I don't know what is."

It did feel good to get out of the truck and stretch the legs. Ike was tentative when Leo first put him down in the parking lot, but once he realized Leo wasn't going to leave him, he found his feet and was bravely investigating on his own. Never more than twenty feet away, Ike would smell a few things and then scamper back to Leo.

"Ike, check this out." Leo clapped and the pup bounded toward him. Leo's eyes sparkled as they swept across Field 1, pausing at the in-ground dugouts, the bleacher seating along the first and third baselines, the covered pitcher's mound, the 10-foot outfield fences, the digital scoreboard. "Man. I've coached at high school fields that weren't this nice. Amazing, don't you think?"

Ike let out a little bark and jumped up on Leo's leg.

"I guess you agree." Leo scratched Ike's head. "You're a smart one, aren't you?"

Ike barked again.

"Good idea to keep players off the field." Leo pointed to the Stay Off Until Further Notice sign on the entrance gate. "That infield needs a good week of heat and sun to firm up. I hope they pull that tarp off the mound during sunny hours."

The facility was smartly organized with three baseball diamonds set off from a central hub of buildings. Leo and Ike walked past the concession stand, maintenance building, umpires' room and bathrooms. Everything was locked up for winter. Adjacent to each baseball field was a warmup area and batting cages.

Initially, it was the thrall of colors that caught Leo's attention: the grass, straw-colored, with a faint memory of green contrasted by a bright mint-colored skirt, a red pail of baseballs and a boy's stark white undershirt cast against an indigo sky. Like a painting, the bold colors lifted off the landscape. And as they took on the familiar movements of baseball, it stirred ashes in the coach that had gone cold.

Ike stopped at Leo's heel. They both watched the pair in the distance. Leo was rapt by this ballet of baseball. The woman in the skirt reached into the red pail, tossed a baseball in the air and struck it with the bat, sending a grounder streaking to the boy in his clean white undershirt who scooped the ball, spun, hop-stepping before firing a chest-high dart into the net of the batting cage. One after another after another.

The woman had her back to Leo and Ike. Suddenly, the boy paused, gripping the baseball. He lifted his glove to shield the low sun, trying to distinguish who was in the distance watching them.

Ike's butt lifted slowly off the ground and his tail began to wag. With hardly an exception, since Leo had found the pup on the highway, Ike had remained glued to him. Now the dog's tail pumped, he began to quake, crouched, his legs loading, and BAM! Ike shed all trepidation and bolted toward the boy. The mother, noticing her son had stopped practicing, turned to look over her shoulder.

Despite the distance between them, Leo felt something that made his breath catch.

Ike, oversized floppy ears pinned back, sprinted past Jess and ran directly to Truman, who dropped to his knees. "Hiya pooch," he said. "What's your name?" The pup wiggled and licked and writhed and jumped. Leo shoved his hands in his pockets and slowly made his way across the practice area to catch up.

"Sorry," Leo said as he approached Jess. "I didn't think he'd run off. He's pretty shy."

"I can see that," Jess teased as the pup and Truman played. She was facing the sun, looking at Leo, causing her to squint. Jess knew most people in town but she didn't recognize this man. He was tall, a bit unkempt with a shaggy beard, longish black hair that curled any way it pleased, wearing a T-shirt that was either purchased small or the man had gained weight. She thought maybe he was visiting family.

"Is that your son?" Leo asked. Jess was front-lit by the sun, offering Leo a much better look at her. She was attractive in a baseball cap and the way she squinted made her even cuter. "Good mechanics," he said. "Fine little ballplayer."

"Yeah. Thanks." They looked over as the boy sent a baseball rolling and Ike bounded after it. "Try not to get any dirtier, got it Truman?" His undershirt showed multiple paw prints.

Leo didn't want to stare, but the woman had a riveting quality. "You sure do get dressed up for baseball around here."

Around here, she thought. That's when it hit her. She knew who the man was. But she had to silently admit: The mystery baseball coach didn't exactly live up to the picture she had formed in her head.

WADE

W ade came into the world with a full head of vivid red hair. That set the stage.

It was only a matter of time before the redhead stood out on the playground in a way he didn't care for. Wade became an easy target. *Hey, Cheeto-head! Look, it's Little Wade Riding Hood!* Now, prematurely balding at age 38, Wade found himself pining for that red hair in ways he never imagined.

"Steaks look ready for the grill," he told himself, sprinkling a last shake of Lawry's Seasoning on them. He checked his watch. Five minutes to six. "They'll be here in no time." He went outside to set up a few chairs.

Last week, he'd purchased a gas grill for his brick patio out back. The actuaries at corporate had routed a memo to all State Farm agents about fire risk and how it spiked in households with traditional charcoal kettle grills when compared to gas grills. Wade thought it prudent to switch. It was important to exemplify, as he put it, "a life that prioritized safety." But he missed the ritual of starting coals in his Weber grill. He enjoyed building a proper stack of briquettes, the smell of smoldering coal, the patient creep of glowing red spreading throughout the pile. Now, just turn a knob and press a button.

Wade felt a stab of guilt as the garage door lifted and he saw his kettle grill neatly tucked away in back, next to the hanging rakes and shears. A canvas cover was pulled over it, like it had been abducted. Wade was prone to occasional episodes of melancholy but there was a remedy. Wade began to whistle. He had a four-octave range.

In Wade's garage, three matching aluminum folding chairs with blue and white striped nylon webbing hung side by side on 10-penny nails. He took each down, carrying them out to the apron of the building. Each squeaked upon opening, with months of winter still lingering in their joints. Wade returned to the garage for a spray can of WD-40.

As he settled into the second of the three chairs, Wade relished his view of the quiet street. He knew not only the owners of the cars that drove by, but in many instances, the make, model and year of the vehicle. He held their auto insurance policies. Wade let his hand rest on his stomach, giving it a pat. "Going to have to do something about this winter spare tire," he told himself.

It didn't escape Wade that he was plain-looking and growing pudgy and soft. He had a rowing machine gathering dust in the basement. He'd bought it four years ago, not coincidentally, after Jess had come back to her hometown with her young son.

She had received a chilly reception in Dannaka. An unwed mother is looked at with a sharp eye in a God-fearing town such as theirs. While it's fair to say she wasn't shunned, she was looked down upon. But not by Wade. When Jess walked into his office and sat down in front of him, he didn't even attempt to dodge Cupid's arrow.

She was looking for life insurance, Jess told Wade. She had a son. Above all, he needed to be provided for should anything happen to her. God forbid, Wade told her, which she took to be a pat response. No. He truly meant it.

Money was tight, Jess said, but she'd find a way to pay the premium. She was looking for work. Herein was one of the rarely spoken perks of the insurance business: an agent quickly becomes privy to a great deal of personal information about someone. Wade told her he'd be happy to work out a flexible payment plan, and that Doc Gifford at the vet clinic had a technician recently leave his employ to raise triplets.

Wade created reasons to schedule Jess for appointments. Like, he'd found her a better deal on her policy. And, I've got a few money-saving ideas on car insurance. Each time they met, he'd ask how Truman was doing in school and how her new job was going up at the clinic. Jess was happy to have someone looking out for her. It had been a while.

Next thing you know, Wade was driving to Sears in Des Moines to get a rowing machine. In part the purchase was motivated by an insurance risk statistic that came across his desk. Exercises were ranked according to the amount of calories a participant burned, and their correlation to healthier lifestyles and longer lives. Top of the list: rowing. But the real motivation was the fact that Jess was active and slim and if he was to keep up with her, he needed to get into shape. Wade also stopped by the Sears sportswear department for a headband, wristbands and a pair of royal blue exercise shorts. He was all in.

Regarding their personal relationship, he and Jess began as friends, although Wade's hopes were more ardent. They would meet for lunch now and again. Or, when Doc's clinic was boarding a dog that needed to be walked, somehow Wade would be out walking at the same time. (He did a lot of business with the auto body shop across the street from the clinic. They would tip off Wade with a phone call.) Finally, Wade worked up the nerve to ask Jess out on a date: *Top Gun* had just come to the theater.

On their second date Wade told Jess he loved her. What a mistake, at least that's what people told him. But it was the truth. In Wade's book, the truth was never a mistake. Jess did her best not to look stunned at his admission. She told Wade she was a long way from any such commitment. He said he understood—that it was okay. He told her he was as patient as the moon.

And now, he waited patiently, in his driveway, drumming his fingers on his stomach. Wade reclined, his chair between two unoccupied ones. Raising a hand, he waved at Mike Ruhland's 1981 gold Lincoln Town Car as it cruised past. He adjusted his posture. He crossed his feet in front of him. He soaked in the last of the day's sunlight. Wade could wait. For as long as it took.

"Go get it!" Truman rolled a baseball onto the grass in front of them. The puppy sprinted out, grabbed it in his jaws, but somehow got tangled and did a cartwheel. Letting out a yip, Ike regained his mettle and pounced on the baseball. He was trying to carry it in his mouth, but the size of the ball only permitted him a few awkward steps before he dropped it. Truman walked over to his mom. He had a pretty good idea to whom she was talking. "You're the new baseball coach, aren't you?"

"Truman," Jess scolded. "Be polite and introduce yourself."

"I'm Truman. You're the new baseball coach, aren't you?"

Leo appreciated the boy's directness. "I guess I forgot my manners, too." He addressed Jess. "I'm Leo," extending a hand to her. "And that's Ike."

"I'm Jess. Pleased to meet you." His handshake was not nearly as firm as hers.

Leo turned and looked down at the boy. "You're right. I am the new coach."

Truman pressed on hopefully. "Of the 12-year-old traveling team?"

"That's correct. How old are you?"

"I'm 12." Truman lifted his heels off the ground to gain a couple inches.

"Then I guess we'll be seeing more of each other. Your mechanics on ground balls looked good." Leo leaned down and picked one of the baseballs out of the beach pail. Like the others beside it, the ball was a mess. Scuffed, a broken lace, somewhat waterlogged. "Looks like you get some use out of these."

Truman was ashamed. "I guess."

"That's excellent," Leo encouraged. "I used to have a few balls that looked like this when I was your age. Would throw 'em and hit 'em against the backstop till they wore out."

Truman brightened. "Until they got so tattered you could tear off the cover and unwind all the string—"

"To get to the cork in the middle." Leo smiled at the memory.

Ike proudly trotted up to the group with a baseball. Somehow his front teeth were able to sink into the frayed laces. He dropped the ball into the pail. Truman's eyes lit up. "Did you teach him that?"

"Wow," Jess said.

Leo was equally astonished. "Can't say I did."

Jess bent to stroke the pup. "Skinny little fella. What breed is Ike? German Wirehair?" She examined him, not at all impressed by the string collar or unattended coat.

Leo shook his head. "I'm not sure. Found him on my way here. Sitting plunked down in the middle of the road."

Jess frowned. "That's awful. Any sign of the owner?"

"'Fraid so. He had a note attached to that makeshift collar. Said the pup was the runt of the litter and unsellable. The owner said he had no use for him so he tossed him out for the coyotes, unless someone found him first."

"Oh, you poor little dear." Jess bent down and scooped up Ike.

"Mom," Truman said. "Your shirt."

"Ah, crap," she said. "Forgot about that." Jess rearranged the pup so his dirty paws rode astride her forearm. "Oh well."

"You know your way around dogs."

Truman spoke up. "My mom works at the vet clinic."

Leo paused. "So you know Doc Gifford."

Now it was Jess's turn to be surprised. "How do you know Doc?"

"He's the one who recruited me to coach here. Came all the way to Illinois to do it."

Jess's cute crooked smile appeared. "That's Doc. Nowhere's too far where baseball's concerned."

"Yeah, he told me about this Little League complex. I thought he was talking the place up to get me interested but it's everything he said and then some." Leo took a long look at the fields. "I'm hoping Doc can help me find a home for Ike."

Truman looked at Leo. "You're not gonna keep him?"

Leo shook his head. "I wish I could, Truman. But I need to focus on teaching, coaching and getting settled."

Truman asked, "You're going to teach, too?"

"Yep. Social studies." Leo gave Truman a wink. "Your favorite subject, right?"

Truman smiled. "Is now, Coach."

"Suck up," Jess said, laughing.

"I'm having lunch with Doc tomorrow. Then there's some sort of baseball meeting with parents and players … up at the school."

"Yep," Jess interjected. "Three o'clock in the gym."

"We'll be there," Truman told Leo.

"So, I need to get some food for this little guy. Is there a grocery store in town that sells something for him?"

Jess explained. "The main road off the highway that goes through downtown is First Street. On First and Third there's a grocery store. They have Puppy Chow, chicken flavor. He should handle that well. Sometimes it depends on what he was fed after he was whelped." Jess lifted Ike's upper lip and looked at the pup's milk teeth. "He looks about three months old. I'd try the Puppy Chow. They should have a dog bowl, too."

"Bowl. Yeah. Would have forgotten that." Leo pointed, "So back to First and then a left to Third."

Jess nodded. She looked at her watch. "Shoot! We need to get going." It was 6:15. She set Ike down. "Truman. Go get your shirt off the fence."

"It's my mom's birthday," Truman said, looking at Leo. Truman didn't want to be anywhere but where he was right now.

"Get a move on," Jess told him. "Sorry," she said to Leo. "We're late."

"Happy birthday," Leo said, thinking their baseball wardrobes now made sense.

For the first time he was positioned to the sun so Jess could get a better look at his face. He had deep blue eyes that sparkled despite a trace of sadness. There was a cupped scar under his right eye. "Today has been a day of coincidences." Leo looked off as Truman ran across the practice area to get his shirt, Ike bounding after him.

"How's that?" Jess said.

Leo made eye contact. "Today's my birthday, too."

"Sorry, sorry, sorry, sorry," Jess said, coming out of the car with her chocolate cake. Wade stood up from his folding chair. "We're late. I know. Again." She gave Wade a quick kiss and headed for the kitchen. "Let me put this cake down. I see you have the chairs out." She was moving fast. "Woo-hoo," she said, glancing at Wade over her shoulder. "First sign of spring."

Wade had to laugh. "She sure gets to moving when she sets her mind to it." He gave Truman a pat on the back. "Hey slugger."

"Hey ya Wade," Truman said. "How's the beer coming?" Wade's latest hobby was brewing beer. His basement was loaded with fermenters, funnels, tubing, bottles, cappers—Truman thought it was the coolest thing.

"Wanna see?" Wade asked.

"For sure."

Jess set her chocolate cake on the kitchen counter and glanced out the open window. There was a perimeter of lilac bushes that Wade dutifully pruned every spring after they blossomed. Three blue chairs stationed in front of the garage, like a little family. There was Wade, his hand resting on Truman's shoulder, walking toward the house as they talked excitedly about something.

"You're a lucky girl," she whispered to herself. Wade and Truman saw her in the window and waved. Jess was distracted, but then waved back. Her thoughts had drifted to the baseball fields, to Leo, to the sadness in his blue eyes.

HOME

---

oc found a cozy one-story house for Leo to rent two blocks from the baseball fields. He'd phoned Leo about a week ago and said the Little League Association would take care of the first few months' rent, while he got settled. Leo began to object but Doc was insistent. He said there was a good chunk of change from the trust fund earmarked for auxiliary costs, so not to worry.

You'll like the place, Doc assured him. Completely furnished. Owned by an elderly widow, Mrs. Hilburn, who was starting to forget things like water running in the tub and chicken in the oven that baked overnight. She had agreed to move three blocks over to live with her daughter's family—on one condition: Her house would be rented to a qualified tenant and the revenue would go to her daughter and son-in-law. She's stubborn Iowa stock, Doc said. There was no talking her out of it.

It was the only yellow house on the block, Doc told Leo. Hardly need the address. If Leo had a pencil ready, Doc said, he'd give him the number. Turned out, Leo didn't need to write down that address. 1479 Oak Street. In fact, Leo asked Doc to repeat it; he thought he had heard it wrong. 1479, Doc repeated. Leo shook his head at the happenstance. On the back of an envelope he wrote: Yellow. Oak Street. Unbelievable. The last word was underlined twice.

The front door was unlocked, as Doc said it would be. Leo set two bags of groceries on the kitchen table next to a key ring marked House and Garage. A note read:

Welcome Leo! Delighted you're here.
Any questions, call. 782-0213.

65

Otherwise see you tomorrow at my house. Plan on lunch at noon. My wife, Margaret, will have sandwiches. We are four blocks west, corner of Rose and Fourth. It's baseball weather!

Doc

"Come on, Ike." Leo whistled, holding the door open, scanning the yard. It was almost dark but Leo thought he saw movement by the shrubs along the front of the house.

Ike, relatively unacquainted with steps, was careful coming down. Once in the yard, the pup locked up, holding point, body rigid, tail straight, nose jutting toward the bushes, right paw off the ground hinged at the ankle.

"That's pretty cool. What do you have there?" Leo walked down the steps. Ike, statuesque, focused his every molecule on the bushes.

As Leo made his way across the grass, Ike's head turned ever so slightly to check in with him.

"You got something in there, buddy?" Just then a rabbit darted from the brush. Ike let out an excited yip and took chase.

"Wait! Ike! Stop!" Leo broke into a sprint, hollering after Ike. A string of shadows headed up the street, the rabbit putting distance between the other two. For three blocks, Leo continued to holler and Ike continued to yelp.

"You can't do that to me." Leo was breathing much harder than Ike. "No. You hear me?" They were back on the front stoop of the house, now, Ike in Leo's lap, panting, his little rib cage pumping like a bellows. Ike cocked his head, trying to decipher the meaning of Leo's words. Leo meant to be stern, but failed. "I've never seen anything like that." He coughed and spat. "Shit. I gotta get in shape." Scratching Ike behind the ear—which the pup leaned into with pleasure—he said, "You're a hunter, aren't you? It's in you. Maybe Doc can find you a home in the country where you can chase stuff without somebody running you down."

The two of them took their first tour of the house, absorbing the new sights and smells. Cozy, just as Doc had described, the home was neat as a pin and plenty big enough for Leo. There were two small bedrooms on the main level, separated by a bathroom. Off the kitchen was, as best as Leo could label it, a TV room with a reclining chair and a small couch. Space in the kitchen was tight, with a sink, countertop and cupboards on one wall, stove, refrigerator and pantry adjacent to that. Facing two small double hung windows was an oval table and two chairs with a view to the street.

"Let's scope out the basement," Leo told Ike. He stepped off the landing through the doorway and BANG! "Damn," Leo saw stars.

Ike's tail tucked.

"It's not you, boy. Just a low bridge." Leo rubbed his forehead. "God that hurt," He let the pain judder through him. "Shake it off," he told himself.

At six-two, Leo spent much of the basement tour hunched under enclosed ductwork. There wasn't much to see: An unfinished utility room, old cement laundry sink, washer and dryer and a small room behind a divider curtain with empty shelves except for a few forgotten canning jars. Ike sniffed around but found nothing to hold his interest.

Back upstairs, Leo unloaded the grocery bag of Puppy Chow, a feeding dish and a small red collar. "Well, Ike, time for your first real collar."

Leo let the pup sniff it.

"No. Not for chewing." Ike got the collar in his sharp milk teeth and thought a game of tug of war would be fun. "Let go. No, Ike." Ike obeyed, under protest, giving Leo a full dose of sad puppy eyes. "This is for your neck, not your mouth."

Finding no scissors, Leo carefully used a steak knife to cut Ike's twine collar. "That's better." Leo's tone put Ike's tail in motion. After a little squirming and rearranging, the pup was proudly parading around the kitchen with his new red collar.

"Bet you're parched." Leo found a square Tupperware container and filled it with water. "Sorry I didn't think of that sooner." Ike happily lapped while Leo tried to determine how much to feed the pup. He decided to fill the bowl and call it good. Ike gave the food one cautionary sniff, but that's where any hesitation ceased. The kibble was devoured.

With only three cardboard boxes to unpack, Leo started with the one that had bath towels. He found an old red towel with green and gold stripes. After folding it over on itself, and then again, he placed it on the kitchen floor. "That's for you," he told Ike, patting the towel. "Come try your new bed." The food, an exciting rabbit chase and playing ball on the field all converged as the pup stepped onto the soft towel, walked a tight circle and dropped. He was watching Leo as his eyes closed.

It was no accident that Leo packed lightly. A person looking for a fresh start can't lug all his history with him. He had two boxes with clothes, bedding, a pair of dress shoes and two neckties for school. And the last box had odds and ends, including a bathroom scale, his baseball card collection, shaving kit and a royal blue Cubs jacket with its bold red C sewn on front.

When Leo signed with the Cubs in 1979 as an 18-year-old straight out of high school, the jacket was one of the items in his welcome package at the hotel. He was fine jettisoning the rest of his baseball memorabilia, but the jacket marked the beginning of his pro career—a turning point similar to uprooting and coming to Iowa. The baseball cards reminded him of his childhood passion, his belief in the possibilities of baseball. Leo hoped to rediscover that in Dannaka.

With three eggs scrambled alongside fried ham, Leo waited for two slices of toast to pop. He poured his second glass of milk thinking he made the right decision at the grocery store to remove the frozen pizza and two-liter bottle of Coke from his shopping cart. It was time, Leo told himself, for discipline to return to his diet. He vowed to eat slowly and fully chew his food. In the end, Leo inhaled his dinner much like Ike had.

His bathroom scale had made the move with him for dubious

reasons. He brought it to chastise himself for the weight he'd gained. But when he unpacked the scale and stepped on it in the bathroom, the 221-pound reading became more motivating than shaming.

His fungo bat, glove and bucket of baseballs went in the front entryway closet. He put away his few changes of underwear, socks and T-shirts in the chest of drawers in the larger of the two small bedrooms. Hung forlornly in the bedroom closet among the many empty wire hangers were his three dress shirts, two sport coats and two ties for the classroom.

Wrapped in a Chicago Bears stadium blanket was the only thing that really mattered. A framed team poster of last year's State High School Baseball Champions. It was the same team Doc and his pals watched Leo coach to a comeback victory.

He carefully took it out of the blanket, reading the small silver engraved plaque cut into the framing mat:

COACH LEO HAMILL. 4X WINNER!
UNDISPUTEDLY, BEST IN THE COUNTRY.

He scanned the smiling faces beneath the red ball caps tipped up for the camera. The team sat in the middle rows of the gymnasium's wooden bleachers. His eyes stopped in the same places, as always: First row, second in from the left. Third row, fourth in from the left. Leo knew all too well where those two faces were among the twenty-one. "Sorry boys," he whispered. He carefully laid the framed poster on the top shelf in the closet.

When Leo returned to the kitchen, he was startled by Ike, who was sitting erect just off his towel, waiting for him. "Hey there," he said, his voice loud in the quiet space.

Ike stood and his tail got busy. He yawned almost big enough to swallow himself, shook off the sleep and trotted over to squat near Leo's shoes.

"No no no no no." Leo scooped up Ike and ran him out the door. The pup was frightened by the sudden transport. The intensity in

Leo's voice dropped.

"Here's a perfect spot." He set him on the front lawn.

Ike glanced at him, uncertain.

"Go potty," Leo said. "That's the spot."

If a pup could say aloud, "Oooh, I get what you're saying," that's what Ike said in action—an action, as it turned out, that went longer than Leo would have guessed possible from a tiny puppy bladder.

"Impressive." Leo smiled at the dog. "Good boy. Good potty." Ike enjoyed both the praise and the relief. "Well pal, time to shut it down for the day. C'mon boy."

Ike peered at the shrub that held the rabbit a few hours earlier. Then he looked at Leo.

"Let's call it good for tonight, okay? Let sleeping rabbits lie."

Ike bounded ahead and waited at the door, with Leo just behind. The steps were floodlit, as was the house address. Seeing those numbers was just as unfathomable now as when Doc had recited the address last week over the phone. Fate? Coincidence? Synchronicity? Leo and Ike stood on the front stoop soaking in the endless quiet. A night breeze whispered to the stars.

"Wanna know something strange, Ike?"

The pup's ears pricked up as he focused on Leo.

"When the Cubs drafted me I was taken in the first round, fourth pick, in 1979. Check out our new address." Leo pointed to it. Ike cocked his head.

Beneath a night sky of countless stars, Leo wondered if somehow they had aligned for him in finding this new home. He shrugged and gave the address a good luck tap. Leo crossed the threshold, pulling the door shut.

The front light went out on house number 1479.

Morning

L eo was in the hospital for rotator cuff repair when the surgeon, Pete Rose, amputated his entire limb. That's how asleep Leo's arm was.

When Leo awoke from the bizarre dream, his arm was dangling off the bed toward the floor where Ike slept pressed against it.

Last night—and into the early hours of morning—Ike slept only if he felt contact with Leo. The dangling arm did the trick, ending continuous whimpering, mostly from Ike.

Leo pulled his deadened arm onto the bed and looked at his watch: 9:14. They'd been out twice in the dark of morning when Leo thought Ike was whining because he needed to relieve himself. One time he did. The other time he just sniffed and sniffed and sniffed and sniffed and sniffed and sniffed. Leo picked him up and brought him in.

With returning circulation burning through his arm, Leo rubbed his face with fingers he could not feel. What a lousy night's sleep. Leo wondered how puppy owners did it. He'd ask Doc for tips when they met for lunch. Right now, Leo needed to get the blood flowing. Maybe a jog to clear his head. The sunlight spilling through the bedroom window was inviting, despite a sleep-deprived headache.

"Feels like I drank a case of beer last night." Leo sat up slowly in bed. Conversely, Ike sprang to his feet; the sound of Leo's voice was music. "You look no worse for the wear." Leo's temples throbbed. "Did I just have my teeth drilled for hours? Huh, did I, boy?"

Ike was ecstatic to be awake and spoken to. He tried to jump up on the bed but ended up falling backward. He bounced, contorted himself to his feet and let out a sharp bark. Then he tried again but the bed was too high. Leo looked at the pup. "I like your grit, but don't hurt yourself. Should we go outside?"

Barefoot, in shorts and a T-shirt, Leo let Ike out into the yard. "Keep away from those bushes," Leo said in a low voice. Ike looked back at him, his posture slumped. "C'mon," Leo said cheerfully. "Let's try in back. Remember? Where we had quality time last night." The pup sprang after him.

The backyard offered one treasure after the next. A downspout edging the house connected to a drainage gutter, which was rich with the scent of chipmunks that had scurried inside it to hide. The base of a maple tree was ringed with brown, curled leaves to paw. A bird nest had blown out of a row of lilac bushes and—bonus!—rabbit poop to munch on. "Don't," Leo scolded, pushing Ike away with his bare foot.

The grass was cool on the shady fringe, but in the open, flat square of the backyard it was warming. "Another beaut of a day," Leo told Ike. Ike didn't have time for small talk. He was ... busy. "I'll be careful not to step in that," Leo said. "Good dog. Good potty."

Generous sunlight fell across the yard. Leo bowed to it allowing his neck and shoulders to relax in the warmth. Chickadees flounced after one another in a large pine tree near the one-car garage.

"Hello. Excuse me there." Leo flinched and Ike barked at a voice that sprang out of nowhere. In the next yard stood a neighbor with a roll of green garden hose over his shoulder. "Sorry. Didn't mean to give you a fright."

Before Leo could call him back, Ike dashed enthusiastically through the straw-covered rose garden that separated the two lawns. His neighbor didn't seem to mind. Leo pegged the man at retirement age, mid- to late-sixties.

Putting the hose aside, the neighbor bent to meet Ike. "Well aren't you the wiggle wart." The pup writhed in joy as the man scratched Ike's withers, sides and flanks. Ike repaid the man's hands in alternating licks and nips.

"Sorry about that," Leo said, carefully making his way through the winter-cut roses. Absent shoes and socks, there were better places for him to tread. "He's getting more and more used to people. And he's got energy to burn."

The neighbor looked up. "Yeah. I heard you guys out here last night. Thought it was raccoons."

Leo shook his head. "I apologize. Couldn't get him to settle down."

"Might try a hot water bottle. Pups like to lie next to something warm. Reminds them of mom." The neighbor stood. "You must be the new baseball coach Doc told me about."

"So you know Doc."

"Doesn't everybody? At least everyone of my vintage. The name's Fredrickson. LaMar Fredrickson."

Leo stuck out a hand. "Nice to meet you. I'm Leo Hamill. And that's Ike." The pup sniffed around the neighbor's bird feeders before moving on to the central air conditioning unit.

"Doc told me you'd be coming. Never mentioned a dog."

"Yeah," Leo shrugged. "Picked him up about 50 miles back. He'd been abandoned and was wandering on the highway. I thought Doc would know what to do with him. Find him a good home."

"Well that's a fine thing you did, Leo. Fine indeed. We need to take care of God's creatures."

Leo agreed, overtaken by a yawn.

The neighbor asked, "You'll be running the 12-year-old traveling team, I take it?"

"I will," Leo said, surprised that something like that would be public knowledge.

The neighbor seemed to read Leo's thoughts. "Baseball is big in this town. Real big. Kids start playing when they're hardly taller than their mitts and play through town ball until their wife or doctor or both says it's time to hang up the cleats."

"You sound like you played a bit yourself."

"Sure did. Some of the best memories of my life. You know?"

Leo had a more complicated relationship with the game, but he smiled and nodded.

Ike came over for some more of that good scratching.

"Look who's back," the neighbor said, squatting down, this time finding a spot behind Ike's ears that all but tranquilized the pup.

Leo spoke up. "LaMar, you wouldn't happen to have a piece of rope I could borrow? I need to get this little guy over to the baseball fields and I don't want him running out into the street on our way there."

LaMar was only too happy to help. "I got a garage full of lengths of nylon rope. My wife tells me I could toss half of them and still have too many." He paused as a twinkle filled his eyes. "I tell her I will do that … as soon as she thins the herd of shoes she has penned in her closet." The neighbor gave Leo a sly grin. "Now, let's see. What do you need? Ten foot or twenty? I'd say to avoid gettin' that pup wrapped around every tree, pole and hydrant, we get you a ten. Be back in a jiff."

Leo pulled on socks and tennis shoes and started up the tree-lined sidewalk in the direction of the baseball fields. The air was crisp but a south wind was shaking the cool out. It was the first gorgeous weekend of pre-spring and folks were making the most of it.

"See you got a rope on that pup," a man called out. He was taking storm windows off his porch and replacing them with screens. "That was quite a race you had last night. I'd say the rabbit won." The man chuckled, enjoying his sense of humor.

Leo waited while Ike sniffed a tree trunk. "Yeah. I took third place."

The man leaned a window against the porch. "So I'm guessing you're our new coach for the Little Leaguers?"

"That's right."

"Welcome to ya." Then he shouted across the street to a man raking the thatch out of his front lawn. "Hey Gibbs! This here's the new coach. For the Triple A Twelve team."

Gibbs leaned on his rake. "Did you say he's the new coach for the Triple A Twelves?"

"That's right."

"Well, nice to meet you," He shouted at Leo. "And good luck."

Leo thanked him.

"Because you're gonna need it. I have a nephew from Des Moines with a kid on the Twelves. That boy can knock the ball into next week."

Leo wasn't sure how to respond. "Oh, okay. Thanks for the tip."

Gibbs worked a twig out of his rake tines. The window man took his thumbnail to a stubborn spot of bird poop on the glass. Leo and Ike stood there, not sure if the conversation was officially over. "Be seeing you then," Leo said, leaving them with a wave.

"You sure will," the nearest neighbor said. "We'll be up at the meeting today. At school."

"Oh," Leo said. "Do you have a grandson playing?"

"Heck no," the window man told him. "We just want to see if there will be any fireworks."

"Yeah, fireworks," Gibbs said hopefully.

"Not sure I follow you," Leo said.

The window man explained. "Coach Dixon has a temper on him."

"He's a barrel of fishhooks," Gibbs added loudly.

"Who's Coach Dixon?"

Gibbs took that one. "He's the man you're replacing."

The other added, "And he's not the replacing type."

Leo nodded. "Hmm. Good to know."

Ike managed to wrap himself around a tree a couple times over. It made Leo wonder if that might be how the day was going to go.

But a morning like this Sunday morning was incompatible with disquieting thoughts. It wasn't yet 10:00 and the temperature was in the high 60s. By the time Leo got across the street, through the park and to the ballfields he didn't have a care in the world. It was difficult to say who was more excited, puppy or man.

It may have been the angle of light, but the baseball fields looked greener than yesterday. After a lengthy stretching session on the grass, which Ike turned into a game called climb on Leo and chew on his beard, they started a slow jog around the outside perimeter of the fields.

The complex was laid out with its buildings centered and the baseball diamonds radiating out like three flower petals. As they jogged around the outfield fences, Ike, now untethered, stayed close by. "Need some loft to get one over these fences," Leo said to the pup. "They look like 10-footers. We'll work a little uppercut into the boys' swings."

Jog around the fields 10 times—that was the plan. Leo accomplished half of that. His lungs burned, stomach cramped, sweat poured off him. He and Ike found a shady spot under a tree to lay down. Ike pulled at Leo's shoelaces before plopping down in the cool grass. "Damn, I'm a load," Leo panted. "Before this summer is over I'm going to be running, not jogging, around these fields. Ten laps minimum."

Leo hooked his hands behind his head and looked up through the boughs of a pine tree at the thin watermark clouds stretching across the blue sky. He felt a nap closing his eyelids, but he pushed back.

"Let's move," he said to Ike, who was more onboard with the nap idea. Leo stood, mentally scrolling through his to-do list: Shower; get ready for lunch with Doc; ask about finding a home for Ike; get the story on this Dixon guy.

Leo wasn't up for a turf war. He hadn't even fully unpacked his boxes yet.

CONFESSION

Sunday Mass times at Saint Joseph's were at 8:30 and 10:30. Truman knew it was fruitless to argue about going. Instead, at bedtime, he only asked if they could go to the 8:30. He wanted to get to Bale's as early as possible to practice before the Little League meeting. Jess gave him a non-committal "let me think about it." When morning arrived she decided it was best for him to sleep. They'd go to the second Mass. Sleep might be the magic ticket to a growth spurt.

Up early with a slice of sourdough toast swiped with raspberry jam, Jess sat on the porch steps and submerged into the quiet. The insects would be making an appearance soon, but for now it was just her, sunshine and a breeze with no leaves to rustle. A golden thread of morning light outlined her barn and pole shed.

"Good morning, step," she patted the wooden tread next to her. "I'm 29 and one day old today." For Jess this spot was a safe place to say aloud what she might otherwise swallow.

Jess wore pajama bottoms and her new "I miss the 70s" birthday T-shirt. Drawing a reflective breath, she was learning to be prouder of herself, or at least trying. Jess recognized she had a wonderful son "most of the time," she would say to tease him. But more so, she understood that Truman was about to go over a waterfall known as puberty with its accompanying acne, cracking voice and deluge of eye-rolling attitude. Right now he was mostly an innocent, trusting boy. Unconditional love enables a child to grow up slower.

"I have a good job. Doc's a great boss. Not retiring—ever—according to him." As she spoke her thoughts ricocheted to Wade. "And Wade's a good man. Very sweet. That should be enough. Right?" A frown creased her brow. "He's fine with being engaged to be engaged. At least he says so. But how or when that evolves into something more, I'm not sure."

Jess and Wade had had a few physical moments together when their kissing became passionate—actually, more so for Wade. But he was a staunch believer in saving further advances for marriage. Jess was aware that many happy, romantic relationships ripen out of friendships. Her hope was this would be true for her, too.

Jess's gaze turned to the pole shed that once housed the septic trucks. For her, the gauzy morning light carried an undertone of sadness. Her busy mind put her in a crossfire of thoughts.

"I'm sorry, Pops. I had no idea what it could feel like to be on the parent side of my leaving. If Truman took off at 17…." Jess shuddered. "No wonder your heart gave out."

The needle on the oversized thermometer had pushed past 60 degrees. Jess looked at her watch. She could shake Truman out of bed and get to 8:30 Mass before the first reading, but she sided with her earlier instinct to let him sleep.

For the last year Jess had been going to confession every month. It hadn't dawned on her how much she was repeating herself until a few weeks ago. The priest had told her quite frankly, "My child, I have absolved you of that sin. Clearly you are sorry for the past neglect of your child. You were young. Your judgment, underdeveloped. Please, you have atoned for your mistakes. You can't let this pattern of thinking become your life. You must move on." It was the first time Jess had ever heard the priest speak above a whisper in the confessional.

Her thoughts came full circle: learning how to be proud of herself versus accentuating the negative. She had deeply hurt her father when she ran away. Not long after, though Jess didn't know it at the time, her mother left him, too.

"All you were doing was providing for your family. And we left you. Why?" Jess had always found it simple to say she left for love and her mother left for the possibility of a more glamorous life. "Why did Mom really leave? How do I know? Did you two fall out of love? Was she ever really in love? She was always critical of you." Jess squeezed her eyes shut. "I don't have a damn clue."

Since the day she left on the back of a motorcycle, Jess and her mother had hardly spoken. Jess had told the truth; she was pregnant. They had a horrible fight. They both said regrettable things. Jess's mother said get out. Her dad tried to mediate. Always the peacemaker.

Now her mother was remarried and living in Arizona with a man who was once the family dentist. Jess tried to patch things up when she and Truman settled in Dannaka, but her mother's righteous indignation was a cancer. She acknowledged her daughter's attempt to reconcile in one sentence. "My daughter and her bastard son passed away some years ago."

Jess's smile was slow in coming and a bit crooked when realized. Most considered it to be spectacularly cute. But really, it was an expression tangled in caution and regret.

"We'll meet Wade for 10:30 Mass. Truman will ride his bike and leave after communion to play ball with Bale and the guys. Wade says he has egg bake ready to go in the oven for brunch." Jess shifted on the step. "Maybe I'll just rip his clothes off and we'll get on with it." She thought for a moment. "Never happen. Especially on a Sunday."

Jess put one hand over her closed eyes and conjured up a mental image. It was a photograph of Truman, tall, handsome, smiling in his high school graduation robes. And then the photograph morphed into Truman graduating from college. She'd visualized this countless times, always raising the same disturbing question. The photographs had Truman in them and they had her in them, but where was Wade? How was Truman going to college without Wade?

"Well," she set her palm down on the sun-warmed wood, "maybe there's more to the picture than I'm seeing." She leaned into the sun like a windowsill plant. "Some girls talk to their husbands. Some talk to a shrink. I've got a step."

LUNCH

"Come in! By all means!" Doc cooked up an excited tone, belying the fact that he didn't immediately recognize the coach. When he did, he was concerned with what he saw. Ragged beard. Extra weight. Dark circles under Leo's eyes.

The inspection was not lost on Leo. "Lousy night's sleep last night," he said. Then he tugged on a rope and Ike came in on cue. "My bunkmate. A light sleeper."

"Well look here now." Doc's eyes sparkled. He bent down, mindful to remain higher than the pup. "What do we have? C'mere you." Ike melted under Doc's practiced hands. Then in a flash, Doc had the pup flipped on his back, pinned to the floor. "No bite," Doc commanded. Ike's legs flailed, but Doc knew just how much pressure would prompt compliance. "Easy now." The edge on Doc's voice softened. Ike calmed. "Good boy," Doc told him, letting the pup back on his feet. Ike shook, his big ears flapping. Doc addressed Leo. "A dog needs to know you're the alpha in the pack. Elsewise, he'll be training you."

"Got it." The pup found refuge in Leo's legs, eyeing Doc warily.

"Didn't know you were bringing a dog."

"That makes two of us. About an hour out of town, I came around a bend and there he was. In the road. Sitting. I nearly didn't stop in time."

"Come here, you." Doc made a clicking sound in his mouth, a curiosity that caused the pup to angle his head. "What's his name?"

"Ike," Leo told him.

Doc tongue-clicked again. "Ike. Come."

Which was precisely what Ike did.

Doc continued. "Good come." He laid on the praise thickly.

"Looks like a German Wirehair. Pointing breed. Undersized. Likely abandoned. Hold still a minute. Easy." Doc's voice was soothing, just above a whisper. He inspected the pup's teeth. "Good Ike. Good dog. Okay, no more poking and prodding from me."

Leo asked, "How's he seem, Doc?"

"Skinny as a worm. Little malnourished. What are you feeding him?"

"I got Puppy Chow at the grocery store," Leo said.

Doc grimaced. "We'll go up to my clinic and get him something better than that."

Leo's shoulders sagged.

"Ah, it's not the worst thing," Doc waved a hand. "Just a lot of filler. Ike, you need protein. I'll write a note. A couple weeks of boiled chicken and rice mixed with his kibble and he'll sturdy up."

Leo cut to the chase. "Well, Doc, I don't know about that. I was hoping you could help me find a good home for Ike. I can't keep him. I don't know the first thing about dogs. Growing up, our family spent all our time on baseball fields."

"Let's go sit in the kitchen," Doc said. "Nice breeze in there. We'll sort this out."

Doc had a manner about him that was soothing, even classy. His blue eyes were welcoming and spirited. What was left of his hair was neatly trimmed. With his legs crossed at the kitchen table, lanky and angular, he folded easily into a chair. Effortless—that was the word Leo was looking for. Doc's disposition had an effortless quality.

Ike sniffed around the kitchen while Leo leaned back in his chair. "Were you a pitcher back in the day?"

Doc's eyes twinkled. "Now how did you know that?"

"You've got the frame. Long arms and legs. Big hands. You rangy ones, I have no sympathy for. Towering on the hill, blowing the heater by us."

Doc allowed a gentle laugh. "Boys like you sent plenty of 'em right back the way they came. We called those a chuck and duck."

Leo smiled at the memory. It was nice to talk baseball without any remorse. "So there's a meeting at three in the gym?"

Doc didn't answer. He was looking out the window at his wife. "Margaret will have my hide, not calling her in, you sitting at the table. But she's a gardener and hasn't had her hands in the ground since last October. She's happy as a lark. Let's give her a few more minutes. Allow us to get better acquainted." Doc turned to face Leo. "Where were we? Oh, yes. Three sharp. Expect quite a turnout in the gym."

"Everybody I run into seems to know about this meeting. You weren't exaggerating when you said this was a baseball town."

"Oh and then some." Doc nodded. "How about this weather I arranged as a welcome? And have you been to see the fields?"

Leo lit up. "Unbelievable. Weather, fields—everything good as advertised. Better. I never had anything like that facility growing up. These kids don't know how lucky they are."

"Amen," Doc said. He paused, and his voice grew more serious. "So how's things, Leo? I must say I hardly recognized you. With the beard," he added somewhat clumsily.

Leo pinched his stomach flab with both hands. "Got work to do. Didn't have my best fall and winter ever." That's as detailed as he got.

"Well here you are now." Doc's enthusiasm buoyed the conversation. "Right on the fringe of the best season of the year, when hope springs eternal for every ballplayer. No matter the age." Crow's feet radiated from the corners of Doc's eyes.

"I was planning to hit the barbershop today for a haircut and have them shave off this mess." Leo tugged on his beard. "But I'm not sure there'll be time. That little guy sure keeps me busy, though you wouldn't know it now." Leo gestured toward Ike.

The pup had found a nice napping spot on the kitchen floor, pressed to the side of the refrigerator. Doc smiled. "You know why he sleeps there?"

Leo said he did not.

"The motor is on the bottom, so the refrigerator is a little warmer in that spot. Plus the security of something to lean against and the low whir of the fan likely reminds him of sleeping next to his mother and litter mates."

Leo shook his head. "Poor little guy. To get tossed out like that. Do you see much of that around here?"

"A shameful amount," Doc said. "Most strays aren't so fortunate to have someone like you come by."

Leo told Doc about the note around Ike's neck.

Doc grit his teeth. "That pup is lucky the coyotes didn't get him. Who knows, maybe he's a lucky charm."

"Doc, do you think you can help find him a good home?"

"I do, yes. We can put a plan together. But first, let's talk a little baseball, before my wife discovers you're here and takes after me with the hoe."

The two men split a Coke and talked inside baseball. Doc asked the questions that filled his head every spring when warm breezes carried the rhythmic pings of batting practice, the lively chorus of diamond chatter and the hopeful surge in a crowd's voice when a ball was well-stroked.

He asked what situation Leo liked best for a safety squeeze? Leo told him tight game, first and third, tough lefty pitcher, lefty batter, 2 and 0 count; lay it down the first baseline. Doc asked when the bases were loaded, single to right, how does your defense rotate? Leo's fingertip traced the choreography of player movements on the kitchen table as he spoke. First base goes to the infield grass for the cutoff. Second covers first. Short takes second. Third stays put. Pitcher backs up home. Center fielder backs up right. Left fielder backs up third. Doc asked if Leo had a favorite trick play? Leo smiled and said every coach has one or two up his sleeve, but that's top secret.

"Speaking of coaches," Leo said, "I hear there's some guy named Dixon I'm replacing. Any politics there I should know about?"

Doc chose his words carefully. "Dixon. Well, he's a handful. But I think if you make him your assistant coach, everything will be jake."

Leo tapped the table, thinking. "I don't want to create an issue, but my assistants—that's not a decision I make too fast. They have to be on the same page, which is my page."

"Dixon is a lot of bluster. But he knows our kids. And the other teams' strengths and weaknesses. Might be helpful."

"I'll give him a look. But no guarantees on him or any of the old guard. Our agreement was fresh start. New thinking, no baggage, no favoritism. Right?"

"Yep. That's our deal." Doc wanted to change the subject. "Do you mind talking about your time in the major leagues?"

"Pretty short conversation," Leo quipped.

"I don't mean to pry," Doc told him, taking a swallow of his soda.

Leo shrugged. "I got drafted right out of high school at the ripe old age of 18. Went directly to the Cubs A-Ball team."

"What year was that?"

"1979," Leo told him. "By 19, I was playing Triple-A in Wichita."

Doc thought for a moment. "Was that the Aeros?"

Leo was impressed. "You do know your baseball. So, September call-ups came, I'm hitting .320, next thing I know I have all my stuff jammed in my roommate's Ford LTD and I'm driving up to Wrigley."

Doc shook his head pensively. "Nineteen and going to the bigs. Were you nervous as all get-out?"

Leo looked off. "Strangely, no. Had every reason to be, but one thing I'd learned—got this from my high school coach, who was probably the most influential coach I had—was the importance of relaxing in sports, and how to relax."

"So this is ten years ago, right?" Doc said. "Must seem like forever."

"And a day," Leo told him.

Just then Doc's wife Margaret came into the kitchen through the back door. Startled from his nap, Ike let out a high-pitched yip, bouncing to his feet. Perspiring, Margaret wore an old Cardinals baseball cap. She had a stripe of dirt across one cheek.

"Our lunch guest is here?" Margaret kept her tone upbeat despite being surprised. Noticing her muddy rubber boots, she pulled them off and left them outside the door. She tossed her gardening gloves alongside them.

Leo stood while Ike took careful steps toward Margaret.

"Who do we have here?" Margaret asked.

"That's Ike," Leo said. "And I'm Leo."

Margaret shot her husband a reprimanding glance. "Were you planning to let me know we have visitors?"

Doc scratched his neck. "I was getting around to it. We were just catching up while you finished in the garden."

"Aren't you the cutest thing?" Margaret's warm tone released Ike from all caution. He bounded over and jumped up on her legs. She lightly stepped on Ike's back paw. "No. Down." That immediately brought Ike's four paws to the floor. "You are a darling," she praised, before coming over to the kitchen table.

"Leo, my wife, Margaret," Doc said. "I told him you'd have my hide but you seemed so—"

"Nice to meet you, Leo. It's great to finally see that the new coach my husband has been talking about for the last six months is real."

"It hasn't been six," Doc said.

Margaret extended a hand to Leo. "Okay. Nine then."

"Pleasure to meet you, ma'am," Leo said.

"Oh please," Margaret told him. "I feel old enough without you calling me ma'am."

Leo was on the receiving end of a very firm handshake. "Hello, Margaret."

"I know we're to have lunch. Just let me wash up … using the basement basin, where I wish my husband would clean up … I hope you like tuna fish." Just like that she was gone from the kitchen.

"Sounds good to me," Doc shouted out, giving Leo a wink.

She peeked back in the doorway. "Careful you don't end up with a heel of bread and nothing more."

Sandwiches. Potato salad. Jell-O salad. Cut carrots and celery. Milk. Margaret was not to be outdone when it came to lunch. And that was before she broke out the fresh baked brownies.

"Is this bread homemade?" Leo was on his second sandwich.

Margaret frowned. "It should be. But I sent Doc up to Eilleen's bakery after Mass. I could not keep away from the garden another second."

As lunch wound down, Margaret scooched her chair away from the table and held Ike on her lap. The pup happily licked her fingers, eyes half closed. Doc didn't like any dog this close to food, but he kept his mouth shut. It had been too long since they'd had a puppy in the house. He could see she missed it.

Margaret was a naturally beautiful woman. Three years younger than Doc, she not only gracefully accepted her gray hair, she celebrated it. The afternoon humidity added a bit of wave, which she side-parted, exposing her forehead, allowing her face to be framed in long, elegant sweeps.

Margaret shifted a now napping Ike in her lap. "Have you had a chance to see much of our lovely town?"

"A little. I've been up to the fields, which are very impressive. I've also been to the grocery store. The one on … First, I think it is?"

"The one and only," Doc confirmed.

"And you're planning to teach here in the fall, is that right?" Margaret asked.

"I am. There's a final certification to take over the summer and then I'm good to go."

"That's just super." Margaret's smile was honest and open. "Now you tell me if I'm asking too many questions or being too nosy, but is there a girlfriend or fiancée in the picture? I don't see a wedding band."

Doc spoke up. "Margaret would've made a fine prosecuting attorney."

She remained matter-of-fact. "There will be questions, sure as I'm sitting here. While you men shrug and grunt, we women will have a few answers."

"You'll also have all the questions," Doc said in defense of his sex.

Leo spoke up. "No. Nothing serious." He didn't mention his breakup with his fiancée. Or, more accurately, her breakup with him.

"Well gentlemen," Margaret said, "I'll leave you to talk baseball, but one more question before I do." She raised her eyebrows to see if

Leo wouldn't mind.

"Sure," he said, distracted by the idea of a second brownie.

"Since you're all alone here in Dannaka, would you consider having dinner with us on Wednesday nights? We used to have Fried Chicken Wednesdays with our four girls, but now all except one are gone, spread through all creation. I miss the chance to make a mess of my kitchen."

"That's awfully kind." Leo wasn't sure if he was ready to be that social. He had spent most of the last six months alone. "Can I see how the baseball practices shake out before I give you a firm answer?"

"Why sure," Margaret told him. She did her best to keep her smile from sagging. "Okay, sleepyhead. Up we go." Margaret slowly stood, feeling the hours of gardening in her joints. Ike let out a mighty yawn, not happy to leave a warm lap for the cool linoleum floor. "It was so nice to—"

"Stop stop stop." Leo was out of his chair, scooping the squatting pup and through the back door quicker than Doc or Margaret would have thought possible. Just in the nick of time, Ike made use of the backyard.

Requiring very little prodding, Leo went on his way with a small Tupperware container of brownies. He never did get to finish telling Doc about his short stay in the majors and what happened to end his season and ultimately, his professional playing career. Nonetheless, Doc knew all too well what happened. It was one of those stories that got him angry or made him sad, depending on the day.

His friend Jerome had originally found the news story. As a member of the Newspaper Guild, Jerome had access to the Associated Press computer archives. After Doc had decided to recruit Leo as a coach, he asked Jerome to dig into Leo's baseball career. There wasn't much to find but the old-school newspaperman kept at it. He'd endured hours of microfiche articles in the *Chicago Tribune* sports section until his eyes gave out. It took about a week before he found the article. A photocopy of the nine-year-old story now sat before Doc at his kitchen table. He read it for the umpteenth time.

The Tough Hop Kid
By Woody McCoy

Most fans who follow the Cubs have heard of the Tough Hop Kid. If you're like me, the story makes you shake your head at the presumption of an all-loving God. But this is not the place to examine the vagaries of faith. We're here to delve into sports. For this story, that means going back almost exactly a year, to the beginning.

Fresh-faced 19-year-old Leo Hamill is a September call-up from our Triple-A club in Kansas. Unlike the local big-leaguers donning a Cubs uniform, the kid is having a terrific year. In Wichita, he is in the top 10 in numerous categories: home runs (18), doubles (26), triples (7), stolen bases (12). Further, his .327 batting average leads the league. No doubt. The kid has earned his ticket to the show.

But cynics—and I include myself in that distinguished cohort—are thinking, *Those are minor league stats. This is different. When you first step on a diamond in the Bigs, it's boy against man.*

I interviewed young Mr. Hamill before his first game. It was after batting practice and I remember the kid spraying line drives across the green outfield like an irrigation machine. "Are you nervous?" I asked Leo, a handsome athlete who reminded me of a young Gary Cooper. "Nah," he said with a shrug of his broad shoulders and a smile that eligible girls (even in the upper deck) would swoon for. "I learned," he told me, "back in high school that this isn't brain surgery. It's baseball."

I remember telling the kid "good luck" but it was more tinged with warning than well-wishes. Turns out this highly skilled ballplayer didn't need luck. In fact, the only luck he got was the bad kind.

In Leo's first at-bat, he stroked a double. The youngster never looked back. He put together a five-game hitting streak, batting .395 including two home runs. Defensively, he handled everything that was hit at him at third without an error.

Since high school, Leo Hamill was known as Hammer, and he

was showing us why. He nailed every ball that ventured near the strike zone. I remember writing a piece about how the Cubs could "build a future" with a Hammer like this one.

And then, literally in the blink of an eye, it was over. One minute the rookie was on the balls of his feet at third, the next he lay on the infield dirt in a pool of his own blood. A fluke bounce, that's what everyone called it. The kid was victim to a ball launched by exactly the wrong mix of power, topspin, and a seemingly harmless pebble in the infield.

Eighth inning, bases were empty, two outs. A hard hit—but seemingly routine groundball—was laced to third. As Leo bent to field the ball, the second hop inexplicably shot straight up and into his eye socket. In that split second, the prospects of a 19-year-old phenom went black.

Surgery re-attached the damaged retina, but Leo's eyesight was never the same. He had virtually no peripheral vision, his depth perception was off, and he suffered from floaters and flashes. The following season, he never got out of the minors, batted .101 and made 32 errors. His professional baseball career was over.

Leo stepped between the Wrigley chalk lines only once more. It was a few weeks after surgery. The season was over and the stadium was closed, but the manager arranged it so Leo could clean out his locker. Leo, duffle bag slung over his shoulder, made his way onto the sunlit infield. He put his bag down near the third baseline and got on his knees. With his hands he sifted through every inch of infield dirt around third, looking for the reason why this happened to him.

The groundskeeper saw Leo and came over. He quietly expressed how sorry he was. He said after Leo's fateful game he'd found a pebble the size of an olive pit in the infield. Night after night, the groundskeeper said, he'd lain awake thinking. He concluded the only way that pebble made it to the infield was by being lodged in a visiting player's cleat.

A pebble the size of an olive pit in over 4,000 yards of soil and four acres of bluegrass. And they call Wrigley Park the Friendly Confines. Try telling that to Leo Hamill. Good luck to you, son, wherever you are. You deserved a better hop.

Doc pushed the article aside. The kitchen was quiet. From the living room, the ticking of a Dutch longcase clock marked time. Through the screen door, the early afternoon air was alive with birdsong. Chin in hand, Doc pondered the reality of loss. He accepted the notion of silver linings because he'd seen enough to know they existed. But they didn't come around for everyone. No. As Doc knew, that only happened in fairy tales.

GYMNASIUM

"Mom. Let's go. The meeting's at three. We're gonna be late!" Truman had his Cubs cap on as well as his Ryne Sandberg T-shirt.

"Since when do you care about being on time?" Jess backed out the front door with apple slices in one hand and keys in the other. She turned around to find her son on the porch waiting for her. "Whoa," she said, taking in Truman's outfit. "That's a lot of Cubs gear. Aren't you overdoing it a touch? You'll look like a total suck-up."

Truman ripped off his cap. Then stuck it back on. "I've bled Cubs blue my whole life. And what do I get for it? Nothing but last place finishes and crap from all the Cardinals fans in town. I'm wearing my stuff."

"All right," Jess said, de-escalating. "Locking the door now. Last chance for changes." She looked over her shoulder.

Truman's face was stone.

During the five-minute drive to the gym, Truman hardly stopped for a breath. "Are we too late to get a good spot in the bleachers? Do you think Coach will remember me? How many kids do you think he'll take for this year's team? Am I looking any taller to you? Do you think Coach meant it when he said I have good mechanics? What time is it?"

"What time is it?" Leo rolled over, cloaked in a nap fog. His watch came into focus. "You gotta be shitting me." He sharply tapped the dial knowing fully the futility of the act. "Oh no." The tautness of Leo's voice got Ike to his feet. "3:10. It can't be 3:10."

Leo's watch was slow. Actually it was 3:13. The bleachers in the gym were packed, and a few groups stood off to the side. Everyone watched the big round clock on the wall. The minutes dragged by. The space was stuffed with the murmur of uneasy voices.

"I'm getting a drink," Truman said to his mom. Wade sat next to her. On the other side, Truman had saved seats for Bale and his parents. As Truman made his way down the row of bleacher seats he saw, near the end, coach Dixon and his boy, Billy. He would have to pass by them. He didn't really need a drink. He had to pee. He'd left the house in too much of a rush.

Just as he was about to cross in front of the Dixons, Billy moved his feet to block Truman's path. "Heya Runt," Billy said, using the only name he'd ever called Truman.

"Dixon," Truman said, enunciating the name: DICK-son.

Billy left his big feet in the aisle. He took an extended look at what Truman was wearing. "Do you have your Cubs lipstick on, too? For kissing the new coach's ass?" He and his dad got a good laugh at that. After delaying further, he pulled his feet back and let Truman pass.

Leo told himself he never should have let his head touch the pillow. But last night's lack of sleep, overdoing it on lunch and the afternoon's warmth were in cahoots. The last thing he remembered he was on the bed looking at his speech notes, his eyelids getting as heavy as patio bricks.

Ike's tail tucked as he looked up at Leo. They were in the backyard. Leo, barefoot, in athletic shorts, pulled on a golf shirt. "Okay Ike. No time to lose."

Ike looked at Leo. Leo looked at Ike.

"C'mon big boy." The more urgent Leo's voice got, the less relaxed the pup became. "Please. Be a hero."

Nothing.

"Okay, you're going to have to hold it." Leo scooped up the pup and ran toward the truck. Then, remembering he needed shoes and the rope leash, Leo veered for the house, smashing his big toe on the brick walkway, which was slightly above grade.

Ike nearly came flying out of Leo's arms as he stumbled, somehow managing not to fall. Hopping on one foot, he came to a limping, agonizing stop.

"Son of a ..." The words squeezed through clenched teeth. He dared not look at his throbbing toe. Leo knew a thing or two about foot pain. When a baseball player fouls a ball off his foot it feels like a stake has been driven through it. With intense pain like that, Leo learned not to fight it; that makes matters worse. You have to embrace it. Almost love it. Trick the brain.

Leo rocked back and forth. "Nice. Nice. Nice. Nice. Nice." He settled his breathing. The conflagration of pain subdued. He exhaled fully. "Okay. Ike, let's go wash that thing up." There was a pool of blood gathering around his big toe.

Doc wished he knew a good joke, a lengthy one at that. Courtside, standing at a table that held the basketball PA system, he pressed a button on the mixing board with the word ANNOUNCE taped next to it. He took the wireless microphone and walked out onto the gym floor. He had a couple ideas on how to stall, as the tension was palpable.

Switching on the mic, he tapped the head. "Good afternoon everybody. Is this working? … yeah? … okay good. Thanks all of you for coming on this beautiful afternoon. Tough to be indoors. Sorry about the delay. We'll get started here in a second."

A voice yelled out from the stands. "Did your coach get lost? Dannaka's not that big." Doc knew the braying of Dixon's voice all too well. As the ripple of laughter subsided, Doc started into a short list of agenda items.

He told the crowd to make sure to fill out a registration form and leave it along with a $50 check at the table. He said by his best guesstimate, Dannaka would field two in-house teams that would play against other 12U teams in the Southwest Iowa in-house league. Doc would be coaching one team, Jerome another.

Doc made it clear that all interested twelve-year-olds, including girls, were welcome and encouraged to play baseball. Everyone makes a team and everyone bats and plays pretty much equally.

He continued, "With regard to the traveling team, there will be one 12U Triple-A team. I'll leave it to Coach Leo Hamill to tell you about roster size, costs, time commitment, tryouts, as well as his philosophy on coaching the team."

Sneaking a peek at the wall clock, Doc thought *Where the hell is he?* It was 3:20. He walked back to the PA system and searched the buttons on the mixer. One button had the letters SSB next to it. It had been a long time since Doc ran the clock at a basketball game but he thought he remembered how things worked.

"Please stand and remove your caps," Doc said into the mic before switching it off. Then his finger pressed the SSB button. *Here goes nothing.*

"The Star-Spangled Banner" piped out of the gymnasium speakers as people scrambled to their feet and turned toward the flag at the south end of the gym. The crowd held hats and hands over their hearts and sang along. This was the last delay tactic Doc had up his sleeve.

A door in the far end of the gym swung open and Leo stumbled inside. The anthem swelled, reaching its last stanza. For Leo, it was a long, painful walk across the parquet floor to where Doc stood in front of the bleachers. Step, limp. Step, limp. Step, limp.

One by one, the singing voices dropped away. The last recorded, amplified notes rang out across the gymnasium, unaccompanied. The silence of the standing-room-only crowd was not lost on Leo.

Doc switched on the microphone to a shriek of feedback. With wind-tossed hair, a hillbilly beard, a golf shirt tightly stretched at his midsection, bloodstained shorts, a gimpy foot and a puppy tucked under one arm, Leo held the audience rapt, but for all the wrong reasons.

"All right folks. I'd like to introduce Coach Leo Hamill."

The only sound was Leo's tennis shoe squeak as he put Ike on the wood floor to accept the microphone.

Ike promptly piddled.

Leo closed his eyes to a gasping crowd. He tried humor. "And I thought I was nervous," he said.

Dead silence.

Russ Dixon adjusted his baseball cap. "What is it you got there, Coach?"

"That's our team mascot," Leo said without hesitation.

Ike finished his business.

"Mascot? He's not very well coached," Dixon announced.

"Yep," Leo said. "Still a rookie."

Dixon spoke to those around him in a confiding tone. "This is our new wonder boy?"

Doc spoke up. "Can someone run to the bathroom for paper towels?"

"I'm on it." Truman nimbly stepped around and down through benches of people, descending three rows before jumping to the gym floor. The boy kneeled. "Ike, come," he said crisply, adding one clap of his hands. Recognizing Truman, the pup had every kind of difficulty getting traction on the parquet floor. He skittered, bounded and finally sprang into Leo's arms. An "ahhh" gushed from the crowd, releasing some tension. Just then, Leo realized he'd left his speaking notes back on the bed.

With the floor attended to and Ike sitting on Truman's lap in the bleachers, Leo took a deep breath and started over. Instrumental to his success in sports and in the classroom was Leo's composure. He called on that now.

"First, let me apologize for being late. I'm not making excuses—but by way of explanation—I found the puppy you just met abandoned on the highway yesterday en route to Dannaka. Spent most of last night trying to get him to settle down."

More sympathetic ahhs from the crowd.

"Then, this afternoon, lack of sleep and a couple of Doc's wife's sandwiches … well, I picked an unfortunate time to close my eyes. But—and I say this for the kids who intend to play on my team— if you're late you run. So I'll be doing laps around the field after today's talk."

From the bleachers, Jess watched Leo slowly gain momentum. Yes, he had a trace of pitiful charm, but she couldn't help but be underwhelmed. He was billed as this super-coach who won state championships at will and played for the Cubs. She wasn't convinced.

Leo reviewed the schedule for tryouts and explained how he'd ultimately pick a final roster. His approach, which Jess did appreciate, was quite different. In previous years the team was all but chosen by the head coach before tryouts even began. Clean slate, Leo emphasized. No one was a lock to make the team and everyone would get a fair shot. Two things that he mentioned raised immediate questions, if not hackles.

Leo repeated back the two-part question. "For those of you who didn't hear that, the question was why carry two alternates on the roster and why recruit kids from outside Dannaka to try out for our traveling team?"

A grumble grew from the crowd.

"Two alternates are there for injuries. You might think with 12 primary ballplayers you can absorb a few injuries. Yes and no. Depends on the position. Depends on how the strengths of the injured boy match up with the strengths on the bench. Things can change substantially in the five months we'll be together. A kid who starts the year as number thirteen on the roster might leapfrog to number five come playoffs. I've seen it before. Also, two extra players help with intrasquad scrimmages.

"Second part: Why would I reach outside of Dannaka for more players? We need a larger pool to draw from. From what I'm told, we're playing against teams with five to 10 times as many kids to look at, Des Moines being the perfect example. More kids trying out helps our players learn to respectfully compete. That's a real life skill. One thing you'll hear me say is if we're going to spend this much time working on baseball—and it will be a commitment—then the kids better be learning more than just baseball."

Bale's mom raised her hand.

"Yes. In the middle."

"Isn't that cut-throat?" she said. "To bring kids to play here on our beautiful new fields and not even be from here? That's not the Dannaka way."

More than a few voices in the crowd audibly agreed.

Leo considered his response. The coaches he admired were honest from day one, even when it stung. "No disrespect meant to anyone, but I was brought here to challenge the Dannaka way. That doesn't mean all the good ideas get tossed out with the bad. But as I understand it, just last year you had a nearby city reach into Dannaka and pull a top kid off your roster. Seems we can do the same."

"Just because they do it doesn't make it right," Bale's mom said. There was another swell of support behind her.

"No ma'am, it certainly does not. And that's not my point. It means if we want things to change, we can't keep doing things the same way. For the last two years this age group's traveling team hasn't advanced out of districts."

"Last three years," someone in the crowd said. "But who's counting?"

"To get out of districts, advance through regions and win state, it's my firm belief we need a bigger pool to draw from."

Leo looked into the crowd. Some heads were nodding. Others not.

"I'll wrap this up with a couple points directed at the players, and then a question for parents. Players: I'm going to coach you like a high school varsity team. You'll be on the big field soon enough, may as well start learning the right way now.

"Another thing. I started playing T-ball when I was five. When I was 12 and 13, our team won Little League state championships. That's when I knew baseball was not just a hobby for me. I was drafted in high school and I played for the Cubs when I was 19. I got hurt. It ended my playing career. I was a scout but my heart wasn't in it so I decided on college instead. Got my degree and teaching license while I was coaching JV at a nearby high school. I got a job teaching, took over the varsity team and won four state titles in a row.

"What I'm saying, boys, is I have spent more days on the baseball diamond than any other single place in my life. That makes the baseball field my home. I will not allow any player of mine to disrespect my home. I will not allow you to come into my home and tell me how you think the furniture should be arranged and what the rules should be. In my book, a baseball diamond is a place where you're not afraid to make a mistake, and where you trust everyone around you. It's home."

Leo let that sink in. "Okay. In case you in the back are just waking up, tryouts start in two weeks. First Monday of April, after school at the fields. See you there."

"Coach," a man standing by the bleachers said, "what about the question?"

Leo was confused. "Sorry?"

"You said you were going to wrap up with a few points for the players and a question for the parents."

"Right. Thank you." Leo cleared his throat. "The puppy, our mascot, Ike, who you met earlier … I can't keep him. I won't be home enough. My question, is there anyone interested in taking the pup?"

The words struck Truman. He elbowed his mother. "Mom, we should."

Jess frowned. "Are you kidding?" she whispered. "You're hardly home in the summer. It's always baseball or off somewhere on your bike."

"I'll take him with me. Like Coach said. He'll be our mascot. You saw him retrieve that baseball the other day and put it in the bucket. He's a natural."

"Truman, I am not going to spend my summer taking care of your dog."

"Bale," Truman said to the boy next to him. "Ike can come play ball with us, right?"

Bale shrugged. "Sure."

"Dogs are good company," Bale's mother added.

Jess gave her a please-shush look.

"C'mom mom. Ike needs us."

Jess looked at the pup who seemed to understand it was no time to be a slouch. Ike sat up straight in Truman's lap and put the puppy eyes on full blast. Then he stretched over and gave the back of Jess's hand a lick. "The both of you," she said. "Such unbelievable suck-ups."

Outside, breezy eddies frolicked. Idyllic, it was a refreshing relief from the tang of sweaty-sock odor that cloaked the gym. The crowd dispersed to mixed reviews. Doc heard some grumbling. Jess's opinion of the coach stayed more middling. Wade thought Leo was super great.

Together, Jess and Wade walked to the baseball fields just one block away. Truman and Ike had run ahead. One could almost hear the trees waking up, stretching for the blue sky. As the ballfields came into view, Jess and Wade squinted through the brightness, finding Leo, wrapped in sunshine. True to his word, he was limp-running laps around the outfield grass. Truman and Ike ran happy zigzags beside him.

That's when Wade's opinion of Leo changed. It went from super great to maybe not so super great.

BOOK

TWO

THE TEAM

"Baseball is a game of inches. Give or take a foot."

—*Tom Tink, Dannaka assistant coach*

IKE

Anyone questioning the concept of renewal need only come to Dannaka in early April. The limbs of every tree and bush make an extraordinary case. Two short weeks ago, these branches looked as alive as barbed wire. Now every tip had opened a tiny green hand to the sky.

Jess walked down the sidewalk carpeted with bud husks carrying a baseball bat and her red pail of old baseballs. The tree canopy above held her gaze. She wondered if God ever ran out of the color green.

"Stay close, Ike," she commanded. Ike picked his head out of a shaggy patch of grass and scooted over. She couldn't help but smile; it was the puppy effect.

Ike had been with them for two weeks. Truman, good to his word, took the pup virtually everywhere during non-school hours. And Doc said it was fine if Ike came to the clinic with Jess, so long as he was kennel trained and didn't cause a ruckus with the visiting dogs and cats. The first week of kennel training was rough, but Ike soon learned that his kennel was his safe place. And a place where he'd find a treat tucked away in a corner.

Weather permitting, Monday through Friday, Jess planned to take her lunch break at the baseball fields. Truman would join her after he'd eaten in the school cafeteria. They would use the remaining lunchtime to continue cramming in practice sessions as tryout week got underway.

It would be a busy, anxious week. The players would be on the field or in the gym every day after school. For the weekend, the schedule was morning practices followed by intrasquad scrimmages under the lights. Leo, true to his promise, would take a long look at the players in virtually every situation. But to make the number of kids manageable, first cuts would be posted Thursday morning.

Tryout numbers were up. Significantly. In past years, among this age group, there had never been more than 20 kids to go out for the traveling team. This year, 42 were registered. Certainly Leo's star power as an ex-big leaguer had a lot to do with the surge. And his clean-slate approach to choosing the team helped. But a great deal of player interest outside of Dannaka could be credited to Tom Tink.

Tom had been on the coaching staff last year. Never much of a player himself, he had a son blessed with one of the liveliest pitching arms in the state. So last season, Tom was given a team cap and the title of assistant coach to ensure that his boy played for Dannaka.

Turned out, Tom got stuck with most of the grunt jobs—raking and chalking the field, managing the team's paperwork at tournaments, wrangling snacks, keeping the scorebook. But Tom Tink was a team guy, through and through. Never a complaint. He was simply delighted to be part of the inner circle. Baseball had left him in the dust growing up. He was making up for lost time.

Leo met Tom at the first coaches meeting and immediately liked him. He had such a pure love for baseball. And unlike Dixon, he had no ego, no agenda.

The plan, Leo reiterated at their meeting, was to increase the depth of the pool of competitive ballplayers trying out. Leo asked for ideas on how that could be accomplished. Dixon told Leo not to worry about it. They'd be fine with the numbers they usually got. Tom raised his hand, a formality, Leo told him, that wasn't necessary. Tom shared his recruiting idea.

Four-color flyers. Posted in grocery stores within a 30-mile radius of Dannaka. Why grocery stores? Tom explained it was the best place to reach moms, and no kid was going to play baseball with an association outside their local community without mom's stamp of approval.

Best of all, Tom Tink drove a bread truck for Pepperidge Farms, delivering bakery and snack goods to the area grocery stores. He told Leo he was on a first-name basis with all the store managers and was sure they would post Dannaka tryout flyers.

When Tom Tink pitches a heartfelt idea, stand back. Gesticulating hands chopped through the air as he explained how the flyer would emphasize the positive coaching philosophy and unprecedented experience the kids would get when taken under the wing of a four-time state high school championship coach WHO ALSO JUST HAPPENED TO HAVE PLAYED FOR THE CHICAGO CUBS! We'll double our tryout pool, Tom promised.

Dixon said it would never work. He said he spent years pulling the strings of promotion and PR. Waste of color ink, he predicted. Leo disagreed. He liked the idea and suggested that Jerome at the newspaper would do a good job with the text and layout. Ten days later, 42 kids were signed up for tryouts, and even more could walk on for late registration.

Jess sat on the first row of bleacher seats. From her sweater pocket she pulled out half of a cheese sandwich wrapped in a paper towel. The week was off to a cool start. As she ate, Ike investigated smells that lined the backstop. Suddenly, he was a statue, body erect, focused on the distant hilltop.

First, there was the faint rattle of bike fenders.

Ike's ears lifted.

Then a whistle.

Ike's tail blurred.

Truman crested the hill, standing as he pedaled, his bike surrounded by green grass and blue sky. His glove was looped onto the handlebars and his baseball cap was turned backward so it wouldn't fly off. Ike nearly levitated at the sight. He rocketed toward Truman.

Jess's heart also took flight.

"Come here, boy!" Truman shouted.

Ike let out a happy yelp.

Swinging his bike into a skid, Truman hopped off before it came to a complete stop.

Even though Ike's stride was beginning to lengthen, his running motion was still a jerky choreography of adorable hops, his rear end slightly out of alignment with his front end. His tongue leading the charge, Ike couldn't reach Truman fast enough.

Jess had resigned herself to a "better later" approach to life, but she had to admit: This moment was hard to beat. Truman and Ike tumbled in the grass.

"Who's happy to see me?" Truman asked as they rolled around. "Who's full of pepper?" Truman laughed. "Ike is."

"Hi Mom," Truman said as he walked over to the bleachers. The way his hair was mussed, the sunshine on his freckles, the unguarded ease in his voice because he wasn't trying to make it sound deeper, these things made Truman her little boy again.

"Hello you." Jess smiled. "How was your first half of school?"

"Meh."

"What do you want to work on?"

"Let's do soft toss. I'll hit 'em into the backstop so we don't have to shag."

"Sounds good."

"First, I want to show you something."

Jess was intrigued. As a preteen, Truman was usually less open with his mom.

"C'mere Ike," Truman said. The two of them jogged excitedly to home plate and got in the batter's box. Truman looked over to make sure his mom was watching. "Ike, sit."

The pup obeyed.

"Wow, great." Jess clapped from the bleachers.

"Ma. That's not it! Just watch." Truman stretched his legs. He looked down at Ike. "Reaaady?" he said, his tone lighting a fuse.

Ike's body remained sitting but Jess could practically feel the pup's muscles loading.

"Go to first!" They sprinted out of the batter's box down the base-line running the 60 feet between home and the bag. Ike was getting faster but was too young to keep up. Truman slowed to make the race close. They both stopped at first, with Ike sitting on the corner of the base.

"Right here." Truman adjusted Ike's butt so he was sitting on the center of the base. "That's it boy," he praised. "You did it. Good go to first. Right? Very good go to first!"

Jess clapped and whistled from the bleachers. Upon hearing that, Ike stood and went running to her.

"No!" Truman said. "Don't get picked off." But Ike was gone, pulled by the excitement that Jess whipped up. "Crap, Mom." Truman threw his cap in the dirt.

Jess waved from the bleachers. "Sorry. That was still super good." She stroked the writhing pup who was having such a time playing baseball. Jess's voice sing-songed. "Who got picked off first base? Who got picked off? Ike did!"

Ike was in heaven.

The key to soft toss is to underhand a short throw into the batter's strike zone while remaining far enough to the side to avoid being hit by the ball coming off the bat. Jess had it down to a science. She raised a baseball in her hand. Truman cocked his bat in preparation. Underhand, on one knee, she lobbed the ball right into his wheel-house. Truman uncoiled, striking the ball dead center, driving it into the backstop. Their red pail only held eight baseballs so for the last one, Truman faced the other direction and hit the ball through the infield into the outfield grass. Ike gave chase. Truman and Jess gathered the balls scattered around the backstop. Ike retrieved the last ball—with a few drops along the way. Just like the first day they played, Ike carried the baseball directly to the pail and dropped it in.

"Where do you think he learned that?" Truman asked. "Coach said he didn't teach him. And if he was ditched, I doubt his owner taught him anything."

"Don't know," Jess said. "One thing I've learned from working at the clinic is dogs do the craziest things. And the smart ones, they will amaze you." Truman was perspiring from the rounds of swings he'd taken. "How 'bout a break?" she said.

They walked to the bleachers.

"Ike is smart. But I think it's more. He loves baseball. A natural." Truman smiled at his pup.

Jess nodded. "Just like his owner." The two of them sat down.

Truman's face tightened, a bead of sweat running down his face. "Mom, do you really think I have a chance in hell to make the team?"

She gently corrected. "Yes, I think you have a chance in heck to make the team. Are you nervous about today?" Jess looked intently at her son, who didn't make eye contact.

"I really want to make it," was all he said.

In the distance the lunch recess bell rang out.

"You and Bale have been working extra. We've been working extra. You're ready."

Truman stood and lightly swung the bat, thinking.

Jess continued. "You have a full week of tryouts. Plus the coach knows you—"

Truman's eyes fired. "He's playing no favorites, Mom."

"I never said that. It just doesn't hurt that he knows you," she said.

"Mom, that makes no difference. And it shouldn't make any difference." Truman was adamant. "Knowing the supposedly right people was what screwed up the traveling team in the first place."

Jess nodded. "You're right. I'm proud of you for seeing that."

"A fair shot, that's all I want." Truman's eyes narrowed, waggling the bat head. "Fair shot."

"I think you're going to get it, honey."

"I should get back," Truman said, hearing the second and final lunch recess bell. "Hey, where's Ike?" The intensity of the conversation had wrested their attention away from the pup. Truman's eyes raced around the field. "No way," he said, relieved.

"What?" Jess was still searching.

"Look."

Jess followed Truman's sightline to home plate. Ike was sitting erect in the batter's box. "Ha," she said in amazement.

Truman slowly got in a batting stance in front of the bleachers, locking eyes with Ike. He stretched out his words like taffy. "You reaaady?"

Ike was more than ready.

"Go to first!"

Ike let out a yip and burst from the batter's box. Flopping ears, churning oversized paws, whipping tail, the pup tramped down the first baseline giving it everything he had. Truman swung at an invisible pitch, dropped the bat and sprinted. It was a race for first base. Ike never looked back. "I'm going to beat you," Truman hollered.

Not this time. Panting, tongue lolled out in what could have been interpreted as a taunt, Ike was sitting squarely on the center of the white base by the time Truman arrived.

BUTTERFLIES

As if the hands of a school clock don't move slowly enough. It was a beautiful spring afternoon. And tryouts began at the fields after the bell rang.

Truman sat in his last-hour science class trying to pretend it wasn't his stomach that was making all the noise. But the gurgling was getting louder. Classmates were staring.

"Truman," his teacher asked, "did you have lunch today?"

"Huh?" Truman said, as if the question couldn't have made less sense.

"Lunch? Did you eat? Your stomach seems rather hungry."

That got a laugh from the class.

"Ah, yeah. Sorta."

It wasn't clear to the teacher if this meant Truman was sorta hungry or he sorta ate lunch. Truth was, both. He took three big bites of his sandwich and tossed the rest of his lunch in the garbage so he could get to the fields sooner.

The teacher persisted. "Do you need to get a drink of water?"

"He needs to take a dump," Billy Dixon said loud enough to make the kids around him laugh, but out of earshot of the teacher.

"Shut your mouth, Dixon," Bale said. That quieted things.

"Yeah," Truman said. "I'll get a drink." His chair skidded as he stood to leave.

Bale felt Truman's hand graze his shoulder as he walked down the aisle. He assumed it was a quiet thank you for sticking up for him, until a folded note dropped into his lap.

Bale was stoked for today. To have a former major leaguer taking over for Dixon's old man—a guy many of his players secretly called Coach Dickweed. And for his buddy Truman to have a legit shot at making the roster—it was awesome.

He unfolded the note and smiled. Truman was one of a kind. He'd written: I do have to take a dump. But I'm saving it for Dixon's helmet.

The fields had been mowed, infields dragged, foul lines chalked. Tryouts.

Truman wasn't expecting this kind of turnout. The boys were standing shoulder to shoulder along the first baseline, each with a number pinned to the back of his T-shirt. "I count 46," Leo said. "So that's four of you who aren't registered yet. If you don't have a number, go see Coach Tink. He'll get your names, set you up with a number and give you a waiver form."

"And a registration form," Tom Tink raised his hand, interrupting.

"Oh yeah. Get them both signed or you can't be on the field tomorrow." Leo looked at the kids. "Clear?"

They mumbled a response.

"Clear?" Leo asked more crisply.

"Yes Coach," they said.

"Guys—and this is for everybody—we're going to be talking about a lot of things over the next seven days. Drills, techniques, ways to play the game the right way, lots of stuff. So if something the coaching staff says is not clear, you need to speak up. Tell us it's not clear, or yes, coach it's clear. That way we know we're communicating. Communication is a skill. It must be learned and practiced—just like hitting and fielding—if a team is going to succeed. Clear?"

"CLEAR!" The boys were learning already.

Leo strode along the line of boys, tapping his clipboard. He was glad to be rid of his bushy hair and beard, even if his clean-shaven face did expose a few more chins than he cared for.

"It might be a pitcher telling the middle infielders who has the bag on a come-backer. It might be me at third telling you the delayed steal is on." Leo stopped pacing to emphasize his point. "Do you think I'm going to yell across the infield," Leo cupped his hands around his mouth, 'Hey, Jimmy, the delayed steal is on?' And you're going to yell back, 'Got it on the delayed steal, Coach.'" Leo tipped his cap back and scratched his head. "Is that how you think we'll communicate?" Leo's question hung in the air like a fat curveball.

"No Coach," Bale said.

"That's correct. How will we communicate?"

"You'll have a sign, like touching your nose."

"Right," Leo said. "And you'll have a sign that says either, *Tell me again, I missed it.* Or *Yep Coach. Got it.* That way we have good communication and we play good baseball. Teams that are quiet, that don't communicate on the field, are making the game so much harder and a lot less fun than it should be." Leo took a breath. "Okay, got sidetracked there."

One hand was raised sheepishly.

"Go ahead," Leo said.

"You said earlier a come-backer. What's a come-backer?"

"Now that is a good question. Anyone else not know what a come-backer is?"

A few more tentative hands went up.

"Anyone else? If I ask you and you don't know and I catch you on it, you're doing laps."

A few more hands came up.

"Okay, you. What's your name?"

"Billy Dixon."

"Billy, what's a come-backer?"

"It's when a ball is hit right back to the pitcher. If there's a runner on first, you want to get the force at second so you have to tell the shortstop or the second baseman who's covering."

"Exactly right."

Billy, showboating, gave himself a pat on the back with his glove.

Leo continued. "So how do you decide who's covering?"

"Huh?" Billy said, still hamming it up.

"Who do you have cover?"

"I have the shortstop cover because he's better than our second baseman."

"No," Leo said. "That's not doing it the right way. What's the right way? Anyone know?"

Bale knew but he elbowed Truman because he knew he also knew.

Truman spoke up. "Depends on the batter. If he's a lefty, then the second baseman is positioned closer to first and the shortstop should take it. If the batter's a righty, the shortstop is farther away from second and the second baseman covers."

Leo nodded. "Yes he does. And that's good baseball and that's how we'll play it." Leo could see a few pairs of eyes beginning to wander.

"All right. Enough talking. Light jog around the field twice, sticking by the fences and backstop so we make the widest circle. No cheating. Leave your gloves." Leo dropped his clipboard and started to jog. "C'mon coaches," he said to the men standing by the backstop. "Whole team runs."

Tryouts were scheduled from three to five. By 4:00 Dixon was ready to blow. To him, the kids had done everything *but* play baseball. They hadn't thrown. Or hit. Or taken infield. Those were the basics. How can you learn anything about a player's ability from relay races, agility courses and push-up contests? Now the group was laying on their stomachs working on three stretching exercises for the arms and shoulders. Dixon shook his head at this colossal waste of time. These kids had rubber arms and didn't need to hear mumbo jumbo about muscle mechanics.

Just as Dixon was walking over to say something, Leo got off the ground.

"Okay guys, up." The boys stood. "Eyes here. This is going to be our way to do jumping jacks." Leo demonstrated as he talked. "Instead of standing in place and jumping like this, we're going to move, making a little square with our feet. One forward, one right, one back, one left. One forward, one right, one back, one left. See, a little square."

The boys nodded.

"Let's do five squares. How many jumping jacks would that be?"

A tall, stout boy in the back had his hand up just as Leo finished the question.

Leo pointed to him.

"Twenty, Coach."

"Very good. You know your math."

"He's a wizard," one of the kids said.

"Okay," Leo nodded. "From now on, you're known as Math. Eventually, everyone on the team will have a nickname. Math, I'm not saying you made the cut, but you cleared the first hurdle. You earned your nickname."

Math tipped his cap.

"Hey coaches, you're in on this, too. Everybody does square jumping jacks. Team deal."

Some players put together the parts of the exercise instantly. Others had trouble coordinating scissoring hands and feet while moving in a square. And some used it as an excuse to goof around and bang into each other. None of these details escaped Leo. Everything in tryouts was purposeful.

With no clouds to duck behind, the sun left the boys in a lather of sweat. "Everyone hit the hose," Leo shouted. "Drink."

Stretching the hose from the equipment room spigot onto the grass, the boys lined up. Leo took off his cap and wiped his forehead. He watched as two boys pushed to the front of the line. One he recognized as Billy Dixon. The other he didn't know, but he found his number on the clipboard roster and put minus signs next to their names. Other notations on the chart were filling in: Fast. Quiet. Natural. Cocky. Strong. Agile. Competitor. Cheat. Goof off, 110%.

Dixon approached. He was decked out in Oakley athletic sunglasses, a Nike sport shirt and matching shorts, wearing last year's traveling team cap. "Just wondering, Coach, when the baseball tryout is gonna start." He said it with a just-kidding laugh, giving Leo a slap on the back.

"What do you mean?" Leo squinted into the sun. The first few days of tryouts he never wore sunglasses. He wanted to make eye contact with the kids.

"Ah, nothing," Dixon said. "Just more kumbaya than batting practice."

"There's plenty of time, Dixon. You can learn a lot about a baseball player by watching how he handles himself."

Dixon looked at Leo. They stood about the same height, and even accounting for the extra weight Leo was carrying, Dixon had 25 pounds on him. "Coach, I understand you have a lot of catching up to do, but I know everything I need to know about these boys." He reached into the pocket of his shorts. "Here are your 12 players, with the first nine in the correct batting order. You can send the rest of 'em to grandma's for ice cream."

Leo didn't glance down at the note Dixon held out to him.

"Clean sheet of paper, Dixon. For everyone." He gave him the same hardy pat on the back that Dixon had given him. Then he went for a drink of water. He needed to wash the bad taste out of his mouth.

"Bring it in boys." Leo created urgency with handclaps. When the group finally assembled around him near the pitcher's mound, Leo set things straight. "Boys, 'bring it in' means you hustle in. We are a team of runners. We are going to run to our positions on the field and off. Baseball is a game of bursts. Readying your body for those bursts is something you can always do. Hustle. All the time. Got it?"

"Yes Coach," they replied emphatically.

Grabbing a bucket filled with baseballs, Leo dumped the contents and flipped it over to make a stool. "Before we move on, a quick question for the group. Was anyone nervous before we started today?"

About half the hands went up.

"Really?"

Most of the other hands went up.

"Who's nervous now?"

All hands dropped.

"Here's the lesson. Because you got your body going, your mind became engaged in the activity and was too busy to be bothered with other stuff. That's why we run and compete before we transition to baseball. Warmups can't just be BP and groundballs. When we race, when we compete before each game, the nerves—the butterflies—scatter. A little bit of nerves, that's normal. That means you care. But too much nervousness holds you back.

"One of our advantages—and this was big on my high school teams—will be that the first time you get a base hit won't be the first time you sprinted all-out. And the first time you compete against an opponent, that will happen way before we meet the other team. You'll be ready."

"All right, everyone pick up a ball. I'm going to show you how to bond with the baseball."

The players looked questioningly at Coach.

"That's right, bond. B-O-N-D. But not James Bond." Leo picked up a ball. "Before we throw, before we hit or field, we bond with the baseball. Every time. Every day." Leo was lightly tossing the ball back and forth between his hands. "We watch it into our hands. We slow the ball down mentally so there's no fumbling or drops. Go ahead. Back and forth between hands."

The boys started to toss the ball from one hand to the other. Dixon just closed his eyes and shook his head. A five-year-old could do this.

Leo fell into the routine he learned from his high school coach; the routine he did in the minors and in the majors. He focused on every detail of the baseball.

"Math, when you see a baseball, what color do you see?"

"White," the boy said.

"Truman," how about you?"

"Same."

"Coach Dixon?" Dixon had his hands in his pockets, refusing to take part in yet another touchy-feely waste of time.

"Last time I checked, a baseball was white."

Leo reached down for two more balls. He tossed the three in perfect cascading arcs as he began to juggle. "Boys, when you see a baseball from now on, the color to see is red. See the laces. That means you're not just looking, you're focusing. Seeing red is how you connect and bond with these five ounces of corked cowhide." Leo's juggling became more complex with switches, cross-unders, reverses, reach-overs and more. "Everyone who makes this team will learn how to juggle. Your hand-eye coordination and your focus will be better than you ever dreamed of. Learn to track the ball from one hand to the other. See red, not white."

The first tryout ended with the boys warming up their arms and playing catch. Above the green outfield, clouds lounged in the vast blue sky. Players stretched out throwing distances slowly, starting close together, tossing with just the wrist, to eventually finish with long, arcing throws. There was no hitting. No fly balls. No ground balls. As the boys threw, Leo jotted down which kids were left-handed, a list that included Truman.

They wrapped up with no further speechmaking. Everyone jogged in, made a tight circle, put their hands in and Coach Leo counted down a Dannaka-on-three cheer.

Truman and Bale took their turns at the drinking hose, removing caps and letting the cold water pour over their heads. As they walked to their bikes, Bale spoke first.

"Not what I expected," he said.

Truman let Bale's words hang. "What did you think of the bond with the baseball stuff he talked about?" He looked up at his friend.

"Kinda weird," Bale said.

"I liked it. Especially the part about seeing red." Truman nodded to himself. "When we were playing catch, I watched the laces spin into my glove. It clicked."

"So you bonded with the baseball?" Bale gave Truman a playful bump.

"I guess so."

"Are you like boyfriend-girlfriend?" Bale bumped him again.

Truman didn't say anything. He just kept thinking about those red laces, spinning toward him, disappearing into his glove.

JESS

Creating busy work, Jess told Doc she'd lock up. She dawdled around the reception counter, putting pens in a holding cup and filling the dog treat jar. She straightened a frame holding an illustrated print by beloved *New Yorker* cartoonist Leo Cullum of a dog being served a drink at a bar with the caption, *"Scotch and toilet water?"*

Heading for the door, Doc looked at his watch. "Day one of tryouts. Probably just about finishing up."

"Yeah." She restacked the tri-fold brochures on summer fleas and ticks. "Coach says tryouts are closed to parents. Might take a walk up there with Ike in five minutes or so. See if Truman is hanging around."

Ike was lying on his pad behind the counter. Hearing "walk" brought him quickly to his feet.

Doc nodded. "Smart of Leo to keep the *adults* away." His tone made it clear how he felt many of them behaved. "The kids don't need the pressure and the politics." Doc paused at the front door and squinted at the cash register. "How are we on receipt paper?"

"Good," Jess told him. "Put in a fresh roll earlier today."

"See you mañana." Doc tossed up a hand. "I expect a full report on the tryout in the morning."

Jess looked up. "I thought you said it's best for the adults to steer clear."

"Yeah," he said, stepping out the door. "But that doesn't apply to us."

Ike knew exactly where they were headed. He pulled his red leash and Jess's arm taut. The strain on his collar left the pup breathing like a mini Darth Vader. "Easy boy." Jess worried about his windpipe.

"We need to get you a walking harness."

As they crossed the parking lot of the baseball complex Jess didn't see Leo right away. The three fields appeared empty and there were no bikes against the fence. Secretly, she was relieved. She didn't want to come off as a spying parent preoccupied with how her child compared to the competition—even if it were a little true.

Ike froze in his tracks, eyes zeroing in on something. Before Jess could follow his line of vision, the pup broke for the field, yanking free. He ran through an open gate, dragging the leash. Jess lifted her hand to block the sun's glare. If she wasn't mistaken, Leo was in center field, doing sit-ups.

What a reunion. Leo hadn't seen the pup in the weeks since Jess and Truman took him in. Judging by the rolling in the grass, they missed each other.

It had been weeks since Jess had seen Leo, too. As she approached, her chest tightened and her throat dried. He had transformed. Without the bushy hair and scraggly beard, Leo seemed to have shed years and concerns. Jess walked up to the perspiring, smiling, blue-eyed man. Something in her heart whispered, but the message was unclear.

Jess waved. "Hey there."

"Hello to you." Leo stood, brushing grass clippings off his shorts. Ike let out a happy bark and turned a tight circle. "I already said hello to you."

"Sorry." Jess looked at Leo like she was meeting him for the first time. "Puppy jailbreak." She clapped her hands and Ike immediately came. She unclipped the leash so he could run freely. "No more bolting like that," she scolded halfheartedly.

"He's gotten bigger," Leo said. "Look at you." Ike happily went back and forth between them. "How's he doing? Hey you little rabbit stalker."

"Still chasing rabbits. The farm is lousy with them, especially around the barn. And with spring in the air, their numbers are about to quadruple." Jess studied Leo. "You look … so different." As soon as she said it she wished she hadn't.

Leo shrugged and scooped his baseball cap off the grass, putting it on backward like a catcher wears it. "Cleaned months of shagginess off my head and face. Trying to lose some of the weight I gained." His voice trailed off. "Starting to settle in, I guess. Taking deep breaths. It's good getting back to baseball."

"I bet. Although I know we can't talk about it." Jess dramatically crossed her arms and spoke with faux seriousness. "Tryouts are off limits to parents."

"Yeah. Sorry to make a big deal. But it's best for everybody to let the team figure itself out … without too much assistance."

Jess nodded. "No, I get it. Just giving you a hard time." She smiled at him and he remembered from when they first met—how her smile came to her face carefully with a cute, crooked reluctance.

Ike pranced toward them with a baseball in his mouth. He'd found it back by the outfield fence. "Hey," Leo said. "Looks like we have another center fielder in contention." Ike dropped the ball at Jess's feet.

They walked toward home plate where Leo had his ball bucket, glove and clipboard. They were comfortable not forcing words back and forth. With the temperature in the mid-seventies, Jess had changed into shorts before leaving the clinic, but still wore her teal V-neck technician's shirt with a pattern of colored paw prints. She bowled the baseball through the infield grass and Ike went after it like it was the first time he'd ever seen such a thing.

"How do you like working with Doc?" Leo stopped to pluck a long piece of grass that the mower missed. He stuck it between his teeth as the sun shone on his face.

"Doc's been a blessing. And Margaret. Have you met his wife?"

"I have. The last two Wednesdays they had me over for fried chicken dinner. Not great for my diet, but a very welcoming couple."

"For sure," Jess agreed. "They're the best."

"Sounds like I'm not the only person they've adopted on behalf of Dannaka."

Jess looked up at Leo. Why she suddenly wanted to tell him her story, she had no idea. It was crazy. She only knew two things about this man: He was a baseball coach. And they were the same age, to the day.

Ike walked alongside them carrying the baseball. Leo grinned. "Now there's someone who has really found a home in Dannaka."

Jess nodded, keeping her words to herself.

"Hey Coach!" A boy came running onto the field but the bright angled sun made him difficult to identify. "Did you find a glove? I think I left mine."

As the distance between them shortened, Leo recognized the Dixon boy.

"I found one by the hose. Check next to the bucket of balls."

"Yep, that's it. Glad you found it." The boy slid the glove on and pounded it a few times.

"You should write your name on it."

Billy Dixon frowned. "Everyone knows it's mine. No one else in town can afford a Wilson A2000." He spat in the pocket and knuckled it into the soft leather, paying no attention to Jess.

Russ Dixon's Dodge Ram idled in the adjacent parking lot. The diesel engine rumbled impatiently. Dixon had been watching the field since he and his boy pulled into the complex. *Well looky here,* he thought. *Who is that with our new coach? He's made himself a friend.* A disingenuous smile spread across his face. *Fast worker, this one.*

He sent his son to the field to look for his glove telling him to find it or walk home. All the while he kept his eye on Leo. The closer the coach got to the backstop the more certain Dixon was of Leo's companion.

That's Runt's mom. Jess ... what's her face. He searched his memory for her last name. *She was a good six years younger in school ... that's it! Younger. Jess Younger.* A gleam came to Dixon's eye. *A lot of dogs have chewed on that stick. Now, sure as shit, she's working the coach—greasing the skids for her pipsqueak kid.* Dixon leaned back in the truck and scratched himself. *Clean sheet of paper for everyone, huh? Yeah, my ass.*

Day Three

Tom Tink loved his job and wasn't shy about telling people so. Many privately scoffed: How could anyone love driving around southwest Iowa in a box truck stuffed with loaves of Pepperidge Farms bread and buns and Goldfish Crackers. But as Tom said, "Hand to God, I was made for this job. I love people. I love baked goods. It's a match made in heaven's oven."

Tom's non-judgmental, easygoing nature made him very popular with the grocery store managers and employees on his route. He knew them all by name—a feat one might think unlikely for a self-described scatterbrain. Tom was known to drive for miles with his turn signal on. But he never forgot that Marcy at King's Grocery in Clarinda had a grandmother who was born next door to the famous bandleader Glenn Miller, and she had a son, Nelson, who was exceptionally musical himself.

Tom had a guffawing laugh. If Tom had a shirt on inside out, it wasn't the first time. But what Tom was most known for was his brain-numbing mixed metaphors, one of which he was waist-deep into as Wednesday's tryouts were about to begin.

The boys had gathered around the coaches. It was another high-sky sunny day, perfect for baseball. Leo complimented the kids on how the first two days had gone. He said after today he would cut the team down from 46 to 30. He reminded the boys to play loose while remaining focused. Have confidence in yourself. That's the secret.

Leo had asked if any of the other coaches had anything to add. That's when Tom Tink fired up a verbal tangle that was harder to grasp than a short hopper with topspin.

Tom had his World's Greatest Dad T-shirt tucked into his gym shorts as he paced in front of the kids. He had begrudgingly left his

Wisconsin Dells fanny pack at home. His son, whose pitching arm made him a virtual lock to make the team, talked him into leaving it behind.

"What Coach Leo is talking about," Tom Tink said, "is like a shower curtain. No, that's not it. It's like the liner thingy behind the shower curtain, you know what I mean?"

No one did.

"Right? You have it or you don't. That's what we're talking about. Am I right?"

Tom Tink scanned the blank faces.

"That liner, is back behind the main one. No one really sees it. Like behind the scenes." Tom nodded, sure that his grain of sand would grow into a pearl of wisdom. "But you know what it does …?" Tom's eyes widened. "That behind-the-scenes liner … is confidence. Confidence your bathroom floor won't get wet so you won't slip and fall. Don't be afraid to slip and fall on the baseball diamond during these tryouts. Because you have your liner back there. Your confidence. And that's what Coach Leo is talking about. With confidence you won't fall on your face. Am I right?"

The kids nodded, hoping that would end it. For those on last year's traveling team, this wasn't the first time they were left dizzy by the twists and turns of Tom's pronouncements. He dubbed them Tomifestos. If you hung in there long enough, his circuitous pep talks usually came around to making a semi-comprehensible point.

"All right, then." Leo clapped his hands—to clear his head, too. "Two laps. The long way." The boys got to their feet and started a light jog in the direction of the outfield fence. "Coaches," Leo shouted over his shoulder. "Everybody runs."

After jogging, Leo told the players to form the same teams as yesterday for the relay race. He reminded them that Team 1 took two out of three. It was time for Team 2 to prove that was just luck.

Coach Dixon had had enough. "C'mon coach. Can we take off the training wheels and get down to baseball?"

"Excuse me?"

"We're here to play baseball. Let's play baseball."

"Yeah," Dixon's son added.

Dixon glared at him. "You shut up."

Leo pressed on like a word hadn't been said. "Boys, you know how to set it up. One group runs the first baseline. The other, third. A baseball glove on either side of the pitcher's mound. Etcetera."

Dixon walked toward Leo. "So we're not going to play baseball? We're going to play games?"

The boys stood, gripped in tension.

Calmly but firmly Leo said, "Set it up." The boys got moving.

Dixon kept coming, shaking his head. "I just don't get it, Coach." He took off his sunglasses, putting them up on the brim of his cap. "How you gonna evaluate ballplayers when we do just about everything but play ball?"

There was something about Dixon's pompous, shit-eating grin that made Leo want to wipe it off his face. But he would never go there in front of the kids. The way Dixon cocked his head, smirking, his disingenuous sing-song tone lacquered in sarcasm—it pushed all of Leo's buttons.

"Dixon," Leo said just loud enough for the two of them, "I'm the head coach of this team. *You* are an assistant. For the time being."

Leo jogged over to the infield where the boys set up a relay race. He jogged because good baseball teams don't walk, they hustle from station to station. He also jogged to get away from Dixon before he said things he wouldn't be proud of.

Compete before game time—that was one of Leo's secrets to success. The boys ran their relay races, cheering, battling, running forward, backward and sideways in the drill. They were learning more than agility and footwork. They were having fun in the midst of full-on competition; when that skill gets transferred to baseball, a team becomes dangerous.

When Leo announced that they were moving to the batting cages, Dixon grabbed his chest in a mock heart attack. Leo evaluated hitters on his clipboard as Dixon pitched. Every kid got 10 good swings.

Batters were scored 1, 2 or 3, with 3 being the highest. The kids who mostly got 1s and 2s for hitting, fielding and throwing would be the first cuts.

There was a tiny part of Leo that secretly hoped Dixon would toss lousy batting practice but that wasn't the case. He zipped one pitch after another right in the batter's wheelhouse. Until Truman stepped into the cage. For him, every pitch was high in his strike zone. And the velocity was dialed up. Truman didn't swing. He had a good eye.

"Swing the bat, Runt," Dixon shouted.

"Throw a strike," Truman said back.

The next pitch was high again, but Truman, feeling pressured, swung and managed only a weak pop-up into the top of the cage. He stepped out of the batter's box to regain his composure. Dixon snarled at him. "Get in there and hit. You're holding everybody up."

Leo, who was sitting outside the cage evaluating hitters, approached the netting so they could speak privately. "Dixon. Bring the pitches down. Give the kid a chance to hit."

"I'm pitching 'em where I pitched everybody else. It's not my fault the Runt has no strike zone."

Leo spat out a sunflower seed. "Bring 'em down and slow 'em down."

Dixon laughed. "What? You want me to give him special treatment? I thought it was supposed to be the same fair shot for everyone."

"You thought right. So put the ball in his strike zone the same way you did for every other kid." Leo walked away.

Dixon put the next pitch in Truman's wheelhouse and he ripped a come-backer. Dixon ducked behind the protective pitcher's screen as the ball whistled past his ear. Leo couldn't help but chuckle.

For ground balls, each player was scored on their fielding and throwing. Leo had Tom Tink hit so everybody's grounders would be the same speed. Dixon caught off. Each kid got six grounders. There were some very smooth fielders, and kids who struggled with footwork and staying down on the ball. Tom was hitting balls about as hard as he could because that separates the wheat from the chaff.

Some kids would rifle throws to Dixon after fielding the ball. Others tossed it, just hoping to be accurate.

"Fire that ball," Leo told them. "No lollypops. We're gonna be facing fast kids on short basepaths." He nodded to himself as he watched Bale glide to ball after ball and throw darts to Dixon, stinging his hand.

Leo told the boys they'd finish the day with a pitching evaluation. "Not everybody's a pitcher. I get that. But if you like life on the mound and you think you can pitch, line up. Or if you know you're not a pitcher, if you don't enjoy it, that's okay. Go get a drink. But stick around. I know it's almost five but I want to talk to the group before we wrap."

"Dixon, grab the catcher's mitt and a pail to sit on. Tom, you stand in the batter's box like you're gonna hit. But bring your glove, not a bat. If you can't get out of the way of an inside pitch, use the glove to catch it. I'll take the umpire's position. Let's go. Let's go. We're running out of time."

Twenty kids considered themselves pitchers. They lined up behind the mound. Tom Tink's son was the first to take the hill and toe the rubber. He had been the best pitcher in this age group since the kids started pitching, so everyone expected him to throw first. Billy Dixon bumped past Truman. "This is the pitching line. The water line is over there." He took the number-two spot in the pitching order.

Bale stood next to Truman near the back of the line. "You should be the next one to pitch," Truman said. "Go up there."

Bale took off his cap and wiped his brow with the neck of his T-shirt. "No biggie. Coach doesn't pay attention to any of that."

Leo shouted out from behind home plate. "Seven pitches. First four are fastballs. Next three are off-speed. Those can be curves or straight changeups. You guys have to learn to change speeds. Keep hitters off balance. At the level you're playing now, just throwing fastballs is going to get you rocked."

The Tink boy was relaxed and lanky and could really pitch. His fastball sizzled and popped the mitt. Then he dropped three big curves across for strikes. Leo had to recalibrate his mindset from the 60-foot-six-inch pitching distance used in high school to the significantly shorter distance of 46 feet played in Little League. Wow, the ball got on a hitter in a hurry.

Billy Dixon threw hard but was wild. His curve was good but it was almost the same speed as his fastball. If he were to have success pitching, he'd need more separation between those pitches.

There were bright spots and lowlights as pitchers shuffled through. Leo kept track of the big details—righty or lefty, number of strikes thrown—but also watched for more subtle indicators of pitching acumen like good mechanics, calm tempo and a full follow through. Three things surprised him enough to merit special note.

Twin brothers, Hispanic boys, not from Dannaka, could throw the ball through a barn wall. They needed some polish, but were very athletic. He needed to get their stories.

Bale was the second-best pitcher of the bunch, but in his delivery, his stride to home was too short. If he could correct that and throw more with his legs, he could be their ace.

The final notation was about Truman. His pitching speed wasn't fast or slow, but he was extremely accurate. In every level of baseball, walking batters comes back to haunt a pitcher. Leo liked Truman's control. But what compelled him to write down the word WOW came on Truman's last pitch. He had thrown two slow curves, which would mix well with his fastball. But his final pitch was a dazzler. Truman uncorked a knuckleball.

Nighttime

———————————

They didn't talk about tryouts during dinner. Jess was bursting with questions, but she assumed Truman would broach the subject when he was ready. Meanwhile, the slurping of spaghetti and crunching of garlic toast was intrusively loud.

Truman said he had homework to do. Jess excused him, saying she would take care of the dishes. *What happened at that tryout that left him mute?* She tried to think about other things while she did the dishes and swept the floor but her thoughts circled back to the same place.

"Truman," Jess hollered up the stairs. "Let's take Ike for a walk before it gets dark." She waited. "Did you hear me?"

"We'll be down in a minute."

Just then the phone rang. Jess went to the kitchen. It was Wade.

"How's my favorite gal?"

"Good. Just cleaning up the dishes. How are you?"

"Excellent. Putting out Easter decorations for Sunday's brunch."

"Oh my gosh," Jess said. "Is that this weekend already?"

"Sure is. I can't wait to grill you guys one of my famous slow-cooked hams."

Jess stretched the phone cord and walked toward the stairs, covering the mouthpiece. "Let's move it up there," she hollered.

"What's that?" Wade said.

"Oh, I'm trying to rustle up Truman and Ike for a walk. And by the way, thanks for cooking for Easter. We don't deserve you."

"You certainly do. And you're certainly welcome." Wade shifted gears. "So what's the tryout report for today?"

Jess's voice dropped. "I don't know. Not a word about it. I'm worried something bad happened."

"Ah, I'm sure it's fine. He's a good player. And now he has a coach willing to recognize that."

"I hope you're right. Oh, here they come now. I should scoot."

"Okay. Call me after you talk to Truman, if you need to."

"Thanks. If not, talk to you soon."

"How about lunch tomorrow?"

"I think I'm hitting Truman pop-ups at lunch. But I'll call from the clinic in the morning to confirm."

"Okay, bye..."

"Bye."

"Darling."

But Jess had hung up before Wade got his last word in.

Ike scampered down the ditch and into the cut soybean field. Corn would be planted early next month and the beans right behind that.

"Stay close," Truman commanded. Ike didn't venture far. "Don't need you getting into a skunk."

Jess and Truman walked down the quiet blacktopped road. The ambient light was beginning to drop off and house windows flickered from across the empty field.

"Honey," Jess said. "You haven't said boo about your tryout today."

"I know."

"I know? That's it? That's all I get?"

"Ma. I don't want to hex it. It's bad luck to talk about something good in baseball. The minute you do, you kill the mojo."

Jess stopped walking. "Something good happened? Tell me."

Truman turned around to face her, walking backward. He couldn't hide his smile. "But what about the mojo?"

"The mojo will keep mojoing. What happened?"

"After tryouts Coach came up to me and said he liked the way I pitched. He said he liked my control. He likes that I'm a lefty." Truman was practically shaking with excitement. "And he said he especially liked my knuckleball. He called it the Dazzler. He said he wanted me to keep practicing that pitch because it can tie good batters in knots.

He said, 'We're gonna need some of that.'"

Jess thought that was all well and good, but didn't see why Truman believed it was such a big deal.

"Don't you get it, Mom?"

"I guess. Maybe not, really."

Truman looked at her emphatically. "He was talking to me in the future tense. 'We're gonna need some of that.' It means there's a possibility he sees me on the team."

Even in the fading light Truman could see a sparkle come to his mother's eyes. "You're right," she said, running up to him and hugging him. "That's so great, Tru. I'm so proud of you."

Truman enjoyed the moment, but only for a moment. He wiggled out of his mom's arms. "You have to promise not to tell anyone."

"Okay. Even Wade?"

"Yeah. I mean everyone. I wasn't going to tell you, but I had to."

"Damn straight. No secrets between us, right?"

"Yeah, yeah, I know." Truman picked a rock from the road and fired it into the field. "Tryouts are a long way from over and I haven't made anything yet. You should see the competition. A few new kids—man they throw smoke and thump the ball a mile. I just need to show Coach that I can do some things that other kids can't."

Ike came trotting over with a stick. Tail wagging, hoping to play.

"Who wants to get chased?" Truman's tone got Ike happy-growling. "I'm gonna get that stick," the boy said. Ike started to trot, watching Truman very closely. Truman lunged for the stick, purposely missing, which sent the pup running, playing keep-away. Ike loved this game. Getting chased. "Who's full of pepper?" the boy said, dashing after his pup.

Back at home, Jess got her book and Truman flipped through the channels on TV. Nothing good was on. The Cubs were playing in St. Louis so he'd listen to that up in his room.

"We're heading up," he said to his mom.

"Wow," Jess said, looking up from her novel. "Early. But that's good. School and tryouts, that's a lot."

"Can we work on bunts tomorrow at lunch?"

Jess stretched her pitching arm dramatically. "Think you can handle my stuff?"

Truman just shook his head. "Good night."

"It'll be good night for you at the plate tomorrow." She continued to loosen her pitching arm.

"Ike," Truman said as they headed upstairs. "Mom's dreaming. And she's not even in bed yet."

Truman's room was neat, like always. Folded, stacked next to his backpack were his clean baseball pants, socks, T-shirt with his evaluation number pinned to it and his Cubs cap.

"See," Truman showed Ike. "All ready to go for tomorrow." Ike sniffed the clothes but they were too clean to be interesting. Truman turned on the radio. "Let's check how the Cubs are doing." The tuning dial on his radio never moved. When he clicked it on, Harry Caray and Ron Santo came crackling across the airwaves. The reception was never great, but for Truman, this was the background music that lulled him to sleep, spring through fall.

"I have to brush my teeth. Wanna try to jump up on the bed first?" Truman was teaching Ike to jump up on things—to learn to be bold—and Ike was a willing participant, even if most attempts came up short. Truman patted the bed. "Come on, boy. Hup! You can do it. Hup!" Ike's weight loaded onto his hind legs, his eyes widened in anticipation and POW—a mighty leap. One paw made it topside, but Ike's head and shoulder didn't clear the mattress, sending him backward in a heap. Ike let out a yip and tucked his tail. "Ah, that's okay." Truman scratched the dog's head. "We'll get it tomorrow. Lie down while I brush my teeth."

When Truman came back to his room Ike was gone. He figured the pup had gone downstairs to be with Mom. Then something caught his eye. On the bed, taking up residence on Truman's pillow, was Ike.

They made eye contact. "You made it!" Truman said.

Ike stood. And then the size of the accomplishment filled him.

He pranced around the bed's perimeter, tail high. "You made it," Truman practically sang. "You made it. You made it. I'm so proud of you." He went over and hugged his pup. "What a jumping bean. Who's a jumping bean?" Truman paused. "Ike is." Ike licked him as they rolled on the bed.

Truman closed his door before stripping down to his underwear and T-shirt. Last year's in-house team picture stood on the corner of his dresser. He scooped it up and plopped down on his bed next to Ike. In St. Louis, the Cubs and the Cards were knotted at three apiece. Harry Caray was singing his famous rendition of "Take Me Out to the Ballgame" for the seventh-inning stretch.

"See this picture?" Ike lifted his muzzle off the pillow. "That's me. Right there. See?" Truman tapped his location. Ike looked, sniffed. "Nothing against these guys, but I am so done with in-house teams." He rolled onto his back and laid the picture on his stomach. "I'm tired of being told I'm not good enough and looked down on, you know, like literally. Just because I'm small doesn't mean I suck. Coach Dickweed doesn't even give me a shot. There are almost 50 kids trying out for 14 spots, and two of those are alternates. Ike, I don't know, but I think I can do it. Do you think I can do it?" The pup looked at Truman, hanging on his every word. Then Ike licked his cheek.

Truman hugged his friend and confidant. There were things he couldn't tell his mom. She'd just worry. She did enough of that without him piling on.

"You know how you kept trying to jump up on the bed and now you made it?" Truman locked eyes with the pup. "You made it up here." Truman patted the bed, causing Ike's tail to thump. "Just 'cause someone says you're a runt and throws you aside doesn't mean you're no good. You didn't let that stop you. You kept at it till you made it. At tryouts when I think I can't do something, I'll remember you up on this big bed." Ike was trying to keep his head above the pillow but his eyes were heavy. "It's been a long day, boy. Let's listen to the Cubs and get some sleep."

After tryouts had finished earlier that day, Leo had instructed his players to tarp the mound and home plate. A 40 percent chance of overnight rain persuaded him to err on the side of caution.

When Dixon was done ordering kids around he mostly leaned on his infield rake. Tom Tink leveled the area around first base while Leo worked between short and third. Dixon strolled over to Leo.

"So, first kids on the chopping block tomorrow."

Leo winced, raking out divots and dings in the infield clay. He had informed the kids that he would post a list outside the gym in the morning specifying who should continue coming to tryouts. As for kids from other schools, he'd call to notify them if they didn't make the cut. He thanked everyone, regardless of the outcome, for their efforts.

Dixon picked at the infield with his rake. "Should we sit down and go over the cuts?"

Leo kept raking. "No. I got it. If I get stuck, I'll jump on the phone with Tom or you to get a second opinion."

Dixon's large fleshy face looked like he bit into a lemon. "Tink? Tink doesn't know his ass from deep center field. I only let him in the dugout to make sure his kid doesn't jump ship."

Leo glanced over at Tom Tink on the opposite side of the infield, hoping he didn't overhear that. "He knows more than you give him credit for. The man pays attention."

Dixon scoffed, toeing his rake. Then his tone softened. "You know baseball, but I know these kids. Let me help you pick the ones that don't shit the bed under pressure."

Holding the rake still, Leo looked up from the infield at Dixon. "That's why we have a week. That's why we practice game scenarios and have multiple scrimmages—daytime and under the lights. By the time the week's up, I'll know the boys' strengths and weaknesses ... what pieces fit together to make the strongest whole. I'm not looking for a bunch of independent contractors. I'm building a team."

"Sounds like more mumbo-jumbo, Coach. To be honest."

"Call it what you want." Leo considered mentioning his resume of baseball accomplishments, but he realized that was quicksand. "Looks good, Tom," Leo shouted across the infield. "That's it for today. Let's get out of here."

The padlock clicked shut. Leo gave it a yank and walked away from the shed where he stored his equipment for tomorrow. When Leo first made the tryout schedule, he included Sunday. Tom Tink quietly let him know that Sunday was Easter. Oops, Leo told him, admitting he needed to get a life. Tom invited Leo to have Easter supper with his family. Leo fibbed. He said he had other plans.

Walking home from the fields, Leo couldn't shake Dixon from his thoughts. *I can't do it. I can't go through an entire season with that ass giving me attitude at every turn.*

He cut over a block early and headed for Doc's place. The houses on this street were larger, many of them stately American four-squares with flags hanging from the front porches. He passed a son and father playing catch in their yard. "Hey ya, Coach," the father shouted out. To his knowledge, Leo had never met the man. "How they coming along?" It took Leo a split second. The man was referring to the boys trying out for the traveling team.

"I like what I'm seeing so far," Leo said.

"I'll have this one coming your way in two years."

"Good to know. Let's see what you got, kid." Leo looked on.

With his father squatting in a catcher's position, the boy went through a deliberate windup, high leg kick and zipped a fastball into the mitt. Thwump.

"That's a strike," Leo shouted out. "Just remember, keep your back straight at your balance point. Like this," Leo demonstrated, "Not bent over like a nail."

"Thanks, Coach. How's this?" This time the boy stayed taller through his delivery. "That's the stuff," Leo said. "Have a good night," he told them.

"Good luck, Coach," the boy called back.

Honestly, it felt good to be recognized as Coach again, without any of the accusatory stares. Leo cut through the alley thinking he might catch Doc in the backyard. A garage door a few houses from Doc's had a strike zone on it for pitching practice with a tennis ball. What impressed Leo was the strike zone wasn't taped on, or chalked on. It was painted. That's commitment.

Sure enough Doc was in the backyard, on his paver patio, sitting at the wrought iron table drinking a Budweiser. In front of him, on a blanket, his granddaughter played with Legos.

"Knock, knock," Leo said, so as not to startle Doc as he came up behind him.

"Huh? Oh, hey Leo. I thought you couldn't make it." Wednesday was fried chicken night. Leo had called a few days back saying he'd be busy deciding the team's first cuts. He'd have to take a rain check for this week.

"No. Can't stay. Just need to talk to you for a second. If that works."

Doc stood. "Sure. Want one of these?" He held up his empty bottle. "Mine evaporated somehow."

"That'd be great." Leo went over to Milly, Doc's granddaughter. She was a precocious two-year-old who had gotten to know Leo over the last weeks of Wednesday dinners. "Hi Milly. Whatcha making?"

She remained focused. "It's an animal hospital for Grandpa and me to take care of hurt birds and horses and dogs and frogs."

"Are you going to be an animal doctor when you grow up?"

"I already am. See?" Inside her Lego hospital was a miniature plastic horse with gauze wrapped around most of its body.

"Oh," Leo said. "What happened to your horse?"

"She got a tummy ache. But it's better now."

Leo patted her gently on the back. "Good work, doctor. If I see any hurt animals I'll bring them to you."

"Thank you," Milly said.

Doc and Leo sat down at the patio table. "Gorgeous evening," Doc said, handing Leo an ice-cold beer.

"And getting better by the second." The men clinked their beer bottles together. The smell of fried chicken wafted out of the kitchen window, reminding Leo how hungry he was. Trying to lose weight had him cutting back to a half sandwich at lunch. No chips. Just nuts to temper the salt craving.

"So what's up? How do the kids look?"

Leo took a long pull off his Bud, nodding. "Still pretty early in the process. But some good athletes."

"And I think you said first cuts get posted in the morning. That's never easy, for anyone."

"It stinks. Cutting kids."

Doc interjected. "But we have a good in-house program to pick them up, brush them off and keep them playing. They'll be fine. Kids are darn resilient."

Leo nodded. "Doc, I know you have dinner coming up so I'll get right to it. I'm going to cut Dixon loose."

Doc's brow furrowed. "I thought that kid could wallop the ball. I'm a little shocked."

"No," Leo said. "I'm not talking about the kid. He's not cut. I mean his dad. I can't coach with that guy. He wears me out." Leo rubbed his face. "I wanted you to know—if you have any advice—before I do anything."

Doc sat back in his chair. "Wow. Yeah. Hmm."

"Not the easiest advice to work with." Leo picked at the label on the neck of his beer bottle.

"I'm surprised. And I'm not."

Leo let that comment spin while Doc came to grips with what he'd just heard.

"Dixon does leave a lot to be desired. I had a truckload of complaints about him from parents, umpires—even parents from opposing teams. He doesn't represent the community very well."

"I don't know about that. But it's obvious to me he's not good for the kids. They play tight around him. He's always hacking on them and tearing them down. You can't play good baseball in fear. Baseball, highly motivated baseball, is fun and challenging and exciting."

Doc nodded. He could see this wasn't easy for Leo, which was as it

135

should be. "Dixon has given a lot of time and energy to the program, that shouldn't be overlooked. But end of the day, I think his coaching is more about him than it is the kids."

"Coach eats last," Leo said.

"How's that?"

Leo watched Milly building her animal hospital.

"My high school baseball coach was an amazing guy. Somehow he showed everyone that nice guys don't finish last. When I decided to coach high school, I called him. Asked if he had any advice." Leo made eye contact with Doc. "'Coach eats last,' he told me. "It's about the kids," he explained, "filling them with confidence and skills. Once they have a full plate of self-esteem and pats on the back, then you can get a little for yourself."

Doc liked that. "Sage advice." The two of them sat quietly. "Honestly, what you're saying about Dixon is not very different than what Poodle Lady Thomson told me when she set up our Little League trust fund."

Leo finished his beer. "So," he said standing to leave, "you've known Dixon a lot longer than I have. Any advice for when I go to his dealership tomorrow and give him the news?"

Doc cocked his head. "Yeah. Stop by the fields first and get yourself a batting helmet."

"That's all you got for me?"

"No," Doc said. "Get a bat, too."

Thursday morning

"Hello Wade," Jess said, snatching the phone from its cradle, not waiting to hear his voice. No one else would be calling this early. "I had to hang up fast last night. Sorry."

On the other end of the line someone replied in a poorly disguised voice. "Sorry? Sorry nothing. Oh, baby. I got every aching thing I needed from you last night."

"Who is this?" Jess demanded.

"It's Wade, your tiger cat, you delicious naughty—"

"Nancy. You sex-deranged weirdo."

"Well," Nancy said, in mock aghast. "I take exception to the word weirdo."

Jess shouldered the phone against her ear as she poured herself a cup of strong coffee. "What are you doing up so early? I haven't even had my coffee yet."

"Slow night at the bar. We closed 12:30-ish. So I got my beauty sleep. Been getting up earlier, now that Danny Boy is out of the picture."

"How you doing with that?" Jess asked.

Nancy took a second before replying. "Mostly good." Then her voice brightened. "How about lunch today? I have some banking to do and we could meet at Eileen's. She's serving croissant sandwiches now. Have you tried?"

Jess stretched the cord as far as it would go, from the kitchen to the landing going upstairs, and muffled the mouthpiece on her hip. "Truman. You awake up there?" Then she brought the phone back to her mouth. "Sorry about that."

Nancy asked, "Is the little superstar up?"

"I hear movement, but haven't gotten a verbal."

"What about lunch?"

Jess said she was sorry. "I'm pitching to Truman. He wants to work on bunts."

"Crap," Nancy said. "I'm craving a flaky tuna fish croissant." There was a pause. "Must be a symptom of waking up with the roosters."

"I can't see you as a morning person."

"Well, like I told you, I've been painting. Morning light is magical. I just might change my ways."

"I want to see what you've been doing."

"Not yet my dear. Not good enough."

"I'm sure they're amazing. I still remember the horse you did in high school that won at the county fair."

"Ahh, I'm phone blushing. Okay. You have a household to run and I need to be a little less literal with my color palette today. Damn, I almost forgot. How are tryouts going?"

Jess needed to get the bacon frying so she avoided going into details. "Good. So far. First cut today. New coach seems to like him. Cross your fingers."

"Toes too. Tell him good luck, honey."

After she hung up, Jess's thoughts lingered on Nancy's wellbeing. *Should I have had lunch with her? Maybe this breakup is tougher than before. Or was it an innocent craving and a spur-of-the-moment call? Am I so obsessed with Truman's happiness that there's no room for anything else?*

Bacon solves everything. Soon Jess was humming as she put eggs, bacon and toast in front of Truman. He went to Catholic school, so every day required a uniform. His blue collared shirt and gray shorts looked a little dingy. She'd have to let it go. Truman was wolfing down his food. He wanted to get to school early and see if the first cut was posted.

Leo tossed and turned most of the night. He even called Tom Tink to ask about a few players, which flattered Tom mightily. Then Leo made his cut from 46 players to 30. But that wasn't what kept him staring at the ceiling for half the night. The thought of confronting Dixon filled him with dread.

He stopped at school on the way to the Dodge dealership. After pounding on the door and explaining himself to the janitor, Leo got the most recent roster taped to the wall next to the gymnasium doors. He pulled his finger slowly down the list, nodding as he went. The first cut, Leo knew, was relatively easy. The next two, not so much.

When he pulled into Dixon Dodge, Leo couldn't help but utter the words aloud. "Holy shit." The front of the dealership featured an enormous glass showroom with brand-new pickup trucks. Lit from the floor and ceiling, they sparkled like jewels. Leo drove past a spotless eight-bay service shop. In back, there was more inventory, both new and used vehicles.

Leo pulled into guest parking, which was overshadowed by an adjacent hill. There, two full-sized, tricked-out new Dodge Rams were positioned side by side—one black, one red—with their front wheels rolled up landscape boulders. As Leo walked into the main entrance of the showroom, the trucks appeared ready to pounce.

Of course, the salesmen inside saw Leo's clunker of a Chevy pull in. They licked their chops and almost fell over one another to see who could greet him first. Leo asked for Dixon, explaining that he coached baseball with him. The salesmen gave Leo a *so you're the asshole we've been hearing about* look. They pointed to Dixon's office, the first on the right of the reception desk. His door was open. Approaching the large, brightly lit office, not only did Leo wish he had a bottle of water, but he replayed Doc's advice about bringing a helmet and baseball bat.

"Coach," Dixon said, swiveling in his chair behind a large glass desk stacked with paperwork. "Welcome to my home field."

"Awfully nice." Leo's eyes swept around the expansive office. Struggling for something more to say he settled for, "Looks like you have a lot on your plate."

"Damn straight." Dixon cracked his knuckles. "I sell more Dodge trucks than anyone in the state of Iowa, give or take. Right here in little old Dannaka." Dixon reached across his desk and held up a glass paperweight shaped like a pickup truck. It was large enough to do bicep curls with. "1989 Dodge full-size truck salesman of the year." He rocked the award back and forth admiring the dance of light.

"I don't want to take up much of your time," Leo said.

"Hell that." Dixon gestured to the chair beside his desk. "We call that the electric chair. Once I have someone in it, if they don't sign on the dotted line they don't come out alive." Dixon laugh-snorted.

Leo stuffed his hands in his pockets.

"Have a seat," Dixon said. "So what's up?" Dixon tried to guess. "Did you come to go over the cut list?"

Leo remained standing. "No. Already posted."

Dixon's face fell. "You got a couple of bubble players you want to talk about?"

"That's not it either."

Dixon crossed his large arms, which came to rest on his belly. His chair groaned as he leaned back. "Spit it out then."

"I'm going ahead with the team without you." The walls of the large office started to squeeze in on Leo.

Dixon shook his head like he wasn't hearing right. "Do what?"

"I'll be coaching the team myself. Along with Tom Tink. I appreciate your willingness to help, but I'll take it from here."

Dixon's face reddened. "You'll take what from here?"

"The team."

"The hell you say. That's my team." His voice came to a quick boil.

"It's Dannaka's team," Leo said, holding his tone flat.

"I am Dannaka!" Dixon's voice reverberated out into the showroom, turning the salesmen's heads. The office chair wheels shrieked as Dixon pushed back from the desk to stand. "Did Doc put you up to this? Or was it that shit weasel, Frank?"

Leo's heart raced as Dixon began to come around the desk. "It was my call."

Dixon's red face contorted, lifting his upper lip to show his neglected teeth. "No one comes into my office in my town and takes my baseball team."

Thoughts stampeded through Leo's mind as Dixon strode toward him: *This guy is a whack job. He actually wants to fight. DUCK!*

The two men were rolling on the gold linoleum flooring when the salesmen ran in and tried to detangle them. Dixon kept flailing punches while Leo told him to stop because he wasn't there to fight, but he was about to change his mind. They took out a coffee table along with its accompanying sales literature and oversized cactus. The cactus ended up under Dixon's back with Leo on top, his fist cocked and ready.

Gasping for air, Leo warned, last chance. Stop this now before I do. Dixon tried to sneak in a left hook but Leo's short right landed first. Dixon, Leo thought, as the two salesmen pulled Leo off their boss, looked at peace, unconscious, with bits of a terracotta pot in his hair.

"The asshole came into my office and jumped me." Dixon held a dripping ice bag to his eye as the sheriff's deputy jotted Dixon's statement into a small spiral bound notebook. "My salesmen will back me on that." They were nodding yes before the sentence had left Dixon's mouth. "I want him arrested and run out of town."

The deputy glanced over his reading glasses. "Which one will it be? Arrested? Or run out of town?"

Dixon growled, "Don't get cute. This man's a menace. Dannaka isn't safe when an innocent man can be attacked in his place of work. Isn't that right, boys?"

The salesmen agreed, repeating the word menace.

Leo leaned against the wall, as far from Dixon as he could get and still be in the same room. He rubbed his swollen left cheek. His eye was starting to swell shut. He was offered no ice.

The deputy turned to Leo. "What's your story?"

"I'm the new baseball coach for the 12-year-old traveling team."

"Hell, I know that. Everybody in town knows that."

Leo continued. "I came here this morning, calmly, and told Dixon I'd be coaching the boys without him this season. He didn't care for that."

Dixon interrupted. "That's a forked-tongue lie."

The deputy spoke to Dixon with what is best described as firm acquiescence. "Russ, would you please let the man give his statement."

"When I told him my mind was made up, he came around the desk and sucker punched me."

Dixon was furious. "I ain't never sucker punched a man in my life. Never had to."

The deputy didn't dispute this aloud, but he could remember one occasion at the Timber Grove bowling alley that proved otherwise. And another popped into his mind: the farm auction at the Sandeen place. "Well, based on what I'm hearing, and there being two corroborating witnesses, I'd say I'm going to have to arrest you."

Leo shook his head. "Witnesses? Really? These guys are on Dixon's payroll."

The deputy asked Leo to turn around and put his hands behind his back. "Only witnesses we got." He handcuffed Leo and ushered him out of the office.

Thank goodness for nosy people. As it turned out, there was one more witness. A retired sugar beet farmer in well-worn overalls had wandered into Dixon's dealership. Telling the salesmen he was just browsing, they had quickly dismissed him as doddering. When the shouting in the office commenced, the beet farmer, a habitual eavesdropper, posted himself perfectly for a clear view through Dixon's open door. He got to see the donnybrook from start to finish, tipping his seed cap back and slapping himself on the knee for his good luck.

The handcuffs were removed once the beet farmer set the record straight. Dixon agreed not to press charges as long as Leo didn't. Leo was going to point out the backwardness of that arrangement, but he needed fresh air more than justice. He could only focus on one thing—and that wasn't because one eye had swollen shut. He needed to get to the ballfields and jog. His pent-up adrenaline and anger were in need of wide-open spaces.

Truman made the first cut. About the same time Leo was pulling into Dixon's dealership, Truman was re-re-re-rechecking the list. He'd get halfway down the hall, headed toward homeroom, and yo-yo back to confirm, again, he was among the current roster of players.

Emotions ran over. Truman sprinted into the empty gym, jumped in the air and screamed "YES!" He pumped his right arm back and forth like he was bucksawing firewood. Spinning in a tight circle, Truman again jumped, landing with both fists clenched. "Yes. Yes. Yes."

"So you made the cut."

Truman was startled. He'd thought he was alone. "Oh, hey Bale." He attempted nonchalance.

Bale leaned against the gym doorway and waited a moment. "Are you kidding me?" Bale shouted. "You made the cut. Hooyeah! Kickass!"

The boys ran toward each other as Bale's words echoed throughout the vast space. They grabbed each other, shook each other, and without uttering a word, looked into each other's eyes. That said everything that needed to be said.

At lunchtime, Jess sat on the warm bleacher bench beside her mitt, pail of balls and an uneaten tuna fish sandwich in a brown paper bag. Ever since Nancy had mentioned it early this morning, Jess had tuna on the brain. But the uncertainty of Truman's tryout outcome curbed her appetite. She unconsciously tugged her earlobe, a pacifying ritual from early childhood. Splayed out on the foul line, gnawing on a stick, Ike soaked up the sun as it separated from the scattered clouds.

Truman's bike crested the hill. Jess squinted to see: smile or scowl? The boy raced toward them with his bat firmly tucked under one arm and his glove looped on the handlebars. Thin arms poked out of his rippling navy blue school shirt. She saw freckles and big ears beneath his cap. His smile shouted from the hilltop.

"I made it," he waved joyfully. "So far," he tempered.

Jess stood and jump-clapped. Ike forgot about the stick, ran to home plate and sat erect in the batter's box.

"You wanna race me?" Truman's voice was spiked with challenge. "You can't beat me to first." He leaned his bike against the backstop. Jess couldn't believe what a fast learner the pup was.

She crossed her arms. "So tell me what happened."

"In a minute." Truman got in the batter's box opposite Ike. "Reaaaady?" Ike's body coiled. "Go to first!" They burst out of the batter's box and a real race was on. Every day the pup was getting faster and more coordinated. Truman let up a bit at the end as Ike plopped his little hindquarters on first, tail sweeping off the dirt.

"Attaboy," Truman praised. From his pocket he pulled out a napkin holding the last bites of his sandwich. He tore off a hunk. "Good Ike." Truman gave his pup a reward while stroking his coat. In a low, calm voice he said, "Stay."

Truman walked to second. Ike could hardly resist, but he remained sitting on first, focused on the boy. Holding up his last sandwich bite, Truman placed it on the middle of second base. Ike's butt began to lift, but he was commanded to stay. Walking back to first base, Truman crouched down to the pup's level. "Go to second!"

Infield dirt flew. Ike's legs pumped furiously, ears flopping, as his small chestnut-colored body made good time to second base. Skidding to a stop, the pup quickly dispatched with the bite. Panting, long pink tongue jabbing the air, Ike was proud as could be. And so was Truman.

As she unwrapped her sandwich, Jess was so thankful she caved to Truman's wishes and took in the pup. *Tests are good. Being out of your comfort zone is good.* Which rerouted her thoughts to Wade.

"What's with the frown?" Truman asked, strolling up to the bleachers.

No response.

"Earth to Mom."

"Huh? Oh, sorry. I'm back." She stood up and hugged the love of her life. "So super proud of you."

"Ma, don't get tuna fish all over me." Truman wriggled free. "Can we work on bunts?"

Jess's eyes widened. "Can I eat first?"

"Oh. Sure." Truman grabbed a raggedy ball from the red pail and bowled it underhand down the third baseline. Ike went after it like it was the last ball on Earth.

Before the final school bell of the afternoon rang, a rumor began to circulate.

It started when the deputy who had been dispatched to the Dixon Dodge melee said something at the lunch counter of the diner. It went from there to Ray's service station, where, along with a patched tire, it traveled with the gym teacher. He mentioned it to a colleague in the school men's room while unbeknownst to them, Ricky Roper was hiding in the stall inking the state capitals onto his forearm. By the time Ricky told the story, Coach Leo had knocked Coach Dickweed out cold with a single punch in the parking lot of Dixon Dodge and was hauled away in handcuffs.

Doc heard a slightly different version of the escapade: A knockdown drag-out fight had careened through the showroom floor and ended with Dixon unconscious, stretched over the reception desk.

"I have to go out to the Cunningham place and vaccinate the broodmares," Doc told Jess. He was patting his pockets. "Keys? Have you seen my keys?"

"Check next to the printer."

"Oh, yeah." Doc had gotten the vaccine record off the printer when he came back from lunch. "I'm clear the rest of the afternoon, right?"

"After you help me with Harley," Jess told him. Harley was a miniature dachshund that despised getting his nails trimmed.

"Is this the one who nipped you last time?"

"Twice."

Doc lightly wrapped one arm around the dog's neck and the other around his stomach. "That's a good Harley," he praised. The dog accepted his fate.

"Did you hear about the big fight?" Doc asked.

"What fight?"

"What fight? How could you not have heard?"

"Nobody tells me anything." Jess focused on not trimming the nail too deep. If she did she had the styptic ready.

"Leo and Dixon went at it."

Jess finished the last paw. "Leo? You mean Coach Leo?"

"That's the one. Guess he took it to Dixon pretty good. Not sure how much I heard was true, but I know he was going over to the dealership this morning to tell Dixon he was no longer one of the coaches of the team."

"Holy crap," Jess said. "King Dixon, dethroned?"

Doc chuckled. "That's one way to put it."

Jess was ecstatic. "Yay, Harley! King Dixon is out!"

The dachshund slid through Doc's arms, happy to be free.

"I didn't know you disliked him so much." Doc got up slowly. His hip didn't approve of kneel-sitting on the floor.

"The man is indecent."

Doc nodded but said nothing more. "Well, I think I'll drop in on Leo on my way out to the farm. Find out what really happened."

"Ouch," Doc said, as Leo stood in the doorway. Leo's eyelid was red and swollen shut. The area under the eye socket was beginning to bruise, showing a grisly green-purple hue.

"Come on in," Leo said. He held the storm door open.

"I told you to bring a bat," Doc joked. They walked toward the kitchen.

"Should have brought a catcher's mask. I'm just about to have a bowl of cereal before practice. Can I get you anything?"

"No thanks," Doc said, pulling out a chair at the kitchen table. "You should put ice on that thing."

"Ice trays are one of the few things I couldn't find in this house."

Doc got up, took a dishtowel off the counter, got it wet under the faucet and put it in the freezer. "Next best thing."

Leo nodded and spoke through a mouthful of Wheaties. "Neber taught of dat."

Doc was pressed for time. "I'd ask how you're liking your place and other small talk, but the word is you and Dixon mixed it up but good."

Shoveling in the last of his cereal, Leo picked up the bowl and drained the milk. "Well," he said, wiping his mouth, "not exactly. You sure you want to hear this?"

Doc couldn't mask his sophomoric fascination.

"Okay." Leo rubbed his stiff neck, trying to decide where to start. "Dixon is a crazy man," he said, leading with the thought that had obsessed him since leaving the dealership.

Doc only managed a grunt.

"I mean certifiable." Leo shook his head in disbelief.

"What happened?"

Leo stood, clearly agitated, and went to rinse his bowl. "One minute—no, one second—I'm telling Dixon I won't be needing him as a coach, and the next he's yelling that Dannaka is his town and the team is his team and he's coming around the desk and he suddenly throws a punch. If I hadn't seen it coming and started to pull away, he would have got me flush and I think we'd be talking in the hospital right now."

Doc felt terrible. He was so enthralled to hear how Dixon got his comeuppance he didn't stop to realize how shook up Leo might be. "Damn, Leo. I'm sorry. I never thought it would come to blows."

Leo took a deep breath. "Not your fault. It's just … the guy's, like, unstable. He's dangerous. You should have seen the look on his face. Then we're on the floor of his office wrestling and I kept telling him to stop, that I wasn't going to fight him. The son of a bitch keeps flailing away so I finally let him have it. Nearly broke my hand on his cinderblock of a head." Leo tried to make a fist, wincing.

"Did the sheriff show up?"

"The deputy. Some buddy of Dixon's. Before long, the three of them convinced the deputy to cuff me. I was this close to being arrested." Leo showed Doc a very small gap between his thumb and forefinger.

"Three?" Doc said.

Leo explained. "Dixon's two sales guys vouched for his BS story and said I jumped him in his office. Luckily one customer saw the whole thing and told it back exactly like it really happened and said he'd swear on a stack of bibles that Dixon and his employees were lying through their teeth. Dixon quickly made up something about not pressing charges because I'm new in town and everyone can make a mistake. It ended as fast as it began."

"I don't know what to say." Doc shook his head, looking at the box of cereal between them. "I guess, keep eating your Wheaties."

SATURDAY NIGHT

Yesterday's tryout included a doubleheader intrasquad scrimmage: one six-inning game was played after school, the second began after dinner, finishing under the lights. Parents were not allowed in the stands, but a few of the more enterprising ones parked on a hill a block away and broke out binoculars. Afterward, Leo had the boys rake and tarp the field in the cool night air. They weren't as chatty as usual because they knew while they did their work, Coach was paring down the roster to 20 from 30. Truman survived that second cut. He was playing a lot of second base, right field and he pitched one scoreless inning in both scrimmages, using guile rather than gas to get outs.

By Saturday, Leo's fight had become old news for the kids, though they thought Coach looked cool with a black eye beneath his baseball cap. Leo thought he looked dumb. On a positive note, the past two days of tryouts had a different vibe without Dixon there—better, looser. Dixon's son Billy had not been in attendance since the fight, and Leo had a feeling he'd soon find out why. Dixon had called a meeting of the Little League board of directors at the VFW for 8:30 tonight. Leo was requested to attend.

Home. On the couch. That's where Leo wanted to be. If he were lucky there'd be a Saturday night Cubs game on television. Put his feet up. Rest his aching body. It had been a full week of drills, throwing BP, hitting infield and fly balls. Plus the fistfight. Leo's legs wanted to sit, his core muscles wanted to recline, his brain wanted to shut off. But there was the VFW meeting. Doc said it was important that he be there, along with Jerome and Frank from Doc's end.

But first, Leo needed groceries.

"Hi there. Are you the coach of the 12-year-old Little League trav-

149

eling team?" A woman a few years older than Leo approached him in the produce section. The grocery store was mostly empty. "I'm certain you are," she said. "I'm Donna Lundberg. My son is Arnie." She looked at Leo, hopeful that he might recognize the name.

"Nice to meet you." Leo shook her hand. It was cold.

As she pumped his hand with more force than her size suggested, she said, "I want to say I'm so proud of the fact that you knocked that Dixon idiot flat onto his ass. Thank you. Very happy."

Leo wondered if she'd been drinking. Just as Leo started to say she was welcome, the woman opened a carton of eggs and smashed the leading edge against his chest. Yellow yolks drained down his shirt. "And that," she said, "is for cutting my Arnie. Good evening then." Her tone was as pleasant as if they were bridge partners.

Another woman was pushing her cart past them as the encounter happened. She stood in disbelief for a moment. "It appears you've been egged," she said, approaching Leo. Her cart was loaded with frozen pizzas topped off by five rolls of paper towels. She tore the plastic off a package of Bounty and proceeded to wipe Leo's front. "What a mess." She started laughing. "Sorry."

Leo couldn't help but laugh, too. "What a day," he said, holding up his arms as she mopped his shirt.

"You better take it from here." The woman glanced at egg dripping down the waistband of his shorts. She handed the roll to Leo.

"Thanks for the rescue," he said. "I'm Leo."

"No problem. I'm Nancy."

Leo wiped his shorts, noticing the contents of her shopping cart. He said nothing, but Nancy could see how it would look odd.

"Little weird, huh?" she said. "Those aren't all for me."

"No. I'm sure."

Nancy explained. "I run a bar just north of town, the Sundown Saloon, on the highway. Freezer crapped out. Big mess. Tonight, only frozen pizza on the menu."

"Didn't know there was a bar out there. I'm new—in Dannaka." As soon as he said that, he knew it must be obvious.

"Well the bar isn't much to see. Locals call it the Rundown Saloon. So the freezer is no great surprise."

Leo nodded.

"Let me guess. You're the new baseball coach."

"That depends." Leo smiled, "Do you have a boy on the team who I recently cut?"

Cute and funny, Nancy thought. "No. No kids. Not me."

"No wedding band, either." Leo hadn't flirted with a woman since his fiancée walked out. He wasn't sure what had gotten into him. Nancy was an attractive woman, but not immediately so. He liked her confidence, the way she stepped in to solve things.

Nancy confirmed, "No wedding band."

"That's surprising." Leo wasn't sure where to go with this so he just went. "Attractive woman. Small town." He shrugged as his voice trailed off.

Nancy looked at Leo. Tall, square-shouldered, baseball cap tipped back, a smudge of dirt on his face. She was going to ask about his black eye, but decided against it. "Leo ... you said your name was Leo, right?"

"Yep," he said, with the trailing edges of a smile still on his face.

"Because you're new to town, and kinda cute yourself, I'll let you in on a local secret. Okay?"

"Okay."

"In Dannaka," Nancy said, "women become the men they wish they'd married."

Leo allowed a moment for that to sink in. "Hmm. Good to know."

A stock boy arrived with a mop and bucket.

Nancy stepped over the eggs, closer to Leo. They looked at each other as she reached, taking the paper towels from his hands. "So, you know where to find me, new Leo." She smiled and tapped him once in the chest with the roll of paper towels.

"Sundown Saloon." Leo nodded. "Best pizza in town."

"That's right," she said in a way that made Leo forget he had egg all over him.

He watched her push her cart toward the two checkout lanes, wondering if she might stop to look over her shoulder. Instead, Nancy used her pants to wipe the remaining egg off her hand.

Usually Truman would protest. Saturday night. Watch TV with his mom? No way. But he was wiped out from the pressure and exertion of tryout week. Plus he had a homework assignment.

At 7:00, PBS was showing a documentary called *Adolf Hitler and the Rise of the Third Reich*. Truman and his classmates were required to tune in and write a 500-word report on the show's lessons. The essay was due on Monday, and tomorrow was Easter Sunday. He was determined to get it all done tonight.

Wade came over 15 minutes before the documentary began. He said he'd take care of making popcorn. Wade believed resoundingly that popcorn was nothing without extra butter and extra salt. Jess was usually against soda in the house, but she stopped for a two-liter bottle of A&W Root Beer on her way home from work. Truman had his pen and note pad on his lap, with a bowl of popcorn balanced on top. Ike was in heaven. He sat at the foot of the couch, ready. Handfuls of popcorn rising to mouths meant fluffy white kernels would soon be raining down on the rug below. The joy!

Truman managed to scribble notes, stuff popcorn in his mouth and drink soda with mechanical precision. Wade's hand exited the large yellow mixing bowl of popcorn only long enough to make a deposit. By the time Jess got settled with her soda, she reached into a nearly empty bowl.

"Slow down, you two," she insisted.

"There's more," Wade said, popcorn tumbling from his mouth.

"Shh!" Truman was listening as the narrator spoke about the power of language, and what made Hitler such a masterful orator. The program cut to a 1939 speech, recorded on scratched, grainy black-and-white film. There was Hitler, on a raised dais, in uniform, swastika on his sleeve, fist hammering, head jerking, bottom lip jutting, his eyes as dark as his brush mustache. His percussive

German staccato thundered in the auditorium. English subtitles ran below.

WE ARE DESTINED BIOLOGICALLY FOR LEADERSHIP
OUR DUTY IS TO CLEANSE THE FATHERLAND
OF ALL INFERIOR BLOODLINES
THE JEWS, THE GYPSIES
THOSE THAT WILL DEFILE
OUR GREAT ARYAN NATION

Hitler's voice escalated, words lashing out like nightsticks.

NOW'S THE TIME!
GIVE ME YOUR COURAGE!
GIVE ME YOUR STRENGTH!
YOU ARE AN UNDEFEATABLE FORCE
THIS IS OUR DESTINY
THIS OUR RIGHT
NO ONE CAN STOP US
WE WILL BE VICTORIOUS!

Ike spun, barking wildly at the television. Powerful, guttural, it was unlike anything they had heard come out of the puppy.

Truman's eyes widened. "Mom, what's going on?"

Jess's skin tingled. "I'm not sure, honey."

Hitler kept shouting.

Ike kept barking.

Louder. Louder.

Truman yelled, "Something's wrong. Help him."

Ike's back hair stood in the glow of the television. On four legs, Ike, with the force of each bark, was brought closer to the screen.

"MOM!" Truman begged, covering his ears.

Jess sprung off the couch, wrapping her arms around the lunging pup.

It was unstoppable.

Until Truman yanked the TV cord out of the wall socket.

The room reverberated in silence. Truman's ears were ringing as he joined his mom on the floor. Ike's chest rapidly expanded and contracted as he panted. His rigid body began to ease. Ike sat. Then he flopped down.

"Is he okay, Mom?" Truman stroked the overheated pup.

Jess looked him over. "Seems to be."

"That was completely crazy," Wade said.

They all looked at each other, speechless. There would be only one other time when the pup would bark like that again.

The VFW was jammed. Doc received plenty of hearty slaps on the back as he made his way to the bar. Before he could say yes, someone had already bought him a beer. Jerome and Frank had taken up two stools and were half-watching a game of pool. The place smelled of cigarette smoke and barbecue sauce. Saturday night was rib night.

Doc took a swallow of his Budweiser and gave a soft salute to the old-timer across the bar who'd paid for it. "Any sign of Leo?" he asked.

His friends said no.

"How about Dixon?" Doc watched the old-timer who had a rib in one hand and a lit cigarette in the other.

Before either could answer, the door swung open and Dixon filled the doorframe. He squinted through the smoke until his eyes fell on Doc, Jerome and Frank.

The closer Dixon got to the bar the more you could see that he, too, was sporting one hell of a shiner. He had attempted, badly, to cover it with some of his wife's pancake makeup. "Come here often, ladies?" Dixon said, trying to be funny.

"You're the one wearing makeup," Frank replied. Jerome looked the other way, thinking he might have to spit out his beer.

"What'll you have?" Doc said to Dixon. "It's on me."

Dixon pushed past to the bar. "You can't buy me off that easy."

"Suit yourself." Doc slid over. He kept an eye on the front door.

Dixon pulled out a money clip thick with twenties. "Where's Coach Kumbaya?"

"Leo should be here any minute," Doc said.

Awkward silence.

Frank couldn't help himself. "Heard you took a swing at our new coach? Nice of you to welcome him to town."

Dixon turned his large frame to Frank. "The kid came into my office and started the whole thing. But I figure he's under a lot of pressure, so bygones are bygones."

Jerome raised his gin and tonic to Dixon. "That's magnanimous of you."

Dixon wasn't sure if magnanimous was a good thing or a bad thing. "Yeah," he said. "Guys," he continued, "let's cut to the chase. What your coach is doing is stupid. It's going to backfire and the kids will pay the price."

"What makes you think so?" Jerome asked.

Doc said, "Do we really want to talk about it here?"

"Why not?" Frank added.

"Let's just wait for Leo, go in the back and hear what you have to say. It's your meeting." Doc nodded at Dixon.

When Leo walked in, the VFW went from boisterous to eerily quiet. Evidently everyone had heard about the fight. Now the two combatants were in the same room.

Dixon stepped away from the bar. "Don't worry," he said to the crowd. "I'm not going to hurt the lad."

The wooden floor squeaked under Dixon's shoes as he walked over to Leo. He shot out a hand, causing Leo to flinch. "Just want to shake hands and bury the hatchet," Dixon said, loudly enough for those in back to hear.

The men shook hands and the bar patrons applauded. Both men's right hands hurt too much to sustain much of a grip.

They settled around the same table they'd used three weeks ago, just before Leo arrived in Dannaka. The dent in the sheetrock where

Dixon threw his Bloody Mary glass had been repaired and repainted.

"Jerome," Doc said. "Will you keep the minutes?"

"Really?" Dixon said. "This crap again?"

Jerome flipped open his notebook and clicked his pen.

Doc continued. "Leo, thanks for giving us a piece of your Saturday night. I'm sure it's been a long week."

"No problem," he said.

Frank came back with two beers and handed one to Leo, who started to dig a few bills out of his pocket. Frank told him that wasn't necessary.

"So, just for the record, this meeting was called by Russ Dixon who is in attendance along with the Little League Board, fill in the names later, and Leo Hamill, our head coach for the 12U AAA traveling team."

"So noted," Jerome said.

Doc looked at Dixon. "The floor is yours."

Dixon leaned back in his chair and looked around the table, nodding dramatically. "We're all baseball guys here." Dixon's big hands talked along with him. "We love the game. We love the competition. We love the kids. I think we just got off on the wrong foot. I think we should go to plan B. Do a one-year transition where Leo works under me, gets to know what's best for the kids, learns the ropes of Iowa Little League baseball and then we review the situation next year."

Doc was flabbergasted. "You called this meeting for *plan B*."

Dixon nodded with certainty. "Yes. Let's reboot this thing before it's too late."

Leo sat up straight. "Too late for what?"

"Young man, okay, I don't want this to get personal. But I think you've shown you don't have the temperament to lead impressionable 12-year-old boys." Dixon pointed at Jerome. "That's for the record."

"And I've shown this how exactly?"

Dixon's voice tightened. "You run ridiculously un-baseball-like practices, you cut the only guy on the coaching staff who knows what these kids need to win in this state and then you jump a man in his place of business." Dixon shrugged. "In my book, that's not leadership."

Leo sat back and crossed his legs. Slowly he removed his cap and hung it on his knee. He had a terrific headache. "Doc. Jerome. Frank. I'm not going to argue with this man, I—"

"Why not?" Dixon blurted. "Aren't these kids worth it to you? They are to me."

Leo met his interruption with composure. "I'm not going to argue because arguing never changes anyone's mind. It just digs him deeper into the same position. So I'm asking you, as the board's representatives, do you want me to coach this team? I'm happy to do so. But without Dixon. Circle that last sentence, Jerome."

Doc spoke first. "I want you as coach, and accept the condition you just mentioned."

Frank followed. "I second you as coach, and applaud the condition you just mentioned."

Jerome looked up from his notes. "It's unanimous."

Dixon scratched the back of his head. He was getting hot, his voice clenched and hissing. "Big fucking mistake, boys. Believe me, huge fucking mistake." Dixon stood, rocking, forcing a chuckle. "You don't know what you're doing. You leave me no option. I'm going to take Billy and go to Des Moines and coach those kids. We will come back here and wipe the floor with Dannaka. You guys," he pointed a thick finger at each of them, "will be to blame. You did this. You and Coach La-la land."

"I think that's great," Frank said.

Dixon laughed. "You think getting crushed is great?"

"Well, if Des Moines crushes us that means at least we won districts, something you haven't been able to do in the past three years."

Leo got his feet under him. Dixon was about to go after Frank, which meant Leo was right back in it with Dixon again.

"Frank," Dixon said, "if you weren't such a helpless old man I'd kick your ass."

Frank jumped up, pulled off his eyeglasses and started coming at Dixon.

Doc horse-collared Frank.

Dixon laughed. "Just try me, old man."

Leo stood. "Shut up. Show some respect."

"Yeah. What are you gonna do about it?"

As Leo stepped closer to Dixon, he seemed to get taller. "You know damn well what I'm going to do. I'm going to drag your ass into that bar and in front of your hometown I'm going to beat you to where you'll be dining through a straw for the summer."

It was obvious Dixon did not want any part of Leo again. "Yeah, summer. No doubt, you'll be seeing me this summer." Dixon sneered. "You're in waaay over your head, Coach." Then Dixon scowled at the rest of the men around the table. "The brain trust. More like brain rust. Congratulations. You just lost last year's top RBI kid. And a coach that knows all your kids' weaknesses."

Dixon knocked his glass of beer over on the table and walked out.

FINAL CUT

Getting out of bed Monday morning, Jess was still stuffed from Easter dinner. Wade's grill-smoked ham was a masterpiece and the Gruyere and Gouda cheeses in his au gratin potatoes had the power to communicate. They whispered, "Another bite. Another bite. Another bite."

As Jess poured a cup of coffee, Truman shuffled groggily into the kitchen. "Is it going to rain today?" Ike came bouncing in at his heel.

"Good morning to you, too."

Ike came over and wiggled around Jess's legs. "Now there's a good morning. Yes, good morning. Good morning." The pup leaned into the butt pats.

Truman stretched his arms high over his head. "Yeah, good morning. What about rain?"

"Turn on the radio. You're not helpless. And let Ike out. Please."

Truman clicked on the radio and slid it across the Formica countertop toward the window to improve reception. "C'mon boy. Outside." That word got Ike's attention. Truman held the side door open and Ike slowly crept out, nose twitching in the air, each paw lifting and setting down in slow-motion. The pup was all pointer: observe, evaluate, step. Repeat.

"You okay?" Jess asked, watching Truman trudge to the table. "You seem especially out of it."

"I was up late finishing my paper."

Jess did feel for him. He had been up late. And he was still unsettled by Ike's barking episode. "Did you write about Ike in your Hitler report?"

Truman said he did not.

"Okay," her tone warned. "It would be memorable if you did. Very

159

original. Teachers reward originality."

"Not Miss Farley. She stands at the chalkboard and writes: Structure, Structure, Structure."

"I like Miss Farley."

"You can have her," Truman said. "Pancakes today?" He saw a box of Bisquick come out of the pantry.

"Pancakes," she confirmed. "I want you battle-ready for the last scrimmage."

Truman dropped his head into his hands and mumbled, "From 20 to 14 today. Oh, man. Coach lets us know after the tryout."

"You'll be fine," Jess said, trying to sound sure.

It would take just about two hours to drive to the state capitol building. Leo recalled passing through Des Moines on the way to Dannaka. Funny how the same road changes once you've traveled it.

Leo's test was at 10:00. If all went according to plan, he'd be licensed to teach in Iowa this fall. He was ready. Easter Sunday had been perfectly quiet; he got up late, went for a run and spent most of the day poring over his study guide for the last time.

Turning his red pickup onto the highway, Leo went north. The accelerating truck made it obvious it could use a new muffler. That was money Leo didn't have at the moment. He rolled down the window, spat out a few sunflower seed shells and took a swallow of Gatorade. What a beautiful day with uncluttered horizons, black fields and a temperature already reaching the mid-sixties.

Leo flipped thorough his small pile of cassettes on the front seat. He had pretty much worn them out so he tuned into a local country station hoping to see if the weather was going to hold for this afternoon's final tryout. The last cut is the hardest cut.

Six players had to go. The kids who won the final roster spots had to bring something to the party that others couldn't: Great speed. Unusual pitching control. Stellar defense. Flawless bunting. Boundless enthusiasm. Big-time power. Things like that. He planned to put the bubble kids in some sticky situations today to see if their distinguishing skills would rise or fizzle under pressure.

The highway hooked north and there it was. "Now I see why they call it the Rundown Saloon." Leo took his foot off the accelerator to get a full look at the place. He smiled thinking about Nancy and the egging. What had she said about the roadhouse? *Our drinks are stronger than our building.* As Leo drove past, it looked like the roof might collapse under a strong wind. Near the entrance of the gravel parking lot, a portable roadside sign read: WELCOME BIKERS. Below, in the little remaining space for text: COLD BEER.

"Succinct." Leo said. "Brevity is the soul of a parking lot sign."

He settled in for his drive north and then east to Des Moines. It seemed to Leo that every time he turned around, someone else was telling him what a powerhouse the Des Moines 12U AAA team was. If he didn't have tryouts to get back for, he'd find out for himself. Chances were they'd be on the diamond, too.

Jess had encouraged Truman to take a full lunch period at school today. Sit with friends. Goof off. Don't wolf down your food and race over to the field to practice. Truman looked at her like she was speaking Latin. Breaking their string of lunchtime practices, he explained, would put his streak of surviving the cut at risk.

He said he wanted to work on the Dazzler, as Coach had dubbed it. Jess refused to catch Truman's knuckleball for one simple reason: she couldn't. The thing would start at her shoulders and dive to her knees. Or out of the blue, take a right or left turn as randomly as a teenage driver. She did agree to stand behind the backstop and call out balls and strikes and tell him which pitches packed the most movement. Truman was experimenting with different grips on the laces, each with unique results.

As Jess walked back to work after their lunchtime practice, she idly hummed a John Denver tune until suddenly she didn't. Her thoughts jumped to yesterday's Easter dinner at Wade's. They'd planned a 4:00 mealtime. Wade said come over whenever. Jess, Truman and Ike, plus a tossed salad and dessert, arrived around 2:00. Wade, per usual, had the supper details running like clockwork.

They had time for a game of canasta while the ham grilled and the au gratin potatoes baked. It was Cubs versus the Pittsburgh Pirates, so they listened to that on the radio. Truman took Ike for a few runs around the block when he got bored. Wade went to the basement for some of his homemade beer. The sun was shining, the windows were open to a clean breeze and life on their little corner in their little town could not have been more pleasant.

At dinner, the conversation hopscotched from topic to topic: Truman's paper on Hitler's rise. A new small business insurance policy that Wade could offer. A three-legged cat at Jess's clinic that liked to jump into people's arms.

Eventually Truman started talking about tryouts. How excited he was to still be on the team. How great Coach was. How cool Coach's drills were. How Coach made baseball much more fun. How Coach gave everyone a fair shot. How Coach being a big leaguer gave their team such an advantage.

Wade snapped. Enough with the Coach stuff, okay? It's getting a little old. And by the way, Coach is not a big leaguer. He's an ex-big leaguer.

You could've heard a crumb fall off a fork.

Wade had never used a cross word in their presence. Ever. He immediately apologized and said it must be the homebrew talking. He went into the kitchen for a glass of ice water.

Dinner didn't nosedive but it never got back to cruising altitude, either. Truman cleared the plates and went to the backyard to throw Ike a tennis ball. Wade and Jess did the dishes. Wade said he was so sorry. Jess asked him if anything was wrong at work. Wade was an honest man and he told her what triggered his outburst. He had never heard Truman speak so glowingly about another man. He was jealous. Jess put her hand on Wade's arm and said Truman thought the world of him, that Wade didn't have to worry about Truman's affections. Wade shook his head and said no; he was jealous of how *she* might be feeling about the impressive young coach. She assured him he had absolutely nothing to be jealous of. But now, so absorbed in her thoughts as she walked back from the baseball field, Jess overshot the clinic by two blocks. She stood in the middle of the sunny sidewalk wondering. *Was I entirely truthful with Wade?*

"Timeout," Leo said, stepping out onto the baseball field. They were in the third inning of the final scrimmage of tryouts. Leo was feeling great. He sailed through his teacher certification test and ran into virtually no traffic coming back from Des Moines. There was nothing on his mind now but baseball.

Walking to the pitcher's mound, Leo looked at the bases. They were loaded. "How many outs?" he hollered to the infield.

"One dead," they answered sharply, turning to hold one finger up to the outfield.

"Truman," Leo shouted to the right fielder, "you're my relief pitcher."

Truman stood there like Coach might be talking to some other Truman.

"Get in here," Leo said. "Warm up."

"Holy shit, holy shit, holy shit, holy shit." Softly, the words bounced out of Truman as he jogged in. "Bases juiced," he whispered. "And Bale's coming up." Truman tried to regulate his breathing.

While Truman took his eight warmup pitches, Leo had a conference with the infielders at the side of the mound. "Just the third inning, so let's play the infield back. Go for the double play. Give up a run for an out if you have to."

The boys nodded. None of them said what they were thinking: *A lot of kids throw harder than Truman. Why him in this spot?*

Truman told Coach he was ready to go. He stepped off the mound, did a few deep knee bends and thought about his pitch sequence. *Bale is going to be geeked up. He would love to give me crap about hitting a grand slam, so I'm going to start him with a slow deuce. If he bites on that, the next curve will be slower. Then I'll get him to chase high cheese.*

When Bale walked to the plate he had a countrywide grin on his face. He stepped into the batter's box and pointed his bat in a trajectory that indicated he was going to deposit Truman's pitch deep over the centerfield fence.

Leo jogged off the field, curious to see how Truman would handle the situation. He was one of the bubble kids, who, when the tryouts began, Leo thought wouldn't get past the second cut. But Truman had pluck and Leo liked pluck. And the boy consistently threw strikes— at least in the scrimmages so far. But now the bases were full and the team's best hitter was in the batter's box.

Truman shook off the catcher until he got the sign for a curve. He focused on the target, wound up and delivered a slow yakker that started high and off the plate but dropped into the strike zone. Bale pulverized the pitch. It was long and gone. No, wait. It hooked … foul. Nothing but a long strike.

Bale smiled but Truman remained impassive. He stared in and again shook off the catcher until he got the sign he was looking for. He threw an even slower curve. Bale took a mighty hack but drove the ball helplessly into the ground where it spun foul. Strike two.

Truman planned to work fast when the ball came back from his catcher. He didn't want to give Bale time to think. Then Truman stopped himself, slowing the game down. He stepped off the rubber. Coach always says nothing good comes from rushing. *Bale knows I'm going to throw a high fastball to try to get him to chase it out of the strike zone. Everyone tries that pitch when it's 0 and 2. Maybe I can fool him.*

Truman called timeout, which was granted by umpire Tom Tink behind home plate. The catcher jogged out for a conference.

"High cheese," the catcher whispered to Truman.

"No," Truman said. "He knows that's coming. I'm going to throw the Dazzler."

"What in heck is that?" the catcher asked.

"You're about to find out." Truman instructed, "The ball is going to start high. Whatever you do, don't reach up for it. Just keep your glove in the strike zone."

"You're sayin' the ball will drop?"

"Right into your mitt," Truman said. "Got it?"

"Um, you sure?"

Truman looked at the catcher calmly. "You're gonna want to reach up. But don't. It'll drop in." The catcher nodded dutifully and jogged back to his position.

Bale stared out at Truman, waggling the bat. "This dog needs to eat," he shouted. "What do you got for me, Runt?"

"Ooooooooh," Bale's team taunted from the dugout. "What you got, Runt?"

Truman knew Bale was just messing with him, but the nickname pissed him off. Rather than fight it, he channeled the anger down his shoulder, through his pitching arm, past his fingertips and into his fingernails, which dug into the laces of the baseball in his glove. Truman's knuckleball grip was hidden from sight.

Standing straight on the mound, Truman came set, brought his front knee slowly upward, found his balance point, pushed powerfully off the pitching rubber with his back leg, striding hard toward home. His arm whipped forward and he released the Dazzler.

The baseball flew toward Bale high in the strike zone. Bale knew a high pitch was coming and he wasn't going to chase. Then, as the ball closed in, Bale froze. There was no spin. Five feet before crossing the plate the baseball dipsey-doodled, right into the awaiting catcher's mitt.

Jaw-dropping silence hung over the field. Tom Tink, struck mute behind the plate, pulled off his umpire's mask in disbelief. A smile grew on Leo's face like he hadn't experienced in months.

"Steeeee-rike three!" Tom shouted. Truman's team erupted. Jumping, laughing, pumping their arms. Bale squared his shoulders to the pitcher's mound and removed his batting helmet, his other hand at his waist. He gave Truman a theatrical bow before walking back to the dugout.

When the cheering settled, Truman got the last out on a changeup that was rolled weakly to the third baseman who stepped on his bag. He walked off the mound taller than when he had taken it.

That night in bed, Truman was the happiest he'd ever been. He made the team. He was a first alternate but he didn't care. Like Coach said, every team is fluid, changing, adjusting. Starters who don't perform will sit. There will be injuries. It's a long season. Everyone must be ready to play when their name is called. Every one of you made this team for a reason. We'll only dress 12 on game day. If you want to be one of them, keep improving.

Ike was curled at Truman's side in bed. The pup's sleep was rhythmic and surprisingly noisy. But more so, it was comforting. Truman wondered why when dogs had a long, exciting day, they fell right to sleep. But when he had the same kind of day, he'd lay awake counting nailheads in the ceiling. It didn't matter. Nothing mattered. He made the team. And he struck out Bale. Truman closed his eyes and in his mind, he pushed Play, watching the Dazzler dance through air.

"Hey, bartender. Gimme a frozen pizza."

Nancy had her back to the bar, stocking Bartles & Jaymes into the knee-high cooler. She hated when customers weren't patient enough to wait for her to turn and face them when they ordered.

"And can I get eggs with that?" the man added.

Nancy went from irritated to delighted. She turned to Leo. "Hardly recognize you in a clean shirt."

"Dressed up just for you." Leo gave her a sly smile, which Nancy could see was capable of doing considerable damage.

"Nice to see you, new Leo," she said. "What can I get you?"

"How 'bout a Bud."

Nancy twisted off the cap and set the bottle down in front of him. "Just between you and me, don't drink the tap beer."

Leo nodded and reached for his wallet.

"That one's on the house. The second one will cost ya." The way she said it was more than a little provocative. Nancy moved down to the waitress station to get a drink order.

A twangy old Hank Williams tune poured out of the jukebox, getting a few couples out of their booths to make turns on the dance floor. Leo was surprised by the size of the Monday night crowd. A buzz of voices mixed with the smack of pool balls breaking.

Nancy made her way back to Leo. "You haven't found yourself a pretty girl to go dance with yet?"

"I'm not much of a dancer."

"Not much of a drinker either," Nancy said, holding his bottle up to the light to see it was more than three-quarters full. Leo watched her. Her face was plain, her nose large and her vibe was hard, tough. She was the type of woman who might challenge you to arm wrestle, and if she did you'd be wise to decline. But there was a hint of softness, some invitation in her eyes.

"Nope. Not much of a drinker," Leo answered.

Nancy smiled at him and her smile said good for you. "Are you going to eat?" she asked.

"No. I just had a good day and I wanted to come out and see a friendly face before calling it a night."

Nancy blushed a little. "Ah, that's nice. What happened on your good day?"

"I went to Des Moines for my teacher's certification test. I know that went well. And I made the final cut for my baseball team. Now the real fun begins. The roster is set and we can get jelling as a group."

Nancy searched her memory. "Did I hear you had a particularly good coaching record in your past?"

Leo picked up his bottle of beer. "I was fortunate to coach some really good kids." He took a swallow.

"Hey," Nancy's eyes sparkled, "I have a friend whose son was trying out. Wonder if he made your team?"

Leo didn't like these conversations. More often than not they ended in disappointment. "What's his name?" Leo asked.

"Do you mind me asking?" Leo looked like maybe he did.

He shrugged. "Who is it?"

"Truman. Truman Younger."

Leo's smile was answer enough.

Nancy clapped her hands and rolled up on her tiptoes. "Ho ho! Truman made it?"

"He sure did," Leo said. "He's a scrappy one. Smallest kid. Maybe the biggest heart."

Nancy's face transformed. The hard edge gave way to something more open and attractive. "You, new Leo, have made a boy very, very happy."

"How do you know him?" Leo asked.

"I went to high school with his mom. Been friends forever."

"Small world," Leo said.

"Small town, actually."

Leo sipped his beer. "That puppy they have, Ike, do you know him?"

Nancy said she did.

"I found him on the way to Dannaka. Jess and Truman were good enough to give him a home."

"That was your dog? I thought she got it at work. How did you find him?"

"Poor little guy. Got dumped on the side of the road because he was the runt of the litter."

Nancy shook her head. "Human beings never fail to disappoint. But, on the other hand, there's you: all-American puppy rescuer." Nancy's face became more serious. "Are you one of the good ones, new Leo?"

"Depends on who you ask," he said in a voice drained of earlier cheerfulness. Leo looked past Nancy at the bottles shelved behind her. "Well, thanks for the cold one. And the talk."

"Anytime," Nancy said.

"The natives are getting restless over there." Leo looked down the bar where a few couples sat with empty glasses. "Have a good night."

From the other end of the bar came a voice: "Can any of the rest of us get a drink around here?"

Nancy didn't bother to look at the customer. "Not if they act like that."

"Pretty please," the voice added.

"Goodnight, new Leo," she said, picking up his half-empty bottle.

Parking lot gravel crunched under Leo's flip-flops as he walked to his truck. Muted music punctuated by jackhammers of laughter drifted through the screen windows of the honky-tonk. The night air was damp. Leo tipped up the bill of his cap and turned his gaze to a sea of black above, bedazzled with piercing stars. This far from the lights of town, the night sky was undeterred.

"Are you one of the good ones?" Leo softly re-asked Nancy's question. A dog from a distant farm found something to bark after. Leo locked his fingers on top of his cap, head cocked back, looking into the sky of stars, wishing he knew for certain the answer to that question.

Book

THREE

Coming together

"Baseball is one-third preparation, one-third perspiration and one-half standing around."

—*Tom Tink, Dannaka assistant coach*

New Leo

"Hey, bony ass," Nancy hollered after Jess, who was walking in front of her with a sidewalk full of dogs. Jess was too busy playing marionettist with the leashes to pay attention. But Nancy picked up the pace, cupped her hands around her mouth and upped the volume. That got Jess to look over her shoulder.

"Oh hi," Jess said, unsuccessfully trying to wave while the dogs yanked her in the other direction.

"Here. Let me take a few of those mongrels." Nancy walked fast to catch up. They untangled the leashes and in no time were striding down the sidewalk together. May's bountiful sunshine showered down.

"Long time no Nancy," Jess said, happy to see her friend. "Where've you been?"

Nancy said her mother had glaucoma surgery. Right eye. "It was getting to where she could hardly see out of it. She told me, what the hell. Worst case they take the eye. I always admired pirates."

"Your mom's a trouper."

"I stayed at her house for a week, till she kicked me out. Said I was cramping her style."

Jess laughed. "How's her vision?"

"Much better. Amazing. I don't think I would have the guts to let someone operate on my eyeball." Nancy shook off the thought.

The oak trees above were fully leafed. A breeze shimmied through them. The women and dogs followed the slow bend in the sidewalk, which led to picnic grounds in the park. Bub was on a lawn tractor mowing grass, producing one of the most pleasing aromas of the new season. An American flag waved lazily on its pole near the covered pavilion.

Ike began pulling the pack, knowing resolutely where he wanted to go. As the pace picked up, it became obvious that Jess was purposely avoiding stepping on the sidewalk cracks. Nancy called her on it. "You don't step on the cracks? Since when?"

"Since I began living with the world's most superstitious 12-year-old. The kid has more quirks." Ike pulled harder as the sounds of baseball eddied in. "Truman's team is practicing this afternoon. Do you have time to stop for a sec?"

Nancy's shift at the bar didn't start until 4:00. She checked her watch. "Yeah. I've got a few minutes."

They cut through the park and made their way to the cyclone fence along the third baseline. The dogs plopped down on the grass, panting. Except for Ike. He stood erect, scanning the boys. His tail did double time when he picked Truman out of the group.

"What are they doing?" Nancy asked. "This isn't baseball like I remember it."

Jess looked on, trying not to laugh. "Truman says they do a ton of fun drills."

The team was split into two lines on either side of home plate. On "Go," one boy would sprint up the first baseline, the other up the third baseline. They would touch the bags, and proceed to do somersaults across the infield until they reached the pitcher's mound. Then popping up, they would sprint to home and touch the hand of the next kid in their line, setting him in motion. The group that got all seven kids home first was the winner.

Leo noticed the women by the fence. "No cheating," he told the boys before walking over. "Hello sports fans," Leo said, looking not only as happy as Jess had ever seen him, but less pudgy, too.

"Wow," Jess said. "You've lost weight, haven't you?" She was stunned by his transformation.

"Twenty-two and a half pounds," Leo said. "But who's counting." He pulled his cap off and wiped his brow. "Hi Nancy," he said, giving her a warm smile.

"Hello new Leo," she said.

Jess was confused. "You two *know* each other?"

"Had eggs together," Leo said.

"You wish," Nancy shot back.

They looked at each other like two people who shared a secret.

"And no fair, by the way," Nancy said.

Leo asked her what she meant.

"Losing 22 pounds in like whatever weeks it took. Guys have it too easy."

Jess tried to catch up. "Wait. You two know each other how?"

Nancy told the story about how they met. "I haven't seen you out at the bar lately," Nancy scolded.

"Gave up beer for a few weeks. Lot of wasted calories."

A cheer went up from the field as the relay race winners celebrated. Leo looked over at the boys. "Five minutes at the hose," he shouted. "Winners drink first. Then outfield for fly balls."

Ike, watching the boys run for the hose, strained on his leash. "Hey there, Ike," Leo said, bending down to scratch the pup through the fence. "Remember me? Look who's growing up so fast." Ike tried to lick Leo but got mostly fence.

"Well, I am so glad you two met," Jess said, but her words hung there.

Leo stood, taking the opportunity to stretch his back. "Tough keeping up with those goofballs. But they're a blast."

The three of them looked at each other.

"I'm going to get back at it," Leo said. "Be seeing you around." He gave them a youthful grin, his eyes radiating laugh lines, before jogging away. His movements were smooth and athletic.

"That man was made to run," Nancy said, appreciatively.

"He sure seemed happy," Jess said, slightly mystified. "C'mon dogs," she commanded. They all rose, ready to go. Ike stayed glued to the fence.

"Ike, let's move."

The pup whined but did as he was told.

They walked back the way they came. Nancy broke the silence. "New Leo is hot, don't you think?"

Jess pondered. "He's okay. Why do you call him new Leo?"

Nancy laughed. "Because when we met, when Donna Lundberg smashed eggs on him, he told me he was new in town. It was cute, him thinking he could be new in Dannaka without everyone knowing it."

"Is this place really that small?"

"No. It's smaller." Nancy paused. "So, you honestly don't think he's hot?"

"Are you interested in him?"

"Nah. I don't think so. Maybe." Nancy shrugged. "The last thing I need is another fling."

They came through the park, headed up the sidewalk and crossed the street toward the clinic. There was very little traffic except for Steve's Carpet Cleaning van, which drove past with the windows down; Steve was back smoking again. "I can take the dogs from here," Jess said. "Thanks for the walk. And say hello to your mom from me."

"Will do." Nancy handed over the leashes. "Truman looked like he was having the time of his life, by the way. He's in for a great summer."

Jess's crooked half-smile cautiously appeared. "That boy is on cloud nine."

As the two women parted, Jess wondered why she hadn't been more direct. She did think Leo was attractive. What was the harm in saying so?

They sat at the kitchen table. Leo declined the offer of a beer. When he explained why, Doc was impressed.

"It's good for men to have goals like that," Doc said. "Too many guys on cruise control. How many pounds you shooting for?"

"I feel best at about 195. That leaves eight to go. Those last few, they're glued on."

"Wow. So how many will that be total since you showed up on my doorstep, what, seven weeks ago?"

"Eight more would be 30 pounds."

Doc grinned. "That's a big bag of dog food you're no longer lugging around."

Leo smelled dinner cooking. Meatloaf. Heaven on a plate. Leo declined the invitation to eat with them because he felt he was over there too much as it was. "So just a couple financial things and I'll get out of the way."

Doc asked, "What do you have first?"

Leo was keeping a notebook on the team, with bookkeeping in the back. He flipped it open and started at the top of the list. "Uniforms," he said.

"How long did they say it would take to have 'em ready?"

Leo told him three weeks. "Final cuts were just over a week ago, so we're still a couple weeks out."

"We put half down, right?"

"Yep. And rather than the trust paying the rest, I want to have the kids raise the money. They should have some skin in the game."

Doc liked the thought. "What do you have in mind?"

"It's actually Tom Tink's idea. He knows all the local grocery stores. So he's been asking managers if they're okay with our players vacuuming and cleaning the interior of cars while customers shop. Five bucks a vehicle. We'll pick a Saturday, set up a few generators in parking lots, corral some Shop-Vacs and be in business."

Doc signaled thumbs up. "Good bonding for the team," he said. "And responsibility to boot."

Leo went over his list of other items. He needed boxes of game balls, new catcher's gear, batting tees, wiffle balls and two portable batting screens. There was one big-ticket item. "I'd like to get a pitching machine," he said. "I worked with the JUGS company when I was in Naperville and they were great. The have one product they dub the ultimate pitching machine, and it truly is. Super accurate. But it's not cheap."

Doc was listening.

"Six hundred bucks, not including tax."

"Ouch," Doc said. "You say it's worth it?"

"Every penny. On rainy days it goes inside with us in the gym. Fires tennis balls 70 miles per hour. That'll speed up the kids' hands so they're ready for pitchers who throw straight heat. And on the field when we're working defensive game situations, I need hitters to get strike after strike. Kojak delivers."

"Kojak?"

"That's what my high school kids named the machine. It has a big white tire that shoots baseballs. When it's spinning it looks like a bald pitcher."

"Funny." Doc said, "Well, if we need to spend it we need to spend it."

"On the other hand, one way we could save money is my pay. It seems high. It's over twice what I got for coaching high school. Plus, you guys are picking up the rent on the house. I feel sorta guilty."

Doc could see Leo meant it. "Believe me, this money is doing what it was intended to do. I appreciate your offer, more so your integrity, but this town essentially won the baseball lottery—and you're in on the winning ticket."

Leo's shoulders relaxed. "How'd I get so lucky?"

Doc raised his eyebrows. "Maybe luck is in the air here."

Tom Tink

A plain-spoken man, known to occasionally be too honest, Tom Tink was frustratingly great. His heart was always in the right place. His brain, oftentimes, was harder to pinpoint.

"If a tree falls in the forest and no one is there to see it, does it make a sound?" The players had taken a knee on the infield grass in front of the coaches. They were in the thick of a Tomifesto. "I'll tell ya if a tree falls on the baseball field and the whole town is in the stands to see it, it sure does make a sound. Do you know what I'm getting at?"

The boys' blank faces communicated: *No, Coach Tink. Not in the foggiest.*

"Adversity. Adversity is that tree falling on your field. Might be an error. Or a strikeout with the bases loaded. That's the TIMBER! And now what?" Tom paused, looking for the boys to answer.

Silence.

"I'll tell you what. Use that adversity. Rise up. Gut it up and cut it up and use that tree to light a fire inside you! Am I right? Yes. Right as TIMBER!"

Leo cocked his head, thinking he got the gist of the thought. Maybe. "Okay boys," he said, "let's get at it. What time is it?"

In unison the team replied, "Time to bond with the baseball."

Leo tipped over two buckets of balls. Everyone got three. They knew the drill. Start with one ball, toss it to yourself from hand to hand in a shallow arc.

"What's our favorite color?" Tom Tink shouted out.

"Red!" the team belted back.

"Focus on the laces," Leo instructed. "Baseball is a game of details."

Then they moved on to juggling with two baseballs, each passing the other in mid-flight, arcing up and dropping into the opposite hand. "Track it all the way. That's the secret to bonding."

The coaches did the drill as well. Everyone on this team knew he had to learn to juggle. Hand-eye coordination, soft hands, slowing down an activity in one's mind—these were the rewards of juggling.

"Let's go to two balls in the right hand. Remember the trick. After tossing the first ball up, hang on to the second one until the last split second. Then toss it up and catch the first one."

The boys had been practicing at home for a week. They had it down. Tom Tink was still struggling, balls banging into each other. He laughed it off. His philosophy: Enjoy life. Don't try to control it.

Tom's mother passed away when he was 13, an impossible loss for a boy just beginning to develop emotionally. His mother, an OB-GYN, believed stridently that life is predictable for the prepared. Her career and habits were guided by rigorous science and textbook certainties, by fertility cycles and nine-month gestation periods, by five-minute contractions and eight-centimeter cervix dilations. Every condition, she believed, informed an act.

On an early December morning, before leaving for the hospital, she tapped the glass face of her den barometer, as was her custom. Falling pressure and a glance out the bay window at a south wind heaving through the neighbor's evergreen proclaimed to her clearly, loudly, that snow was imminent. The first of the season.

As Tom's mother stood by the side door, on the landing above the basement steps, pulling on her mid-calf snow boots, the zipper became stuck in the fur. She had no time for such nonsense. She gave the zipper a stern jerk, causing the pull tab to detach from the slider. One moment, Tom's mother was stooped over her boot, struggling with the closure on the top landing, and the next, with the unexpected release of the zipper pull, she was tumbling backward down the stair flight. Her neck snapped on the third tread, the impact sending her half-on boot airborne. She was found dead on the basement landing. Her boot stood midway down the flight, upright like it had been placed there.

It did not snow that day.

"Good progress," Leo said. "Let's move on." Leo caught his last descending ball as carefully as an egg. "When you slow down the game of baseball and focus on controlling details, it gets a lot easier. On defense and offense."

Nearly every one of Leo's drills involved competition. The boys loved it. It was friendly competition, but there were consequences. There was a winner and a loser and the sooner the boys learned how to do both with class, the faster this group would jel as a team.

The boys were getting to know each other. Not all of them had grown up in Dannaka. As a group, they'd been together, including tryouts, for three weeks. Leo had been observing closely. Leaders were emerging. Some boys were carefree, others deliberate; some were an open book, and a few were so quiet that Leo would have to wait for their personalities to unfold.

The two quietest kids were the Hernandez brothers. Identical twins, they were new to the team, living in New Market, 15 miles east. The brothers were extremely self-sufficient. Nobody dropped the twins off for practice or picked them up. They rode their bikes—raced actually—up and down the rolling hills of the county highway to get to Dannaka.

Leo learned that their parents worked at New Market's poultry processing plant. For years, the population of this neighboring town had been like a slow leak. Businesses were degrading or disappearing. And you couldn't drive a block without seeing a For Sale sign in someone's front yard.

Then the largest local chicken farmer purchased the processing plant, sunk his life's savings into renovations and signed a deal to be a hub producer for Gold'n Plump Poultry out of Minnesota. He organized the area's other chicken farmers into a co-op.

The new owner promoted the plant's best worker, a young Hispanic family man, to manage his operation. That man had just fathered twin boys. He would provide for his family and show them that there was opportunity and mobility for anyone who worked hard in America.

As the processing plant grew so did the demand for employees. The manager tried to hire more workers but many of the locals were busy farming or not interested in processing chickens. So he reached out to family and friends. A slow influx of Mexicans came to New Market where the houses were affordable, the work was abundant and the pay was good.

Some of the locals saw this as a threat to their way of life and traditions. Others saw a revived downtown with a busy grocery store, a full school and a church that once again had long lines for communion.

The Hernandez twins were raised to be respectful but not to let others determine their goals. Their parents said the future favored those who worked the hardest and kept their eyes open more than their mouths.

The two brothers approached Leo while the rest of the team was at the hose. One of them talked for both.

"Excuse me, Coach. We were wondering what happened to Billy Dixon? And Coach Dixon?"

Leo had been meaning to explain the Dixons' absence but he wasn't sure how much of that to get into. "They decided to leave the team," Leo told the brothers.

The boys blinked in unison. "You mean they're not coming back? Gone for good?"

Leo told them yes.

"You're sure?"

"I'm sure," Leo said.

This news was transformative. Apprehensive when they approached, now the twins were shaking with joy. They threw their baseball gloves into the air and embraced. Then they pushed apart.

"You're not joking with us are you, Coach?"

Leo grew concerned. "No. No joking. What's wrong? Did something happen?"

The talkative brother spoke up. "Once after tryouts we were riding home. A big truck came up behind us on the road, very close. The horn started honking, almost pushing us into the ditch. We rode as fast as we could. They pulled up right next us. It was Coach Dixon and Billy." As he told the story, the boy's face tightened. "They said stop so we did. They got out of the truck and said nobody wanted twin wetbacks on the team. They said the only thing we did good was run fast because we were always running from the police. They said to swim back across the Mexico River and stay the hell out of their country."

Leo's mouth went dry, his temper rising. "Did you tell your parents?"

"No. Coach Dixon said not to tell anyone. Or else."

"Jesus," Leo whispered.

"Please Coach, don't tell our parents. They'll take us off the team."

"We should go to the sheriff."

The boys' eyes grew wider yet. "No. Not the police. Our parents and the families who work with them do not trust the police. Please, please," they pleaded.

"Did you feel like the Dixons wanted to hurt you?"

"Only with words," the brother said. "If there was real trouble, we would have dropped our bikes and run. We're like rabbits. They're turtles."

Leo leaned down to be closer to the boys' height. "You let me know if there is any more trouble. Promise me."

The boys said they promised.

Leo was still having trouble getting their names right because of their strikingly similar appearance. "Okay, remind me again who's who."

"I'm Juan ... I go by John," said the talkative brother.

"I'm Marcos. Mark."

John explained. "Our mother is a big fan of the Gospel writers."

"Tough act to follow," Leo said.

They nodded as if to say *don't we know it.*

"So everybody on this team is going to get a nickname. Who's the fastest of you two?"

Mark pointed at John and John pointed at himself.

"Good enough. John, from now on, you're Rabbit." Leo looked at John, noting that his face was slightly broader than his brother's and he was a skosh shorter. "Mark, I don't have a nickname for you yet, but the baseball gods will help me with that."

John asked seriously, "Coach, who are the baseball gods?"

Leo explained. "You know in baseball when things go your way? Like you take a full swing and a little dribbler spins down the third baseline and stays fair? Or you sky an easy fly ball and the outfielder loses it in the sun? Or you dive to snag a line drive and you catch it even though half the ball is sticking out of your glove?" Leo nodded. "That's the baseball gods on your side."

"Really, Coach?" John asked.

"Rabbit, you gotta believe. That's how you get the baseball gods on your side." Leo smiled at the boys in a way that let them know that he, for sure, was on their side.

They finished practice with an intrasquad scrimmage. It was another sunny day, which made Leo wonder if Dannaka had some sort of monopoly on baseball weather. Tom Tink's son was on the mound throwing BBs and no one was making decent contact at the plate.

Truman stepped into the batter's box. Bale was playing shortstop and he razzed his buddy. "Let's see what you got, Runt."

Truman had decided rather than fight the nickname he'd embrace it. It whipped up a fire inside him. A lot of ballplayers have a chip on their shoulder and use it to their advantage.

"Runt is going to knock one down your throat," he shouted back. That drew some oohs.

Truman was sitting on a fastball because, so far, nobody could catch up to it. The first pitch was hard and high. Truman laid off. The second pitch was the fastball he was looking for and he took a mighty hack. But he got under it and sent a harmless pop-up floating out toward Bale at short. It was a sure out but Truman ran every ball out regardless. He put his head down and took off for first base.

Bale eased back under the ball calling "mine, mine, mine," put his glove up, pounded it—then stumbled—appearing disoriented. The ball dropped a good foot behind him. It was the cheer from his team-mates that raised Truman's head. The ball had found some grass.

As Bale picked up the ball, Truman thought he saw him wobble.

Everyone said the hit was a gift from the sun. Truman said it was the baseball gods. But in the next inning, with Truman playing second base, that's when he knew something was definitely wrong with his friend.

Bale laced a line drive that got to the center fielder quickly. If Bale tried to stretch it into a double, there would be a play at second. Truman sprinted to the bag, positioning himself for the throw. Bale churned for second, but not with his usual speed. The throw from the center fielder was high. Truman leaped and caught the ball. As Bale began his slide, the heel of his front foot gouged into the dirt. Truman came down with the tag. In a grotesque microsecond, show-ered in dust, Bale's leading leg broke halfway up the shin.

Truman screamed for help. Bale writhed in pain. Leo bolted from the dugout. And on a sun-soaked afternoon in May, a routine slide into second had become anything but.

HOSPITAL

From Dannaka, the University of Iowa Hospital was almost a four-hour drive. Truman was insistent. He needed to see his best friend before he had surgery.

The doctor at the local clinic in Dannaka had set the tibia bone but before the cast had dried and his teammates were done signing it, Bale was referred to the University Hospital in Iowa City. The doctor didn't like the ragged nature of the fracture, especially considering the minimal trauma that had caused it.

In Iowa City, Bale had seen a revolving door of specialists in what was a two-day blur of blood tests, X-rays and conferring doctors. Then Bale was put inside an MRI scanner where the loud hammering and claustrophobic confines made him sob. Bale was not one to cry.

The doctors told his parents first. Bale had osteosarcoma. Imaging had identified a tumor and the biopsy concluded it was malignant. They said the tumor was three centimeters in diameter—about the size of a 50-cent piece. They needed to do surgery as soon as possible. No trace of cancer was detected in any other part of Bale's body and they wanted to keep it that way.

Telling Bale was the hardest thing his parents had ever done.

Truman and Jess were okayed to come for a visit the day before surgery. Bale needed to spend time with a buddy, talking about 12-year-old stuff, getting away from the adult realities of what he faced.

When they arrived at the fifth-floor nurses' station, Truman and Jess were told Bale and his parents were talking with the surgeon. They were ushered into a small waiting area.

"How're you doing?" Jess asked her son.

He stood at the window and looked down at colorless cement.

Cars, parking ramps, stories of glass windows reflected a gray sky. An ambulance pulled over and parked at the yellow painted curb. The driver got out for a cigarette. Everything outside was soundless. Foreign. Truman wanted to be home, blurring past green sprouting fields, bikes rattling as he and Bale rode to baseball practice.

He turned to his mother. "It sucks and it's not fair." Truman didn't care about the other people in the waiting room or the dumbass soap opera on TV or the ugly polished green and tan tile flooring that reflected the overhead florescent lighting. "Bale wasn't hurting anyone. Why would God give him cancer?"

Men and women in blue scrubs walked purposefully past the open doorway. Jess wanted to be angry, too, but now wasn't the time. "You need to be strong for your friend," she told him. "Can you do that?"

When Truman stepped into Bale's hospital room it didn't smell like anything. His bed was in one half, separated by a curtain. "I didn't get the window side," Bale said as Truman approached carrying a small wrapped present.

"Still pretty cool." Truman gestured to the wall-mounted television. "Got your own TV."

"Watch anything, anytime." Bale held up the remote. "Thirty channels."

As the distance between them shrank, each friend gauged the other's reaction. Bale looked different with his cast sticking out of a hospital gown. His hair hadn't been in the wind for a few days so it was plastered oddly to his head.

Truman sat in a chair next to Bale's bed. He looked at a styrofoam coffee cup stuffed with balled-up Kleenex on his bed tray. "Pretty cool you being on the fifth floor, even if you don't have a window."

"How so?"

"Because five is your favorite baseball number. It's good luck."

Bale let his head fall back on the pillow. "Not exactly feeling lucky."

"Sorry about that. About your … your leg and all."

Bale looked at Truman. "You can say it. Cancer."

"Yeah. Cancer." Then he remembered what his mom told him in

the waiting room. "But you'll be okay. You'll get better. You're strong … but smell isn't everything."

Bale half-smiled. "Ha, ha."

"How do you feel?"

"I'm fine. I mean my leg hurts, but it's been hurting a while."

"Was that from the bone cancer?"

"Yeah. The tumor grows and pretty soon it hurts and then the bone gets weak. That's why it broke so easy. I was safe, by the way."

Truman laughed. "So how do they fix it?"

"The doctor says out with the bad and in with the good. So they cut out the tumor and stick in a small piece of my rib bone—like a bridge—so my leg bone can grow back together. It's called a rib graft."

"Weird."

Bale nodded. "No crap. When my leg feels itchy I might end up scratching my armpit."

Truman laughed. "They do it tomorrow?"

Bale nodded.

"You scared?"

Bale hardened his countenance. "What scares me is losing my leg … like if the cancer keeps growing. I'd rather die than be a freak show."

Truman was resolute. "Don't say that. None of that's going to happen. This hospital is the best. They'll fix your leg. You'll be back playing ball in no time."

Bale's voice got quiet. "They say I could be in here for a couple months. And a year of rehab."

"I'll come help you. Anything you need. I'll quit the team to help you."

Bale's eyes flashed fiercely. "Don't ever say that. Ever! You got to go out and do better. For me. You have to work harder for me. Practice more for me. You're lucky to be playing. All you guys are."

Truman nodded. "I promise. But maybe you can still help me."

Bale sat up, putting a pillow behind his back. "Yeah?"

Truman continued. "Coach says my fastball needs to be faster. Not enough separation in speeds between my pitches. Maybe you can be my pitching coach. Help put a few miles per hour on my heater. We got three months till the state tourney."

A slow smile appeared on Bale's face, the first real sign of hope Truman had seen all day.

KOJAK

For 10 seconds, in unison, the entire team was juggling base-balls. Even Tom Tink. It was a first. More than just an accomplishment, the synchronized orbiting of dozens of baseballs was a sight to behold.

Leo was practiced enough to keep his three balls in the air while watching the others. To see their utter concentration, tracking the exact arc of each baseball, remaining under control—he loved it. Lessons were sinking in. They were learning the first principle of baseball—focus—while having fun.

Then a ball dropped. Like a daisy chain, others followed.

Leo let his balls fall to the ground and applauded. "Way to go, boys! We did it. The whole team was rolling at the same time. We'll have it figured out before our first real scrimmage next week."

The boys high-fived.

"Line up for quick-toss," Leo said.

Quick-toss was a relay race that Leo invented to get kids to throw the ball accurately under pressure, much like the situations they'll encounter in a game. With Bale out, they were down to 13 players.

"Team one, since you have six and they have seven, whoever goes first in your line will go again as the last guy."

The boys formed two lines. Leo and Tom Tink placed a baseball on the ground about eight feet ahead of each line. The coaches backed up eight more feet, putting down a second ball. Eight more feet, a third ball down until there was a string of seven baseballs between each line of boys and each coach.

"Let's do this!" Leo shouted.

The first boy from each line sprinted to the closest baseball in front of him, snatched it off the ground, shifted his body, front shoulder pointed to his target and let the ball fly to the coach at the end of his line.

"Go! Go! Go!" the boys yelled to their teammates.

The throw had to be on target. If a ball sailed over a coach's head or bounced wildly past him, that boy's line automatically lost.

The balls sizzled into Leo's and Tom's gloves as the first throwers raced back and touched the glove of the next boy in line. He then ran out to the second ball, picked it up, got into throwing position and fired it to the coach.

"We got 'em! C'mon!" the leading team cheered.

The last boy in each line had the farthest to run to his ball, but the shortest throw to the coach in front of him. The trick here, Leo had taught his players, is to execute a firm underhand toss to the coach's glove. In games, he explained, there are many instances when a ball is fielded close to a base and the infielder's best play is a quick, accurate underhand throw to his teammate.

Four weeks ago, when the boys started this quick-toss drill in tryouts, throws were flying out of control because the kids were only focused on going fast. What they had learned since was to play with controlled urgency, eliminating many of the errors.

After a few rounds of quick-toss, the kids learned they had a surprise waiting for them. Abuzz with suspense, they followed Leo to the equipment shed. He pulled open the door. It was like Christmas morning. There stood a brand-new pitching machine.

"Men," Leo said, "I want you to meet Kojak. Kojak, these are the Dannaka 12U AAA All-Stars. Your job is to help them learn to eat fastballs for lunch."

The pitching machine was heavy, with a cumbersome tripod of metal legs. Working as a group, the players managed to move it from the shed to the apron of the pitching mound. Leo followed behind with a long extension cord.

Truman asked the obvious question. "Why is it called Kojak?"

Leo explained. "See that white tire? When that thing gets spinning to shoot baseballs, it looks like a bald-headed pitcher." Leo smiled.

The kids were too young to understand the reference. "Huh?"

Leo felt old. "Kojak was about the coolest bald police detective ever on TV. Just ask your mom or dad."

Truman sized up the pitching machine. "Is he fast?"

"Fast and deadly," Leo said.

The boys liked the sound of that.

"Who's ready? Race to the center field fence and back. Fastest guy gets the first shot at Kojak."

Kojak was dialed in and spitting out one perfect strike after another. Leo told the group in round one that they would be going up against 55-mile-per-hour pitching. "To start, everyone only gets one swing."

Standing behind the machine, Leo held up a baseball to signal the batter, then fed it to Kojak. FFWUMP! The ball rocketed out, sizzling toward home plate. Ten of 13 batters missed the ball entirely. Three managed to foul one off. Leo made full use of the moment.

"Who walked up to the plate with a plan?" he asked the boys who stood around home plate. "Raise your hand if you did."

A thickset kid that Leo had dubbed Pot Roast simultaneously raised his hand and spoke. "I planned ... to rip a home run," he declared, getting a laugh from the team.

"How did your plan go?" Leo asked.

"Not so great," he said sheepishly.

"Because that's not a plan. Right? Going to the plate and looking for and swinging at a certain pitch, that's having a plan. When you step in the batter's box with no strikes on you, your plan is as simple as it gets: I'm looking for a such-and-such pitch in a such-and-such location. A plan says you won't swing at any other pitch."

The team listened intently as Kojak's wheel whirred on the pitcher's mound, ready to be fed another baseball.

"Pot Roast, what should your plan be against Kojak right now?"

"Choke up on the bat ...?"

Leo shrugged. "That's a good idea, but that's a tactic. Not a plan."

Another boy raised his hand.

"Go ahead," Leo said.

"Look for a fastball down the pipe."

Leo smiled. "Exactly. Right? We know what Kojak is going to throw. He's like those fastball pitchers you're gonna face who want to blow away every batter. One-dimensional. Early in the count, you know odds are he's going to throw his go-to fastball. Since you have no strikes, you can be very choosy. Don't swing at a high fastball. Don't swing at a low fastball. Don't swing at a curveball. Look for something hard right here."

Leo demonstrated with his hands. He shaped a small box at his beltline. "Fast and right here is your plan. You need to visualize that pitch before it's ever thrown. Because by anticipating it you have a much better chance of hitting it. With no plan, a batter gives all the advantage to the pitcher.

"Today, we start batting with a plan. Right now, we know Kojak is a fastball pitcher, right? I told you he was dialed in at 55 miles per hour. So ... look for that, plan for that, and when it comes, punish it. Got it?"

"Yes Coach!" the team responded.

The second time around they each got two pitches to hit. The third time, three. The batters became selective. They got their timing down. Baseballs were getting stung and laced and launched and ripped.

Once all the balls were shagged, Leo told the boys that Kojak had been knocked out of the game and was headed to the showers. The pitching machine went back in the equipment shed.

They gathered in the bleachers. Perspiring. Red-cheeked. Buzzing with chatter. Baseball smiles abounded. These were the faces, voices and moments that Leo needed to restore him. He stood in front of the boys.

"Listen up."

The team went quiet.

"That," Leo said excitedly, "was a line-drive fest. Well done. What did we learn?"

"Capitalize on a pitcher's tendencies," Math said.

Leo told him to say more.

"A fastball at 55 miles per hour was the constant. A hitter's plan should be a mathematical equation. We hit against 2xF."

Leo was intrigued. "How did you get that?"

"Kojak equals 2xF because he's twice as likely to throw a fastball than any other pitch. So looking for that pitch gives me the best odds of success. Every pitcher is different. You have to study your opponent. Just like schoolwork."

All the boys groaned upon hearing that word.

Leo was impressed. "Interesting way to think about it. What's your equation for a pitcher who has a great fastball and a decent curve, but is wild?"

Math didn't hesitate: "W-2xF-C."

"Explain," Leo said.

"W starts the equation because wild is the most important factor—it leads to walks, wild pitches and hit by pitches. Those are free bases so I'll sit back, won't be too aggressive early. Great fastball means he's twice as likely to throw that pitch. That's what I'll be looking for when he needs to throw a strike. You said he has a decent curve. So at the back of the equation—always in the back of my mind—is to watch for a C. W-2xF-C."

"I like it, Math," Leo said. "That's a great way to classify pitchers. Let's add that to our plan at the plate." Leo clapped his hands, changing gears. "Boys, we have one last surprise. Coach Tink, will you do the honors?"

Tom went behind the dugout and from under a tarp he pulled out a cardboard box big enough to hold a mini-fridge. A buzz swept through the boys. What's in there? What could it be? Before long, one word arose.

"Uniforms!"

Truman's skin tingled. He had waited years to put on a traveling team cap. He had dreamed, literally, of having that badge to wear to school and around town. He was overcome with happiness, but there was sadness, too. He wanted to share this moment with Bale, his best friend who practiced with him and pushed him and believed in him, but he was recovering from surgery. His surgeon had successfully removed the tumor, inserted a graft into healthy bone and screwed a metal rod to align and support the tibia. Bale would be in the hospital for four weeks.

The box of uniforms opened and the boys crowded in.

"Look at those jerseys!" Pot Roast said. "Wicked."

The word Dannaka was lettered in gold script across the front of the charcoal gray button-down jerseys. The design was old-school—including the D on the cap—replicas of the uniforms Doc and his teammates wore during their legendary championship streak in high school.

Tom and Leo began to organize the uniforms on the grass. "Just wait guys," Leo said. They crept closer yet, calling dibs on their favorite numbers. "Let's get these arranged by size."

"That cap is retro sweet," someone said, which got Truman thinking. "We should pull one out for Bale," he said. The team agreed as Leo took one cap out of the pile and tossed it back in the box. He also quickly scooped up two jerseys, numbers 7 and 10, and dropped them in the box, too.

As the boys jostled for position the coaches arranged the uniforms by size, including a jersey, two pairs of white pants with gold piping and gold stirrups. Tom Tink was puzzled. He said to Leo, "I think we're missing a couple numbers."

Leo quickly shook his head and replied quietly, "I pulled two jerseys along with Bale's cap." When Tom asked why, Leo didn't answer.

That evening when Truman got home from practice he put on his uniform to show his mother. She was proud, but more so, grateful. Today was a milestone for her son. He had learned that when the odds are stacked against you, you knock them over. This moment in their living room made her boy stand a little taller, even if his jersey, bearing the number 1—the smallest of the bunch—was still too large.

She was going to say he looked cute but amended herself. "You look like a real ballplayer." She loved the uniform's throwback design and imagined that Doc and the gang would appreciate it even more.

Ike followed as Truman bounded up the stairs to do his homework. His uniform remained on. Jess hit play. Her standby CD, John Denver's Greatest Hits, whirred to life. Calming guitar chords and lyrics about country roads taking her home felt truer than ever. She could hear Truman and Ike quietly walking down the hallway to her bedroom and wondered why.

With his mom's closet door swung open, Truman looked at himself in the full-length mirror. Truman hated mirrors but for tonight, at least, that had changed.

Leo finished dinner, trying to convince himself it was better than it was. A turkey sandwich on wheat toast. Big salad. Two carrots, peeled, washed and quartered. Glass of skim milk. He closed his eyes and imagined sliding two frozen pepperoni and sausage pizzas into the oven.

"Nah," he said aloud.

Out at his truck, Leo lowered the gate and sat down. Night had fallen and stars swept across a matte black sky. A lilac-scented breeze found its way to him. "So unbelievably quiet." Straining for a sound, he heard broken traces of the 10:00 news scattering from a house up the block. It was a night for sleeping with the windows open.

One hand rested on his thigh, one pressed on his chest. Leo relaxed his shoulders and tuned into his breathing. His back was straight, a posture that allowed his diaphragm to easily contract and expand. Leo had been required to see a therapist last year—eight sessions over two months. It did him no good because he'd decided before stepping into the therapist's office it would do him no good. But he did learn conscious breathing. He liked how that slowed down his mind, his body and the world. He was a believer in that.

"I like it here," he said. "Really do." Up to this moment Leo had been afraid to commit, to say that out loud. He thought about his team and the gallery of baseball smiles that appeared when the new uniforms came out of the box. In the dark, Leo smiled to himself.

He reached for the cardboard box. In the moonlight Leo pulled out the two jerseys and the cap. He planned to drive to Iowa City to see Bale in the next few days, so he left the cap in the truck's back seat.

Walking into his house, Leo had the jerseys hung over his arm. In his bedroom he carefully folded them, number 7, then number 10. He pressed them to his chest, taking a deep breath. Leo opened the closet door and carefully laid the jerseys on the top shelf.

DOUBLE DATE

They agreed to meet for lunch at Eilleen's bakery which, due to popular demand, had added a third small wrought iron table to its sidewalk seating. Ever since sandwiches came on the menu, the place found new life after 10 in the morning. Townsfolk strolled past, stopping to say hello, reflected in the plate glass window with *Eilleen's* in gold script across the front.

Nancy arrived early. Sunny lunch hours had a way of filling those tables in the blink of an eye.

Jess waved as she crossed the street. Her hair swung in the sunshine, her body lithe and relaxed.

"Are you getting younger or am I just getting older?" Nancy said as her friend approached the table. She got up for a hug.

"You are a ... robust hugger." Jess's voice was muffled in Nancy's shoulder, as the embrace lingered. Nancy seemed to need it more than Jess did.

"That's better," Nancy said. She stepped back from Jess. "Let me look at you. What is it? You got your hair cut." Jess nodded self-consciously. Her once shoulder-length hair now curled under at mid-neck. "And highlights."

"The works. I was feeling drab," Jess confessed. "Decided to celebrate spring."

"You're blooming," Nancy said. "Shorter is cute on you. I could never pull it off. My face is already big as a potato sack."

Jess cringed. "Don't say that. It's not true and it's not nice."

Nancy shrugged. "I come from healthy stock." She changed the subject. "So how's life, starting with your little future Hall of Famer and his four-legged sidekick?"

Jess's cautious smile made an appearance. "Inseparable, except for school hours. Ike is the team mascot so he runs alongside Truman every day as they bike to baseball practice."

"Practice every day?"

"Yep. And twice on Saturdays. Early and then under the lights."

"Isn't that a bit insane for 12-year-olds?"

Jess shrugged. "He loves it. And when he's not at formal practice, he's working on his pitching or getting me to hit him pop-ups or racing Ike from home to first base. I swear he's getting faster. The coach constantly has them running and doing push-ups. The kids are getting real conditioning."

"Are you talking about the cutest coach in Page County, new Leo?"

"Yeah. I mean, that's who I'm talking about." Then Jess conceded. "And he is kinda cute."

A counter girl came out with water and took their lunch order. Both of them chose the BLT on a flaky, morning-fresh croissant. They'd split a salad.

Nancy picked up the conversation. "So, speaking of our new coach, I've been wondering…." Nancy let the thought drop.

"Yes?" Jess said.

Nancy studied her reflection in the window.

"Wondering what?" Jess nudged again.

"Ah, just some stupid idea," Nancy said.

Jess stared at her friend until her persistence pried loose the words.

"I was wondering if you and Wade and me and Leo could, like, you know, go on a double date?"

Jess's surprise was obvious. "Uh, yeah. Why not? It'd be fun."

"Do you mean it? You don't sound so sure."

"No. I mean yes, I'm sure. Just, you caught me … wasn't expecting it."

Nancy hedged. "It would be just as friends. Kinda a *Welcome to Dannaka* dinner. We could go to the Ranch House. Treat ourselves to a T-bone and the cowboy potatoes."

The more Jess thought about it the better it sounded. "Cool. When?"

"I don't know. Maybe tomorrow night?"

"Don't you work Fridays?"

Nancy said she hadn't taken a Friday night off in two years. It was long past time she did. "When is practice today? Maybe I'll trap him in the parking lot with my car. It'll be 'yes' or I'll run the poor sucker over."

They both laughed.

Jess said, "Practice is after school. Usually till 5:30-ish."

"Shit," Nancy said. "I have to be at work by then." She looked genuinely disappointed.

Jess's eyebrows lifted. "This a little weird, but I could bring up the idea after practice today. If Leo likes it, he could swing by the Rundown and ask you."

Nancy mulled it over. "I feel a little chicken for not doing my own bidding. But, upside, if Leo isn't interested, he can get out of it without thinking feelings got hurt. You sure you don't mind?"

"Nah. Like you said, just a friendly get-together."

Nancy perked up. "Right," she said. She looked at her reflection again. "Feels kind of tingly," she said with a smile. "Almost like when we were in high school."

Jess didn't say it then, or when they said their goodbyes after finishing lunch, but it did feel tingly. A distant emotion was stirred, one that perhaps did go back to her teens.

Silly, she told herself as she walked to the baseball diamonds to catch the end of practice. Silly or not, there it was: a full-body fizz of anticipation. *Where did this come from? Or*, she asked herself, *where had this feeling gone? Is it me? Is it Wade? Is it the two of us? We're good, right? What we have is enough. I've had my crazy days. Living for the moment was a disaster. Except for the Truman part. He's my center of gravity. His security and happiness come first. I will have better later—*

Jess almost tripped on a sidewalk crack, which she was usually careful to avoid. *Slow down and pay attention.*

Leo was jogging in the green space surrounding the three fields. Athletic shorts, ball cap backward, T-shirt stuck to his perspiring back, he waved, recognizing Jess.

Her heartbeat sped up as he veered in her direction.

"Hey there," Leo said. He put his hands on his knees, half bent over, catching his breath.

"Hi," she said. She was at a loss for what to say next.

He filled in the empty space. "I was just thinking about you."

She hadn't expected that.

He took a few steps closer. His dark eyebrows, hair and tanned face truly offset his blue eyes. "That son of yours," Leo laughed, "what a great kid. He surprises me constantly." Leo's bright smile was easy and beguiling. "You're doing a great job with him. I was thinking, it can't be easy but it has to be special."

No one had ever put it that succinctly. Those words captured their lives exactly.

Jess nodded and said thank you. Words dammed up behind a barrier she had been building.

Leo stretched his quads as he continued. "So today, at lunch, I came over to rake the infield and who do I find here?"

"Truman," Jess said.

"Yeah. It's his school lunch break and here he is. He didn't see me so I stayed back a few minutes to watch. Do you know what he was doing?"

Jess shook her head.

"He was playing long-toss. By himself. He had a bucket of balls at home plate. One after another, he fired those balls as far as he could toward another bucket out in center field. When the one bucket was empty, he sprinted out to center, put all the balls in that bucket and threw them back home."

Jess watched Leo as he talked about her son. "He's working on his arm. He said you said he needs more speed on his fastball."

Leo thought for a second. "I did say something about that, now that you mention it."

Jess's forehead creased. "You're not just giving him false hope, are you? He really believes he's going to get a chance to pitch this year."

Leo's smile disappeared. "I would never do that," he said. "I respect any kid who works hard for goals and I treat him as I'd want to be treated. That said, there are no guarantees on this team. Every player has to earn his place. And re-earn it. And re-re-earn it." Leo touched his toes a few times. Sweat rolled off his face onto his shoelaces. "We've got a scrimmage next Saturday and I'm still moving kids around. I won't really know who my group of pitchers is until mid-season, after they've dealt with some bigger ups and downs."

"I don't mean to snoop. I know you don't like parents getting too involved. It can get super political."

Leo took a moment before he spoke. "I don't have children so I'm not here to judge parents. I just want them to stand back and let their kids' talents shine. I don't know what it's like to watch my child succeed or fail on the ballfield. But I do remember my parents stayed out of it. We would talk about a few baseball things, mostly the fun moments because I wanted them to enjoy 'em, too. But it's a two-way street: I don't tell you how to parent, you don't tell me how to coach."

Jess said that sounded fair.

"From my vantage point, though," Leo's voice was wrapping up, "you must be doing something pretty okay because Truman's a heck of a kid. My hope is to do an equally good job coaching him."

Jess smiled her reluctant half smile. Leo had not forgotten its appeal. She squinted through the sunlight. "From what I hear," she said, "the kids think they have the best coach in Iowa."

Leo looked away. He inhaled the green fields. "Iowa. I'm not sure, really, how I ended up here. I've never put much credence in the concept of luck, but maybe."

The two of them looked at each other. "Crazy our birthdays are on the same day," Jess said, unguarded. Then quickly, "Not sure why I just said that."

"I think it's cool." Leo upped the volume in his voice. "Well, better get back at it. I promised myself 10 laps. I have six to go."

Jess could see Leo didn't just talk about honoring his obligations. "Okay," she said. "Oh, shoot. Almost forgot why I came out here in the first place. Um." Jess scrunched up her nose in a way that bugged her but was undeniably cute. "You know my friend Nancy…."

Leo had the look of someone who was answering the question in front of him while skipping ahead to see where it was leading. "Sure. Nancy's great."

"Well, I had this idea that maybe you and Nancy and Wade and I might go out to dinner on Friday night."

Leo took off his cap and scratched his ear. "Are you trying to set me up with Nancy?"

"No. It's not like that. It's just, you're new to town—you know, the whole new Leo thing—and I thought it might be nice for you to get away from the 12-year-old hooligans and have a night out with adults. Just as friends. For sure."

Leo put his cap back on. He nodded. "Dinner, you said?"

"Yeah. There's a steak joint called the Ranch House just 10 minutes west of here. Great meat. Old-school supper club, if you like that kind of thing."

Leo smiled. "I love that kind of thing." He thought for a moment. "First, I need to talk to Nancy. Make sure we both understand what this is."

Jess nodded. "Good idea. But Friday night might work?"

Leo licked his finger and pantomimed paging through his calendar. "Friday night. Friday night. Friday night. Look at that. It's open. A little too open. We have practice after school. Wrap up around 5:30."

"I hope you'll come," Jess said. "It'll be fun."

Leo's face gave no indication of which way he was leaning.

"But no pressure," Jess added. She didn't mention that meanwhile she'd get a reservation for four. Fridays at the Ranch House filled up fast.

"Okay," Leo said.

"Good seeing you." Jess was suddenly anxious to get her feet moving.

"Yeah. You, too." Leo watched her turn and go. "Oh, and thanks. Thanks for making the effort." He grinned. "On behalf of the Dannaka welcoming committee."

She waved and headed back the way she'd come.

The parking lot of the Rundown Saloon was surprisingly full for 6:30 on a Thursday. Rusty pickups were the vehicle of choice but a line of a dozen Harleys on kickstands made a muscular fence by the entrance.

"Wouldn't want to tip those dominoes over," Leo said to himself as he entered the bar. It was dark in the club, and smoky. His eyes had difficulty getting a full picture of what was in front of him. He nearly walked into a woman who, if it weren't for leather, would have been naked.

"Watch it there, cutie," she said. Leo made a quick stop to let her pass. The six bottles of beer she held by their necks made a glassy rattle as she strode toward the pool tables.

Nancy was busy lugging two buckets of ice to the steel beer bins behind the bar. She wore cutoff shorts and a black tank top beneath an unbuttoned flannel shirt with the sleeves rolled up. Leo watched as she handled the buckets like she handled most things in life: with easy impatience.

He paused, thinking about this single woman, close in age to himself, at a roadhouse just outside of her tiny hometown. He wondered what kept her here. Was she happy? What dreams did she worry would never come true? What from her past was she ashamed of or afraid of? As Leo's eyes adjusted to the low light and cigarette smoke, it was like wiping dust off a light bulb. Now he saw everything brighter and clearer. This was a woman who'd been given very little and had no illusions of that changing anytime soon. Her looks were plain, as were her expectations. She was honest and accepted nothing less in return.

"Do you know that creep?" a woman at the bar said to Nancy. Nancy finished loading in the ice, looked up and saw Leo, halfway to the bar, staring at her.

Nancy snapped her fingers a few times. "Hello. New Leo. Anyone there."

Leo offered an embarrassed wave. He approached the bar.

"He's pretty cute for a statue," the bar patron said.

"Your shoes get stuck to the floor back there?" Nancy smiled, straightening her shirt.

"Sorry. Bright outside. Took me a minute."

"A long minute," the bar patron said.

"Why don't you get some popcorn," Nancy told her. The regular picked up her greasy paper boat and headed for the popcorn machine in back.

Leo chewed on the inside of his mouth. He finally spoke. "It's good to see you."

Nancy wiped down the bar in front of them. "It's good to see you, too."

Nancy watched Leo shift his weight from one foot to the other. She knew why he was here. But he didn't know that.

"Can I get a lemonade?" Leo asked. "I mean, do you have something like that?"

Nancy nodded. "Yeah. It's a mix that usually gets overrun with vodka or tequila, but it's passable." She reached for the mix. "Ice?"

"Please."

She spun out a coaster and put his lemonade on top. "Go easy on that."

"Thanks."

"So how's the team?" Nancy said with forced pep.

Leo drank half his glass of lemonade. It knocked the dust back and lubricated his vocal chords. "Is it okay if we don't talk about baseball?"

"Yeah. Sure."

Leo took a breath and scratched an eyebrow with his thumb. "See, I've come here to ask you to dinner. It's something Jess brought up. I guess there's a place called the Ranch House. She and Wade are going tomorrow night and thought it would be fun if we joined them."

Nancy said, "That does sound like fun."

Leo looked at his lemonade, then at Nancy. "I should be really clear about, you know, where I'm at. Um. I'm asking you out as a friend. I don't have a lot of friends in my life right now—being new Leo and all. I'm not looking for anything more. This is not a reflection on you; it's me. I'm just not too great for anyone right now."

Nancy's face softened and her eyes found a sparkle in the dreary bar. "You're stealing all my lines, Leo. Usually it's me setting the let's-just-be-friends ground rules."

Leo shrugged.

She leaned across the bar, closer to him. "I sincerely appreciate your honesty. In fact, I feel a little dumb because truthfully, the group dinner was my idea. I asked Jess if she'd bring it up to you. Partly because she runs into you more. Partly, I guess, I was hedging a little. I thought if you didn't like the idea you could back out gracefully without me standing there asking."

Leo chuckled. "So I'm asking you out when it should be you asking *me* out?"

"That about sums it up."

"Looks like you're paying for dinner then."

Nancy's mouth opened in surprise.

"Joking," he said.

She threw her bar towel at him. "We'll split it. Just like a couple of senior citizens." When she got playful, her hard, independent face transformed into something more attractive.

"I'll take that deal." Leo put out his hand.

"Deal," she said, completing the handshake. And a firm handshake it was.

RAIN

Jogging across the puddled parking lot, Leo held something under his shirt. It was the only thing that wasn't struck by relentless raindrops. Today's baseball practice would have to move to the gym. Hopefully things would dry out for tomorrow's scrimmage. Leo ducked into Doc's clinic.

Jess was at the reception counter when Leo pulled a brand-new baseball cap out from under his damp T-shirt. She gave him a curious look.

"You must really like that cap," she said.

Leo smiled, pulling back his wet hair. "It's a surprise. For Doc."

Ike, upon hearing Leo's voice, was instantly out of his dog bed, into the waiting area, writhing through Leo's legs.

"Hey ya, boy." Leo looked at Jess. "He's getting big, huh?"

"Eating me out of house and home. He and Truman, my wolf pack."

"Oh, before I forget. I talked to Nancy last night. We're good to go." Ike got a hold of one of Leo's shoelaces and quickly had it undone.

"I heard. She called—Ike, stop!" Jess gave the pup a cross look. He was torn between the fun of the shoelace and the wrath of his owner. "That pup is a bundle of pent-up energy—staying mostly inside today—but we need the rain." Jess finished her earlier thought. "Nancy said she told you it was her idea about dinner."

Leo grinned. "We straightened it out. Kinda like my shoelace." Leo didn't elaborate.

"I thought I saw Doc's truck in the lot," Leo said. "Is he here?"

"Yep. We just had a tooth extraction. I think he's on the phone with the dog's owner."

Leo crouched to tie his lace and that turned on the licking machine. "Ike. Yes. I'm happy to see you, too. Okay." Leo went to plan B. He set the ball cap on a chair and sat opposite it. "About tonight. Do I need to do anything like get a reservation?"

"Nope. It's all set up. Everyone is meeting at my place at 7:00. Dinner is at 7:45. Does that work?" Before Leo could say anything, the office phone rang. Jess held up her index finger.

Just then Doc appeared through the door of his examination room. He lit up when he saw Leo. "Well hey there. Look what the cat dragged in." Leo quickly stood to block Doc's view of the baseball cap on the chair. Doc continued. "Farmers are happy today but I don't imagine baseball coaches would say the same."

"We've been lucky with weather. We'll head into the gym with our pitching machine and let kids whup tennis balls."

"How is that new machine?" Doc asked. "Don't you have a name for it?"

"Kojak. It's great."

Doc laughed, shaking his head. "I sure loved that show." He rubbed his face. "So, what brings you here?"

"Got you a present."

"Since when?" Doc scoffed. "You still owe me a six-pack from horseshoes last Wednesday."

"You sandbagged me. I didn't know I was going up against the county fair champ."

Jess watched the two men. She hadn't realized how close they'd become.

Leo reached behind his back. "This is for you." He held out the Dannaka All-Stars cap, size XL. Doc was struck by the sight.

"Holy moly," he said with reverence. "That's the same D from our caps back in the day." He reached for it. "Leo. This is amazing."

"I hope the boys and I live up to it."

Doc's finger traced the raised D stitched into the cap's crown. "I can't stop looking at it. The colors are perfect. How did you get it to match so well?"

"I had Margaret slip me your cap one night after fried chicken. Jerome got me an old jersey. Wait till you see how the new jerseys turned out. They are a sight to see."

Doc's practiced hands curved the cap's bill, taking some of the newness out. "Can't wait to break this baby in."

Leo assumed Doc would like the throwback caps but he hadn't guessed how touched he'd be by the gesture. It was well worth the hassle he went through to do the uniforms this way.

"Thank you, Leo." Doc came over and gave Leo a hug. "Thank you for coming to our little town and pouring your heart into these kids. Win, lose or draw, you're giving them baseball memories. You know how enduring that will be. For the rest of their grown lives, whenever they drive by an empty baseball diamond, they'll fill it with memories." Doc pulled on his cap. "In their minds, they'll dig into that batter's box, rip a screamer down the line, stab a wicked backhander off the dirt, dive across the outfield grass to rob a hit. Even when they're old farts like me, they'll pull on a dusty cap and their fingers will itch to pick up a bat, to launch a baseball through the sky, pulling a chorus of cheers behind it. Only baseball sticks with you like that."

Leo forced a smile. He didn't have the heart to tell Doc he had stuffed his baseball memories in a trash can and left them on a curb back in Illinois.

With hands and toes on the gym floor, they shouted as a team: D-A-N-N-A-K-A 1-2-U A-L-L S-T-A-R-S G-O. Every letter and number represented one push-up. When they were finished, the team had ripped off 20.

"On the line," Leo hollered. The boys and coaches hustled across the basketball court to the baseline. "How many today, Rabbit?" Leo asked Juan Hernandez.

"Eleven!" he shouted.

"Thank you, Rabbit," the team shouted back, army style.

They did 11 full-court sprints to the opposite baseline, jogging backward when returning. Baseball is a game played forward, sideways and backward with agility and speed. All the races, drills and games were giving the kids what Leo called "good feet."

Sweat dripping, adrenaline surging, the true test was about to begin. "Thirty-second juggle," Leo announced. "Math, how many drops will we allow?"

"Three," Math said, out of breath.

"How many?" Leo repeated.

"Two!" he shouted.

"Two it is. Or we're back on the line."

Every boy knew if more than two balls hit the gym floor during 30 seconds of juggling, they were back doing full-court sprints.

"Calm your breathing," Leo said. "Visualize. Slow everything down. Be easy. Be purposeful. Know your plan." Leo zeroed-out his stopwatch. "Go!" he barked, intentionally adding a burst of immediacy, watching to see if it would impair their performance.

The boys all got off to a smooth start. Most of them were smiling, as Leo had taught. "Tight face, tight body," was one of his lessons. "Smile your nerves away."

At the 15-second mark, a ball thudded onto the parquet floor. Everybody heard it. Everyone knew they were one drop away. "Ten seconds left," Leo said. "Don't blow it. Nobody wants to run again."

Two more balls struck the floor. Leo clicked off the stopwatch. "Twenty-three seconds. Seven away from victory. Back to the line."

The kids didn't groan or complain. They merely set the balls down by the wall and lined up on the baseline. Leo asked, "Math, how many?"

"Eleven!"

They got their feet set on the baseline and crouched for takeoff.

"Truman, who dropped the balls?" Leo watched Truman for his answer. He knew the boy was a good enough juggler to look away and see whose baseballs hit the floor. "We all did," Truman said.

"That's right," Leo repeated. "Lose as a team. Win as a team. Work hard as a team. Have fun as a team. Go!" They were back to sprints.

After a break at the drinking fountain, Leo brought out two buckets of tennis balls. "Soft-hands drill," he announced.

Everyone got a tennis ball, stood back 20 feet from the gymnasium wall and let it fly. Each boy sprang into a fielding position—legs shoulder width apart, knees bent, hands out front—and watched the bouncing ball into his hands. No gloves were used. This was about tracking the ball all the way in, hands giving slightly when it struck the palms, then hop-stepping into a throwing position and zipping it off the wall again. Throw after throw after throw, made and received. If a player fumbled or dropped his ball, he stepped back and sat down. He was out.

After three minutes, half the team was sitting. "Okay!" Leo shouted. The last of the tennis balls echoed off the walls and bounced back to their players. "About half of you made it three minutes. That's not good enough. Pot Roast, what happened to you?"

The thickset boy puffed out his cheeks. "Bad throw so it didn't bounce back to me right."

"Havoc, you?" Havoc wasn't the most technically sound ballplayer on the team, but he was all athlete. When he was on the bases, his combination of speed, savvy and fearlessness made him a perpetual threat to score. In one game last year, Leo was told, Havoc drew a walk. He sprinted to first and didn't slow down rounding the base, speeding for second. The opposing team screamed out an alarm, the pitcher spun and promptly overthrew the second baseman. Havoc rounded second, put his head down and made for third. The throw from the center fielder beat Havoc to the base by 10 feet. Havoc slammed on the brakes and got happily entangled in a pickle, caught between second and third as the ball went back and forth as well. Finally, Havoc committed to taking third with a head-first dive. The throw sailed over the fielder's glove. Havoc sprung up and sprinted home. A walk turned home run. Nobody playing against him was comfortable when he was on base.

"I didn't watch the ball all the way in," Havoc said. "Bounced off my hand."

Leo didn't say anything. Picking up a tennis ball, he fired it at the gym wall. The ball quickly skipped back to him as he effortlessly bent, scooped, turned and zipped the ball back at the wall in one fluid motion. Over and over and over. "We can't give the other team more than three outs. We have to make the easy plays. We have to bond with the ball, watch it in, make good throws." He said these words in time with his movements.

"All right." Leo put the tennis ball in his back pocket. "Who here knows how to get hit by a pitch?"

The kids looked at each other, then laughed. Havoc was the first to raise his hand.

"Get a bat," Leo instructed as he placed a portable home plate under the basketball hoop. He grabbed a bucket of tennis balls and as he walked out to the free-throw line, the gym grew quiet enough to hear his tennis shoes squeak. "How far am I from you?" Leo asked as Havoc tapped home plate with his bat.

"Too close," Havoc quipped, drawing a chuckle from the boys who stood behind Leo, watching.

"I'm 15 feet from you. That's one-third the distance I should be. I can't throw these balls as hard as a baseball, but I can throw them pretty hard. Ready?"

"Yep," Havoc said.

"Nope," Leo replied. "Where's your helmet?"

"Oh yeah." Havoc jogged to the equipment bag and grabbed a helmet. "Ready," he said, this time more assuredly.

Leo brought his hands over his head in a big windup, raised his front knee to his balance point, strode hard toward home and let the tennis ball fly right at Havoc's head. Instinctively, the boy sprawled onto the wooden floor, the aluminum bat dropping out of his hands, a clang reverberating throughout the gym.

"I thought you said you knew how to get hit?"

Havoc got up on all fours and looked at Leo like he'd lost his mind. "You almost beaned me in the head!"

Leo grinned. "That's why you have a helmet. That tennis ball isn't going to hurt you. And if your helmet fits right, a baseball isn't going to hurt you much either. Just ring your bell a little. Okay switch places. I'm going to teach you how to get hit. Because a free pass in baseball is too good to jump away from."

Havoc went to the free throw line and Leo went to the equipment bag, got the XL helmet and worked it on. He picked up Havoc's bat and squeezed in on the plate. "Men, there are times to really crowd the plate. To test a pitcher's accuracy. Will he hit us? Will he throw outside to avoid hitting us and give us a walk? We don't care. We just need a base and we're going to take it any way we can."

Leo nodded at Havoc. "Let's see what you got. Can you hit me?" Leo waggled his bat, practically standing on home plate. "Nah. You can't."

The first pitch sailed way outside. "Ball one," Leo said. "C'mon. That's the best you got?" The second pitch bounced in front of the plate, drawing a smattering of boos. "Ball two. Walk me or hit me, I don't care."

The third tennis ball was located perfectly. Havoc rifled it inside, closing fast on Leo. The coach turned his head, eyes to the floor, earflap to the ball, dropped his shoulder, bent his front knee and took the pitch on the bicep with a loud thud. "Free pass," he said.

"Sorry." Havoc waved tentatively.

Leo rubbed his arm. "Come in here, you guys. I want you to learn how to get hit. It might sound strange, but has anyone showed you this before?"

They shook their heads no.

"First thing: Don't lift up your arms and jump away from an inside pitch. That opens up your ribs, neck and face to the baseball. Exactly what you don't want. Stay in there. Don't bail out. It might be a curve that's going to cut over the plate. If you recognize it's not, you're about to get a free pass. The key is to look down at your back foot. That way the big part of the helmet is turned to the ball." Leo rapped the side of his helmet to demonstrate. "A ball isn't going to hurt if you get hit here. Also, your shoulder and arm should tuck into your body, like so, to protect your ribs. And get your hands and bat out of the way. Lastly, bend your front knee so your legs have some give."

Leo had the boys circle up and go through the motions slowly, only visualizing a ball that came at them in their imaginations. "Identify the pitch. Look down at your back foot. Shoulder and arm to the ribs. Hands and bat out of the way. Bend leg." Again and again and again they went through the steps.

"Okay. Line it up behind the baseline. First four guys, get a helmet." The boys were a little hesitant. Truman grabbed a helmet and was first in line.

"Number one paratrooper out of the plane," Leo said as Truman took a few practice cuts at home plate. "I'm only going to throw half speed today. Just so everyone gets comfortable standing in there and taking one for the team. Truman, you ready?"

Truman pushed his helmet down and nodded.

"You did what?" Jess asked, nearly spitting her drink across the table. Wade was wide-eyed. Nancy was frankly astonished. At the table next to them in the Ranch House, an older couple looked up from their shared onion ring appetizer.

"I drilled Truman in the helmet with a tennis ball," Leo repeated. "Only half speed. And once in the shoulder. If you're going to play baseball, you have to learn how to get hit properly. It's a part of the game that fewer and fewer coaches teach anymore."

"Probably because of the liability," Wade commented.

Leo shook his head. "Players get hurt every year. I've seen it all the way up to the pro level, because they don't know how to defend themselves from a wild pitch. Or maybe even an intentional one."

"What do you mean?" Nancy asked.

Leo was on his second beer of the night. It had been weeks since he'd drunk alcohol and it was making him more talkative than usual. "Human instincts shout 'Jump back!' as the baseball bears in on you. Often as not, that just opens vulnerable parts of your body to getting hit. I teach them to protect themselves best they can."

"How?" Wade wanted to know. Jess grew more uncomfortable with the topic by the second.

Leo stood up and demonstrated.

Jess was appalled. "You want them to just stand there and get hit in the helmet?"

"No. But better that than to get hit in the face if the ball is head-high."

"How about ducking?" Nancy said.

"There's not always time. Or it could be a curve and you end up ducking right into it."

"Can we just change the subject?" Jess said. To her, the idea of Truman being hit anywhere by a baseball was disturbing.

The waitress came by and asked how they were on drinks. Jess, usually a light drinker, was ready for another. Leo lifted his empty beer to say he was ready, too. "Probably not the best dinner topic," he said.

"To be fair, I asked how practice went," Wade said. "Truman was so fired up tonight. Maybe he liked being—"

"Wade," Jess said curtly. "Changing. Subjects."

"Roger that." Then a gleam appeared in Wade's eye. "I could tell you about an interesting new variable term life insurance product—"

"NOOO!" Jess and Nancy cried in unison. Everyone laughed, sat back in their chairs and let the ambience and the happy clatter of background noise take them away.

Dinner was brought to the table by a young waitress who wore a narrow golden promise ring on her wedding finger and far too much mascara. The food came in courses: Bread and relish tray. Appetizer. Salads. And just when they were feeling full, medium-rare steaks and cowboy potatoes. Their conversation was lively. Sometimes all four were involved. There were side chats between just the women and just the men. Leo talked with Nancy; Wade with Jess. But it wasn't until the dinner plates were whisked away and the four-piece band kicked into Glenn Miller's "Little Brown Jug" that Jess and Leo had their own conversation. Neither of them were much for dancing, so Wade and Nancy sashayed to the floor, waving back at them.

"I think I'm a little buzzed," Jess said, her smile less cautious than usual.

"I know I am," Leo said. "I haven't had alcohol in a while. Cheap date."

Jess had noticed other women throughout the night sneaking looks at Leo. He was striking. Tall, dark thick hair, the scar under his eye adding ruggedness. His simple blue-and-white checked button-down shirt was tucked into his jeans. She spoke frankly. "Does it feel odd to be here?"

Leo crossed his legs. "You mean in Dannaka or with our group or with you right now?" His eyes had a casual intensity. She couldn't hold his look for long.

"Take them one at a time." Jess watched the dance floor. Wade and Nancy were laughing in their struggle to swing together to the music.

"Dannaka feels good. Friendly. Almost surreal. I'm loving my team. It's very manageable. That's the phase I need right now."

Jess nodded, relating to the idea of manageable.

"As for our double date—as friends—I'm real comfortable with Nancy. She's low-key and funny. She puts it out there."

"I love that girl," Jess said. "She's been a true, true friend the last few years." Jess's brow creased slightly and the chandelier light sparkled in her eyes. "When a person comes back to a small town, it gets even smaller."

"Hmm," Leo said. "That's a cool thought." They looked at each other. For a moment it was just them. "As for sitting here with you, I have to say I feel lousy about mentioning the tennis ball beaning thing. Like I let you down or something."

Jess shook her head. "No. It's not you. I'm overprotective. He's all I've got."

"What about Wade?" Leo said.

"Yeah, and Wade. But that's different."

Leo left it at that.

Jess was a discreet user of lipstick but tonight she wore a shade of red that brought out the shapeliness of her lips. "Doc was really touched by that cap you brought him," she said. "He was wearing it around the clinic today like he was on the team. Awfully nice of you."

They listened to the music and watched a couple in their late seventies swing and twirl, effortlessly gliding hand in hand across the floor like they were born to dance together.

Leo asked, "Can you imagine yourself out there, when you're old, dancing like that?"

Jess looked at Leo and said yes.

SCRIMMAGE

Leo had gotten a call from Russ Dixon. It had been weeks since he and his boy Billy joined the Des Moines association to play ball there. Water under the bridge, Dixon had said. Let's get our teams together for a scrimmage. I'll have the Des Moines kids drive over. It'll be a good tilt.

At the time, red flags were popping for Leo. Des Moines had such a large number of elite 12-year-old players that they could field two traveling teams—with enough left over for great in-house competition. Why wouldn't Dixon just scrimmage in Des Moines instead of having his team drive two hours? Was he hoping to show Dannaka it was a big mistake to push him off the coaching staff?

Leo had told Dixon he'd call him back, but Dixon pressed. Good scrimmages weren't easy to find in Dannaka.

What the hell, Leo had thought. It would be good to see how they stacked up against Des Moines. He'd been hearing about them since he got to Dannaka. Okay, he'd told Dixon. Let's do it.

Now, as Leo opened the equipment shed early Saturday morning to chalk the field, he questioned the wisdom of his decision. Not that he didn't have confidence in his team. Not that he cared about winning or losing, which was his last concern when scrimmaging. He just had a bad feeling about anything to do with Dixon.

On a brighter note, he would get his first look at Ryan Rippen, the Dannaka boy who'd left the traveling team last season to play for Des Moines. Leo's players said he was even better than Bale, which Leo found hard to believe.

Putting down morning chalk lines will fix a guy. It's just you, the birdsong and the game's lineup flip-flopping in your head. A field is blissfully silent as the wheels of the chalker slowly turn, powder sifting from the hopper, setting a stark, straight, two-inch white line.

Bub had been to the fields yesterday afternoon when the rain pushed north. He'd fired up the riding mower, cut the grass and dragged the infields. Now, for Leo, as the morning warmed, fresh-cut aromas were resurrected. He sat on an overturned bucket, duct taping wiffle balls.

To say Leo was a mere believer in the wiffle ball and its ability to build excellent hitters was a sizable understatement. Leo revered the wiffle ball. If he was pressed for time before a game and had to choose between a batting cage and zipping wiffle balls from 20 feet to his batters, he'd take wiffle balls, easy. More control meant each batter got more reps. And throwing with velocity from close proximity helped a hitter develop fast hands.

In the minors, Leo had a hitting coach named Machine Gun Strom who would pepper batters with wiffle balls every day. He'd start with five pitches right down the middle. Then locate five pitches outside so batters could work on staying back and shooting the ball to the opposite field. Then five inside, where batters had to be early with the bat head yet keep the ball fair. Then golf shots, low, just off the shoe tops. Finishing with five high pitches where a batter needed to get his hands high and stay high through the ball.

Of course, those plastic wiffle balls took a pounding and would quickly split in half if not properly prepped. This involved a roll of duct tape, some patience and a little time to yourself.

Leo pulled a 12-inch strip of tape off the roll and tore it in half lengthwise, creating two long narrow strips. One strip went firmly around the center seam to keep the ball from cracking in half. The other strip went around the other way, top to bottom. This made the ball much more durable and faster when thrown. Just like his hitting coach before him, Leo zinged these doctored wiffle balls from close range, targeting all areas of the strike zone. He was excited. After taping balls for the past week, today Leo would finally break them out.

Dixon and Billy were finishing breakfast. The scrimmage was set for 10:00, with warmups starting at the Dannaka fields at 9:00. Most of the Des Moines traveling team lived two hours away by car, which meant they had to be up and on the road early.

"We still have a little time," Dixon said to Billy. "What do you say we swing by the golf course?"

Billy raised his eyebrows. "Really?"

"Yeah, if we hustle." Dixon checked the clock on the kitchen wall. "They teed off a half hour ago."

The Dixons lived close to the municipal golf course in Dannaka. On Saturday mornings the women's league had tee times locked up from 8:00 until 10:00. Dixon had made it clear to course management that this was an abomination of a prime golfing window. Women, he said, played too slow and hit the ball about as far as he could throw it.

To further declare his protest, last year, if he and Billy had an early Saturday morning baseball game, they would make a quick detour to the course. Sneaking ahead of the league's first foursome, they'd toss the women's tee markers into the rough. Or pull a flag and plant it in the ground just off the green, tittering all the way back to the truck.

Today they left the vehicle running by the par-three seventh hole, crept through the roadside tree line and got busy in the sand trap just in front of the green.

"Women always end up in here," Dixon scoffed.

"They can't make it to the green," his son replied.

They each had a trap rake turned backward, using the top of the handle to draw in the sand. They quickly finished and stood aside to admire their work, doubled over in laughter. "That'll wake 'em up," Dixon said, high-fiving his son. They had drawn a five-foot penis and scrotum in the sand trap.

The Des Moines team arrived sporadically, a truckload here, a vanload there. Generally, the team looked big. Leo watched their faces as he said hello to a few of them in the parking lot. None of them were smiling.

Dannaka's players came mostly by bike, with the Hernandez twins getting to the fields first despite having the farthest to pedal. As a reward, they would hit first and second in the batting cage. But Leo liked to finish in the cages rather than start there.

Leo heard a bark. Truman's bike crested the nearby hill with Ike running beside him. The pup had little trouble keeping up, quite a change from his first weeks here. Truman's freckled face was brightened by sunshine, his big ears sticking out from his traveling team cap, which, for aerodynamics, he wore backward. His bat stuck out of his backpack, which also held his glove, cleats, batting gloves and water bottle. The unofficial start to the season wasn't long off.

Leo reached into the back pocket of his baseball pants and pulled out a bag of sunflower seeds. He watched as his team organized themselves, tying their cleats, stretching, joking, laughing. Tom Tink smuggled a jumbo bag of bubble gum past the players for post-game festivities.

A boy in a white T-shirt and baseball pants rode over to the Dannaka dugout and leaned his bike against the fence. Leo didn't recognize him. They all fist bumped along with some friendly shoving and laughing. As Leo walked over, it occurred to him this must be the legendary Rippen boy.

"Listen up," Leo said, "let's get ready to run." The team began stretching in earnest. "Hey there," he said to the boy. "I'm Coach Hamill."

"Hi Coach. Ryan Rippen." The two shook hands. "I go to school with these guys. I hear you're gonna be our teacher next year."

The boy had an easy confidence, looking Leo in the eye when he spoke. He was immediately likable. "That's right," Leo said. "So you play with Des Moines?"

"Yep," Ryan said.

"Well, good luck."

"You're gonna need it," Havoc added.

Ryan just grinned as he walked his bike to the visitors' dugout.

After running, Dannaka had a best-of-three relay race in the outfield. Every member of the losing team had to do cartwheels with Ike giving chase. Dixon and the other Des Moines coach, hearing laughter and barking, looked on from the batting cage.

"Pretty loose group," the coach commented.

Dixon sneered. "Coach Disneyland."

Next they paired up and played catch, starting with short tosses just using their wrists and eventually spreading out to make long, arcing throws.

With their arms warmed up, the Dannaka team raced in. "Get your bats and form two circles in left," Leo instructed. "Tom, grab those buckets of wiffle balls. I'll be out there in a sec." Leo jogged over to the visitor's batting cage to introduce himself to the second Des Moines coach. Dixon was throwing BP while the other coach worked soft toss. "Welcome," Leo said, pulling up from a jog. Leo always hustled on the baseball field.

"Thanks," the coach said, introducing himself. "I appreciate you having us over. Your facility is amazing." They shook hands.

"Pretty unbelievable," Leo agreed. "Can you imagine being twelve and having this?" Leo waved at Dixon who was hollering at the kids to swing like they meant it.

"Here's for the ump," Leo said, handing the coach $10. "Dixon said he's 20 bucks. Figured we'd split it."

The coach said that wasn't necessary but Leo was firm.

"How should we work home and away—flip a coin?"

"Nah," the coach said. "It's your field. You guys go ahead and be home."

Leo nodded. "Well good luck, Coach. Perfect day for baseball."

In left field the boys were in two circles, leaning on their bats. Leo was in the center of one with a bucket of wiffle balls, Tom Tink was similarly set up in the other circle.

"What's that, Coach?" Truman asked.

Leo held up a taped wiffle ball. "Our secret weapon," Leo said. "Okay guys, Tom, listen up. We're going to pitch clockwise around the circle. The first pitch is going to hit the batter. Work on your technique for that. Next two pitches are bunts. Then we swing away. Math, how many pitches do you see before swinging away?"

"Three," Math replied.

"Everybody got it?"

"Yes Coach," they barked back.

"Okay. This drill is called Circle of Death because once you guys start swinging, Coach Tink and I are directly in the line of fire. Anyone who rips one back and hits us gets a point."

The boys liked the sound of that. Before long they were loose, swinging hard and determined to drive wiffle balls back into the coaches. Every time they did, hoots and hollers sang out. The players didn't fully realize they were working on hitting line drives; that was the only way to get the ball on the coach so fast that he couldn't side-step it. Ike ran around pouncing on skittering wiffle balls.

Leo kept a close eye on his watch. Thirty minutes before first pitch. "Rabbit, you and your brother were the first ones here, so you're number one and two in the batting cage. The rest of you go to Field 2 with Coach Tink for infield and fly balls. Let's keep running. You got a good pace going." Leo took off his cap and wiped his brow. "Tom, when I send a finished batter over, you send me a new one."

Jess and Wade came to the field 15 minutes early. Truman had put Ike on a leash and told him to lay down in the dugout shade. When the pup saw Jess, he was up and straining.

"Hello boy," she said. Ike shook with excitement. Jess unlooped his leash and headed to the bleachers, which were starting to fill. One advantage of Poodle Park was dogs were always welcome.

And they weren't alone. Parents, grandparents, aunts, uncles, brothers, sisters—as well as a number of Dannaka residents who had heard the buzz about this new coach—wanted to see if he lived up to the hype. A few of the younger kids spotted Ike. They came over and asked if they could pet him. The pup soaked in the affection. A dog that grows up around baseball quickly becomes socialized, getting endless lap time.

With five minutes to go, the team gathered in front of their dugout.

"Take a knee," Leo said. "Our first scrimmage. I want everyone to relax now and slow the game down. Just do things the way you've been practicing and you'll be fine." Leo looked at the boys' faces.

"What's the most important muscle we need to keep loose?"

"Smile muscles," they all said.

"Let's bond with the baseball for these last couple minutes." On the grass in front of the dugout, Leo dumped out a full bucket of balls. "Take three and focus on red."

Leo and Tom Tink remained on the dugout steps as each boy picked up three balls. They formed a line on the infield grass. "Have at it," Leo said.

Skyward, simultaneously, baseballs left the hands of the 12-year-olds. Like magic, balls took flight, arcing from hand to hand, eyes focused, arms flexed at the elbow, a ballet of synchronized juggling. Calm. Ease. Confidence. The scale of the activity seized the crowd. Even the Des Moines team stood rapt.

Leo looked at his watch. "Okay guys," he said. Each player caught the last descending ball in his cap. The crowd burst into applause, which reddened the boys' cheeks. "Take the field."

Leo had addressed positions and the batting order with each boy when he threw him batting practice. Everyone would play at least two positions. Scrimmages are for learning, he repeated.

Tom Tink's son, who earned the nickname Q-tip for his long, thin body and mop of blond hair, took the mound. His warmup pitches were intimidating.

Des Moines' leadoff hitter approached the batter's box like he was 10 feet tall. Digging in, he spat, waggling the bat. He could hardly wait to take the game's first hack.

Pot Roast was catching. He peered into the dugout to see what pitch Leo wanted thrown. Leo flashed three fingers. Changeup. That request was relayed to the pitcher, who nodded.

Q-tip wound up like he was going to chuck the ball through a barn wall, then pulled the string upon release. The Des Moines kid, amped up, looking for a fastball, was way out front. He popped up a harmless duck fart to the first baseman, who didn't have to move to make the catch. One pitch, one out.

The next two Des Moines batters saw a nasty mix of fastballs and curves, both striking out. Jess, Wade, Doc, Margaret, Jerome, Frank and bleachers full of Dannaka's faithful sprang to their feet. The team ran off the field goosebumped by an ovation. Des Moines' vaunted powerhouse had gone down in order without a ball so much as leaving the infield.

Jess was shocked to see Truman come out of the dugout to bat first. When they were talking at home, he thought he might hit last. Truman knew the leadoff guy's job. Coach had been clear. Get on base. Walk, bunt, hit by pitch, base hit—whatever. Put immediate pressure on the Des Moines pitcher. Nothing does that like a leadoff baserunner.

Even though Truman planned to bunt, he took big swings from the on-deck circle. He thought this might help sell the notion that he was going to the plate to hit.

"Batter up," the umpire hollered.

Truman, one foot in the batter's box, peered down at Leo coaching third, looking for the sign. Leo went through some motions, touching his nose and the bill of his cap. Then he went to the belt. Belt starts with B as does bunt. The bunt was on.

Truman set up in the batter's box, crowding the plate. If the pitch was inside, he would take one for the team. He uncoiled his biggest practice swing.

"No sweat with this Runt," Billy Dixon shouted from first base. His pitcher smiled, tugged on the bill of his cap and looked for the sign from his catcher.

The first pitch sizzled by Truman, a blazing fastball right down the center of the plate that froze him. "SteeeRIKE!" the ump called, shooting out his right hand.

Truman stepped out of the box and fiddled with his batting gloves, watching Leo for the sign.

"Let's do this, Runt," Pot Roast encouraged from the dugout. "Get us going!"

"Yeah, let's go Runt!" other teammates shouted.

In the bleachers, Jess was a mess. Her boy was facing a pitcher twice his size. He was being heckled by that oaf, Billy Dixon. And suddenly "Runt" had become a term of endearment from his teammates.

Meanwhile, Truman was swimming in thoughts as Leo went through his signs. *Where's your plan? That was your pitch to bunt. Fast down the middle. Don't blow it. Okay, the bunt is still on.*

The pitcher uncorked another fastball. Truman squared to bunt, but pulled back only to watch it blow by him. "SteeeRIKE TWO!" the ump shouted.

"C'mon Runt, no problem," Pot Roast shouted.

Leo clapped his hands at third and encouraged Truman. "C'mon, One. You can do this. I believe in you. Just slow it down." Again, Leo gave the bunt sign.

Truman was verging on hyperventilation as he stepped out of the batter's box. But when he heard Coach say I believe in you, he let that flow through him. *Two strikes. You bunt it foul it's an out. But if you just stand there and watch strike three, that's even a worse out. Slow it down. Lay it down. Slow it down. Lay it down.* Truman stepped back in the batter's box and crowded the plate.

Jess could see Truman's lips moving as he talked to himself. She clasped her hands together and squeezed. *Please. Please. Please.*

Another fastball came humming in. Truman squared to bunt. *Slow it down. Lay it down.* Truman focused on the baseball, finding the red laces. He let the ball come to the head of the bat and directed a bunt down the third baseline. Because batters rarely bunt with two strikes, the third baseman had backed up and the catcher and pitcher were caught off guard.

PING! A perfect bunt angled off the bat head. The ball shot to the grass, deadening, rolling slowly just inside the chalk line. The third baseman, pitcher and catcher all broke for the ball at the same time. Truman dropped his bat and bolted for first.

Ike had been playing with kids on the grass between the bleachers and the infield fence. But the moment he saw Truman sprinting, it was like a starting gun had been fired. The pup darted through the open gate, ears pinned back, hind legs kicking up dirt, past the home team dugout, tongue lolling as he raced toward first base, too.

The fans in the bleachers watched, mouths agape, not sure what to focus on: The slow-rolling baseball just inside the chalk line. Truman, head down, legs and arms pumping toward first. Three Des Moines players converging unyieldingly on the bunted ball. Ike bounding after Truman, hell-bent to beat him to the bag.

The Des Moines players collided at the baseball, caps, gloves, feet and arms momentarily filling the air like contents in a blender. Truman's right foot slammed down on first base, just in front of Ike. Shocked by the sight of three Des Moines players piled on the ground and the unattended baseball sitting on the chalk line, Truman didn't miss a beat. He went hard for second.

Coach Dixon yelled at his team to get the baseball, but the players standing were as dazed as those on their butts. Ike, seeing Truman heading for second, skittered around first, his rear end fishtailing until he got his nose pointed to second.

The fans were a cacophony, oohing at the collision, laughing at the puppy, cheering for the small leadoff batter and screaming to get the baseball. Truman rounded second and headed for third.

The pitcher, catcher and third baseman found their legs, blinking the game back into focus. The ringing in their ears was replaced by screaming. Instantly, simultaneously, it became clear to each of them: Someone had to grab that baseball and get to third before Truman did.

Where moments ago none of the boys hesitated, now all three did. Each was certain the other would spring into action. As it turned out, all three stood there as Truman reached third with a bunt triple. Ike came in behind him and sat on Truman's foot on the bag.

Pandemonium.

The Dannaka fans cheering, whooping, stomping their feet on the bleachers were not entirely sure if what they just saw had actually happened. Wade hugged Jess as they jumped up and down. Doc had a smile on his face like Margaret hadn't seen since high school. Dixon threw his cap on the ground and proceeded to stomp on it like it was on fire. In the dugout, the Dannaka team leaped into one another's arms chanting RUNT! RUNT! RUNT!

At third base, Leo gave Truman a slap on the backside. "Told you I believed in you," he said just loudly enough for the two of them.

When things finally settled down, the umpire made sure that Ike was on a leash and the gate leading to the field was shut and latched. Jess was exhausted and the game had only just started.

Truman tagged up and scored on a fly ball to center field and Dannaka was ahead of Des Moines for the first time since anyone could remember.

Despite the fact that his starter had a dominant one-two-three first inning, Leo put a new pitcher on the mound in the second. His plan was to start a different player every inning regardless of his performance. As Leo knew, it was very early in the season, the adrenaline would be pumping and he didn't want to risk pitchers hurting their arms. Plus this was an opportunity to learn how different pitchers handled themselves against difficult competition.

Rabbit's brother Marcos took the ball next. A pop-up, walk and two errors loaded the bases. Leo looked for frustration in the boy's body language but saw unusual calm. Marcos kept mixing his pitches, never throwing the same one twice in a row. He struck out the next Des Moines batter. Finally, after the following hitter fouled off three full-count pitches in a row, Marcos' changeup was slapped weakly to Truman at second who threw the batter out.

The team hustled off the field to another ovation from their home crowd. "You had ice water in your veins," Truman told his pitcher.

In the third inning, Ryan Rippen hit a two-run bomb for Des Moines to give them their first lead. But in the bottom half of the inning, Dannaka went back ahead when Havoc hit a two-run shot of his own.

The fifth was scoreless. One inning to go. Dannaka was clinging to a 3-2 lead.

"Truman," Leo said. "You finish up."

"Huh?" he said, surprised. "Yeah. Okay." He grabbed his cap and glove, dropping the cap. He tried to spit. His saliva was like pine sap.

"And hey," Leo said, "no throwing the Dazzler." He put his hand on the boy's shoulder. "We'll spring that on them when it really counts. Now go have fun."

Truman jogged to the mound, disappointed that he couldn't use his knuckleball, but excited that Coach trusted him with a one-run lead in the final inning.

The lead didn't last.

Des Moines tied it at three apiece with back-to-back doubles. A ground out advanced the baserunner to third. A fly ball to left allowed that runner to tag up and score the go-ahead run. Truman had two outs.

The next two Des Moines kids hit the ball just out of the reach of Truman's defense. He was frustratingly close to getting out of the inning, but instead, runners stood at first and second with two outs. Next, Billy Dixon strolled to the plate flashing a wicked grin. He stood in the batter's box and pointed the barrel of his bat to center field.

"Runt," he said. "Put a stamp on it 'cause I'm gonna send it to the next county."

Truman's dugout came to his defense. "Ooooh. So scared. Shut up Dixon. Let your bat do the talking."

Truman's first pitch was a slow, looping curve that dropped over the plate for a called strike. His next pitch, a faster curve, spun out of the strike zone just beyond the reach of Billy Dixon's mighty swing. Truman had Dixon in a no-ball two-strike hole. If he could only reach into his bag of tricks and throw the Dazzler. Truman looked into the dugout. Leo, as though reading Truman's thoughts, shook his head no.

His high fastball wasn't high enough to elude Dixon. Truman's pitch was blasted over the fence for a three-run homer. The Des

Moines dugout erupted, arms pumping, feet airborne, bodies over-flowing onto the field, eager to mob Dixon at home plate. They had to wait. Dixon circled the bases in a painfully slow trot.

Truman didn't remember getting the third out. The next thing he knew, he was slumped in the far end of dugout, head in hands.

One after another, his teammates approached, slapping him on the back.

"You had him, Runt."

"He was scared shitless."

"The Dazzler would have locked him up and thrown away the key."

"We still have the bottom half to win this."

With each bit of encouragement, Truman was revived. His posture straightened. He found his feet. Soon he, too, had his cap on inside out and upside down, cheering with the rest of his team.

But the rally caps didn't work their magic. Dannaka lost six to three. Nonetheless, no one hung his head. Coach said there were a lot of positives to build on. He said the team's hard work really showed. He told the boys to go over and shake hands with the Des Moines squad.

As the Des Moines players changed out of their cleats, untucked their jerseys and left the field, they knew the game was much closer than 6-3. They had used only their two best pitchers and batted their top nine players. Dannaka pitched six different kids and let everyone hit.

Ryan Rippen stood straddling his bike by the bleachers. Dirt and sweat streaked his face as a smile formed. In the sunshine, on the impeccably cut infield grass, the Dannaka team stood in a circle with their coaches. They had their arms around each other's shoulders, locked in a final competition. It was no holds barred.

Who could blow the biggest bubble gum bubble.

Ryan Rippen

Jess sat on her warm porch steps. Truman and Ike would be home from the scrimmage any time now. In the past few hours, she had been bombarded with the gamut of emotions. Drained, Jess was left with only one: pride.

"Hello, step," she whispered. "You should have seen Truman today. So brave. Amazing, amazing. He didn't let his fears hold him back."

Jess folded her hands in thanks and continued. "After the game the parents and the kids were mingling in this surge of, I don't know, happiness, accomplishment, optimism I guess, and Truman says to me with this quiet directness coming from I don't know where, 'Mom, you can't be afraid.' And I knew he was talking about himself, about facing those huge challenges in the scrimmage, but now, I'm not so sure."

Jess closed her eyes. "Was he talking about himself? Or my fears? My choice of certainty over something that could be so much bigger. Today was a long shot for Tru, but he chanced it. He chanced it! And afterward, he stood there, holding an imperfect conclusion—but he went for it. Is winning in the daring? Because I've never seen him … he almost glowed. Like he stepped out of an old self and stood there new." She paused.

"I don't know." Opening her eyes, she patted the step. "Something's there. When I see Leo there's something … far-off. It's terrible, I know. Wade has been so good. Patient. I do care for him and I've always hoped we could both get to the same place someday. But now, when I see Leo, something pulls at me."

Jess took a deep breath. "Don't listen to me. I'm talking crazy." She put her head in her hands and smiled her reluctant smile. "Girl, what are you thinking?"

The rattle of bicycle fenders came in on the wind. Truman turned in to the gravel driveway followed by a running, panting Ike.

"Don't be greedy," she said to the listening step. "This is enough."

Leo thought he heard a knock at the door but wasn't expecting anyone. Probably just the wind. He went back to studying the team scorebook. Hits, walks, RBIs, strikeouts, left on base, assists, errors, it was all there. Baseball is a gut-feel sport. But well-kept stats should shape decisions, too. Spur-of-the-moment emotions can get the best of a coach.

Another knock. Leo, in Nike shorts and a Bears Super Bowl XX T-shirt, walked barefoot through the kitchen to the front room. The windows were open and a breeze pushed through the screens. He swung open the door to Ryan Rippen.

"Hey ya, Coach," he said in his easygoing way.

"Ryan Rippen, right?"

"Yes sir. Sorry to bug you. Can you talk for a sec?"

Leo had his Dannaka baseball cap on backward. He nodded. "C'mon in."

Ryan followed him to the kitchen table. "Looking over the stats?" the boy asked.

Leo smiled, tapping the scorebook with his finger. "Lot of answers right here. You can always come back to the book."

Ryan looked at Leo. "As long as whoever is keeping it knows what he's doing."

"We have Coach Tink. He's a stickler. Do you know what the count was when you hit your homer?"

"Two and one," Ryan said, still standing. "Like that count. Pitchers get antsy."

"Take a load off," Leo said, pulling out a chair. "What do you mean antsy?"

Ryan sat. "They're looking to even the count, fast. They're behind and they don't want to get further behind." Ryan shrugged. "They hurry. It's a fastball situation."

Leo looked at the scorebook for Ryan's at-bat. Balls and strikes were recorded in little boxes by the baseball diamond graphic. Two balls were ticked off, one strike. "Two and one." Leo nodded, impressed. "So what can I do for you, Ryan?" He sat back in his kitchen chair, locking his fingers behind his head.

"I want to play for your team," Ryan said, his face becoming serious. He was a handsomely featured boy. Dark hair and eyebrows. Blue eyes. Classic, lean, athletic bone structure to his face.

"We've already made our team," Leo said.

"Yeah, I know. But with Bale going down, I figured there might be an open spot."

Leo watched Ryan. It looked like there might be more to the story. "That's it?"

"I have a lot of friends on the team. I live here." Ryan hesitated to say more. He looked down at the table. "It's Coach Dixon. He's why I left last year's team. He makes baseball pretty miserable. But your team, I watched you guys today. You have a blast. The team loves playing for you. Getting better at baseball doesn't have to be punishment, right?" A small line creased between Ryan's eyebrows.

Leo sat up straight. "Getting better at baseball should never be punishment."

Ryan nodded. "I talked to my mom and dad. Told them what I was thinking. Said I wanted to call you and ask about playing for your team. They said go over. Ask face to face. So here I am. I'd like to come back and play for you. If you'll have me."

Leo took off his cap and put it back on with the bill facing forward. "See that D?" he said pointing to the front of his cap. "If you come back, you don't play for me. You play for Dannaka. I'm just the head coach. Dannaka is the team." Leo cocked his head, looking straight at the boy, making sure his point was understood.

Ryan chewed the inside of his mouth. "I want to come back and play for Dannaka."

"Who's full of pepper?" Truman looked at his pup. "Ike is." He chased him around the living room couch. Ike growled playfully through a mouthed tennis ball. Around and around they went until Ike cut, reversing, dodging past Truman. The pup lived to play keep-away. "Who's ready to wrestle?" Ike's spiked tail shifted into overdrive. Truman made his move.

Ike tried to juke, but the diving boy scooped up the pup and pulled him onto his chest, careful not to roll on him. Ike let out a bark, inadvertently releasing the tennis ball.

"Fumble!" Truman shouted, reaching for the ball as it dribbled toward the coffee table. "Butter jaws." Ike wiggled free and pounced on the ball. Eyeing Truman, coiled in downward dog, Ike happy-growled, daring Truman to resume chase.

"I'm going out for a minute," Jess said, her car keys jangled in hand. "And be careful of my lamp. It's an antique."

"You mean it's older than you?" Truman smiled, catching his breath. "Where ya going?"

"Um, grocery store. Before they close at nine."

"What are you getting?" Truman took a fake step toward Ike, which put his tail back in motion.

"Milk."

Truman looked at his mom. "You just got milk."

"I mean ice cream."

Truman frowned. "We don't buy ice cream."

"Special occasion," she said. "Celebrating a great scrimmage."

"Wasn't so great for me." Truman shrugged. "But that's baseball."

"I'm proud of you. How you did. How you handled things."

"Tomorrow's another day, as Coach says." Truman turned his attention back to Ike. "That's my ball and I'm coming for it!"

Jess walked to her car in the farmyard. The sun had just slipped below the horizon line, striking a match.

Wearing shorts, sandals and a sleeveless striped blouse, Jess really wasn't sure where she was going. But if that were true, why did she freshen her eyeliner and put on a trace of lipstick? Truman's voice from the baseball field came back to her. *You can't be afraid.*

Nancy knew where he lived. For some reason she'd driven by one day as Leo mowed the lawn. Now, making her way up the front walkway, she felt a little silly for showing up unannounced. Deep breath. She knocked on the door.

"Hey Nancy," Leo said cheerfully, holding the door open. "Nice surprise."

"Hi. I caught you at a bad time, didn't I?"

"Not really, no. Come on in. It's a little messy." Leo gestured her in.

Nancy looked around the front room. "Love what you've done with the place," she kidded. "There's a distinct 1970s Iowa grandma influence."

Leo laughed. "I don't dare touch anything. Just a renter."

Nancy crossed her arms. "You know what they say about a man who doesn't hang any pictures on the walls?"

"He's out of nails?"

Nancy didn't let him off that easy. "He ain't planning on staying."

"Hmm," Leo said. "Can I get you something to drink? I have Coke and tap water."

"No. I'm working. Can't stay. I just needed a break and I wanted to ask you how the game went today." Nancy was wearing what she called her hard-ass work clothes. A tank top under a black leather vest, cutoffs and biker boots. It was her way of telling patrons at the Rundown she wouldn't stand for any of their crap.

"It was just a scrimmage. You want to sit for a minute? You should see what I've done with the kitchen."

Nancy smiled and took a breath. The guard she had to put up at work could be lowered here. "Yeah."

They sat at a small wooden pedestal table. As for the avocado-colored refrigerator, the faux brick backsplash behind the cooktop, the frilly orange curtains over the sink and the yellow Formica countertops, Nancy bit her tongue.

"No comment?" Leo said, watching her quietly assess the kitchen.

"Cozy," she offered. What she wanted to say was she expected Alice from the *Brady Bunch* to walk in with a bag of groceries at any moment.

"It's home," Leo said, surprisingly unrestrained. "Where I was, wasn't working. Now, it's like someone turned back the clock and I get to do some things over."

"That's a cool way to think about it," Nancy said. "Makes me want to have a cigarette and an ice cream sandwich. High school."

"What was high school like?" Leo asked.

"For me, a lot like this room. Small. No place to hide."

"Were you a good student?"

"I was. But I was mostly into art and fixing cars."

Leo's eyebrows lifted. "Interesting girl."

"The kids back then didn't think so. They were drawn to girls like Jess. Pretty. Cheerleader. Fearless."

Leo tried to work a knot out of his neck. "Funny. Those aren't the words I would use to describe her. Pretty. She is that."

"Life has a funny way of totally changing some people and leaving others alone."

Leo nodded, looking at Nancy, appreciating her directness, her street smarts.

"You'll make me blush if you keep looking at me like that."

"Nah. You don't blush."

There was a knock at the door. Leo and Nancy looked at each other. "Busy night," he said, getting up from the table.

"That's okay. I need to get going anyway." Nancy got up, too. They both walked to the front door.

It's difficult to say who was more surprised when the door opened. Leo. Nancy. Or Jess.

"Jess?"

"Nance?"

The two women frowned, trying to reconcile how, at this same moment, they both came to be on the stoop of Leo's house.

"What...?" they said at the same time. Then they said nothing.

"Heya, Jess," Leo said, breaking the awkwardness. "Nice night."

"Shoot, sorry," Jess said.

"Oh, no. It's not that," Nancy said hurriedly.

"I was in the neighborhood." Jess was less than convincing.

"I'm just leaving. Back to work."

"No, I can go."

"Really, honey." Nancy laid her hand on Jess's arm. "I gotta go. Leo," she said, turning to him, "thanks for the chat."

"Anytime." He knew it was a poor word choice the moment he said it.

Jess and Nancy had a quick embrace in the doorway. "We'll talk later," Nancy said.

"Um-hum," Jess replied, wishing she could disappear.

Every strike of Nancy's boots on the walkway was amplified. Car door opened. Car door shut. Engine turned over. Car drove away.

"Hey there," Leo said softly.

Jess was looking in the other direction.

"Jess?"

Her eyes met Leo's.

"Just friends," he said. "Just talking." Leo waved his hands like a magician does to show he had nothing up his sleeves. "I'm glad to see you."

Inside, they sat at the kitchen table. It didn't take long before they were able to joke about it. "I feel like such a dork," Jess said.

Leo took a swallow of his Coke. "You should have seen the look on your face."

"It's not funny," she insisted, trying not to laugh.

"Pretty funny." Leo nodded, noticing once again how Jess had a way of smiling while remaining suspicious of the idea. It was beguiling.

The room emptied of chitchat. There was the refrigerator's hum, the neighbor's wind chimes, the two of them.

"I'm curious," Leo said, "why you're here." The words came out in an honest, unthreatening way.

Jess's green eyes sparkled. "You should have seen Truman tonight. Chasing Ike around." She shook her head. "It was hard to tell who had more puppy in him. I would have bet that losing the game today would have crushed Tru. But he shrugged it off. Said he almost had Dixon. Told me he'd get him next time. All positives," Jess said, tapping the table with her finger. "He's a different boy. You're doing something important with these kids. I came to tell you that."

Leo took off his cap and hung it on his folded knee. His dark hair was a mess as his hand pulled through it. "I tell the kids there are two kinds of energy in the world. And only two." Leo looked earnestly at Jess. "Positive. And negative. It took me a hell of a long time to figure that out. Should be obvious, right? Look at every battery in the world." Leo paused to let her consider that. "Could be baseball, could be life. You can go at it with positive energy or negative. I tell the kids, choose positive. Negative doesn't help a bit. Never has."

"It's seeping in," Jess said. "After the game was over, I watched our team and I watched Des Moines. I would have guessed Dannaka won."

Leo's full white smile appeared. Laugh lines radiated from his blue eyes. He looked good in his Bears T-shirt, raggedy in the collar, snug across the chest, tightly stretched around muscular arms, which he folded loosely.

Jess asked, "Do *you* always choose positive?"

Leo's smile dimmed. "Just because you know the answer doesn't mean you always apply it."

"Yep," Jess said, nodding.

They looked at each other. The distance between them was in jeopardy.

"I think I should go." Jess exhaled, holding Leo's gaze. "Before I do something stupid."

"Okay."

"This is when you're supposed to talk me out of it," she said.

Leo swallowed. "I think it's best if you go."

Book

FOUR

Winning ways

"Leaping for a line drive keeps a player on his toes."

—*Tom Tink, Dannaka assistant coach*

SYNCHRONICITY

"Put 'er there," Tom Tink said, thrusting out his hand. Leo shook it firmly. The Dannaka All-Stars had just recorded the final out against their conference rival Glenwood, notching a fourth victory in as many games. Last year's team only won four games all season.

The two teams went through the handshake line, coaches bringing up the rear. Glenwood's head coach, Mike DiNardo, stopped to talk with Leo.

"I was looking back at last year's book," he said, "when I put my lineup together. We whipped you guys 7-1 and 9-3. Gotta say, you're fielding a good bunch of ballplayers. Playing the fundamentals. Impressive."

Leo thanked him.

"I heard you did a stint with the Cubs."

"I was up there for a cup of coffee. Got injured."

"Well, least you got a taste. More than most can say."

"Yeah." Leo popped a few sunflower seeds into his mouth. It was unusually hot under the blistering June sun. He was ready to be off the field.

DiNardo asked, "I was wondering, looking at your lineup. No number 7 or 10. Struck me as peculiar."

"Yeah. Long story." Leo said no more.

"Okay," the coach said. "We'll see you next time at your fields."

"Sounds good, Mike. Good game."

"Yeah. Not nearly as good as yours." He gave Leo a friendly clap on the back.

The boys gathered around Tom Tink, who got out his jumbo bag of bubble gum. They formed a circle, put their arms around each other's shoulders and got busy chewing. Leo didn't unwrap his gum right away.

"Just a couple words, boys. Listen up."

They listened but chewed. If a player was to blow the biggest bubble, he needed to get busy on his rock-hard gum.

"How many errors today?" he asked.

"Zero," they shouted back.

Leo nodded, making a zero with his finger and thumb. "Zip. Nada. Goose egg. Guys, you put on a clinic today. Math, what's the team batting average?"

"I was just working on that, Coach. I have to double check on paper, but I'm thinking it's…" Math squinted, ".425, thereabouts."

Leo whistled. "Wow. Talk about great plans at the plate. Rarely did we hack at anything out of the strike zone. We sat on his fastball and pounded him like Kojak."

The boys cheered.

"And kudos to Rip," Leo said to Ryan Rippen. "Our first grand slam of the season. Golf claps, everyone." The team applauded quietly, the fingers of one hand barely striking the palm of the other.

Leo addressed the two boys who pitched today. "Q-tip and Walter, get to practice twenty minutes early tomorrow so you can run. That's how legs recover. Every big-time pitcher runs the day after he throws."

"Should we ice our arms?" Q-tip asked.

"Ice tonight. Run tomorrow." Leo looked at the boys chomping away on their bubble gum. "All right already," Leo said tearing the wrappers off two pieces of Bazooka. "Let me catch up." Leo chewed as fast as he could.

Jess watched from the bleachers. When you see someone doing what they love, you see them at their best. Leo belonged surrounded by green grass, home run fences and the chatter of ballplayers.

Leo saw Jess as well. Ike was beside her, but no Wade. He made eye contact and waved.

It felt nice to be picked out of the crowd. Jess waved back. The team commenced to blow bubbles. Ryan Rippen had a beauty going until Pot Roast tossed his cap into it.

Before they left the field, the team assembled for push-ups. All hands and toes were on the grass. Tom Tink was in the center of the group, leading the exercise. He told the boys to get cracking.

In unison the team shouted out the letters and numbers that added up to 20 push-ups. "D-A-N-N-A-K-A 1-2-U A-L-L S-T-A-R-S G-O." People heard the boys from a block away.

Ike, straining against the leash, nearly pulled Jess onto the field.

"Let him off, Ma," Truman yelled. The boys were sitting on the infield grass unlacing cleats and untucking jerseys. Jess unclasped the leash. Ike bolted to Truman, pouncing into his lap, rolling him onto his back.

"Who's full of pepper?" Truman said. "Ike is." The pup yipped and licked and writhed. Truman loaded his voice with great expectation. "Want to run the bases?" Ike froze, locking eyes with Truman, wondering if it were true. "Go to home," Truman instructed, including a hand command to direct the pup in the right direction.

Ike ran to home plate and sat down, utterly focused on Truman for the next word.

"No chance, Runt," Ryan Rippen said. "No dog is smart enough to run the bases." Ryan, being new to the team, had not been to all the previous practices to watch Truman training Ike. The pup studied his master who slowly stood up from the grass.

"Reaaaaady?" Truman asked. The pup's hips twitched in anticipation. The Glenwood team and the fans in the bleachers stopped to watch. Truman's arm chopped forward. "Go to first!"

The pup burst down the first baseline, ears flapping, paws shooting up dirt. It appeared that Ike was going run through first and continue into right field. Then a few steps in before the bag, Ike lowered his butt, thrust out his front paws and skidded to a perfect stop at first base.

The crowd and ballplayers let out a wild cheer.

"No friggin' way," Ryan Rippen uttered. "That is such a cool dog."

"Go to second!" Truman yelled. The pup was only too happy

to oblige. Next, as Ike was commanded to go to third, Truman wheeled his arm in the air, the universal baseball sign to round the base and head for home. Ike nearly spun out at third, but quickly got his muzzle pointed to home, his hindquarters coming in line, long strides kicking up dust, his wiry coat laid back in the wind. The pup finished with a butt-skidding stop, coming to rest, erect, tongue lolling, on the center of home plate.

"We're not worthy!" the Dannaka players sang out, bowing with arms extended to Ike. Truman ran to home, kneeled and looped his arms around his pup. It was maybe the best day of his life.

Leo asked Truman to load the catcher's gear and batting helmets into the game bag and haul it to his truck. That gave him a few minutes alone with Jess.

"Hey there," Leo said. The tops of Jess's shoulders were lightly sunburned, her nose freckled. "Now I see where Truman gets his freckles."

"They come out in the summer. Like weeds."

Leo frowned. "I like 'em." The wind played with Jess's hair. "I haven't seen you in a few weeks. I was afraid I ran you off."

Jess squinted up at him. "The last time we talked, you were pretty clear about where you wanted me to be."

Leo kicked at the grass. "Are things really that clear in your life, Jess?" He didn't wait for an answer. "Not mine."

"Truman has never been happier. That's pretty clear. Fun game today."

Leo rubbed the three-day stubble on his face. "I don't see Wade."

Jess looked away. Her eyes moistened. "Wade and I are taking a breather," she said quietly. "I told him I needed to get some things clear in my life." She smiled wryly. "There's that word again."

Leo asked, "Are you familiar with the idea of synchronicity?"

Jess thought for a moment. "The only thing I can think of is the album ... by the Police, I'm pretty sure."

"Meaningful coincidences," Leo said. "That kind of synchronicity."

"Never gave it much thought," she said.

Leo looked at Jess. "Like being born on the same day."

Just then Truman came bounding up, Ike beside him. "What are you guys talking about?" He grinned. "You look all serious. Am I in trouble?"

Removing his cap, Leo playfully swatted Truman. "We're talking about having the same birthday. Which also happened to be my first day in Dannaka. I saw your mom and you playing ball at the fields. Never in my life had I seen two more dressed up baseball players."

A smile spread across Truman's face. "We were going to Mom's birthday party."

"And I had tiny Ike with me. I was telling your mom it's pretty great we were born on the same day."

"Um-hum. Did you see Ike run the bases today, Mom? Totally awesome."

Jess shot Truman a look.

"What?" he said.

"Were we not just in the middle of talking about something else?"

Truman shrugged. "Your birthdays. Same day. Cool. But Ike running the bases, that's epic. He used to stop and sit at third till I started using leftovers."

Jess stuck her hands on her hips. "Don't tell me that's where my extra pork chops went."

"Ma. Pork chops. Poor man's steak."

She was flabbergasted. "Where did you learn that?"

"From Bale."

"Yeah," Jess said. "Whose family happens to raise beef cattle."

Leo got a kick out of watching them go back and forth. He asked, "When's Bale get home?"

"Tomorrow," Truman said. "He had radiation, but no chemo. So he still has all his hair."

"Wait till he sees the haircuts on you guys," Leo said. "He'll get a chuckle out of that."

"He's bummed he can't play this season. I think he's hoping to help out. Like keeping the book or something."

"You tell him he's welcome to keep the book," Leo said. "Or catch-off at practice. Whatever he feels up to."

They walked together to the parking lot, a few parents stopping to shake Leo's hand. It was time for them to go their separate ways.

"Truman, you're starting next game. Have you been working on the Dazzler?"

"Oh yeah. Mom won't go near it. It's nasty."

"Nasty as five-day-old socks," Jess said.

Leo waved his hand in front of his nose. "Looking forward to that. Truman, can you put Ike in the car? I want to talk to your mom for a second."

"Uh-huh," he said, standing there.

"In private." Leo gave him a get-moving tilt of the head.

"Oh. Sure. C'mon Ike. Car ride?" The pup knew those words and off they went.

Leo stuck his hands in the back pockets of his baseball pants. "Now might not be a great time for you … but I was thinking … when you've had time to clear your head … um, if you thought it was an okay idea…."

Jess frowned. "If what is an okay idea?"

Leo bit his lip. He cracked a knuckle. "Um, maybe we try. You know."

"Leo, are you asking me out?" Jess looked at him in a way that didn't reveal how she felt about the idea.

"I was thinking about it. Yeah."

"What about you and Nancy?"

"What about me and Nancy?"

"I saw her at your house, remember? She's my friend."

"She's my friend, too. And that's all there is. Nancy and I have agreed on that since the beginning."

Jess absorbed what he said, looking up at Leo. Her forehead had a little frown, just like it did when she was reading a challenging book passage. Here stood a man born on the same day she was. A man who everyone in town knew but no one really knew. A man from Somewhere, Illinois, who came to Dannaka for God only knows why. A man Doc couldn't stop raving about. A man Wade said was "probably not Mr. All-American after all."

Leo stepped forward and touched Jess's hand. "Maybe we try it."

Jess remained still. "Maybe we do."

DANNAKA BUGLE

The *Bugle* was his baby.

Jerome had returned from the European Theater in 1945 ready for the next big thing. He used the GI Bill to get his journalism degree at Drake University and promptly landed a job at St. Paul's *Pioneer Press*. One of the first colleagues he befriended was about the same age, a Twin Cities native penning a comic strip called *Li'l Folks*. His new pal, Charles Schulz, later used many of those characters to syndicate a new strip called *Peanuts*.

Jerome became the consummate business beat reporter with an unwavering allegiance to his editor and his paper. But he was homesick. The Twin Cities were thick with new-fangled shopping centers and congested streets. Belching busses began to replace electric streetcars. At every turn there was another fancy club or bar barker. He could hardly get a clean, deep breath of air. He didn't know when, or how, but he knew he'd eventually get back to the serenity of Dannaka.

In 1954, Jerome took an inheritance from his parents' farm and the money he judiciously saved in Saint Paul and bought the *Dannaka Bugle*. I never married, Jerome liked to say. But I do have a baby. The *Bugle*.

As he put the finishing touches on his article about the town's Little Leaguers, in his ear Jerome heard the wise advice of his old copy editor at the *Pioneer Press*. *When in doubt leave it out*, a mantra about trimming sentences to the bone. With his red pen perched over each word like a hawk, he gave his weekly opinion piece, *Jerome's Jottings*, one final read-through.

Is This Baseball Magic?

Our Dannaka 12U Little League All-Star team is on a roll. In beating Glenwood 9-2 this week, they stand alone in first place in the Southwest Iowa Conference with a perfect four-win no-loss record. Let me say it now for all of us: Jeepers!

How could this be? Last year's team only won four conference games all season. Undoubtedly, this is a very different team. It starts with a roster of twelve-year-olds who hail not only from Dannaka, but from towns within a 30-mile radius as well. What's more, the team lured back one of our community's best young players, Ryan Rippen, after his one-year hiatus to play for Des Moines.

I phoned Ryan's mother about her son's decision to rejoin the hometown team. "He scrimmaged against Dannaka earlier this spring," she recalled. "He came home and said, 'Mom, Dannaka's good. They have a blast. And they got a new coach who used to play for the Cubbies!' We're a Cubs family," Ryan's mother declared, "not a Cards family. It wasn't a hard decision to come back to Dannaka."

Which brings us to the architect of this impressive rebuilding project: Leo Hamill, a 1979 first-round draft pick of the Chicago Cubs whose career was cut tragically short by an eye injury suffered when he was struck by a batted ball.

Unless you've been living under a hay truck, you've heard about this young, new coach coming to town. He says the secret to baseball is teaching players how to compete at their highest level and have fun at their highest level. "You have to keep it positive," Coach Leo told me, "because baseball is a game of failure. Think about it. If you fail two out of three times at the plate that still gives you a batting average 30 points above the average Hall of Famer's. The game is plenty tough without adding to it."

I've watched a few of his practices. To say they are unconventional is an understatement. But if you pay attention, you quickly see that every drill either simulates a game situation, or is designed to encourage players to full-on compete.

And then there are the haircuts. Coach Leo explained. "I told the kids when we pull on the uniform we are going to look sharp and play sharp. So we all went to Bert's and got haircuts. I had a coach in the minors who said, 'Long hair means don't care.' Our haircuts are a bonding thing—but I do want our kids to understand they are representing Dannaka when they wear the traveling team uniform."

I'll be first in line to give him kudos on this year's uniform design. Coach Leo chose a replica 1940s design to match the jersey and cap that Dannaka wore when we won back-to-back-to-back state high school championships, as some of you of a certain vintage may remember. The D on the cap, jersey and warmup are the spitting image of those once worn by old-timers such as Doc Gifford, Frank Galligan, and yours truly, all members of that record-setting team. That achievement stood, as chance would have it, until last year when a high school team from Naperville, Illinois won four straight titles. Can you guess who coached the team for those four momentous years? None other than our new coach, Leo Hamill.

Which makes me wonder, is all this happenstance? Or is it baseball magic?

I'll leave it for you to discern, Dear Reader. Just know this. Our beloved Dannaka, many say, is home to the finest Little League baseball facility in Iowa. Could it also be said that we have the state's best 12-year-old elite team to go with it?

Come out to Poodle Park and cheer on our boys. Who knows? You might just encounter a pinch of baseball magic for yourself.

The word count of his piece, at 638, was longer than he cared for but with some reformatting, Jerome was able to get the team's schedule next to his column. Below, he would position an article about a farmer from neighboring Red Oak who, while backing up his tractor, was struck by a tree limb, tumbled to the ground and was found dead under his machine. It was Jerome's practice to place difficult stories like that on a page with uplifting stories. Readers need a dash of hope to countervail news that can knock the bark off a person.

The *Bugle* was distributed every Wednesday. Russ Dixon summoned one of his "show floor dollies" and told her to find him a newspaper. He had placed a full-page four-color Dixon Dodge ad in this week's edition announcing his spring closeout sale. He was excited to see how it looked in print.

When she returned with the newspaper, Dixon grabbed her wrist and pulled her onto his lap, nearly sending them over backward in his office chair.

"What do you think of my desk?" he chuckled.

"I'd say it's mighty large," she giggled.

"Don't you know it." Dixon tried to open the newspaper but there wasn't room, given the seating arrangement. "Honey, you gotta move. You're too damn distracting."

"That's my job." She started to loop an arm around his thick neck.

Dixon pushed her off his lap. "Then get out there and distract some rock farmer from looking too close at the sticker price."

"Hey. Okay already. Be nice."

"I don't have to be nice," he said. "I'm the boss."

Dixon never did get to see his new ad. As he was thumbing through the pages, his eyes fell upon a photo of a pup bounding down a chalk line at a baseball field. Below, the caption read: Team mascot Ike runs the bases after another win for Dannaka's 12U AAA All-Stars.

Then Dixon saw Jerome's article. He almost broke a tooth trying to get through it: Underhanded commentary about his record last year. Overblown hype about Leo. Some bullshit about baseball magic. He reached into his desk drawer, pulled out a lighter and set fire to the paper. When he dropped it into his wastebasket, it had the unintended consequence of starting a heap of discarded paperwork on fire.

Dixon sprinted to the showroom lounge, grabbed the 36-cup polished aluminum coffee maker, pirouetted, and bolted back the way he came, tearing the plug from the wall receptacle, nearly getting bullwhipped.

An old farmer chewed a complimentary cookie, browsing the new trucks. "Shame," he mumbled. "Was lookin' to wash down my raisin cookie with a cup of that."

Under the lights

Leo suggested Eilleen's bakery for lunch. Jess was apprehensive, but agreed. She knew Eilleen's was more than a busy place at lunch; it was a busybody's place.

Milly, who was in line for Russian Tea Cakes, took the long way home past Arliss's to tell her she'd never in a million years guess who she just saw eating lunch together. Doris was at the counter having a loaf of rustic sourdough sliced when she turned and watched Jess and Leo's table like she expected a bear to crawl out from under it. Ed was the least subtle of the three. He walked up to Jess and asked where Wade was.

Leo excused himself and went to the counter.

"Heya there, Coach," Eilleen said. "Read about you in the paper. Way to go."

Leo hadn't seen the newspaper. "Oh. Thanks."

"Your sandwiches will be up in a jiff," she said. "Audrey is just putting the finishing touches on 'em."

"Can you put those in a bag to go? We'll open up our table for someone else, what with it being so busy."

"Well bless your heart," she said. "Just give me one more sec."

"No hurry," Leo said, thinking just the opposite.

Leo returned to the table carrying a white paper sack. "What's up?" Jess asked.

"I thought we might go sit in the park and eat. Little quieter."

Jess agreed, picking up their drink glasses. "Paper cups are by the soda dispenser. I'll get these changed out."

At the park the only gawkers were squirrels.

Jess's winsome half-smile suddenly appeared.

Leo watched her. "What are you thinking?"

She shook her head. "Ah, bittersweet Dannaka."

"Sorry about picking Eilleen's. I go there a lot and never got that kind of attention."

Jess tilted her head back to the trees overhead. The sun had burrowed behind gauzy clouds. The sticky warm air came with an intermittent breeze—just enough to shimmy through the leaves. "Feels like rain."

Leo knocked on the wooden bench. "I hope it holds off till after our game." Their sandwiches were laid out between them on napkins. He pulled open a snack-size bag of potato chips and offered it to Jess.

"Farmers are hollering for moisture." She crunched a few chips. "We're way behind this year."

"I hear you. It's like Dannaka is in a bubble. Blue skies and sunny. I've never seen such a stretch of baseball weather."

Jess was in her blue technician's shirt and jeans. She was jealous of Leo in shorts, but shorts weren't a great idea when working with pawing cats and dogs.

Jess asked, "How's the adjustment been for you? Do you miss … where were you in Illinois?"

"Naperville."

"Oh yeah. Do you miss it?"

"To be honest, I've mostly blocked it out. Like, I was trying to remember some things about our house the other day. The layout. How creaky the steps were. Where the TV was set up. It was like the blackboard had been erased. And washed."

Jess finished a bite of her sandwich. "I don't mean to pry."

"No." He shrugged. "I don't think of it like that."

"You said *our*," Jess said quietly.

"What's that?"

"You said 'our' house. Did you live with someone?"

Leo's hand went through his hair. It was one of the few times Jess had seen him outside without a ball cap. As far as she was concerned, he could keep it off more often. "For a couple years. I had a girlfriend.

We got engaged. Then we got unengaged and it was just me. Didn't realize I said *our* house. Weird."

Jess saw some of the pain in Leo's eyes that was there when they first met. She was sorry to bring it back.

"How about you?" Leo said. "Did you miss Dannaka when you left? Is that why you came back?"

"I didn't really miss Dannaka. I came back ..." Jess's shoulders rose and fell in a lengthy inhale-exhale, "I came back because I needed Truman to be in a safe place. A healthy place. As they say, I was up shit creek without a paddle."

Leo nodded. "I've seen a stretch of that water." He looked at his sandwich but had lost his appetite. "I remember you saying something the night Nancy and Wade and you and I got together. It was about returning to a small town. Do you remember what you said?"

"Small towns get smaller when you come back to them."

"Yeah. Why do you think that is?"

"I'd like to believe it's because you've grown during your absence and the small town essentially stood still." Jess looked at Leo. "Can we talk about something else?"

"How about we just sit here," he suggested.

They did. And it was nice.

Truman was in total command on the mound under the lights. He had allowed only one hit and one walk through four and two-thirds innings. The sticky night air gave the baseball laces something to grab onto so his Dazzler was as fidgety as a bank robber. Now he had two strikes on their number three hitter, a big, ropy kid who mashed one of Truman's changeups in his first at-bat, but it went foul.

Pot Roast was catching. The heat and humidity had his jersey soaked through. He looked into the dugout for the sign.

Leo conferred with Bale, who was keeping the book. "What did this guy do last time up?"

"Fly out 8," Bale said.

"What'd he swing at?"

Bale squinted at the details. "The Dazzler."

Leo thought, *There's no way that kid is sitting on a fastball. Not with the Dazzler and slow yakker that Truman has been dropping on kids with two strikes.* A bead of sweat slipped down Leo's temple. He flashed four fingers, then one. They were going with second sign, which meant a fastball had been summoned.

Below his crotch, Pot Roast put down the sign.

Truman shook him off. It was a diversion that Coach told him to use in critical situations to confuse a batter. Truman hadn't shook off a pitch all night. Suddenly he did. This must mean Truman wanted to go with his bread-and-butter pitch. These were thoughts Truman wanted buzzing around the batter's head.

Again, Pot Roast flashed four fingers then one. Truman okayed the sign. He thought about the red brick wall at school that he'd been throwing at since spring. A trace of a smile formed on his lips. He saw the strike zone, a chalked rectangle. He focused on the high inside corner. Truman went into his windup, his smile becoming fuller, found his balance point and drove his front leg and shoulder to home plate, chin pointing to the catcher's mitt. Arm whipping, Truman's hand released.

The baseball, flooded by stadium light, slashed through the night sky. Their number-three slugger was anticipating something soft. By the time he registered fastball it was too late. He took a vicious, blurring hack at the high inside pitch, which spun him around and left him facing the umpire who hollered STRIKE THREE!

Pot Roast squeezed the high hard one and calmly stepped out from behind the plate, rolling the ball back toward the pitcher's rubber. The team let out a collective shout, but it was no match for the eruption that came from the Dannaka fans who packed Poodle Park's bleachers for the season's first night game at home.

Truman made a fist, swinging it downward like a hammer. But he didn't over-celebrate. He wasn't about to show anyone up. He jogged off the mound and met up with his catcher.

"That was a number one with extra mustard," Pot Roast said. He took off his mitt and shook his catching hand like it was on fire.

Leo didn't get to enjoy the moment. The ball hadn't even rolled all the way back to the pitcher's mound when the center field sky fissured with lighting.

The boys hustled in and dutifully took a knee in front of the dugout. Tom Tink bounded up the dugout steps and waited to hear what adrenaline-charged words Leo had for the guys. And waited. But Leo wasn't there. He was inside the dugout, his face sickly white.

Then Leo lost it.

"Off the field right now!" Leo yelled. He studied the sky. Again, distant lightning cracked the blackness. "Now! Concession stands. Inside!"

The umpire ambled toward the dugout. "What's our problem, Coach?"

"That's lightning," Leo shouted. "Tom, get these kids out of here."

"Ah, ain't nothing. A little heat lightning is all," the ump said with a chuckle. "We'll keep an eye on it. No reason not to—"

"Boys. Tom. Concession stand!"

The players looked at each other wide-eyed, more confused than scared.

"C'mon boys," Tom said as the team organized themselves to leave the field.

Someone asked, "Should we grab our bats, Coach?"

"GO!" Leo yelled.

"Hold your horses, Coach," the ump said. "You walk them off the field, it's a forfeit."

Pretty much everyone in the ballpark heard Leo's blurted response. "I don't give a shit!"

GOOD TALK

The boys weren't themselves. Balls were popping out of gloves.
Throws in the dirt. Missed cut-offs. Leo stood at home with
his fungo bat on his shoulder, sweat ringing the collar of his
shirt. The afternoon sun beat down on Poodle Park. He shook his
head. He was mad at himself.

"Tom!" he hollered to Field 2. Tom was hitting controlled pop-ups
with a tennis racquet to the pitchers who sprang off the mound to
make running catches along the first and third baselines. "Water
break. Then come over."

"Water!" Tom Tink shouted out. The kids hustled off the field to
the hose by the equipment shed. It was the middle of June. The boys
had been out of school for two weeks. When the weather was good—
essentially always—Leo was running morning and night practices
on Tuesdays, Wednesdays and Thursdays.

"Hit the water!" Leo shouted. His group ran off the field, but not
with their usual carefree abandon. Bale was standing next to Leo at
home plate, where he had been catching-off. He dropped a ball into
the scuffed five-gallon bucket.

"Me too, Coach?"

"Yeah. Of course."

Bale's face grew tight. "I'm not really a player, so I wasn't sure."

Leo took a deep breath. "Bale, you're a part of this team. Your
cancer didn't change that. You'll be back on the field next year.
Meantime, you're a big help. You're another set of eyes and ears for
me. That's important."

Bale had always been direct. "No bullshit, Coach?"

"No bullshit," Leo replied.

Bale lingered. "Then I should tell you something." He squinted, looking up at Leo.

"What is it?"

"You need to talk to the guys. You can see they're tight. This practice today … isn't us. They think you're mad at them."

"Why?"

"Because the way you screamed at them last night."

"I screamed because I was concerned. This league needs to have a lightning policy. It can't just be left up to some umpire."

"But the rain missed us." Classic, direct Bale.

"Bale, if a player came up to you and said his leg had been hurting for weeks and he'd been feeling queasy on and off, would you tell him to just ignore it? Hope it goes away?"

Bale's jaw set. "No."

"What would you do?"

"I'd tell the kid to go to the doctor and have it checked out. Right away."

"What if the doctor discovered it was nothing? Just growing pains. Was it still a good idea for you to tell that kid to see a doctor?"

"Yeah," Bale said with no reservation.

Leo put his hand on Bale's shoulder. "I agree with you." He patted him on the back. "Now go get some water."

The team was sitting in the shade of the dugout. Leo overturned a ball bucket and had a seat. An unusual silence wedged between them.

"Okay," Leo started, "who here thinks I acted crazy last night?"

Pot Roast's hand shot up faster than he wished it had.

"Well, at least there's one straight shooter on the team. Anyone else?"

Bale slowly raised his hand, as did Havoc, Q-tip, Math, Truman and, reluctantly, Tom Tink. Eventually all hands were up, except the Hernandez twins, Rabbit and Walter.

"What about you two?"

Rabbit spoke for them both. "You were just trying to protect us. Like family."

Leo took off his cap and tapped his knee with it. "Guys, you might think I was being overly worried, but lightning is nothing to mess with. If you're on the diamond and you see it, get your butt in. Go to the concession stand." Leo looked at the boys' faces. "It has a cinder-block foundation, wood siding—not metal. That's a safe place. Clear?"

"Clear," they repeated back.

"Okay. Let's hit the reset button. As for last night, that's behind us. But it bonds us. We look out for each other."

Havoc's hand shot up.

"Yeah," Leo said.

"Did our win last night count? Some of their kids said we lost on a forfeit."

"No. It counted. Since the rain missed us and we came back on the field, that was just a delay."

Truman asked, "How'd ya talk the ump into that? He said forfeit all the way."

Leo grinned. "Ask Coach Tink. He's the one who saved us with the ump."

Tom couldn't have been more delighted to have all eyes on him. "I bribed him," he said, light and easy.

The whole team inhaled at once.

"Well, not really a bribe bribe. No money or anything. More of a favor."

"Time to confess, Coach Tink," Leo joked.

Tom crossed his legs and locked his fingers behind his head. He did enjoy having the floor. "You guys have seen me around town, driving my Pepperidge Farms truck. I've got a ton of great products on board, but my number-one seller is Goldfish. I run out of those little suckers every week." Tom shrugged in a what-can-a-guy-do manner. "Turns out, the ump's grocery store is on my route. He's a manager at Korte's over in Glenwood. I don't get to him until Thursdays. By that time I'm rationing the remaining Goldfish. So last night I said to him, "I'll start putting aside two extra cases of Goldfish for your delivery if we call this a weather delay and forget about the forfeit business. You know what he said?"

Pot Roast couldn't help himself. "He said yes! 'Cause we went back on the field and whipped those whiners."

Tom stood and hiked up his pants. He shook his head no. "He said 'three cases, and you got yourself a deal.'" Slapping his knee in delight, Tom said, "Sometimes you gotta take one for the team."

The boys let out a cheer and when it dissipated Leo said enough chit chat, let's get back to baseball.

"Bond with the ball," Leo shouted to the smiling players. Each took one ball and flipped it from hand to hand, watching the red laces, focused on detail. The drill had advanced beyond just tosses in front of their chests. Balls were flicked behind the back—up and over a shoulder—and caught with the same hand that tossed them. Then, switching, they did the same thing over the opposite shoulder. Focus drills were mandatory for every team Leo had coached.

"Juggle," Leo said, picking up three balls of his own. Each boy had mastered a simple routine. No one dropped a ball. "Pair up." Everyone found a partner and now three balls were juggled by each duo. Coordinated movements and extreme tempo awareness allowed each twosome to act as one. "Boys, you're getting good," Leo said. "Scary good. Get your gloves. Time for Asteroids." The kids let out a collective whoop.

Each pair of boys faced one another, 10 steps apart, balls cocked in their throwing hands, gloves up, opened to their partner. "Go!" Leo called out. Baseballs left the boys' hands at the same time, narrowly missing in mid-flight, zipping into the other's glove. Each pair found a quick throwing rhythm, keeping balls in their own lane. When two balls struck each other in flight, it was like asteroids colliding: thus the name.

"Three steps back," Leo shouted. Then three more. And again. The players had this drill down to an art form. Balls whizzing past each other, the slap of leather, a machine-like cadence of catch, cock, throw; catch, cock, throw. Turning a double play on a Little League field with its short 60-foot basepaths requires quick, sure hands.

They ran relay races, took infield and hit wiffle balls. Leo finished

RUNT

by getting on the mound and throwing the batters curveball after curveball. The more Uncle Charlies they saw in practice, the quicker they could recognize that telltale spin in a game. And straighten it out.

After practice wrapped up, Leo jogged the fields. It was five o'clock hot, so he didn't overdo it. It's just—he'd gotten into a routine. And it was paying off. Leo was down to 190 pounds. He was sleeping great. He felt like his old self.

Tonight, steak. On the Weber grill Leo'd bought at the hardware store a few weeks back. Most of his dinners this month were cooked outside. Ah, June: seemingly endless stores of daylight, add briquettes, it's a griller's paradise.

The grocery story was quiet. Most moms were already preparing dinner, and not many Dannaka dads shopped, beyond picking up milk and bread. Mack was manning the butcher case.

"Heya Coach," he said, wiping his hands on his apron. "Grilling again tonight?"

Leo had come to appreciate that questions like these weren't nosiness so much as friendliness. People cared to notice another person's habits in Dannaka.

"Hey Mack. Did you save me a good one?"

"I got a T-bone," he shook his head decisively. "One bite will tell ya why cows are sacred in India."

"Wrap it up."

Mack asked, "Your boys still undefeated?"

"They are."

"Saw about you in the paper. Need to catch a game. I cut the schedule out. Just need to stop with all the working."

Leo felt the wear of the sun and his arm ached from too many curveballs. "Everybody needs a little time off."

Mack wrapped the steak in butcher paper. He scrawled a price in grease pencil. "I appreciate the work."

Leo tipped his cap back. "I know what you mean."

"Take it to 135 degrees inside," Mack called out as Leo walked away. "Or a bit less."

Leo lifted his ball cap and gave it a shake.

At the cash register, a high school girl was snapping her gum, doing her best to look deathly bored. Leo put down one steak, one potato, one quart of milk, one bag of carrots. "That's it?" she said, taking a peek in Leo's basket. "Looks kinda lonely." She shot Leo a flirtatious look.

Leo reached for his wallet. "You know, you're right." He cocked his head, reconsidering. "Hang on to that stuff a sec."

Jess scrambled for the phone. She had been outside watering her vegetable garden. The broccoli, Brussels sprouts, cauliflower, onions and tomatoes were started indoors in April. June's sun had them growing great but the lack of rain had her watering every other day.

"Hello ... shoot, crap." Jess's hand left a smear of mud on the phone. She tucked the receiver between her ear and shoulder to grab a paper towel. The smear migrated to her cheek.

"You there?" someone said.

Jess recognized the voice, but couldn't place it with all her shuffling around. "Doc?"

"Ah, no. It's Leo. Leo Hamill." Pause. "Coach Leo."

Jess couldn't help but laugh. "I know which Leo you are, you goof."

"Oh." Pause. Leo looked down at his countertop. Three steaks. Three potatoes. A bag of carrots. A six-pack of Budweiser. A bottle of Sprite. A gallon of milk. And a box of popsicles.

"Leo, is there something in particular? Or are we just going to listen to each other breathe?"

"Oh yeah. Um, I'm going to say something." Pause.

"Tonight? Or sometime tomorrow?"

"Yeah. Tonight. I was wondering, since it's so nice out, good for grilling and all ... if you and Runt—Truman—had any dinner plans?"

"Oh." Jess shifted her weight onto her other foot. She was dirty. Sweaty. And most of all, surprised. "When were you thinking?"

"Tonight," Leo said.

"Can you be a tad more specific?"

"Whenever it works, if it works. It's okay if it doesn't."

"Leo?"

"Um-humm."

"That's not a very strong invitation."

Leo scratched his whiskers. "Um. I'd like you to come. To dinner. What time works for you guys?"

Jess smiled, leaning against the countertop. She looked at the wall clock. It was 5:45. "I told Truman to be home at six. He's over at Bale's. We were just going to have leftovers. What are you making?"

"Better than leftovers."

Jess laughed. "Okay. Yeah. We'll be there around 6:30. What can I bring?"

"I forgot to get salad stuff."

"By salad stuff, does that mean dressing, too?"

Leo said, "Just a minute." Jess heard the refrigerator door rattle open. "You guys okay with French, Thousand Island or Italian?"

"You kidding? That's two more than we have."

"Oh, and bring Ike, too. There'll be some bones he'll be interested in."

Jess showered quickly. With a towel wrapped around her, she stood, dripping, her closet door swung open. *Shorts? Sundress? Shorts? Sundress?* She told herself this was the first dinner with just the three of them, reaching for the sundress. But her motto was *short notice means shorts.*

Shorts it was. Jess sat on the front steps, Saran Wrap stretched invisibly over the salad bowl on her lap. Truman was due home five minutes ago. She'd give him five more before driving to Bale's and picking him up.

Jess drummed lightly on the wrap. "Nice night, huh step? Going to Leo's tonight. Don't know what to make of it. Friendly invitation? Something more?"

The sun had slipped westward, leaving Jess and the front steps in shadow. A soft breeze picked up and dropped, repeatedly. "The breeze seems as unsure as me," she told the step.

Across the road, the field was planted in corn this year. Leaves on the short green stalks opened to the evening sunlight. She sighed. The thought of Wade outside starting his grill, alone, stabbed her heart. "Oh, Wade," she said, setting her palm down on the worn step, feeling its stored heat. "I hope I haven't hurt you too much. I never meant to. I tried. I was honest, mostly. I wasn't looking for something else, but my heart was, I guess." She closed her eyes and folded her arms to her chest. "Who is this man who has been sent to us?"

The rattle of fenders was ferried in on a breeze. And an excited yip! from Ike. The two of them curled off the road, onto the gravel driveway, then across the bumpy front lawn. Jess was grateful to have her secret conversation clattered away.

"Hey Ma!" Truman shouted excitedly. Ike bolted to Jess and wiggled his heated body around her legs.

"Now don't you go getting me all a mess." Jess stood, lifting her salad bowl out of harm's way. Ike jumped up and stuck his big, dirty paws on her shorts. "Get down, you." Jess kneed the pup aside. Ike gave her a momentary sad look before heading for the full water dish beside the porch.

Truman dropped his bike on the lawn. "What's with the bowl? You look kinda dressed up." He was sweaty, dirt on his face. The summer sun had doubled his freckles, even on the tops of his large ears.

"Pick your bike up." Jess frowned, adding, "Please."

Ike lapped up water nonstop. "Good idea," Truman said. He leaned his bike on the porch and went to the water faucet on the side of the house. Cranking it on, he followed the hose out to Jess's garden, dropping his ball cap and peeling off his T-shirt as he went. Truman proceeded to run water over his head and squirt it into his face before drinking deeply.

Jess stood there with her green salad bowl, shaking her head. "Whose alien are you?"

With his last mouthful, Truman squirted a fountain of water

through his front teeth. "Careful I don't shoot you with my death ray." Truman pointed the hose at his mom and started walking toward her.

"Don't you even think about it," Jess warned.

Truman clamped down his thumb, making the water spray a few feet. "Aliens don't like being made fun of."

"Truman. No!" Jess tried to keep a stern face. "Drop that hose or else."

Truman kept walking toward the porch. "Or else what?"

Jess, laughing, started to back up. "Ike! Get him. Sic that alien!"

Ike began barking, circling around Truman, who squirted water at Jess as she bolted for the screen door, a few drops nipping her bare calves.

"Chicken," Truman said as he sprayed a pulse of water into the air. Ike, always game, leaped and contorted, chomping into the water stream with abandon.

Dinner at Leo's

Truman watched out the car window as they headed to town. With his baseball glove on, he pulled a ball out of the pocket, quickly spun it to get a four-seam grip and then tossed it back in. "How come we don't go to Wade's anymore?"

Jess, too, was thinking about Wade. She wondered if Truman had somehow picked up on that. "Remember, I told you Wade and I decided to take some time. Apart."

"You guys decided, or you decided?"

Jess took a breath. "I decided."

"Is it because of Coach?"

Jess looked at her son, who continued to take the ball out of his glove, only to toss it right back in. "Can you stop fiddling with that?"

"I'm working on my grip. Coach says when you transfer a ball from your glove to your hand, you need to find a four-seam grip so the ball flies straight."

Jess was half listening. "Tru, I don't know if it's because of Leo."

Truman stopped playing with the baseball. His mom was always decisive and sure. He saw a frown crease her forehead. "Do you still talk to Wade?"

"Yes, we talk. I ask how he's doing. He asks how I'm doing. Then it's usually something about the weather."

"We can talk about something else." Truman watched out the windshield as they passed Poodle Park, the fields aglow in evening light. He loved those fields.

Jess managed a tight smile. "It's okay. It's a kinda confusing time. For all of us."

"Do you like Coach Leo, Mom?"

The turn signal's tick-tick tick-tick sounded unusually loud. "Yes,

I do."

Truman nodded. "Me too." He hesitated. "But we should still be friends with Wade."

Jess reached over and rubbed her boy's shoulder, a gesture he wouldn't normally tolerate. He smiled at his mother.

Leo was on his front stoop with a Rawlings water bottle, wearing shorts, flip-flops, and a blue, short-sleeved Nike running shirt. His hair was wet from the shower.

Ike bounded out of the car door, spun out on the sidewalk, sprinted up the steps and jumped into Leo's lap.

"Hello there, rookie." Leo ducked and weaved as Ike tried to lick his face. "Growing up around baseball means you always have laps to sit on. You're getting good at it." Leo scratched the pup's neck, under his collar. That lessened the writhing. Then, suddenly, a switch flipped. A distant memory came calling on the wind. Ike carefully stepped off Leo's lap, putting one foot slowly down in front of the other. Body rigid, nose pulling him forward, the pup stalked toward the bushes.

Leo spoke quietly. "Looking for that rabbit?"

Ike, now on the front lawn, glanced back at him.

"See for yourself, but I think he found a new address."

Leo stood and watched Jess and Truman come up the walkway. Truman had his baseball glove, but was tentative, something Leo hadn't seen from him since the first day of tryouts. Jess looked fantastic: tanned, hair pulled back, wearing white shorts and a striped navy blouse.

"Welcome," he said. "Thanks for coming."

"Thanks for having us," Jess said.

"Yeah. Thanks," Truman added. "Ike. Hey. Get out of there." The pup was buried in a hydrangea shrub with only his wagging stub tail exposed.

"I'll take that," Leo said, freeing Jess of her salad bowl. "Doesn't your mother look nice?" Leo asked Truman.

Truman shrugged. "Brought my glove. And a ball. Want to play catch?"

Jess reprimanded. "Truman. We only just got here."

"Yeah, we can play," Leo told him. "My glove is on the back seat of the truck. Grab it, will ya?"

Truman jumped off the steps and ran to the truck, which was parked in front of Jess's car. He tried the door. "It's *locked*?" Truman said, like it was an impossibility. "Nobody locks cars in Dannaka."

"Gimme a sec," Leo told him. He stepped through the front door where the keys hung in the entryway.

Jess smiled as Leo came back. "Old habits die hard," she said.

"Illinois gets further away every day." He looked at Jess whose green eyes had a happy sparkle. "Incoming!" Leo shouted to Truman. Underhanded, he gave the keys a high, arcing toss. Golden sunlight glinted off them as they jangled through the air. Truman hardly had to move his glove as he watched the keys drop into the leather pocket with a muffled chink.

The smell of charcoal smoldering to life strung through the back-yard. Layered atop that was the drone of a distant lawnmower and the regular THWUMP! of a baseball striking leather.

Jess sat sideways on the steps, leaning against the iron railing with a can of Budweiser. She rolled an old tennis ball onto the lawn, which Ike chased, pouncing on it with a growl, running back to her with the prize in his mouth. The pup was growing into his paws, getting less clumsy.

Like a clothesline, the white baseball zipped between Leo and Truman. Jess hadn't watched Truman throw from such close range. It was hard to believe this was the same boy she played catch with in early spring.

Leo would position his glove, giving Truman a target either at his right or left shoulder, or his right or left hip. The boy would throw the ball in those quadrants with enough precision that Leo's glove rarely moved once set.

"How's the arm?" Leo asked.

"Good," Truman grunted.

"Any soreness?"

"Not really. It loosens up nice."

·Leo nodded. "That's how it should be. Do you want to pitch a few or are you good?"

"Pitch a few."

"Okay. Let's set up like always," Leo said.

Pitching is about routine, about technique that becomes muscle memory. Leo had his pitchers go through the same process every time they practiced or warmed up before a game.

"What are we going to use for a plate?" Truman asked.

Leo grabbed the empty Kingsford coal bag, folding it to approximate a 17-inch home plate. He stomped it flat. Truman began stepping off 25 feet.

"What's going on over there?" Jess took a sip of beer.

Leo explained, as he got down in a catcher's squat. "First we throw from half the pitching distance. You need three strikes out of four before moving to three-quarters distance, again throw three strikes out of four, then move to regulation distance—46 feet."

"I'll stick to my beer," Jess said. "Don't want to show off."

Truman started pounding the strike zone. He threw two pitches from the windup, two from the stretch.

"That's three strikes," Leo said, standing, working a crick out of his knee.

Truman backed up and promptly threw three strikes in a row from three-quarters distance.

"What's our other rule?" Leo asked.

"No more than two pitches of the same kind in a row." Truman backed up again. Now he would be throwing from the full Little League pitching distance.

"I'll give you a dollar if you get three strikes in a row from there," Jess taunted.

Truman stepped off his pitching rubber, which was a stick. "Make it worth my time. Five bucks."

"You're on."

Truman's first pitch from the windup was his hard curve. It snapped into the strike zone with plenty of juice for a strike.

"That's one," Leo said, firing the ball back to Truman.

Next out of Truman's hand came a slow yakker that bent in for a high strike.

"That's two." Leo said. "Time!" Leo called to the imaginary umpire as he jogged out for a conference with Truman. "Throw the Dazzler," Leo said.

"That's a hard pitch to throw accurately." Truman wanted to win that five-dollar bill.

"Pressure is a part of the game." Leo handed him the ball. "Give me the Dazzler."

Truman nodded.

With Leo squatting behind the Kingsford plate, the razzing began.

"C'mon pitcher. C'mon Runt." Jess smiled. "If you can't take the heat get outta the kitchen."

Truman came out of his windup, struck his balance point, thrust off his back foot, staying narrow as he strode for home. His knuckleball was released to the caprices of the evening air. The ball, laces nearly frozen in space, closed in on the strike zone, only to drop a foot just before reaching the plate.

Leo smothered the low pitch, fooled by the late movement to the point of almost missing the ball entirely.

Jess jumped to her feet. "Ha! A ball. The five bucks is still mine!"

Leo jogged the ball back out to Truman. "Runt. That pitch had a heart attack and croaked two feet in front of the plate. Amazing."

Truman was too locked in to say anything.

"Let's finish with heat. Fastball, right down Broadway."

"I'm going back to the Dazzler," Truman said flatly. "I'm going to start it high. Just keep your glove in the middle of the strike zone. It'll drop in. Trust it."

"Okay." Leo jogged back to the plate.

From the windup, Truman's mechanics were a carbon copy of his last pitch. The only adjustment was a higher release point. The baseball came out of his claw-like grip. By the time the ball was halfway to home, Leo zoned in on the red laces, which shimmied slightly right, then left. The ball was transported through the air as though pulled by a tractor beam. Leo tuned out the alarm blaring at him to raise his mitt. The pitch was coming in head high.

Trust it. Leo recalled Truman's voice.

Leo squinted, bracing himself, ready to bail out if he had to.

Three feet before crossing the plate the ball dipsy-doodled directly into Leo's steady mitt.

"That's a friggin' strike!" Truman flung his glove to the sky.

Leo ran out and wrapped Truman in a hug. "The Dazzler will not be denied!" Ike joined them, jump-barking, tail ablur.

Jess stood on the step, silently absorbing this moment, thinking that her life, of late, was about as predictable as a knuckleball.

The baked potatoes weren't quite done. The steaks were overcooked. Truman pretended to like carrots. But what makes a meal is the company. It was the best dinner any of them could remember.

Leo and Truman began clearing dishes.

"I'll do those," Jess said. "You cooked."

Leo looked at Truman. "How about you walk Ike to the ballfields and back while your mom and I do the dishes."

Truman jumped on the offer. "Deal."

"When you get back," Leo said, "we'll have dessert."

"What are we having?"

"You'll see," Leo said. "Do you need a leash for Ike? I think I still have a rope around here somewhere."

"Nah. He minds me. If I can get him off that bone." Ike lay on the floor, pressed against the refrigerator, gnawing. Truman whistled. "C'mon boy."

Only the pup's eyes moved, looking up at Truman.

"You can bring it. C'mon." Truman waited. "Outside." That word was magic. Ike pranced after Truman, bone in tow.

Leo rinsed the dinner plates, handing them to Jess to slot in the dishwasher. "I usually do 'em by hand in the sink. Don't create many dishes around here."

"It's crazy how many we make. But dishes are a casualty of cooking and I like to cook."

The windows were open but the kitchen had heated up. Baking potatoes in a small space, running hot water in the sink, the proximity of Leo and Jess.

"I have a confession to make," Leo said, setting his dishrag on the counter.

Jess looked up at him. Her stomach tightened.

"I had an ulterior motive, sending Truman off with Ike."

One wisp of bangs clung near her eyebrow. "Okay."

"I was thinking about kissing you. But wasn't sure that was appropriate. Even more so with Truman here."

Jess looked away. "It's complicated. What you're thinking about."

"Is it?"

"A single mom. A son. A dog. That's complicated."

Leo waited for Jess to meet his gaze. When she did he said, "Well, I'm still thinking about kissing you."

"I like that thought."

Leo stepped closer. He tucked a rogue curl of hair behind her ear. They came together at last. The kiss set her nerve endings afire. His left knee buckled. Their bodies pressed together leaving no room between them for even the smallest second thought. It was a kiss that renewed their faith in heaven-sent coincidences. It was a kiss that confirmed they were deserving of something magnificent. It was a kiss with the power to heal.

Blasting through the front door with Ike on his heels, Truman was ready to hear about dessert. In the kitchen, Jess and Leo stood close to each other, leaning against the sink, flushed.

Truman crossed his arms. "Well I hope you kissed her and got it over with," he said.

Leo gave him an I-must-have-heard-you-wrong cock of the head.

"What?" his mom said, trying to suppress a smile.

"C'mon," Truman said. "What do you think? I'm stupid?"

First tournament

Raucous. No word better captured the Dannaka All-Stars as they ate at Tilly's, a Des Moines sports bar. Piercing 12-year-old voices recreated their victory. Hoots. Hollers. Color commentary. It was a hot Friday night and the boys were shoulder to shoulder around a long table with burgers the size of their heads. There was a lot to celebrate, beyond the free refills on Pepsi.

They had just dispatched Urbandale, last year's tournament winner. And it wasn't even close: 5-1, under the lights. The kids were buzzing, still wearing baseball pants but stripped down to T-shirts that carried their team's motto: Choose Positive.

Leo, Tom Tink, Jess, and a few other parents were smart enough to get a table of their own, far enough away to hold a conversation but close enough to keep an eye on their rowdy bunch.

Tom said, "It's like they've never been fed before."

Leo chuckled. "I wouldn't want to get between any one of them and his burger."

A parent chimed in, "You'd lose a limb."

Jess ordered a vodka tonic. "Dannaka looked good out there tonight."

"I'll tell you who looked good," one parent said. "Runt. Couple hits. Couple scoreless innings on the mound. Holy smokes."

Jess blushed. "He's just happy to be on the team."

"We're just happy he's on the team," the parent retorted. "Littlest guy out there. Scrappy. That should be his nickname."

"I like that a lot better," Jess said.

"A person doesn't get to pick his nickname." Leo drained his glass of water. "The nickname picks a person. It's a baseball thing."

Jess shrugged. "That's what I hear."

"Can't argue with the baseball gods," Leo continued.

A father of one of the players changed the subject. "So tomorrow. You've got that A-hole Dixon and his Des Moines hit squad. I'd love to see that guy go down." His wife rebuffed him, saying it was just a game between 12-year-old kids.

"Dixon is the 12-year-old." Her husband polished off his beer and caught the waitress's eye. The parents were doing a little celebrating themselves. It was a hot night. The beer and cocktails were going down easy. Even Jess was getting in on it.

Leo, on the other hand, was sticking to water. He needed to be sharp. The weekend tournament was jam-packed with two more games scheduled for Saturday, and depending on how those went, possibly two more on Sunday. They'd learn a lot about how they stacked up against the elite associations in the state. Teams in the Des Moines regional jamboree came from districts near and far. This was the only way to face them until the best teams met in the state tournament in mid-August.

"Who are you going to start tomorrow against Dixon?" one of the parents asked. "Or is that top secret?"

"Walter will get the ball." Leo grinned.

"He's one of the Hernandez twins, right?"

"Yep. Marcos."

"And he is called Walter why?" a mom asked.

Tom Tink answered. "In honor of Walter Johnson."

The mom frowned. "Who's that?"

"Who's that?" Her husband's eyes widened. "Walter Perry Johnson. The Big Train. A gangly farm kid who pitched in the early 1900s. The story goes, Walter walked to the mound to face Ty Cobb for the first time. Cobb laughed at the hayseed, telling his teammates he was going to make mincemeat outta the rookie. But in an interview after the game, Cobb said that one second he was watching the kid take an easy windup and then something blew past him that hissed with danger. Right then, Cobb said, he knew he'd met the most powerful arm ever turned loose in a ballpark."

"Marcos does throw fast for sure," the mom said.

"You mean Walter," her husband corrected.

She shook her head in frustration. "Here's what I'm gonna do. Jersey number. Name. Nickname. Parents' names. Then laminate. One roster for each family. Hells bells, only way to keep these kids straight."

A waitress came over balancing a huge tray of burger baskets. Noses lifted and inhaled. Just like that, all talk of turn-of-the-century baseball legends ceased.

Leo made quick work of his burger and fries, slammed one more water and stood up from the table.

"Tom, can you organize things here? Make sure about rides back to the hotel? I'm going to catch a few innings of the Des Moines-Ames game." Leo reached for his wallet and pulled out a $10 bill.

A parent held his hand up. "Oh no you don't. Coach, we got this. Least we can do."

"I'll wrangle things here," Tom said. "Which Des Moines team is playing?"

"Des Moines Black. Dixon's bunch."

"Take good notes. So we know what to expect tomorrow."

Leo pulled on his baseball cap. "We know what to expect from them. I'm more interested in Ames. Thanks for the burger, everyone." Leo turned to leave, but stopped. "I know our kids are dying to get in the pool. But only one hour. All right? Big day tomorrow."

Tom nodded. "Got it."

"See you all," Leo said. He took a moment to smile ever so slightly at Jess.

"I might see you at the fields," Jess said. "I need to walk Ike."

"I can take him if you want," Leo said.

Jess shook her head. "As if you don't have enough going on. We'll see you a little later."

A baseball field under the lights at night is a masterpiece of simple green geometry. Circles, rectangles, squares, organized within straight white lines angling away from home plate. In the short lifespan of each game the white lines dictate an outcome. A baseball can land just inside the chalk to shouts of joy, jumping athletes, full hearts. Or a baseball can land just outside the chalk, causing ascending cheers to fall apart in mid-air.

Leaning on a cyclone fence that ran the length of the field, Leo stood near first base. He pondered the chalk lines of his life. Where would he end up? Happily inside the line? Or foul? Had you asked him when he left Illinois on his unlikely journey, he would have said the latter. Now he just squinted at the white line in front of him, wondering.

"Heya Leo," Doc said, approaching in an unhurried gait. He had a contented look on his face. "Don't you just love night ball?"

"Hard to beat," Leo said, shaking Doc's hand.

"Whale of a game your boys played today. Urbandale—those kids are no slouches."

"Yeah. We might have caught them on an off day."

"Could be," Doc said. "You never know with baseball. Enjoy it."

Leo pulled a folded piece of paper out of his back pocket and made a note about number 15 from Ames. A big strong kid who had just struck out on a changeup. "Where are Jerome and Frank?"

"They're scouting the other field. It's Des Moines White versus Cedar Falls over there. Been hearing a lot of cheering."

"Not much of a game here, it seems." The scoreboard read 10-2 in favor of Des Moines Black. "Did I miss anything important?"

"Nah," Doc said. "It's one-sided. I have it all written down. Four home runs. Two by Billy Dixon. That kid's bat has pop."

Leo took Doc's notes. "Yeah. He's going to be a tough out."

Doc looked shocked. "You're not going to pitch to him. Just walk him and take your chances elsewhere."

Leo frowned. "There might be a spot for that. But sometimes if you throw a kid to the wolves, he comes back leading the pack."

"I'd just walk him," Doc said. "But you don't tell me how to deliver a calf so I'll stay out of your hair."

It was the top of the fifth inning, and Ames went down 1-2-3. "How many pitchers has Dixon used?" Leo asked.

"No one has thrown more than two innings. Same as you did."

Leo nodded. "How'd their starter look?"

"Dominant. He's their ace."

"I remember him from the scrimmage. Leans on the curve. Has a decent fastball. No changeup."

Doc pointed to the notes he'd given Leo. "Yep. Started most kids off with a curveball. He's got a knee-buckler."

"Good to know," Leo said.

"I'll get Jerome's and Frank's notes and slide 'em under your door."

"Thanks."

Doc hiked up his pants. "Well, I got to go get rid of a couple cups of coffee." He put a hand on Leo's shoulder. "You're doing Dannaka proud. Fun as all get-out. Takes me back. The parents I talk to, they sure like the way you treat the kids and the game."

"Thanks," Leo said.

Doc headed for the restrooms, telling Leo, because of his frequent visits, he could get there blindfolded.

Leo paid close attention to the throwing arms of the catchers and shortstops. The catcher for Des Moines was a bit lazy getting the ball back to his pitcher, but that could be attributed to the score. Leo made a note. And added that throws from the Ames shortstop were inconsistent.

Jess and Ike made their way past the bleachers. Weaving through parents in camp chairs, she waved. Leo waved back. Ike strained against his leash, pulling toward every chair, thinking he needed to say hello. Or better yet, end up on someone's lap.

Leo watched Jess. Her tan legs braced against the 30-pound pup, her slim, muscular arms doubled up on the leash. Regardless, Ike got plenty of licks in as they stepped through the crowd.

"Pretty lopsided game," she said. Ike raced to Leo, licking, whining with excitement. "Hard to compete with that," Jess deadpanned.

"I doubt you're up for public displays of affection just yet," Leo said, looking at Jess as he knelt on the grass to scratch Ike's upturned belly.

"Probably right," she said. "But I might surprise you."

"Big talker." Leo stood, closing the distance between them.

"Careful." Jess lifted an eyebrow. "I've had two vodka tonics."

Leo looked at Jess intently. She held eye contact. He could feel their kiss from last week. Since then, they hadn't had any time to talk about it, or, for that matter, return to it. Leo's jaw clenched. "I should call your bluff," he said, disappointed in himself. "But I need to keep my mind on baseball."

Jess smiled, less tentatively than usual. Stadium lights kaleidoscoped in her eyes. She let her arm brush against his. She was beautiful, her freckled nose, her one perfectly shaped ear turned toward him. "I'm going to walk Ike. You've got a rain check on that kiss. Don't let it expire, Coach."

She walked away, the overgrown pup pulling her toward a mystery smell as he browsed the taller grass snug to the fence. She turned and looked over her shoulder, a wisp of hair caught in the night breeze. Leo took off his cap and slapped it against his leg for emphasis. Jess waggled her fingers and went on her way.

His team had the game in hand. Dixon's focus wandered. His eyes found Leo and Jess across the field on the first base side. Dixon wasn't completely sure what he just saw—but he was pretty sure. Leo and Jess stood closely by the fence. Talked closely. Something was going on.

"Well ain't that too cute for words," Dixon muttered. He spat and watched as the two of them separated. "Guess I'll have to find the right time to bring *that* up at tomorrow's game."

Rundown Saloon

The Sundown Saloon was looking par for the course. It was raining hard when Wade ducked under the leaky awning over the front door. The bar's lighted sign in the parking lot, with many bulbs burned out, read: undo Soon. The innuendo was lost on Wade. Truth be told, Wade was pretty much lost altogether these days.

His usual bar stool was open. For the last few weeks, he'd been a Tuesday and Thursday guy: one Grasshopper, a few boats of popcorn and the same conversation.

Nancy pierced his ice cream cocktail with a red straw and slid it toward Wade.

"What did I do wrong?" he said, staring down at his green drink.

"Wade," Nancy said, patting his hand. "Wade," she said more tautly.

He looked at her.

"You did nothing wrong. Sometimes people just aren't right together."

He began to respond. "It's just—"

Nancy slung a bar towel over her shoulder and held up her index finger. "I know. You thought you were right for each other. You thought you were unpaired socks who finally found their match."

"Right. How did you know that?"

"Wade, you've told me that close to a hundred times."

Wade looked down at his Grasshopper. Not even layered swirls of green ice cream could entice him out his funk.

"You know what?" Nancy said. "You need to get drunk and pick up a new friend from the bar."

Wade shook his head. "No. Actuarial models show alcohol-induced one-night stands lead to a 30% uptick in unwanted pregnancies. That's not my kind of lovemaking."

"Too much information, Wade. On all fronts."

"Yeah. Sorry."

"Let me get you some popcorn," Nancy said.

When she returned to the bar, Wade was as she had left him. "Don't like my drink?" she said.

Wade mumbled something as the popcorn was set down in front of him.

"Listen Wade," Nancy said as someone on the other end of the bar called out for service. "Don't think for a minute you're the first person on God's green Earth to get his or her heart stomped flat."

"Bet it never happened to you," he said, fiddling with a piece of popcorn that had spilled onto the bar.

"Wade, shit. Don't be ridiculous and don't be pathetic. Sure it happened to me."

He looked up. "Really?"

"Yeah really."

"You're just saying that to make me feel better."

Nancy looked at him and slowly shook her head. "I shouldn't do this, but I'm going to tell you something about me, something I've never told anyone else. First, I got to get a beer for Sherm down there before he goes hoarse." Nancy rapped a knuckle on the polyurethane-coated bar. "But when I get back, if you're still in sad sack mode and not sipping on that drink I took the time to blender to perfection, my offer is off the table."

When Nancy returned, Wade was sucking down his Grasshopper. She asked, "How is it?"

Wade nodded enthusiastically, life coming back into him. "So what's the story?"

Nancy had a look on her face like she was on the end of a dock on a cloudy day about to dive into a cold lake. She took a deep breath, put both hands on the bar, leaning in toward Wade. She didn't want any of the regular neanderthals eavesdropping. "Wade?"

"Um-hmm."

"I'm guessing your health insurance is up to date."

"Yes."

"And you've got an excellent life insurance policy."

"Yes."

"Good. If you repeat a word of this to anyone, you're gonna need 'em."

Wade took a suck off his drink, looking at Nancy, not accustomed to such close proximity. He never knew how pretty her brown eyes were.

"Nancy?"

"Yep."

"You smell nice. Kinda pepperminty and buttery."

"Wade?"

"Uh-huh."

"That's your drink and the popcorn."

Wade's Grasshopper was sucked completely dry. "Holy shitoly." He breathed out a little whistle to punctuate the end of Nancy's story. "I never, ever woulda guessed. A tough gal like you. Crying yourself to—"

Nancy gave him the shut up frown. "The bar has ears, Wade," she said, freezing him in her gaze. "The bar has ears."

Nancy went off to refill glasses as Wade contemplated her story. Nancy was in love once. She was convinced it was mutual. They confided in one another. Shared dreams and disappointments. Even talked about running away, an adventure—maybe to Alaska. They opened a joint bank account and started putting money in.

He lived an hour and a half northeast in a town called Winterset. It was easiest for him to come see her because he traveled in the area selling Pioneer seed. So that's what they did. They made the most of every hour they had together.

Just about the time they were closing in on one year as a couple, Nancy had a friend with severe bunions who decided she couldn't take it anymore. It was time to have surgery. Her friend didn't have family close by so Nancy said she would take her to the hospital in Des Moines. The procedure was scheduled for 10:00, with discharge late that same afternoon.

After helping her friend get admitted for surgery, Nancy did some shopping in Des Moines, treated herself to a late lunch and returned to the hospital. Orthopedics was on the sixth floor. She mistakenly pressed seven: the maternity ward. When the elevator doors opened, whom did she run into? Her confidante. Her soulmate. Her future. Who, as it turned out, was manning a wheelchair for his wife as she held their newborn daughter. At his side stood his three-year-old son, holding a string of helium balloons that exclaimed: It's a Girl!

The douchebag was married. A big walking, talking, fabulous bullshit artist. He had her completely fooled. Nancy was unable to speak as he slipped past her, and hadn't spoken of it since. That moment had another enduring consequence. Nancy protected herself by, as she put it, only swimming in the shallow end of the relationship pool.

When Nancy finally made it back to Wade's stool, he broke the awkward silence.

"That was brave of you to share. I know you did it on my behalf and I'm grateful to you."

Nancy contemplated Wade. He had a polite chivalry to him that was cute. She'd been pelted by more than enough testosterone-laced bravado for one lifetime.

"Yes and no," she said. "I did it for you, but the more I got talking the more I was doing it for me. I haven't felt this good since I cleaned out the garage last fall." She smiled. A small act that wouldn't have drawn a second look unless you were an attention-to-detail type.

Wade saw a different Nancy when she let her mask down.

DES MOINES BLACK

Enjoying a light breeze in the outfield, Leo sat on an overturned bucket. His feet straddled the left field foul line. Head down, checking his lineup card, he lifted a hand. Across the outfield, in center, lined up on Tom Tink, the team crouched, ready for the signal. Leo dropped his hand. It was an all-out sprint.

They raced toward Coach. Reaching the foul line, the boys dropped, did three consecutive somersaults, rose to their feet and raced back to Tom Tink.

There was laughter and friendly taunting.

"One more," Leo shouted. "This time backwards. Both ways." Leo lifted and lowered his hand again.

Leo's lineup card was in pencil, as always. Each name was thoughtfully printed the night before, but not irrevocably. The baseball gods might whisper something in his ear before game time. That's why there are erasers.

Team: Dannaka 12U AAA All-Stars
Coach: Leo Hamill
Assistant Coach: Tom Tink

1) No. 1 Runt 2B
2) No. 8 Rabbit LF
3) No. 4 Money SS
4) No. 13 Rip CF
5) No. 3 Havoc RF
6) No. 2 Seeds 3B

7) No. 6 Walter P
8) No. 11 Pot Roast C
9) No. 12 Math 1B
10) No. 15 Q-tip
11) No. 5 Gramps
12) No. 9 Daze

Leo nodded at his lineup and looked at his boys in center field. A good bunch of athletes, but an even better bunch of teammates. He shouted, "Okay gentlemen, bond and juggle time. Havoc, you run it today."

"Let's go Dannaka!" Havoc hollered, leading them in a sprint to the dugout. Each boy got a baseball out of the ball bucket. "Time to bond, boys. See red and it's dead."

Dannaka spread out on the grass in front of their dugout. They had already taken batting practice, fly balls and ground balls in the outfield. The infield had been dragged and prepped for the game, so no team was allowed to take grounders there.

Each Dannaka player started with his own ball, simply tossing it from one hand to the other, watching the flight, focused on the red laces, seeing it all the way into the other hand.

"Behind the back," Havoc shouted. Now each player tossed the ball from behind his back, over the opposite shoulder, to be caught in front of his body with the same hand that tossed it. Then the ball was flipped to the other hand to do the same behind-the-back toss over the other shoulder. There was an eye-catching, crisscrossing rhythm of action as the ball's trajectory arced sure-handedly over one shoulder and then the other.

"Juggle," Havoc told the boys. "On your own." Each player got three balls and began to juggle. As Leo walked in from the outfield, he soaked it in, watching his boys smiling in the sunshine, clad in handsome gold and charcoal gray old-school uniforms, displaying their hand-eye coordination, making juggling look easy. "No balls on the ground," he said, walking past them to the shade in the dugout.

"Coach?" Havoc asked. "Can we go for three-man?"

Leo tipped his cap back as he sat down on the dugout bench. "You think you're ready, boys?"

"Born ready," the team said on cue.

"Three-man it is."

The team let out a collective cheer.

"Pot Roast," Leo said, "you warm up Walter." Tom Tink went

along to oversee the batterymates.

Meanwhile, groups of three players stood on the infield grass. Every unit formed a loose triangle, giving each boy enough space to juggle his three balls. While the balls looped through the air, Leo counted out, "One … two … three." On three, each juggler tossed one of his balls to the guy on his right, who seamlessly incorporated that new ball into his trio. And on and on it went until one player in the group dropped a ball, which eliminated them. They then sat on the grass, heckling the remaining threesomes.

The gathering fans loved it. Des Moines' players had seen some of this when the teams scrimmaged in May but Dannaka's warmup routine had gone from pretty cool to jaw-dropping. An umpire, looking on, checked his watch. Five minutes until first pitch. He'd never seen a pre-game ritual like this.

Dixon approached the ump. "Hey Cam," he said. "Looks like the circus is back in town." Dixon handed the ump two brand-new game balls, as was required by the tournament.

The ump picked up some dirt, spat in his hands and rubbed up each baseball. "Unusual bunch."

"Who you umping with today?"

"A guy named Johnson. Seems good enough."

Dixon asked, "Where's he from?"

"Ames, I guess."

"Who's behind the plate?"

"He is."

"Well it's good to have one ump on the field from Des Moines. Just to make sure we don't get screwed."

The ump looked at Dixon. "Didn't you used to have the Dannaka team?"

"Yeah. But we never disrespected the game like these idiots. Somersaults in the outfield for chrissakes. Maybe if we were playing girls softball."

The ump chortled. "This new Dannaka coach, he's an ex-Cub for real?"

"Big washout, that's what's real. Another high school star that couldn't cut it. I'm not impressed."

The ump's attention swung to Dannaka's pitcher as he warmed up. Walter was finishing with fastballs for two reasons. One, to get a good sweat going. And two, every time his fastball thudded into Pot Roast's mitt, the Des Moines kids got a little tighter. "That pitcher can bring it," the ump said. "He looks dark complected."

"Friggin' wetback," Dixon hissed. "Never would I take a jersey off a Des Moines kid and put it on some kid who isn't even from here."

The ump nodded. "Don't seem right." Walter kept firing warmup strikes.

Dixon leaned in. "That Dannaka team has two of 'em. Twins. I told that new coach I wouldn't take those kids on my team. Not in a million years. Said I'd sooner quit." Dixon put his hands on his hips, his large belly protruding. "Here I am."

"That's respectable," the ump said.

Dixon spat. "First we allow these Mexicans to steal our jobs. Now we let them take over our national pastime. That's bullshit."

The umpire glowered. "Amen."

"Well, like I said. Glad to have one of ours umping the bases today. Our kids deserve nothing less."

The ump watched as Pot Roast threw his arm over Walter's shoulders, sharing a laugh, making their way back to the dugout.

"Cam," Dixon said, "good catchin' up. And by the way, if that truck of yours is in need of an upgrade, you see me directly. I'll get you a better deal than I'd give my own mother."

The ump liked the sound of that.

The head coaches and captains came out for the coin flip. Leo, who rotated his captains, had Walter and Truman with him today. Dixon had his same two: Billy Dixon and their tall, athletic shortstop, Hud Doran. The Dannaka boys first shook hands with the umps, then with the opposing coach, then with the opposing captains. That was the Dannaka way. The coaches exchanged lineup cards.

"Dannaka, since you traveled the farthest, you can call it." The home plate ump asked Leo, "Coach, who's calling for your team?"

"Walter?" Leo said. "You want it?"

Walter, introverted by nature, said Truman should do it.

"Call it in the air," the ump said, sending a 50-cent piece flipping into the blue sky, flicking sunlight with each revolution.

"Tails," Truman called.

The coin landed in the dirt, heads.

Groaning to retrieve the coin, the ump told Des Moines they won the toss. "Home or visitor?"

"Home," Billy Dixon declared. "Nice call, Runt," he scoffed.

As Dixon, his son and their shortstop made their way back to the dugout, Coach Dixon couldn't help himself. "If that other one could speak English," he said, "we mighta lost the toss." That got a big laugh.

The team gathered around Leo and Coach Tink in the dugout. "All right, guys," Leo said. "It's Dannaka baseball time. Just like yesterday. It can be Urbandale. Des Moines. Iowa City. Dubuque. Cedar Rapids. I don't care. Forget about the jerseys they're wearing. It's time for us to go on offense. Let's pick up right where we left off last night. Take your plan to the batter's box, step out and review it as you go, especially you first three guys. Set the table for us, right?"

Leo spread his hands in disbelief. "I don't see a lot of smiles from an undefeated baseball team." The guys collectively exhaled and grinned. "Math, we faced this pitcher in our scrimmage. What do you remember?"

Math squinted. "2xC-F, I think. Coach Tink?"

Tom looked at his notebook. "Yep. Lover of the curve. Two speeds on it. Fastball is just average."

Leo looked around the group. "So what's our plan?"

"Sit on his curve," Ryan Rippen said. "He'll hang it, we'll bang it."

"There ya go," Leo said. "All right, hands in."

Huddling up, the boys piled hands one atop the other.

"Walter, you lead us."

Walter licked his lips. "One, two, three …"

"Dannaka!" the team shouted in unison.

Leo walked with Truman out of the dugout into the sunshine. It wasn't yet 10:30, but the temperature was already 70 degrees. Truman, helmet on, spat into his batting gloves, clapped once, and began to time the pitcher with warmup swings. Leo stood next to him, saying nothing. The boy needed a quiet space to tune into his upcoming at-bat.

"What do you think about a bunt, Coach?" Truman asked. "Get some traffic on the base paths, pronto."

Leo edged closer, attentive to the swinging bat. "Let's see how they play the infield. Corners back, lay it down. But if the corners pinch, attack early or late and rip it down either line."

A hint of a smile curled on Truman's face. "I hope he comes inside." Truman, a left-handed batter, would smoke that pitch right down Billy Dixon's throat at first.

Leo patted Truman on the back. "Good plan now. Straighten out one of those curves, huh?"

Runt made his way to the batter's box, watching the catcher throw down to second base to complete the pitcher's warmup. The catcher had a howitzer.

With just one foot in the batter's box, Runt looked to third for the sign. Leo went through a series of quick nose touches, cheek taps and swipes down his arm. Along the way he touched the top of his cap with his palm, which meant the batter was on his own to decide: bunt or swing away.

Runt fully stepped into the batter's box and tapped the plate with his bat.

The umpire pointed to the Des Moines pitcher and firmly said, "Play."

Billy Dixon took five big steps in from the first base bag. "Watch for the bunt. He can't hit."

Runt edged closer to the plate. If a curve got too close, he'd take one for the team.

The third baseman snuck in too, but not as close as Billy Dixon.

The first pitch was a big curve, just as Truman expected. But it was thrown at the center of the plate to start, so Truman knew the ball would be outside by the time it got to him.

"Ball," the ump called sharply.

Truman stepped out, got the same sign from Leo, and crowded the plate even more.

"Easy out," Billy Dixon shouted across the infield.

The pitcher looked in for the sign, nodding yes.

"This kid's nothing." Dixon's taunting was incessant.

Truman thought, *Here comes a fat, juicy yakker and I'm going to knock it through Dixon's teeth.*

This time the pitcher started his curveball more at Truman's shoulder. The pitch was going to end up on the inside corner, right where Truman wanted it.

Truman uncoiled. His hips leading his hands, his hands getting the barrel of the bat to the baseball before it crossed the plate, driving straight through the ball so not to yank it foul.

Billy Dixon was still jawing when he heard the unmistakable sound of an aluminum bat squaring up a baseball. The line drive was on him so fast all Dixon could do was blurt out a shriek, throw his arms in front of his face and fall backward. The baseball scorched over his head, landed fair and scooted for the right field corner.

Double or triple. Double or triple. Truman knew he had an extra-base hit. Base running was something he and the team consistently worked on. Truman curled through first, hitting the inside corner of the bag, put his head down—avoiding the temptation to watch the right fielder chasing the ball. He pumped for second. Halfway there, he picked up Coach Leo, looking for his sign.

Leo threw up his hands, which meant Truman would play it safe: stand-up double. Coach wasn't going to risk making the first out of the game at third.

Rabbit batted next. He also smoked a double, which Leo called switching places with the runner. Truman came across home plate for the game's first run.

Money walked and with two on, Ryan Rippen did what a cleanup hitter is supposed to do: cleaned the bases with a three-run no-doubter to center. His old team hung their heads as he trotted the bases, beaming.

Coach Dixon started yelling at his players the moment he hit the top step of the dugout. He marched to the mound, chewing out his pitcher as he went. He yelled for the infield to huddle up and he berated them, too—especially his boy Billy who he called a giant pussy for not getting in front of a little line drive. Then he laid into his pitcher.

"Pull your head out of your ass and throw something other than a first-pitch curveball. Can't you see they're sitting on that pitch?" He grabbed his catcher by the chest protector. "Come here! Do you want to sit on the bench the rest of the tournament?"

An answer leaked out of the catcher. "No."

"Then call a smart game. Mix up the pitches. Let's go. This is Dannaka for chrissakes, not the Yankees."

It was 5-0 after the first half inning, and it could have been worse. Dannaka's last out was a close play at first. It appeared Math beat it out, which would have scored the runner on third. Leo decided not to question the ump at first. He walked over to Bale instead, who was keeping the book.

"About that third out," he said to Bale.

"That was no out," Bale interrupted.

Leo continued. "Circle it twice."

"How come, Coach?"

"I like to keep track of all the close outs, for both teams. So make sure you circle anything close."

Bale nodded.

Through the first two innings, Walter was in complete command. Six up, six down, five by strikeout. His fastball completely overpowered the Des Moines kids. They were intimidated and it showed by how far off the plate they stood as balls hissed past them. Just when they worked up the nerve to get aggressive at the plate, Walter would drop in a slow curve, which they flailed at.

Leo stood at the corner of the dugout with a decision to make. He called Tom Tink over. "What do you think, Tom? Throw Walter another inning?"

"Heck yes," Tom said. "Maybe two. He's got 'em in his back pocket."

"I was thinking of pitching Q-tip next."

"You mean next inning next? Or eventually next?"

"Next inning next."

Tom was flabbergasted. "Why? Walter's in a groove."

Leo looked at Tom matter-of-factly. "Walter is always in a groove. If we're going to win this tournament—bigger yet, for this team to go deep in the playoffs and get to state—we need a lot of pitchers who have thrown in high-pressure situations. It would be good for your boy to get that experience."

Tom was reluctant.

"Is there something I should know?" Leo asked. "Do you think his nerves can take it?"

Tom looked at Leo. "His nerves? Fine. Mine? Not so sure."

Leo gave Tom's shoulder a shake and turned around to the dugout. The players maneuvered past each other, getting ready to bat in the top of the third. "Walter," he said. "Great job out there. You go to first next inning. Pot Roast, warm up Q-tip."

"Yes!" Q-tip ran to the bucket for a couple of baseballs. "Don't worry, Walter," he assured him. "I got your shutout."

In the third inning, with Havoc on first after being hit by a pitch, Leo gave him two thumbs up. Not the most subtle sign, but Leo didn't care. Havoc was to take a big lead after the first pitch, luring the catcher into a pickoff attempt. The moment the catcher released the ball to first, Havoc would break for second. The idea was to get the other team throwing the ball around and force an error. Havoc was nearly impossible to get out when he was in a pickle between bases, and almost without fail, other teams couldn't keep him from advancing.

The play worked to perfection. As the Des Moines catcher rifled the ball down to Billy Dixon at first, Havoc broke for second. By the time the second baseman figured out what was happening, both he and Havoc were racing to the base. Billy threw a bullet to the bag, but with all the confusion, the ball sailed untouched into left field. Havoc never slowed down, rounding second coming hard to third. Leo dropped to a knee and signaled for Havoc to slide as the throw came in to the third baseman too late.

"You're OUT!" the ump hollered.

Leo couldn't believe his ears, and the Des Moines third baseman could not have looked more surprised by the call.

"What!" Havoc screamed, jumping up from the base.

"Ump," Leo said. "You're kidding me. His hand was in before their kid even caught the ball."

"I was SO SAFE!" Havoc grabbed his helmet in anger.

"I said he's out." The ump had made his call from the infield dirt on the shortstop side of second base.

Leo put his hands on Havoc's shoulders and told him to cool down. Then he continued with the ump, calmly. "Come on. Maybe the home plate ump had a better angle. Ask for some help. See what he saw." Leo gestured to the other umpire.

The infield ump took choppy little steps in Leo's direction. "Do you want to get tossed?"

Leo didn't have words. "Tossed?"

"One more word and you're out."

You wouldn't know out if it were staring you in the face! was what Leo wanted to say. Instead he gave Havoc a pat on the butt and told him to get some water.

The game turned on that moment. Dannaka got mad, tightening up. An unlikely error on a double-play ball through Money's legs at short led to two Des Moines runs.

In the fourth inning, Billy Dixon hit a two-run blast to tie it.

Neither team scored in the fifth.

The sixth would be the last inning, even if the score remained tied, because the tournament hadn't advanced out of pool play yet.

Bale looked at the scorebook and announced the hitters due up. "We got Math, then top of the order with Runt and Rabbit. C'mon guys."

Leo had everyone huddle up. "Boys, forget about everything up to this point. We've got a one-inning game against a team we're better than. Just get back to playing our way." Leo looked at the tension in the boys' faces. "There's only one thing we can do. Caps off."

The boys removed their caps.

"Shake 'em to the baseball gods." The players held their caps by the bills, upside down, shaking them back and forth. "Good juju will fall in, but only if you believe."

"Stand up," Havoc said.

"Let's dance," Pot Roast added.

"Baseball gods come to us," Truman said in the deepest voice he could muster.

The group spun slowly in a circle inside the tight dugout, chanting, shaking their caps, laughing. The Des Moines team had taken the field. They stared on.

Math led off the inning with a line shot up the middle that somehow the pitcher speared for an out. That brought up the top of the order. Runt had two hits on the day, which put a cork in Billy Dixon. It did not, however, bring a stop to Coach Dixon's incessant screaming at his players from the top step of the dugout.

Tuning that out, Truman had a definite plan for his at-bat. *Low fastball,* he thought. He dug into the batter's box, crowding the plate. The first pitch whizzed in, high and tight. Ball one. He stepped out, checked the sign from Leo, adjusted his batting gloves and dug back in.

Truman watched a slow curve drop in for a high strike. Not the pitch he was looking for. He was fine with letting it go. *C'mon low fastball.* Truman took a deep breath and blew out, slowing everything down.

The next pitch came at him fast. Truman focused on the spin of the laces: a four-seamer streaking in low. He squared and laid down a firm bunt along the third baseline. Bolting out of the batter's box he knew it would be a close play at first. To be effective, Truman's bunt needed to roll far enough from the catcher without getting too far up the third baseline.

Charging the ball, the Des Moines third baseman stumbled slightly. He managed a barehanded pickup, took an awkward step and rifled a side-armed throw to Billy Dixon at first. The baseball's spin caused it to hook. Billy stretched with everything he had but the throw pulled his toe off the bag as Truman's foot pounded down safely on first.

The infield umpire's fist came through the air like a swinging hammer. "You're out!"

Tom Tink, coaching first base, nearly jumped out of his uniform. "His foot is off the bag! Look! It's off the bag!"

Truman ran through first base in disbelief. The fans booed. Doc and Jerome uncharacteristically joined in. Leo left the coaching box at third and jogged across the diamond.

"I caught it first, then my foot came off," Billy Dixon said.

"Yeah," the ump said to no one in particular. "Caught it. Then foot off."

Mild-mannered Tom Tink was literally hopping mad. "That's complete bull crap!" He got nose-to-nose with the ump. "You should be ashamed of yourself."

"Don't get up in my face," the portly umpire warned.

"Yeah. What are you gonna do about it?"

Leo stepped between the two men. "Tom! Cool it."

Tom spoke in his defense. "His foot was way off the base."

"Was not," Billy Dixon said.

Truman got into it now. "Was so you lousy cheat."

"SHUT UP EVERYONE!" Leo's outburst shocked the group into silence—extending into the stands. He addressed the ump calmly. "What did you see?"

The umpire's voice quavered. "Billy made the catch. Then his foot came off."

"Billy?" Leo said.

The ump nodded. "Yeah. The first baseman."

"What's the name of my first baseman?" Leo asked.

The ump shrugged. "How would I know?"

Leo shook his head. "So that's it. Unbelievable." Leo looked at the Des Moines dugout where Dixon stood, leaning against the fencing, arms crossed, a smug smile on his face.

"C'mon Truman," he said. "You're better than this."

Des Moines got a run in the bottom of the sixth to win the game. The entire team streaked out of the dugout to dogpile the player with the winning hit.

Dannaka jogged in, heads down, some crying, ducking into the dugout. Emotionally, they were wiped out. No one wanted to line up for the post-game handshake.

Truman spoke up. "Guys," he said. "Guys!" He waited. One by one his teammates looked at him. "Dannaka doesn't give in to bad sportsmanship. Dannaka doesn't give in to cheating. And Dannaka doesn't give in to crap umpires. We're better than Des Moines, in more ways than just baseball." He paused as that sunk in. "Let's line up."

Truman made his way up the dugout steps, looking back. No one had budged. Bale stood, dropped the scorebook on the bench behind him, and followed. Then Ryan Rippen stood, and Havoc and Walter and Rabbit. Pot Roast ran his shirt across his eyes and joined Math, Money, Q-tip and the rest of the team as they stepped onto the field.

In the stands, Jess stood up and began clapping. Doc joined her. Then Jerome and Frank. It cascaded and soon every fan, regardless of their allegiances, stood and applauded as Dannaka walked onto the ballfield to shake hands.

As usual the head coaches were last in line. Leo grabbed Dixon's hand and pulled him in close. "You ought to be ashamed of yourself."

"What?" Dixon said, trying to make light of the situation. "A few close ones went our way today. That's baseball."

Leo pushed away, feeling sick to his stomach. "That was not baseball."

In silence, the Dannaka players packed up their gear in the dugout. The team scheduled to play next waited. Dannaka filed out, hearing the same words over and over as they passed. "You got robbed."

The team planned a quick meeting by the batting cages under a giant shady oak tree. Leo said he'd be there in five minutes. He went off to find the tournament director to lodge a formal complaint against the umpire and check the bracket to see when and where their next game would be.

On his way back, Leo went through a mental checklist of what to say to his team. *We have to put that one behind us.* And, *No doubt, that ump stunk and I told the tournament director he can't do anymore of our games.* And, *Time to focus on winning the consolation bracket because that earns a bid to the state tournament, too.* And *I'm proud of how you guys handled yourselves as baseball players and young men.*

But when Leo came up the path toward the batting cages and saw what his team was up to, he knew he wouldn't need to say a single word.

DELIVERING PAPERS

I t was a four-hour round-trip drive from Dannaka to the printing press in Lincoln, Nebraska. Jerome made the trek every Wednesday morning, bright and early, to pick up his newspapers. Weather permitting, by 3:30 that same afternoon, most business and home delivery would be completed.

As he walked to Doc's clinic, Jerome had one folded newspaper squeezed under his arm while he worked on a second. He could fold and deliver papers in the dark—something he had done in Dannaka as a boy. Jerome had a small delivery team on the residential and commercial sides of the *Bugle* business, but sometimes he'd hand-deliver a few. It reminded him that his job was about more than circulation numbers; it was about connecting with readers.

"Hello Jess," Jerome said. She was organizing postcards that reminded customers their pets were due for shots.

"Hi Jerome," she said. "Nice enough day for you?"

"Is it ever. The boss in back?"

"Sure is."

"Any toothy animal with him I should know about?"

"Just Doc. He has been known to bite."

Jerome lifted an eyebrow. "All bark, that one. Say, I have today's paper for you. Hot off the press."

Jess smiled at Jerome. He was a hard nut to crack. Single his whole life—"married to the newspaper" he liked to say. Intellectual. Didn't suffer fools. Seemed to go about his days with a Do Not Disturb sign hung around his neck. But behind his wire-rimmed glasses and clenched jaw, there was a good person. He was just careful who he allowed in. "I appreciate the delivery," Jess said.

"By the way," Jerome added. "There's an Opinion piece that may catch your interest." Saying no more, he left her with a polite nod and went through the door. A hallway led to Doc's office.

"You back here?" Jerome scanned Doc's office, finding it empty.

Doc's desk made a mighty thump. "Ow. Hurt." Doc crawled out from under his metal desk, holding the top of his head. "You gave me a fright."

"Same here," Jerome said. "What are you doing down there?"

"Ah, a button came off my shirt. Margaret will give me the stink eye if she thinks I came to work like that." Doc slapped the pearlescent button on his desktop. "All the same, more trouble than it's worth." The two old friends looked at each other. "To what do I owe the pleasure?"

Jerome approached the desk, carefully slid the button aside and set down the newspaper. "Brought you the *Bugle*."

Doc straightened up, feeling his head for a lump. "I see that. Any particular reason why?"

"Mind if I sit?" Jerome asked.

"Help yourself."

"I'm not keeping you?"

"Not at all."

Jerome sat down. He laced his fingers together, his hands resting at his belt buckle. "I wrote my piece about the tournament last weekend. Wanted to get your thoughts on it."

"Seems a little late for that." Doc opened the newspaper with a snap.

"I don't mean input," Jerome clarified. "I was more wondering how it strikes you."

Doc nodded and paged through to the Opinion section. His eyes settled on *Jerome's Jottings*. "I usually use this section for fish wrap." Doc put on his reading glasses.

"That would require you actually catching fish," Jerome replied. Doc pretended not to hear. He sat back in his chair with the article.

I've never been more proud of third place

I spent last weekend watching Iowa kids play baseball. Gracious sakes, did I learn a lot.

My destination was the Des Moines Regional Little League Jamboree. From the moment I stepped out of my car, the sight of neatly uniformed kids hustling to their positions, the sound of voices rising in unison when a baseball is well-struck, the aroma of hotdogs turned on the grill by dedicated parents, it awakened memories in me.

As a youth baseball player myself, I made the trip to Des Moines with my teammates from Dannaka. The automobiles didn't travel as comfortably and the maintenance of the fields was not nearly what it is today, but the heart of the experience remains undeterred by time.

I traveled with a few teammates from my bygone days: Doc Gifford and Frank Galligan. If you've been around town more than a few years, you'll certainly recognize those names. We had come to cheer on our very own Dannaka 12U AAA All-Stars—a team undefeated in conference play—now scheduled to meet the best teams in the 35-county Central and Southwest regions of Iowa.

Friday night, under the lights, we drew Urbandale, the number one seed and last year's tournament winner. No one thought the game would be close. They were right. Except, it wasn't the favored Urbandale that won by the lopsided margin of 5-1. It was little Dannaka.

Saturday morning broke, offering postcard-perfect baseball weather. Fat white clouds settled over green baseball diamonds and there was just enough breeze to make a person grateful for it. Our next opponent was Des Moines Black, or so we thought. Actually, the real opponent we faced that morning was the umpire.

Let me say now I have no stomach for attributing a loss to "Blue," as umpires are universally called. But in Dannaka's 6-5 loss Saturday morning, all five close calls on the basepaths, all ruled by the same umpire, went against Dannaka. I talked with numerous fans after the game—supporters from both teams. They were shocked by the umpiring. Comments went from the unprintable to a quote one Des Moines parent encouraged me to publish: "I've never seen so many calls be first of all, wrong, and second, go for one team."

My intent here is not to complain about umpiring. The real story is what came next. Leo Hamill, our outstanding first-year coach, will set the stage.

"I submitted an official complaint about the way our game was umpired and requested going forward that that particular ump not be scheduled for our games. I was convinced he wanted us to lose, and I said as much."

Leo continued. "Walking back for a post-game talk with my team, I expected it to be quiet as a wake. Hardly. The boys were standing in a circle, arms slung over each other, having a bubble gum blowing contest—just like after every game. No feeling sorry for themselves. No whining. It took all of five minutes and they were over it. Ready to play more baseball."

Leo says the Dannaka kids realized why they were playing tournament baseball in the first place: Have fun. Get better. Secure a bid to the state tournament in August. They knew if they won the rest of their games, they'd win the consolation bracket and earn that bid.

"I was more proud of those kids at that moment, blowing bubbles, than when we went on to beat Ames, Des Moines White and Council Bluffs to take third. Right then I saw what an unusual group of athletes we have. They learned that baseball isn't always fair, but it always favors those who stay positive."

As for this ex-Little Leaguer, I learned that a third-place trophy can be a greater victory than a first-place trophy. And that a ballplayer is never too young nor too old to be taught something new by the grand game of baseball.

Doc folded the newspaper, set it on his desk and rapped it with his knuckle. "You knocked it out of the park."

"Really?" Jerome said in an unguarded moment.

"Really. Really good."

Jerome nodded. "I appreciate that."

"What do you think happened in that game? Bad luck, or something more?"

Jerome took off his glasses and held them in Doc's direction. "Either that ump was sorely in need of a pair of these or he was from Des Moines, knew the kids on the field, friends with a few parents—probably a pal of Dixon's, too."

"So he threw the game?"

Jerome pursed his lips. "You were there, what do you think?"

"He threw the game. And I bet Dixon had something to do with it."

As Jerome was on his way out, Jess looked up from her newspaper. She stood, walked over to him and hugged him hard.

"I've read it three times," she said.

Jerome wasn't a hugger. He stiffly patted her back. "Okay," he said.

She continued the embrace. "This is going straight into Truman's scrapbook."

"That's good to hear," Jerome said.

Jess spoke softly into his shoulder. "The only way to get rid of bad memories is to replace them with good ones."

SLEEPOVER

Before and after each practice and game, the team did 20 push-ups, led by Tom Tink. Not only did they have a unique manner of counting off the 20, but what they said changed, too. "Ready?" Tom yelled. The boys and Leo were poised off the ground, straight as planks. "Begin."

In unison the team barked out "D-A-N-N-A-K-A 1-2 A-A-A W-I-N I-T A-L-L." Twenty push-ups were nothing for these guys, especially Truman who was both light and a push-up hound.

Next came the good part. The boys unlaced their cleats, took off their socks and stood in the cool grass. They groaned with pleasure.

"Coach, you got the victory balloons?" Havoc asked.

"Sure do." Leo lugged a five-gallon bucket, usually full of wiffle balls, onto the outfield grass. It was a steamy July night at Poodle Park, where every home victory was celebrated with balloons.

"Line up," Leo commanded. The boys scrambled for position. "Bale, you too."

"You sure, Coach?" he said. "You got enough?"

"I'm sure. You kept a meticulous scorebook tonight. Even saw you sweat."

"That's true," Bale said, joining the line.

"Coach Tink, do you have the weapon?"

"Right here," he said, handing an old, dinged-up bat to Money, who was first in line.

"Victory balloons," Leo said joyfully, pulling the first water balloon out of the bucket. There were 30 more where that came from.

The game was simple. From 10 feet, Leo underhanded a plump water balloon into the batter's wheelhouse where it was wholeheartedly smashed into a burst of cool droplets, spraying the batter, face to toes.

Jess watched on from the bleachers with Bale's mom and a few other parents. "No wonder they're so motivated to win," Jess said.

Bale's mom looked on as her son took his turn at bat. "The way he keeps Bale involved, such a blessing. Lot of coaches would have been too busy to bother. We won the lottery with this one." She looked at Jess and gave her a small smile. "Hope he sticks around."

One of the parents said to Bale's mom, "You sure are brave, having the whole team for a sleepover."

She replied, "I asked Bale what he wanted for his birthday." She shrugged. "You only turn 13 once."

One by one the boys stepped up to the folded towel that served as home plate. Dirty, sweaty, most of all happy, they slotted the bat into the loaded position, studied Leo's hand as it swung forward releasing a jiggling, pear-shaped water balloon, until POW! A mighty swing atomized it into a refreshing mist. Every contact was greeted with a team-wide whoop.

Three players from the losing side lingered, standing behind the backstop, their fingers laced through the fencing. "Be a fun team to be on," one of the boys commented. The others just nodded, watching.

As always, Leo jogged around the fields after they were raked, tarped and put to bed. Since shedding excess weight, he was determined to keep it off. Equally important, running helped him unwind.

Suddenly, out of the darkening shadows, Ike appeared beside him, dragging his red leash. The stadium lights cast three dog shadows beneath him. "Hello Ike," he said. "Someone slipped you a Get Out Of Jail Free card, huh?"

Jess was sitting alone in the bleachers. Leo waved.

"You're making us all look bad," she said. Her voice carried to him on the cooling night air.

He made a circling gesture with his finger. "One more. For Ike's sake."

"That dog gets plenty exercise enough," she said.

Leo did his lap, ending at the umpire's building, which also housed the fuse box. He turned off the three breakers for Field 1, locked up the building and headed to the bleachers. One whistle and Ike came alongside him.

Jess sat in the dark, her eyes adjusting to where she could begin to see the stars. Leo sat next to her, closely. "If I stink I could go up a row."

She felt heat coming off him. "You stay put," she said.

They looked at each other. Jess was the picture of summer in shorts, sandals and an old Cubs T-shirt. "Summer looks good on you," Leo said.

"I'm happy." She let the notion breathe. "You've been so good for these kids. For Truman."

Leo leaned against her. "They're the ones doing me good. Got me back on track."

"I'm happy you're here," Jess said. "But it scares me just the same."

Leo sat back so he could get a better look at Jess. A frown creased between her eyebrows. "Why do you say that?"

She shrugged, her voice just above a whisper. "You appeared out of nowhere. You could just as easily disappear."

Leo took off his baseball cap. "You're not getting rid of me that easy." He gave her a smile that was near perfect. "I have a rain check on a kiss I wonder if I can use."

Jess nodded yes.

Leo pulled her into his arms and their kiss rearranged the stars.

Jess invited Leo to a late dinner, blushing slightly when she added that Truman would be at Bale's house for a birthday sleepover. Leo said dinner would be great and yes, he had heard all about the sleepover in the post-game chatter. He asked what he could bring. Beer, she told him.

After showering, Leo put on a pair of blue and white checked shorts, a collared golf shirt and his flip-flops. He thought better of the flip-flops and put on socks and tennis shoes.

"You look nice," Jess said, as Leo walked from his truck to her front porch where she sat on the steps. She was wearing a sleeveless navy sundress with pink flowers and a beige leather tie around her waist.

"Wow. Not as nice as you," he said. He set a paper bag down on the steps. "I like your hair like that." Jess's hair was tied up in a carefree bun.

"Thanks. It helps in this heat."

Leo reached into the bag. "This might help, too." He pulled out a six-pack of Budweisers by its plastic ring. "Want one?"

"Sure. Great."

Leo popped open a can and handed it to her. "Cheers," he said. "To summer nights."

Jess was wearing a trace of red lipstick and small hoop earrings. Leo considered Jess to be naturally cute—dressed in jeans, a T-shirt and wearing a baseball cap—but tonight he saw her elegance. "Cheers," she replied, lifting her beer, waiting for Leo to clink cans together.

Leo just stared.

"You're kinda looking at me funny," she said.

"Oh, sorry. Yeah, cheers." He tapped his can to hers and took a cold swallow.

"It's nice not to hurry with dinner," Jess said. "We're always in an endless sprint."

Ike whined at the screen door, waking from a nap to the sound of Leo's voice. His back end wiggled with delight.

"I got him," Leo said, getting up from the steps. Leo cracked the door and Ike didn't wait, busting out onto the porch, running a tight circle around Leo's legs. "Hey there, toad from the road. Do you remember when we met?"

Jess leaned back, letting her elbows settle on the step behind her. "How can he forget? You saved him." Jess's voice was serious.

Leo shook off the compliment. "More like we found each other. Both lost." Leo sat down next to Jess as Ike struck out on his own, his nose pulled to the grass by scent—maybe a fat field mouse.

Jess said, "Some day we need to talk about our pasts."

Leo nodded. "Yeah. But let's not hurry there." He took her hand in his. "Okay?"

"Yeah. For sure."

Leo drew a deep breath. "Sometimes I get stuck when I'm with you. Not sure what to say. Do I say what I'm thinking? What if it's the wrong thing?"

Jess squeezed his hand. "I know what you mean. But we get to make the rules. So how about if it's true, it's not the wrong thing to say?"

"Honesty is good. But can be tough—leaves you unprotected."

Jess agreed. "But it's better than the alternative. I lived a lot of half-truths with Wade. Half-truths on my side. He was always straight-forward."

"I get what you mean." Leo leaned in. "So can I ask you a personal question?"

Jess stiffened. "You can ask, yeah."

Leo chuckled. "And you'll answer me honestly?"

"I will."

Leo could feel his hand perspiring in Jess's. "Tonight, as you thought about how it might go … with you and me … and Truman's sleepover, did you wonder or think about, maybe, what if one person wanted to go further with this, you know, but the other wasn't ready for that?"

Jess watched Leo struggle to ask his question. "I thought about that a little bit. Then I thought if it's supposed to happen, it'll happen."

Leo nodded. "Okay. In the spirit of honesty, I'm not ready to go further than this right now. Don't get me wrong, I'm attracted to you in a million scary ways. I just want—need—to be deliberate, to settle into this, and I don't want you to misinterpret that, and I don't want it to create pressure between us, like, what is she thinking and what is he thinking and will tonight be the night or will never be the night?"

"Do you think never will be the night?" Jess asked.

"God, I hope not."

Jess smiled. Then laughed a little. "It was easier when we were teenagers. Didn't think, just did. For me that led to a lot of bad but one fabulous good." She shrugged. "You're not what I expected, Leo Hamill. And the more I realize that the happier I am for it. So how about we have a nice long kiss now. Then we'll make dinner."

Book

FIVE

STATE TOURNAMENT

"Get to first any way you can. Even if it's a home run."

—*Tom Tink, Dannaka assistant coach*

FRIDAY WITH DOC AND MARGARET

The late afternoon wind gusts were a welcome relief to the heat. Doc's work shirt was slung over a chairback next to him. He sat in the screened porch with a stone on either side of his newspaper to keep the pages from lifting off the table. He could hear Margaret humming as she stood outside at a nearby trellis of climbing beans, snapping off blue-ribbon dandies. Each one that she dropped into a ceramic bowl at her feet added a note to the music.

August can be unbearably hot in Dannaka. Corn and soybeans grow taller by the day and the vibrating buzz of cicadas pierces through leafy hardwood canopies. Doc had a cool washcloth on his neck as he sipped a glass of ice water. It had been a long week of tending to animals big and small—so much so, he was just now getting to the newspaper. The slightly sweet aroma of cornbread muffins baking in the kitchen visited Doc on the porch before a breeze snatched it away.

Turning a page, Doc landed at the Opinion section and *Jerome's Jottings*.

Iowa state tournament here we come

Confession: I can hardly contain my excitement. After a long baseball drought, Dannaka is headed to Ames next Friday through Sunday for the Little League state tournament, thanks to our 12U AAA All-Stars.

Unless you've been locked in a storm cellar for the past four and a half months, you already know that our traveling team has been playing great baseball, capped off by winning Iowa's Southwest district and finishing third in regional play. To say the least, our kids are poised to make a solid run at the state championship.

Which brings me to the heart of my thesis. Our Dannaka team

has already won the biggest prize, to my way of thinking. We have a cohesive team of young men who perform on the diamond as well as any team in our state and are peerless in the way they carry themselves as gentlemen athletes. There are no angry words shouted from coaches or players. And they accept the highs and lows of each game with stalwart positivity. Certainly, our kids will have moments where they're upset about an at-bat, an error or a close call going the wrong way—but it's just that: a moment. Then it's chins up and make the next play.

We've got a winner here, folks, no matter what happens next weekend. So come out, watch and cheer loudly. (Small town, big diaphragm, I like to say.) When the dust finally settles, what's most monumental about this accomplishment is the grace and exuberance of our Dannaka twelves, and the fashion in which they represent our fine town.

However, bringing home a state championship baseball trophy wouldn't be all bad, either. To each and every one of you, good luck. You deserve it, you really do.

Doc took a sip of water before sitting back in his chair. He thought about luck and if people really do get the luck they deserve. Certainly, up to this point, Leo hadn't. Jerome knew that. He knew what Leo had been through. Jerome was always attentive of the newswire, had a way of finding stories—

"What are you daydreaming about?" Margaret asked, coming into the porch with her bowl of fresh beans. She made sure the spring-loaded door didn't slam. "I simply can't keep up with those beans. Will you take a bowl next door to the Langstons?"

Doc groaned. "Can't you leave me sit?"

"I won't have these beautiful vegetables going to waste. Come now. Help me wash these up. If you're lucky, I'll sneak you a muffin."

That did the trick.

Jess and Leo arrived for dinner promptly at 6:00. Jess brought a cucumber salad fresh from her garden and Leo had a bottle of red wine. The front door was open to the screen door. Leo rapped and stepped in, to Jess's surprise. Then she remembered he'd been having dinner here almost weekly since he arrived.

"Hello," Leo called out.

"Back here." Doc's voice came from the porch. Jess put her salad on the kitchen counter and followed Leo.

Doc and Margaret stood up from the wicker sofa to greet their guests. "Welcome," Margaret said, smoothing her dress. "My, Jess. Don't you look stunning." Jess wore a tiered peach-colored skirt and white linen blouse. Friday dinner out to a friend's home was something you dressed for in Dannaka. Jess had passed that hint on to Leo, who wore a short-sleeve button down shirt and dress shorts. Leo set the wine down on the tableclothed harvest table.

Handshakes and hugs made everyone comfortable. Doc fixed vodka tonics for Jess and himself, Leo had a beer and Margaret was fine with water for the moment. The women went outside to look at Margaret's vegetable gardens and Doc's roses while the men sat at the table and got directly into the topic of baseball.

Doc said, "Holy smokes, can your boys hit line drives. Never seen anything like it."

"Yeah. Thanks. I like how they're swinging the bats."

"What's the secret?"

Leo uncrossed a leg and sat forward. Margaret had put a dish of Spanish peanuts out on the table. Leo popped one into his mouth. "The guys have a real good grasp of the strike zone. We have a thing called the Favorite Four."

"Sounds interesting. How does it work?"

Leo unfolded a paper napkin, spread it out on the table and grabbed a handful of peanuts. "Home plate is 17 inches wide, that's about six baseballs across. Imagine these are baseballs." Leo placed six peanuts end to end across the bottom of the napkin. "For your average 12-year-old, from knees to armpits, that distance is about 10 baseballs high." Leo began placing peanuts vertically. "So I lay out a strike zone just like this, only on the grass with baseballs." Leo kept placing peanuts until his rectangle was complete: six peanuts wide by 10 peanuts high. "I tell the guys, six times 10 equals 60 baseballs in your strike zone. But when you have no strikes, there are actually only four out of 60 you should swing at."

"The Favorite Four," Doc said, catching on.

"I put a square grouping of four balls in the center of that rectangle, like so. There's your Favorite Four."

Doc looked at the small square inside the larger rectangle. "Good focal point."

"Absolutely," Leo said. "We want to eliminate the hard-to-handle pitches early in the count."

Doc added on. "Those are the ones you swing at and miss or turn into an easy out."

"Exactly." Leo moved the grouping of four peanuts. "Now for some kids, those four balls might be a little higher in the zone—high-ball hitters—or a bit lower. Every one of my kids knows where his Favorite Four lives. Those are the balls they attack. That equals line drives."

Doc asked, "What about with one strike?"

Leo grabbed another handful of peanuts. "Now we fill in half of the strike zone, or about 30 balls to swing at. If you like 'em high, attack pitches middle up. Same goes if you like 'em low. Essentially cut the strike zone in half and focus on the half you like. When you played, what was your preference?"

"I liked pitches up," Doc said.

Leo began filling the rectangle from the middle up. "You're like Truman. He's a good high-ball hitter. He won't swing at the low stuff until he has two strikes on him."

Doc asked, "And the kids stick with it?"

Leo nodded. "Yep. Once in a while they get off plan and chase, but rarely. That's why we walk so much. Line drives and walks. That's our game."

Doc nodded. "What about with two strikes?"

"Batter chokes up. Shortens his swing. Foul off anything close." Leo filled the rectangle putting roughly sixty peanuts on the napkin. "Battle. Don't count on the ump to give you anything close. Put the pitches you can handle in play. As you know, a lot can happen when a ball leaves the bat."

"Seems to work like a charm," Doc said. "What's the team batting average?"

"Right around .420," Leo said.

Doc whistled. "And how many games have you lost this year, including tournaments?"

"Three," Leo said.

Doc clapped his hands together and laughed. "Happy days are here again. Fingers crossed, though."

In the backyard, Jess was blown away by the scale and beauty of the gardens. Margaret's green thumb accounted for the majority of it, lush with beans, carrots, tomatoes, corn, lettuce, chard, radishes, zucchini, cabbage, cauliflower, garlic, peppers, potatoes and squash. Doc's roses included white Morden Blush, orange David Austin, Pink Knockouts and peach Kiss Me varieties. Now that it was August he was done fertilizing, but those hungry buggers got fed every three weeks before that.

"We used to garden together," Margaret said, "but that led to squabbles. Now we garden independently together, which may put us out here at the same time, chatting a bit, but mostly we enjoy the quiet company of one another and the bumblebees."

"Sounds nice," Jess said.

"Tell me. How long have you been working with Doc?"

"Going on four years."

"Good gosh, I need to apologize for not getting you over to the house more often," Margaret said. "I mentioned it a few times to Doc, having you and Wade for dinner, but he said he wasn't sure how serious you two were." Jess grew quiet. "I'm sorry, I don't mean to be a busybody."

Jess reached over and touched Margaret's arm. "No, it's not that. Wade is wonderful. I just got, well, I got as serious as I was going to get with him, and it wasn't enough. It took me time to see that.

Perhaps too long."

Margaret was a matriarchal figure. Her elegant, long gray hair gave her an aura of calm wisdom. "Do you mind one more question?"

Jess said she didn't.

"Do you think meeting Leo helped you realize you weren't able to get serious enough with Wade?"

"Maybe. Probably."

Margaret continued. "I ask because I had a beau before meeting Doc. We were pretty serious, but there was a murmur of reservation in my heart. I thought that was normal, given the size of the life decisions we'd be facing. But when I met Doc, that disquieting little voice fell silent. Or actually, started rooting for the other team." A cute nose-crinkling smile came to Margaret's face.

"I think you're a bit of a mind reader," Jess said.

"Not at all," Margaret told her. "I saw something on your face in the past that I don't see here tonight. And I recognized it."

The women shared an appreciative smile. Margaret felt herself blessed to be in the presence of a budding romance. And Jess had no relationship with her mother or exposure to the perspective and care that can come from a woman in her senior years. Both felt fortunate for the other's company.

Cold fried chicken with coleslaw, cornbread muffins, cucumber salad, pickles and iced tea make the perfect dinner when temperatures linger around 90 degrees.

Jess asked, "So you did your chicken early this morning and refrigerated it?"

Margaret nodded, putting her hand to her mouth, finishing her bite.

Doc filled in. "She was up before the birds."

"If there *is* a right time to fry chicken in August," Margaret said, "early morning is it. I did wait to bake the muffins, though. I don't like it when they sit too long."

"They don't sit too long around me," Doc said, helping himself to another.

"So Leo," Margaret continued, "congratulations are in order for taking Dannaka to the state tournament. Although I never had a doubt."

"We're excited," Leo said. "But I have a suspicion the town is even more so."

"No contest," Doc said. "As Jerome put it in his article, our baseball drought is over."

Jess asked, "Do you think the kids feel a lot of pressure?" She was asking about Truman more than she let on.

"All in all, no. They've learned how to compete and stay loose. That's been our focus for the past four-plus months. There will be some butterflies, playing on a bigger stage, but that won't last."

"So how do you stay sharp," Doc asked, "with the season over, but a week to go before the tournament cranks up?"

"We're going to scrimmage tomorrow and Sunday. Playing against kids one year older, which helps get us prepped for bigger, stronger competition. Take Monday off, have lighter practices through Thursday. Friday morning we travel to Ames to check into our barracks before opening ceremonies."

Margaret frowned. "Did you say barracks?"

Leo grinned. "Yep. From what I hear, the Army National Guard puts up temporary barracks for the 16 teams. We sleep, eat and even do laundry right there on the baseball grounds so there's less back and forth for the kids from all over the state."

Doc asked, "Do you share a barracks with another team?"

"Nope. Every team gets one. Bunk beds, just like the army."

"The coaches stay there as well?" Margaret asked.

"We sure do. Two coaches to a barracks to keep the kids from getting ... ah ... overly exuberant."

Jess said, "You guys should be sainted when it's all said and done. Trying to keep all those horses in the barn."

"I hear they call mandatory lights out at 10 p.m. That should help."

"The kids will never forget it for as long as they live," Doc said.

"What an experience." Leo sat back and enjoyed the thought of it. Doc asked, "Did you say you scrimmage tomorrow? They're calling for afternoon storms."

"Really?" Leo said, sitting up. His face tightened. "I hadn't heard."

"Word is tomorrow afternoon. I was out earlier today giving Norb Puckett's mare a shot for Potomac Horse Fever. Norb's a weather junkie. Has anemometers spinning all over the property. He said it's coming out of Colorado with gusto. Probably why the wind is blowing like it is."

Leo bit a fingernail. "Hopefully we'll get our game in first."

"What time do you play?" Doc asked.

"First pitch is at 1:00."

"Well, we need the rain."

Margaret and Jess agreed with that. Leo was silent.

They let the dinner dishes soak in the sink as Leo was given lessons on being an Iowan. For one, Doc told him, you are not permitted to live here and not know how to play cards. Margaret shuffled the deck, saying that a little wager makes every card game more interesting. Tonight's losing partners would do the dishes. They'd play euchre, which Margaret said was easier to learn than it was to spell. Women against men, Jess offered. Margaret wholeheartedly agreed, Doc less so.

Leo was a fast learner. He had a little trouble remembering his right and left bowers—from the German word *bauer*, Doc informed, meaning farmer—but soon got the hang of the game. Before long he and Doc were gobbling up tricks. The two of them kept getting ridiculously good cards, winning easily and mercilessly. As the women pushed away from the table, they wondered aloud what they did to deserve such lousy hands and remorseless men.

"I've been asked to play some music," Doc said, returning to the screen porch with a fresh vodka tonic. He rattled the ice in his glass. "Sure I can't fix you one?"

"No thanks," Leo said.

"So about music, any requests?"

"I like everything, so whatever you think."

Doc ducked his head around the doorframe and sent his question toward the kitchen. "Any music in particular you'd like to hear?"

There was a pause, the murmur of distant discussion. "Put on something toe-tapping," Margaret said. "But no John Denver."

Doc slumped. "Ah, c'mon," he said, situating himself about halfway between the porch and the kitchen. "Back me up on this, Jess. Who doesn't love John Denver?"

Jess's voice came from the kitchen. "I worship John Denver."

"See there," Doc said. He directed his voice back toward the porch, "How about you, Leo? Don't you love John Denver? A little *Rocky Mountain High*?"

Leo answered.

"What did he say?" Margaret asked from the kitchen.

Doc deftly managed the conversation from the living room, although he couldn't see the participants. "He said not really."

"Good for you, Leo," Margaret said. "Find something else."

Doc put on the artist who was only slightly behind John Denver on Margaret's would-you-find-something-else-to-play list. Neil Diamond.

Doc had wired the house so music would play in the kitchen, living room and the screen porch. It took him a month of winter Saturdays to do it, but he loved filling the house with music.

"That was harder than Reagan negotiating the end of the cold war with Gorbachev." He sat on the wicker couch across from Leo, careful not to spill his drink. "What do you think of those Bose speakers?" he asked.

"Pretty amazing," Leo said.

"I do enjoy relaxing out here when it's getting dark. Music and a breeze. Taking time to enjoy." Leo smiled in agreement. "So, before the girls get back out here, can I offer a piece of advice should you run into Dixon and his Des Moines team in the state tournament?"

That got Leo sitting up straight. "Sure."

"Ignore him if your two teams meet. Pretend he's not there."

"That's easier said than done." Leo let his head rest against the back of his rocking chair.

"He is a strong flavor," Doc said. "But don't let him into your head. He's smarter than he looks when it comes to dirty tricks. And he'll do anything to win."

Leo frowned. "This is 12-year-old baseball. It's not like we're battling for a major league contract."

"You understand that and I understand that, but there are coaches out there where a state championship is the pinnacle of their baseball achievements. They don't grasp that youth sports isn't about them, it's about the kids. They get all wrapped around the axle about it."

Leo said, "Yeah, I have seen a few of those this summer."

The evening with Doc and Margaret ended as pleasantly as could be. There was talk of a euchre rematch. Margaret asked Leo to exchange one cassette tape from his truck with one of Doc's. Jess left with a recipe for cold country fried chicken.

With one hand, Leo steered his truck. The other arm was around Jess. They were quiet. Doc's John Denver cassette serenaded them, to Jess's delight. Leo turned the wheel and the high beams swept across her driveway, gravel popping under the tires. Leo clicked off the headlights and rolled slowly up the drive under the light of a three-quarter moon.

Truman was at Bale's house watching a movie. With only a single overhead porch light on at the farmhouse, the darkened building struck her as lonely. She didn't speak of it.

Leo turned off the ignition switch as the truck's hot engine ticked and pinged. Night air flowed in the open windows. The peeping frogs had their orchestra going strong.

Leo looked at Jess and she slid in tightly to him. Only centimeters of fabric separated them as he pulled her closer to him for a full kiss that went on, building in them both, spinning them both, Leo hearing rushing water and Jess feeling her skin hum. Their bodies were at the precipice, but their minds pulled them back.

"Whew," Leo said reclining, the heat of Jess's body lingering.

Jess laughed, tucking her hair behind her ears. "I felt that one in my kneecaps."

"I'll walk you up," Leo said.

"It's probably safer if you say goodbye here."

Leo nodded. They had one last kiss.

"Good night," Jess said.

Leo's smile almost lit up the cab of the truck. "The best I can remember in a long, long time."

THE SCRIMMAGE

Heat. Wrapped in humidity. If the 90-plus degree temperatures weren't enough, there wasn't a breath of wind. Leo, almost imperceptibly, shook his head. He didn't like the look of those clouds. The trees behind the bleachers stood still and silent. *Where were the birds?* It was getting darker.

The catcher, Pot Roast, stood in front of home plate and asked for the second time, "First and third, Coach. What's on?"

Leo's attention jerked back to the scrimmage. Typically in this situation, the baserunner on first tries to steal second, believing the catcher won't risk a throw that gives the runner on third an opportunity to steal home. Leo gave the signal for one of the team's trick plays where it appears the catcher is throwing to second. When the runner on third sees the ball released, he breaks, trying to steal home. The trick is that the throw from the catcher is actually to the shortstop, who has run onto the infield grass. The shortstop's job is to receive the throw, take a quick hop-step, and deliver a bullet back to the catcher in time to get the runner from third at the plate.

The play was executed flawlessly; Pot Roast dropped a tag on the surprised runner trying to steal home. That was the third out of the inning. The score in the middle of the fourth remained tied at four apiece. The small Poodle Park crowd made their appreciation known. Jess was among them. Ike whined, lurching against the leash as the Dannaka team ran to the dugout, exchanging high-fives. They buzzed and chattered about the play.

"Just like we practiced it!"

"He was out by a mile!"

"Did you see the look on that dude's face?"

Tom Tink hollered out the names of the three hitters scheduled to bat as Leo stepped out of the dugout, peering into a dark sky tangled in an eerie green tinge. A few fat raindrops thudded on the dirt next to him. A wind suddenly swirled to life, brushing Leo's cheek cold. A bubble gum wrapper blew across Leo's shoe top, exactly as it had a year ago last July.

Naperville Central high school was just south of downtown, a block from the winding DuPage River. Well-respected, the school excelled in academics and sports. Leo loved it there. And they loved Leo equally. His baseball teams were winning state titles at a record clip, he was the teacher everyone wanted for social studies (especially the girls) and he was engaged to the stunning daughter of prominent local husband-and-wife lawyers. Leo had it all. In fact, if he weren't such a nice guy, people said, you'd have no choice but to despise him.

July was when he took the players he expected would make the varsity team next year and groomed them on his summer Legion ballclub. About half were juniors who'd played varsity the previous spring; the other half were the best kids from JV.

It was a sweltering afternoon. The question wasn't if it would storm, but when. Leo never worried much about weather. He'd been playing ball and coaching his whole life. His philosophy: Let's see what happens because obsessing on it won't change a thing.

The afternoon sky had gradually grown darker, making this change surprisingly difficult to notice for those on the baseball diamond for the past few hours. Practice had ended for all but five players when the first, intermittent fat raindrops began to plop on the brims of ball caps. A slight breeze stirred, blowing a bubble gum wrapper over Leo's shoe top.

"Last thing for today," Leo hollered to his players. "We got a guy on second who's taking waaay too big of a lead. Let's work on our inside pickoff move."

Leo told his guys to set it up. They knew exactly where to go. The catcher got behind the plate. Pitcher on the rubber. The extra pitcher grabbed a helmet and ran out to second to be the runner. The shortstop and second baseman took up their positions on either side of the base.

In the distance, a bolt of lightning fissured the black sky. The players and their coach, focused on executing the play, didn't notice.

Leo placed a batting helmet on the left side of home plate as he shouted instructions. "We have a lefty up. I give the signal to the catcher that the play is on." Leo made a fist and tapped his right hip twice. "Catcher relays the sign to the pitcher," which the catcher then did. "Pitcher sends the signal to his infielders by tapping the ball twice on his hip. Two taps for second base, remember that."

Leo continued, as the rain and wind picked up. "I want our shortstop to do a lame job of holding the baserunner close at second. Runner takes a big lead; pitcher checks him once. Count one thousand one. Pitcher picks up his front foot, runner takes his secondary lead, second baseman sneaks in behind, pitcher spins and fires." The boys executed it perfectly. "Runner is DOA," Leo said. The rain was coming harder now, which everyone welcomed. It felt awesome to cool down.

Suddenly the wind let loose, each burst flattening the grass, whorling up tree trunks, stripping leaves. Leo's cap was ripped off and pinned against the backstop.

"Tarps!" he yelled. The five players and Leo sprinted, splitting duties. Three players dragged a tarp over the mound, fighting the wind. Leo and two others tarped the area around home plate.

Rain sheeted from the ominous black sky. Leo could hardly see from home to the mound. Then in a frightening flash, the field was as bright as if sunlit. Everywhere, lightning cut both vertically and horizontally.

Leo sprinted to the mound, shouting over the wind. "Leave it!" Three players were trying to secure the tarp with old car tires, but the wind kept flapping it back on itself. One boy yelled, "The mound is getting soaked, I don't—"

"Screw it!" Leo grabbed the boy's shoulder, his jersey plastered to his skin. "Guys!" he yelled to the three, pointing at the school. "Make a run for it. Get to the locker room. I'll get those two and be right behind you."

The sky lit. Behind the left field fence, a massive lightning strike sheared off the top half of a tree. BOOOOM! Phosphorescent white illuminated the field. Leo saw pure fear in the boys' faces. He clapped hard to get them to focus on him. "GO GO GO!"

The boys sprinted away and Leo ran to home plate for the other two. They were having the same problem, getting the tires to keep the tarp from being ripped away by the wind. "Leave—"

BOOOOOM! This bolt exploded closer, shaking the earth. The three dropped to their knees as lightning center-split a tree behind the batting cages. Limbs and bark pelted the field. The rain was blinding.

Leo yelled to his players. "We gotta run for it!" Lightning lanced the sky around them. "School. Safe in there!"

One of the boys was petrified. He shook his head, trembling. "Can't. Coach."

"How about the equipment shed?" the other boy shouted.

Leo yelled to the petrified boy. "Can you make it to the equipment shed? Behind the backstop?" He grabbed the boy by the shoulders. "You can do that, right?" The boy nodded.

The two players ran arm-in-arm, hunched, around the backstop toward the shed. Leo threw the last two tires on the tarp before a realization seized him: It's metal.

He screamed helplessly against the storm. "NO! Guys! Don't go in there!"

The boys ducked into the shed.

Leo took a running step toward the building. He was knocked off his feet. ZZZZZZBABOOOOOM! A sizzling bolt of lightning attached itself to metal equipment shed. The building's outline went from blinding to emitting a horrific fuchsia aura.

There was only ringing in his ears. Leo stumbled to the shed. The doors were gone, the roof ripped open to the sky. The two boys lay in one corner, still clutching each other. Their baseball cleats had been blown off.

Rain poured in the roof's jagged hole as the wind blowing through it made a sickening whistle. Leo crawled toward the boys, throwing aside a tangle of field rakes, batting tees and a wheelbarrow. "Oh Jesus Christ almighty. What? No. Please." Leo laid his head on each boy's chest, plugging his other ear. There were no heartbeats.

Shaking, lightheaded, Leo swiped pouring rain from his face.

"What? What?" He tried to formulate a plan. He knew every second mattered. He was spiraling, hyperventilating. "C'mom! C'mom! C'mon!"

In full sprint, Leo burst from the shed. The boys were too heavy to carry. "Get your truck get your truck." Hearing his voice drove some of the ringing from his ears. He splashed wildly across the baseball field, at times through ankle-deep water. Twice his feet came out from under him, putting him on his back in the flooded field. Lightning fissured the blackness, which was moving away now. "WHY?" he screamed at the sky. Spittle and rain flew from his mouth. He raked wet hair away from his fierce eyes. "WHY NOT ME?"

Leo's truck roared through center field, fishtailing, wheels tearing up grass. Rain pelted the roof of the cab, creating a peculiarly unthreatening ping that incensed Leo. His wipers on high hardly cleared the windshield. "I'm coming," he said through clenched teeth. The sky was beginning to lighten and he could see the backstop and the ragged shell of the shed.

Leo stood on the Poodle Park infield, rain drizzling down. Clouds balled on the horizon like filthy fists. His ears thrummed. In the background, Tom Tink's voice shouted out the batting order a second time.

A sliver of lighting split the sky.

Leo's heart raced, his blood pressure spiking. The speed of every moving thing ramped down. His head jerked. Tom Tink's voice became distorted. Leo tried to shout, to warn them, "lightning!" but fear clamped his throat. His field of vision tunneled in. Hands trembling, his eyes fluttered. Leo fainted.

"Stand back. Everybody, back!" Doc fanned Leo with a baseball cap. Frightened players had circled around Leo who was laid out on the dugout slab, his feet elevated by the equipment bag.

Leo's eyes blinked open. He said flatly, "They're dead, aren't they?"

"What? No. Everyone's fine."

Leo, groggy, rubbed his eyes. Doc, dripping wet, came into focus.

"What are you doing here?"

"We carried you into the dugout," Doc told him.

"In Naperville?" Leo said.

Doc frowned. "You're in Dannaka, Leo. Remember?"

"Dannaka?" he said, looking around.

Tom Tink was there, and Jess too. Tom spoke up. "We're here. At our scrimmage. With Red Oak."

The kids didn't know what to make of it. Jess squeezed Leo's clammy hand.

"The lightning. Everyone's safe?" Leo asked, trying to sit up.

Doc said yes and told him to lay still for a moment.

"Everyone's safe?" Leo repeated.

"Yes," Jess said. "Perfectly."

Leo closed his eyes. "Everyone's safe." A tear squeezed from the corner of his eye and ran down his cheek.

Before you

Rain drummed on the roof. Truman lay curled on his bed, his body wrapped around his warm pup. He spoke quietly to his confidant. "Ike, I don't know what's wrong with Coach. It's too weird. He's ... Coach. He doesn't get scared about anything."

Ike's head was up, but he was fighting sleep, his eyes becoming slits.

"What if we lose him somehow? He might leave. I don't know what I'd do. I love Coach."

There was a knock on Truman's bedroom door. "Hey bud?" The door cracked open.

"Hi," Truman said.

"Mind if I come in?" Jess asked.

"Okay."

As if Ike sensed he no longer needed to stay awake, he put his head down on the bedspread.

Jess sat next to Truman and patted his hip. "How you doing?"

"I don't know. Not great."

"That was scary out there today," Jess offered.

"What happened? Why would Coach faint?"

"Maybe the doctor who examined him will be able to say. Dehydration can cause fainting."

Truman gave his mom a puzzled look. "You mean not drinking water?"

"Not drinking enough water," she said. "On a hot day like today, a body sweats a lot."

"Coach is always having us drink. Him too."

Jess rested her hand on Truman's shoulder. "I don't know, honey. Let's not guess. We'll wait to hear from the doctor."

327

"He's done it before." Truman's eyes widened. "Gotten weirded out by a storm. Remember the game he pulled us off the field and it was going to be a forfeit? That storm completely missed us."

Jess nodded. "I think it's more about lightning. Lightning is dangerous."

"Not *that* dangerous," Truman said. "Can you go talk to him? See what's wrong?" Truman looked at his mom urgently. "The team is freaked out. I wish Coach would talk to us about what's going on. What did he mean, are they all safe?"

"Why don't you take a nap with Ike and I'll drive over and see how Leo is. Sound good?"

Truman nodded yes.

"I love you, Truman."

"Me too, Mom."

Jess scampered up the walkway from her car, raindrops spattering puddles. The heat had broken since the rain began some three hours ago. She knocked on Leo's storm door; the front door was open. "Hello? Leo?" she said, stepping in. "It's Jess … in from the rain. Hello?" She waited.

Leo came around the hallway corner, his hair shoved to the side, eyes puffy. He looked at Jess and his shoulders sagged.

"Sorry. Did I wake you?"

Saying nothing, he walked directly to her and they folded into each other, remaining there, just past the entryway, in a long, silent embrace.

"I don't know what to say." Leo looked away, vacant.

"You don't have to say anything," Jess told him.

He sighed. "Yes. I do." Leo stepped back, letting his arms fall to his sides. "Dear God, I've been not saying anything for so long." He looked at the floor. "So much happened before you. I'm not sure you want to hear it."

Jess was firm. "I want to hear it."

They sat at his small kitchen table holding hands. In front of them lay the framed team poster of last year's Naperville high school baseball team.

Already, Leo had been up to get a box of tissues as he told the story of the storm and his two players, the lightning hitting the shed and his desperate drive to the ER. Leo spoke solemnly. "The doctors said a current of electricity went through the shed." Leo closed his eyes. "The boys were together, leaning in the corner. It surged through them, stopping their hearts. They couldn't be resuscitated. Seventeen years old."

Jess's eyes welled as she blew her nose.

Leo pointed. "This is Jacob, number 10." He gently touched the glass frame where a boy stood in the back row, smiling. "Pitcher. Beanpole. Smart as a whip. Never had to tell Jacob anything twice." Tears slipped down Leo's cheeks.

"And this is Mikey." Leo pointed to a boy sitting in the front row with a big, crooked grin. "Number 7. Second baseman. He could really go get it. Flares, line shots, he lived for diving catches and dirty uniforms. We called him Trombone because he had a big Italian nose and when he was in a slump—" Leo's voice broke as he half laughed, half sobbed, "he said he couldn't see the ball 'cause his nose got in the way." Leo's head dropped into his hands. Open-mouthed, nose running, he sobbed again. "You goofball, Mikey." Leo placed a trembling finger on the boy, shaking his head, tears falling on the glass.

Leo wiped his eyes, took a deep breath and let out a ragged exhale. "Whew. So that's why there isn't a number 7 or 10 on our Dannaka team. I put those jerseys aside. I couldn't write those numbers in the lineup card."

Jess said she understood.

"Then came the funerals. Unbearable," he said. "No sooner were the boys laid to rest, and I started hearing things being said."

Jess watched him closely. Leo appeared stuck so she carefully asked, "What kind of things?"

"That it was my fault," Leo said. He stiffened. "That I was always on the field practicing. That I stayed too long. That I cared more about keeping a pitcher's mound dry than the safety of the kids. Worst of it, they said I never should have let the boys go into a metal shed in a lightning storm. Everywhere I went—whispering, staring, shunning. I started just staying in the house."

Jess asked, "Who would say something like that?"

"Parents. Teachers. Students. But not the players. They defended me, too much in my opinion. Then somebody told me I'd be smart to get a lawyer. Said there might be a lawsuit. And that the school was going to fire me."

"Fire you?" Jess said, astonished.

"It happened on school grounds. Even though it wasn't technically a school team, it was our high school kids. They thought I showed poor judgment. Plus, I felt guilty. In a way it was my fault."

Jess shook her head resolutely. "You don't control the weather. You don't control lightning strikes."

"Maybe. But back then ... I was a total mess. I loved those boys. And they were gone."

Leo used a Kleenex and exhaled. "So my fiancée at the time," Leo shook his head, "her parents were well-known lawyers in town. But they wouldn't discuss defending me. They wouldn't even speak to me, other than to say the whole incident was way too hot. Too local. If they got involved, they said it would turn Naperville against them and their business."

Jess shook her head incredulously.

"And their daughter," Leo continued, "the woman I was living with, she supported their decision."

"My God," Jess said.

"So we're done as a couple. My job as a coach and teacher is about to disappear, and probably, there's a lawsuit coming."

"All this happened a year ago?"

"Yeah. Almost exactly a year ago. It was ... way past comprehensible. I essentially detached from my old self, split off, and now there was this new guy. Sitting in the house all day. Gaining weight. Growing a beard. A disguise. Not answering the phone. Not answering the door. Checked out. Totally."

Jess nodded, hardly able to move.

"Thankfully my parents got a lawyer and that lawyer walked around the baseball field. Then he scheduled an appointment with the school principal. The lawyer told him that he should do everything in his power to discourage any legal action because it would be the school that'd be liable for a big settlement. The principal said that was nonsense, and the lawyer told him it was cut-and-dried. The negligence was in having a steel shed, a 10-foot by 10-foot structure—qualifying it as a temporary shelter—within 50 feet of a baseball field. That showed no prudence on the school's behalf. On the other hand, by using what is legally known as an Act of God defense, the school and I would not be liable." Leo's voice trailed off. "In the end, that's what happened. But a lot of people had already decided it was my fault."

"I'm so sorry for what you had to go through. Did you have anyone to help you?"

"I pulled the plug on pretty much everyone. My parents and friends called. Knocked on the door. I didn't want to talk. I didn't want sympathy. I didn't want to be told it was going to be okay. I didn't want to think about it. It was the end of July. I pulled down the shades and locked the doors.

"Next thing I know, it's February nineteenth. An alarm went off in my head. Time to do something. It took me a few minutes to realize: February nineteenth, the day spring training camp begins for all the position players. I hadn't been to major league camp in years, but that day gets burned into you. It's the day that a baseball player gets the chance to start things over. I knew then and there if I didn't do something, I wouldn't make it.

"I pulled all my baseball stuff together—memorabilia, keepsakes, jerseys, game balls, autographed bats, awards, the whole megillah. I made three piles: trash, garage sale, keep. It was time for a clean break. As I picked up one of my team scorebooks, a business card fell out. Can you guess whose it was?"

Jess said she couldn't.

"Doc's. He and Jerome and Frank had come the spring before to watch us win our fourth straight state high school title, which was one more than Dannaka's record from their playing days. Doc told me about the town's brand-new Little League facility and a coaching and teaching opportunity. Gave me his card. Asked me to think about it. Give him a call if I was interested. I remember taking his card and thinking, nice enough guy, but there's no way I'm going to some tiny town in Iowa to coach and teach.

"But there I stood on February nineteenth with Doc's card in my hand. I flipped it over. On the back, there was a small handwritten note. I never saw it before then. It said, If you're lucky enough to be in Dannaka, you're lucky enough."

Jess's eyes welled.

"Here I am. Unspeakably lucky. In Dannaka. Where I've been allowed to see baseball through 12-year-old eyes again."

Jess could see Leo was worn out with talking. "Can I say something?" He nodded.

"I think you should tell your team about what happened with the storm and that two boys lost their lives. I think the kids need to start to understand why you had the reaction you did ... why people need to be very cautious around lightning." Jess pointed to the poster. "I think the team should learn about Jacob and Mikey. I honestly believe it would be good for everyone to hear you talk about them just like you did with me. And maybe, if you think it's appropriate, the team could dedicate the state tournament to them."

Leo looked down, tapping his leg with his knuckles.

"Give it some thought," she said. "Don't close the door on it."

Leo frowned, searching. "Do you think the kids are too young to hear about something like this?"

"No. I don't," she said. "Kids Truman's age will surprise you when you're honest with them. I think it would help them make sense of things."

Leo looked away.

Jess quietly persisted. "Keeping this tucked away on the top shelf of your closet is not really helping."

Leo nodded. "Let me think about it."

Cardboard box

Leo was nervous. It wasn't tonight's scrimmage. Or the state tournament starting at the end of the week. Those were baseball things where the unknown was just a game, not something that kept him up at night.

His red pickup rolled into the main parking lot of the baseball complex. Tapping the brakes, Leo gazed up at the Poodle Park sign, its towering, well-groomed poodle sitting erect, baseball under one fluffy paw, wearing a D-emblazoned cap. Leo, absent any other response, tipped his own cap and drove on.

A person's path is never straight. Even so, Leo could only shake his head upon recalling his arrival here on his birthday over four months ago with a shivering, wet travel companion. And whom does he first encounter? A small, skinny kid in a white undershirt skillfully fielding grounders hit by his mother in a skirt—a woman who shares his birthday. "Damn," Leo whispered. "Talk about your curveballs."

Field 1 had three parking spaces reserved for coaches. Leo took one. He was early-early, meaning he was a full hour ahead of their scheduled meeting time. The team had a rule that everyone could recite: "If you're not early you're late." That meant everyone should arrive 15 minutes ahead of the scheduled time.

Out of the truck, with the driver's seat forward, he pulled out a bucket of jiggling water balloons. Leo set the bucket on the hot blacktop. A silver jet glinted high above leaving a fattening contrail across the open blue sky. Crows cawed. The distant drone of a lawn tractor came in on a breeze. This sprinkle of sounds accentuated how quiet things were here.

From the back seat, Leo lifted a cardboard box. It wasn't heavy but he dedicated both hands to it, leaving the bucket for a second trip. He had time. Leo watched his step as he walked to the dugout.

The team began to arrive, a few here, a few there, mostly on bikes. Each time Leo looked up from chalking the field, more boys were there, like puzzle pieces coming together.

Bale slipped out of his mom's minivan, hoping not to draw attention to his mode of transport. His latest cancer screening had been clean. But his doctors said his leg was still susceptible to a refracture. He was to avoid activities that could lead to a fall or that put too much stress on the bone. More than anything, he ached for normalcy.

The team warmed up with a jumping jack relay race. They were divided into two groups, one on the first base side of home plate, the other on the third base side. These were not stationary jumping jacks. These were moving jumping jacks where one player at a time scissored down the line, touched the base, and scissored back to the next player in line. Usually, this got the guys loose in more ways than one, but Leo could see the players were still anxious over what had happened yesterday.

"Let's juggle," Leo said. Everyone got three baseballs. The team could juggle in their sleep now as the balls arced flawlessly from one hand to the other. Leo began to talk.

"Guys," he said, keeping his balls airborne. "Why do we juggle?"

"Hand-eye coordination," Truman said, watching the flight of his baseballs. "Red laces. Keeps us focused."

"See red it's dead," the team sang out.

Leo nodded. "Yeah. But you can accomplish that just tossing one ball up and catching it."

The team continued to juggle. "No challenge in that," Havoc said.

Leo agreed. "You're right. Baseball … life … they're more challenging. A person needs to learn to juggle a lot of things. Take Bale, for example." Bale juggled next to Truman. "He's had some big challenges. A cancer diagnosis, missing the baseball season, working through rehab, getting stronger. A lot to juggle."

Bale added, "Don't forget I had to juggle being more perfect every day. Not easy."

A groan from the team.

Leo continued. "You guys need to know we're all juggling stuff. On the inside. And when we come together as a team, this is one place we can always talk about it. We trust each other. That's what team is." Leo ended juggling by catching his third ball in his cap. "Let's take a break."

The team gathered in the dugout with Leo on the grass in front of them, sitting on an overturned bucket. The cardboard box was on the ground next to him.

"Do any of you know what a panic attack is?" Leo asked. The boys' only response was a blank look. "Well, I didn't know, either. But the doctors at the hospital said I had one. They said if something traumatic happened in your past, sometimes certain things can trigger a memory that seems so real your heart starts to beat really fast, you can't get a good breath, you get dizzy and in rare situations you can faint." Leo folded his hands. "That's what happened yesterday. For sure, very surprising for all of us. I didn't mean to scare everyone like that."

Bale raised his hand. "Can I say something?"

Leo squinted in the sun. "Sure."

"Sometimes things happen, Coach. Even when you think you're too strong for them to happen to you."

Leo tipped his cap back. "I suppose you're right about that."

Bale continued. "I didn't think I could get cancer. I thought it was for old people. When I got it, I thought, why wasn't I stronger? If I was, I'd be playing and wouldn't be letting the team down." He kicked the dirt. "Stupid leg."

Everyone waited on Bale's next words.

"Then my doctor said to me, life sucks sometimes. And it's nobody's fault."

"Smart doctor," Leo said.

"So, what happened yesterday, Coach?" Bale asked. "What gave you the panic attack thing?" The rest of the team nodded.

Leo began. "Remember the lightning we had at our scrimmage? That reminded me of something terribly bad that happened before I came here."

The boys listened carefully.

"It was last summer, back in Illinois. I was on our high school field practicing with my Legion team. We were pretty much done, most of the team had gone to the locker room. I stayed on the field to work with a few guys when a big storm hit. I didn't see it coming. We were having fun and it started to rain so we went to cover the mound and home plate and suddenly it got so much worse." Leo shook his head. "Lightning was everywhere and by then it was raining so hard you could hardly see and the wind was so loud you could hardly hear." Leo swallowed, determined to get through this. "Three boys ran to the school, and two ducked into an equipment shed behind the backstop." Leo took a deep breath. "The shed was struck by lightning. And those two boys died." Leo paused, looking in the faces of the boys. "Is everyone okay to hear this?"

The boys nodded solemnly.

"When I see lightning around a baseball field, I get very tense. It's hard for me to breathe. All I want is to get my team off. Safe. A month ago, remember how we almost forfeited that game? I saw lightning and thought it was coming toward us." Leo took off his cap and rubbed his face. "Any questions about any of this? Ask away. I want things to be as clear as can be."

"It's clear," Truman said.

"Yep," said Bale.

"Yep," said Havoc.

"You all good?" Leo said. "No questions?"

Everyone nodded, the tension beginning to lift.

"I have a question." Pot Roast tilted his head. "What's in that box?"

Leo pulled the cardboard box to his side. He carefully unfolded the flaps and brought out the framed poster of last year's Naperville team. "This is my squad from last year." Leo rested the poster on the ground. "I want you to see who the two players were. So there are fewer unanswered questions. You guys okay with that?"

The team leaned in, nodding.

"This is Jacob. Come on in closer, so you can see." Leo waited as they huddled in. "He was a heck of a pitcher. Nice mix, working off his fastball. Q-tip, you remind me of Jacob. Tall. Rangy." The boys kneeled around Leo, looking at the photograph.

"How old was he?" Bale asked.

"Seventeen. Going into his senior year. Same thing for Mikey, here." Leo pointed him out. "He was our second baseman. Lotta hustle. Even more heart. Kinda like Runt."

The boys' eyes went back and forth between the two players.

"It's hard," Pot Roast said. "Seeing them smiling and knowing they're dead."

"I know," Leo said, putting a hand on his catcher's shoulder. "Their numbers were 10 and 7. Math, do you remember what you asked me when I assigned uniforms in the spring?"

Math nodded. "How come no number 7 or 10?"

"I kept these two out." Leo took the folded Dannaka jerseys out of the box. "I wasn't ready to see those numbers on the field so soon."

The boys understood that.

Leo continued. "I'm wondering. What do you think of us dedicating our state tournament to Jacob and Mikey? We could put number 10 and 7 on hangers and hook them on the fence by our dugout."

Rabbit said, "To honor them."

"Yeah." Leo nodded. "To not forget."

"We should do it," Pot Roast said.

Leo looked into the boys' faces. They were all nodding. "There will be some questions. Parents for sure will ask. You'll need to tell them the story. Do any of you have any questions about what happened?" Leo paused. "Don't be afraid to ask."

Truman tentatively raised his hand. "How does lightning kill someone?"

Leo answered best he could. "From what the doctors told me, the current—the shock—from the lighting jumped from the shed to the boys and that current was so strong it stopped their hearts. Something called a cardiac arrest."

Havoc asked if many people die from lightning.

"No, they don't," Leo said. "But even though it's rare, that doesn't mean it's safe. Lightning can never, ever be ignored. When you see it, get to shelter."

"Like under trees, right Coach?" Pot Roast said.

Leo shook his head. "No. Never. Lightning can hit a tree or right near it and the current can pass through the ground and come up through your feet. Find a good-sized building. A car is safe, too."

No one had any other questions until Bale asked, "Can we hang the jerseys starting with today's scrimmage?"

Leo wasn't expecting that. "If you guys are up for it, yeah."

The team was unanimous.

Truman went to the umpire's room to collect two hangers. He knew where to look because last season Tommy Dicke's dad locked his keys in his truck and offered any kid who could find a hanger five bucks.

The boys were warmed up and raring to go. This was their last rehearsal before the state tournament starting Friday. Today's scrimmage, like the day before, was against boys a year older. The chance to face faster pitchers and compete against physically bigger players really got the kids on their toes. Over the years, Leo had arranged for his teams to play up in scrimmages. He was known to throw his varsity boys out against junior college teams in Chicago, until their coaches stopped returning Leo's calls. They didn't like getting beat by the young guns.

The Dannaka nine hustled out to their positions as the opposing head coach made his way over to third base. An occasional sunflower seed shell fluttered out of his mouth. He noticed two jerseys hanging on the fence by the home dugout.

"Excuse me," he said to Leo who was rubbing up an extra baseball. "Those jerseys there—hope you don't mind my asking—did Dannaka lose two boys?"

Leo put the ball in his back pocket. "No, but thanks for asking. Last year, I lost two of my high school players in an accident. We're dedicating the rest of our year to them."

The opposing coach reached out his oversized hand to shake. "My condolences on your loss. It's a good thing you're doing, remembering them boys like that. Too often losses get stuffed away and the departed never leave you." The coach's grip softened. "I lost a son. Rollover, just outside Imogene. About to graduate high school. Still have trouble talking about it." The coach squinted into the sun.

Their handshake continued. "I'm sorry for your loss, too. It took me a year to talk about it," Leo said.

"I'm going on five." The coach let Leo's hand go and made his way to third.

The game wasn't close. Dannaka won 9-2. Leo threw six different pitchers, each for one inning. The only damage came off the bat of their first baseman—a towering two-run blast by a boy almost as tall as Leo.

The players went through the handshake line, head coaches being the last to congratulate each other. "Good game, Coach," Leo said.

The other coach grinned and shook his head. "I heard a little bit about you guys through the grapevine. Man oh man. Your kids hit line drives like they got no other choice." Leo thanked him for saying so. "And that little guy, the one they call Runt, you pitched him last … holy ham fat. That's some movement on his knuckleball."

"I call it the Dazzler."

"My boys may as well been blindfolded."

The two coaches watched as the Dannaka kids divided up the groundskeeping. Infielders raked their positions and filled in the lip. Outfielders got tarps and swept out the dugouts. Pitchers raked the baselines and tamped the mound.

"Wish I could get my kids to do that without kicking 'em," the opposing coach said. "You're running a good operation here. I wish you the best in the state tournament. I think you'll surprise some folks."

"I appreciate that. And thanks for coming over with your guys." Leo gave the coach a goodhearted slap on the shoulder before making his way to the dugout. About halfway there, he turned and jogged back for a last word. The two talked quietly for a minute, before one final handshake. Leo had told the coach if he ever wanted to talk to someone about the loss of his son, he would be honored to listen.

Coach Tink had a church softball game, but he rushed to Poodle Park afterward. And just in time. The boys were packing up their gear when he got there with his usual bag of bubble gum. In vintage Tom Tink form, he had taken off his softball jersey, leaving him in a T-shirt that was on backward and inside out. Leo discreetly mentioned it. Tom laughed but didn't seem to care. He tossed bubble gum to the boys who came after it like trained dolphins.

Just then, Jess arrived with Ike on a leash. When the pup saw the team running around in the outfield popping each other's bubbles, it was too much. Jess managed to unsnap the leash and Ike tore after them. He was received like a returning prince.

Crossing her legs, Jess watched Leo lug a pail of water balloons to the outfield grass. Putting his fingers to his mouth, Leo whistled. Instantly a scrum of boys, now barefoot, sprinted to him with Ike keeping pace. It was encore time after another 90-degree baseball game in Dannaka. One after the next, underhand-tossed water balloons were clobbered into a mini-shower by the boys. Jess looked closely, and sure enough: Each spray left a fleeting rainbow. How could summer get any better than that?

"Hiya good looking," Leo said, approaching the bleachers, which were empty now except for Jess. The boys and the bikes and Ike had left. Parents had said their goodbyes, needing to get Sunday dinner started.

Jess pushed her bangs out of her eyes, squinting at Leo. "Hey, aren't you that famous bachelor coach from Dannaka?"

Leo grinned, sitting down next to her. "Can't say about the famous part. Still a bachelor, but less eligible by the moment."

"Good answer," Jess said.

Leo whispered, "Can I tell you a secret?"

"Mm-hmm." Jess was entranced by the look in Leo's eyes.

Leo leaned in, as did Jess. He surprised her with a soft kiss on the lips. "My secret is I'm becoming more comfortable with public displays of affection."

Jess let the kiss shudder through her. "But there's no one here but us."

"Details." He took her hand. "I had a great day today thanks to you."

Jess's face slowly revealed that she understood what he was alluding to. "You told them," she said excitedly.

"I told 'em." Leo's smile widened. His face unburdened. "I told 'em, and you were right. They were great. They listened. Took it all in. Asked questions. Handled it. They want to dedicate the rest of our season to Jacob and Mikey." Leo closed his eyes and basked in the moment. "I'm so relieved," he threw his arms to the sky.

Jess rubbed his back. "Good for you. And good for them."

Leo opened his eyes to Jess. "Thanks for the push, Coach," he said.

Jess's reluctant smile came to her face, but less guarded. "Do you have plans for dinner?"

"I do not."

"Do you want to eat with us?"

"That would be great. Just have to finish here and get cleaned up."

Jess looked at her watch. "How about 6:30?"

"Great," Leo said. "What can I bring?"

"Just you," she told him.

"White bases, green grass, silver water tower, blue sky." Leo spoke to the empty baseball diamond. Sitting beside the infield, legs stretched in front of him, Leo prepared to run. As chance would have it, from his ground-level vantage point, first base aligned with second. His eyes tracked along that line to the green outfield grass and farther until his sightline arrived at the silver water tower with DANNAKA wrapped around its tank. Beyond that, blue sky. He repeated, "White bases, green grass, silver water tower, blue sky."

The water tower was the highest point in town. Jess said she had climbed it in high school. You can see for miles, she told Leo. He imagined the view, how it had changed, but ever so gradually. The big picture was mostly the same. The durability of Dannaka's character drew him to this place.

On the grass next to him lay Leo's coaching jersey. He had soaked through the layer below, his team T-shirt with Choose Positive across the front. On the back it read: 1990 Dannaka 12U AAA—with the roster lettered beneath. He stood with a groan and began his 10 laps. Predictability in life is a balm that you don't appreciate until you need it.

As Leo finished his final lap, he jogged down the third baseline of Field 1. Home plate was in front of him as it had been months ago when he first circled these fields. With each footfall, dust kicked up. Today, instead of ending his run by veering off, as he had always done, Leo brought his foot down firmly on the plate.

"Home," he said.

OPENING CEREMONIES

For the past five years, Ames had hosted the Iowa 12U AAA Little League state championship tournament. Everyone agreed they pulled out all the stops.

In their lighted, four-field complex, each baseball diamond featured the same dimensions: 60-foot basepaths, 46-foot pitching distance and 205-foot fences. Because the city was centrally located, no one grumbled about traveling to play here. What made the Ames complex even more ideal was its adjacent soccer fields. Almost magically, in fewer than 24 hours, that space was transformed into temporary housing for the 16 qualifying teams.

In a stroke of brilliance, the Iowa National Guard coordinated their bivouac training with the tournament date, erecting a baseball village consisting of 16 barracks, a power station, a mess hall and a first aid station. They also hauled in shower trailers and portable toilets.

It was like nothing else the kids had experienced: essentially *the* baseball sleepover of their lives. Each team was assigned its own barracks complete with stacked bunk beds, footlockers and electricity to run lights, fans and two mini-refrigerators.

Wide-eyed, the teams checked in Friday morning. Opening ceremonies were at 10:00 and first games began at noon. There was no time to waste. The tournament was run with army efficiency and discipline.

"Oh my God," Bale said to Truman as they ran through the baseball village looking for their barracks, number 11. "This place is massive." They each had a small suitcase in one hand and a bat and glove in the other. Proudly, they wore their Dannaka caps with the bold D on the crown. They weaved through other kids wearing caps from their teams. "There's number six," Truman yelled, pointing.

Bale, slightly winded, said, "Eleven must be in the next row."

If you wanted to get the best bunk in the barracks, Coach said, you had to get there first. Once your gear hits a bed, it's officially claimed.

Truman gave the stuck door a second push, this time putting his hip into it. The door banged open. They were first to arrive in barracks 11. Four bunk beds stood on the left side of the room, four on the right. Each bed was tightly made, topped with one crisp pillow and a white sheet folded over a blue blanket that was tucked firmly under the mattress using hospital corners.

"Look at those fart sacks," Bale exclaimed.

"That one's golden," Truman said, pointing to the rear of the barracks. His chosen bunk, back left, had a nearby sliding window and a fan.

"You take the top," Bale said.

By the time the rest of the team scrambled in, Truman and Bale were each on their beds, hands tucked behind heads comfortably propped up by pillows.

"You better be faster than that on the bases today," Truman said.

"My granny has better wheels," Bale added.

Excitedly, the rest of the team jostled for bunks.

When Leo and Tom Tink finally strolled in, they bumped Havoc and Pot Roast from the two bottom bunks closest to the door. There would be no late-night escapes on their watch.

For opening ceremonies, each team, in full uniform, walked behind a long, horizontal banner announcing its name. Leading the procession in crisp, high-stepping style was the Ames High School marching band. It was a gorgeous, sunny August morning as the excitement and tension began to build. Teams checked each other out. Comments were whispered through the ranks: "Those guys are flippin' huge," or "They don't look so tough."

Alphabetically, teams proceeded through the grounds to Field 1. Dannaka followed the Ames 12U AAA Tornadoes. Leading Dannaka was their trusty mascot, Ike, tongue out, marching high-tailed. Evidently, the pup sensed the import of the moment.

Parents lined both sides of the walkway, straining to see their teams, applauding, shaking cowbells, shouting out support. Dannaka drew some of the loudest cheers due to an impressive turnout from town. And it didn't hurt to have a puppy leading the group.

Announcing each team as they filed in, the tournament director stood at home plate with a microphone. Once assembled, teams ringed the entire infield looking like a multi-colored fence of boys: uniforms of blue, yellow, red, purple, orange, gray and so on. Next, parents and family were ushered into the stadium's seating.

While the national anthem played, the local Honor Guard raised the United States flag. The tournament director then announced that today's games would be played on all four fields, with eight teams starting at noon and the other eight playing at three. He continued, "A tournament bracket will be posted outside each field. Lunch will be served in the mess hall immediately after opening ceremonies and dinner is served from 6:00 until 6:30. If you're late you're out of luck. So don't dilly dally."

The director took a moment to make sure the boys were paying attention. "We run this tournament with army-like efficiency but does that mean we don't have fun?" He paused for an answer. "I can't hear yoooou," he sang out. "Does that mean we don't have fun?" He held his microphone out toward the players. "No," a few players said timidly. "You can do better than that." His voice raised an octave. "Does that mean we don't have fun?"

"NOOOOO!" the teams shouted back.

"Now you're cooking with gas," he said. "And speaking of cooking, after tonight's dinner, there will be a number of activities including a skills competition right here on the fields." He gave a rundown of the events.

"On Field 1, there will be a Moonshot home run hitting contest. One player is selected to represent his team. That player will get five swings at balls thrown by a pitching machine. Most home runs wins.

"Field 2 will feature the Cannon Arm where players are given three throws from center field to hit a four-foot by four-foot square of plywood. Field 3 will have the Around the Horn competition. A stopwatch will time how long it takes a team of five to throw a baseball from pitcher to home; home to third; third to second; second to first; first to home; home back to pitcher again. And Field 4 will have the Cheetah Championship. What player will be the fastest to circle the bases?

"Now, where was I?" the tournament director's voice rang out from the stadium speakers. He looked at his notes. "Oh yeah. I've been told we have a special guest today who's not only fast but has unusual baseball smarts, too."

Truman flashed Leo a thumbs up. Earlier, Leo had asked the tournament director if he was interested in kicking off the state tournament in unforgettable style. A short conversation later, the director, somewhat apprehensively, said yes.

"From the Dannaka All-Stars," the director's voice crackled, "I proudly give you Truman 'Runt' Younger and his amazing pup, Ike."

A fizzle of applause came out of the crowd, while a boisterous cheer rang out from the Dannaka faithful.

"Ike, come," Truman commanded as he walked to the mound to shake hands with the director. The pup was glued to Truman's heel.

"So you have a dog who knows his baseball?" the director said, holding the microphone to Truman.

"Yes," Truman replied, overly loud. He lowered his voice. "Yes sir, I do."

"How old is he?"

"Not even one yet," Truman said.

"Ahh. A rookie. Okay, show us what he can do."

Truman looked at Ike.

Ike looked at Truman.

"Stay," he said off-mic. As Truman took a slow walk to the third base coaching box, Ike sat statuesque by the pitcher's mound. The crowd noise flattened to a murmur.

"Home!" Truman shouted loud enough for all to hear. Ike's butt popped off the grass, looking at Truman who gestured to the plate. The pup strutted to home plate, circling it once before sitting down atop it.

The fans applauded thinking what a smart dog and what a neat trick. They had no idea what was coming next.

"First base!" Truman shouted, his arm arrowing in that direction.

Infield dirt flew as Ike sprang from home and dug for first. Much of the awkwardness had matured out of the pup in the four-plus months since he was left in a highway ditch. Leo smiled proudly, seeing how Ike had developed. *You never know*, he thought.

When Ike got to first he thrust out his front paws and skidded to a stop, his butt landing squarely on the bag.

The crowd erupted. Ike's eyes fixed on Truman.

"Second base!" he commanded.

Ike thrust forward, striding for second, snout cutting through the wind, his cinnamon coat laid back. He made a perfect stop at second, placing his hindquarters on the white base.

Another big hoot from the crowd. The Dannaka team started to chant, "Ike. Ike. Ike." The crowd joined in. The snare drummer in the marching band couldn't help himself. He proceeded with a drum roll. All eyes were on the panting pup on second.

Truman squinted at Ike, leaning in. Ike's body tightened like a spring ready to snap. "Score, Ike! Score!"

The pup sped toward third. Truman, in the coaching box, pinwheeled his arm, the universal baseball sign for keep going. Ike's front paws hit third base as he cornered, nearly spinning out in the dirt. Muscles hunched and expanded with each stride as he closed in on home plate. Ike was two pup-lengths from the home when his front paws drove forward, his backside lowering, dust pluming. Skidding into home, Ike's body did a gentle quarter turn. When he came to rest, on the plate, he was sitting, facing the pitcher's mound.

Standing ovation!

Truman ran to Ike and threw his arms around him. The fans, players and coaches were exuberant. Except Dixon. He stood stone-faced on the field next to Billy, who was caught up in the moment along with his teammates.

Dixon backhanded his boy in the chest. "What're you clapping about?" he said, through clenched teeth.

"Nothing." His son stiffened.

Dixon shook his head. "I've had it with the Dannaka clown show." He looked across the field at Leo who was high-fiving his players. "Celebrate all you want now. For me, winning this title won't be enough. You gotta lose."

GAME ONE

——————

The tournament bracket was posted. Dannaka, the third seed, drew fourteenth-seeded Storm Lake. Three wins and you're in Sunday's championship game. Four wins and you get to kiss the big trophy.

But that wasn't what Leo talked about in the barracks as the boys dressed for game one. They pulled on their CHOOSE POSITIVE T-shirts as Leo spoke in a relaxed tone. "Gotta have fun today. Soak it in and slow it down. Relax."

Havoc was buttoning his jersey. "I doubt Storm Lake is any good. Ranked fourteenth and all."

Leo frowned. "Coach Tink, what do we say about underestimating an opponent?"

Tom spoke up. "Goliath underestimated David. Look where it got him."

Havoc paused, blinked. "Yeah, but we're David. Being from Dannaka and all."

Leo clarified. "Respect all the teams. If they're good enough to get here, chances are they have a stud or two who can be game-changers."

As Dannaka approached from the batting cages, the four baseball fields were a sight to behold. Ten-foot wooden outfield fences, freshly painted white, were garnished with pleated red, white and blue bunting. Silver stanchions topped with stadium lights rose above meticulously groomed fields. Rows of bleacher seating circled the field from home plate to the outfield foul poles.

Bale threw an arm around Truman. "Can you believe we're here?"

They walked onto the green grass. Truman whistled softly. "I got goosebumps."

"Me too," Bale replied. "And I'm just keeping the book."

Truman craned his head, taking it all in like Coach said he should. "Look at this place. I heard a kid say every seat gets filled for the championship game."

"I dunno," Bale said skeptically. "That's a ton of people."

The infield was dragged and chalked, so teams weren't allowed to warm up there. Instead, coaches could hit ground balls along the fence by each dugout, which Storm Lake was doing.

Leo had led everyone to center field except for his starting pitcher and catcher who threw long-toss as Tom Tink looked on. The outfield was soon filled with the cheering and hooting of Dannaka's relay races, which featured piggyback rides and somersaults along with sprints. The kids loosened up in more ways than one.

It was time to play catch, Dannaka-style. This meant the thrower had to hit the glove—a target—set by the receiver opposite him. First the glove would be positioned in front of the receiver's right shoulder. If the throw hit that spot, then the target moved to the receiver's left shoulder. With that target hit, the glove was held in the center of the chest.

The opposing Storm Lake coach took a breather from hitting ground balls only to be blown away by what he saw and heard in the outfield. The thwump! of baseballs striking leather as a neat line of Dannaka pairs zipped throws to one another, right shoulder, left shoulder, center; right shoulder, left shoulder, center—all the while backing up, making each round of throws from greater and greater distances. The Dannaka throwers didn't miss their targets. And no ball was dropped. It was pinpoint baseball, bordering on machine-like, except for the boys' raucous chatter as they complimented and taunted each other.

As the Storm Lake coach turned back to his players, the whole group was watching, mesmerized. One of the Storm Lake players whispered to his teammate, "These dudes are for real."

The game was never close. The 10-run rule came into effect in the fourth inning before Dannaka, the home team, even got to bat. They had already scored 13 runs in the first three innings to Storm Lake's zero. Q-tip pitched two scoreless innings, allowing only one baserunner who was hit by a curveball that slipped out of his hand. Rip pitched a one-two-three third, striking out two, before allowing a weak pop-up gloved by Truman at second.

Standing in the early afternoon sunlight, the two head coaches met at the end of the handshake line. "Quite a clinic you put on today," the Storm Lake coach said, shaking Leo's hand. "I don't have the best pitching in the state, but the kid I started never allowed more than two runs in a game in the past two seasons. You sure had his number. What, eight runs in an inning and a third?"

"The boys' bats were going good today."

"Don't mind me asking, but what's your secret? Something in the water in Dannaka?"

Leo laughed, pulled off his cap and let the breeze muss his thick hair. "Our boys know how to get on fastballs. Your pitcher throws hard, but we knew what was coming and had a good plan for it."

"Shoot yeah. Line drives are still ringing in my ears." The Storm Lake coach sagged.

Leo encouraged him. "Your kids kept their heads up, hustled, played clean. Tomorrow's another day, as long as you move on. Right?"

"Huh? Yeah."

Leo slapped him on the back. "Short memory. That's what every ballplayer needs. Enjoy the festivities tonight. Start fresh tomorrow."

The Storm Lake Coach was revived. "Hells yeah." He nodded vigorously. "Good talking to you, Coach. My name's Bill."

"Nice to meet you, Bill. I'm Leo." They shook hands again, but this time not because it was compulsory.

After dinner, each of the four fields held a skills competition. Billy Dixon won the Moonshot home run contest, hitting four of five pitches over the fence. The Cannon Arm was won by the center fielder from Storm Lake, which lifted his entire team's spirits after their loss earlier in the day. The other two competitions went to Dannaka. Rabbit registered the fastest time running the bases and when it came to throwing the baseball around the horn, Dannaka's speed and execution were untouchable.

What a night in Ames. The temperature was in the low eighties and the sky was having a slow-moving pillow fight with gigantic white cumulus clouds. The kids had long forgotten if they won or lost, struck out or knocked in a run. They were busy being 12.

There was an egg-and-spoon race, which produced great swells of cheers, and an obstacle course that ended with a Slip 'N Slide belly-flop to the finish line. Another favorite was the clothespin game. Ten kids stood on the grass inside a wide circle marked with white spray paint. Each player had five clothespins clipped to his T-shirt. The object was to get other kids' clothespins and clip them to your shirt without leaving the circle. Once a player lost all his clothespins, he had to leave the circle. The winning player ended up jouncing around with a hilarious number of clothespins on his T-shirt trying to get the last pin off the last kid, to the chant: "Get him! Get him! Get him!"

The tournament director was definitely onto something with this first night of activities. It helped the kids get to know one another beyond the uniform and realize that there was more to summer's final baseball tournament than just winning and losing. Plus, it was tiring. When lights out came at 10:00, the players would be ready. Equally important, it gave the coaches a place to introduce themselves and mingle carefree. Tempers can get short in the heat of a tight tournament game—especially among strangers. The evening events allowed coaches to meet and engage under more relaxed circumstances.

Somehow, Dixon missed the point. He and his Des Moines Black team were busy tallying the score of all the night's events. "We got to win this," he said about the three-legged race. "Who's ready?" All the boys raised their hands, wanting a chance to compete. "Give me Billy and Hud," he said. "C'mon. Let's talk strategy."

The tournament director announced that the race would begin in two minutes. All contestants were told to line up.

Dixon craned his head to see who was gathering at the starting line. "Looks like Dannaka is sending Tink's kid and one of the wetback twins. Here's what I want you to do. Line up next to them, on their left. If they try to pass, *accidentally* bang into them. Send 'em flying. If Tink lands on his throwing arm, better yet. I watched him pitch today. Practically untouchable."

Billy nodded enthusiastically; Hud, not so much.

"Get going already," Dixon barked.

All 16 teams had a twosome ready at the starting line. The tournament photographer quickly jogged to the front of the group and snapped a few impromptu shots. It wasn't until months later, when Leo opened a cardboard tube marked HANDLE WITH CARE PHOTOGRAPH INSIDE, that he saw broad smiles on all the kids' faces—except for the two Des Moines players to the left of his Dannaka pair.

The tournament director held an air horn above his head. "On your mark...."

Billy Dixon and Hud sidestepped a little closer to Q-tip and Rabbit. "Get set...."

With arms tossed over the other's shoulders, their inside legs bound together, the Dannaka twosome agreed they would start outside leg first.

The air horn shrieked and the three-legged runners were off. Some tumbled immediately. Others learned quickly to work together as a unit.

Q-tip and Rabbit got off to a slow start because they were laughing too hard. But they soon found a rhythm and started to catch up. At about the halfway mark, they caught up to the Des Moines team.

"Passing on your right," Q-tip blurted. Then came a white flash of impact before a moment of black.

Q-tip shook his head. Trees and sky spun until locking back into focus. He and Rabbit lay in a heap. Next to them, Billy and Hud were getting off the ground.

"What happened?" Q-tip said.

Rabbit touched his chin finding a little blood. "We got broadsided."

Q-tip braced himself to stand. "Shit. My wrist. I think it's messed up."

Rabbit helped him to his feet. "You okay?"

A few tournament staff members ran toward them, along with Tom Tink and Leo. "Please, stand back," one of the staff instructed.

"That's my boy," Tom said, continuing on. He put an arm around his son. "Are you hurt?"

That's when the tears started.

It didn't take but a minute for the wrist to swell up and announce that it was broken. The tears were not from pain. They were tears of recognition. Q-tip knew his season was over.

Tom helped his son to the first aid tent. Leo was behind them becoming more enraged with every audible sob. Rabbit walked alongside, stanching the bleeding from his chin with the neck of his T-shirt.

"What happened?" Leo asked angrily.

"It wasn't my fault, Coach," Rabbit said.

Leo put his arm around the boy. "I didn't mean it that way. Sorry. When I see someone hurt, I get angry." His tone softened. "Are you okay? Let me see." Rabbit showed him his chin. "Just a little cut," Leo said. "You'll be fine. Do you know what happened?"

Rabbit's eyes welled. "The Des Moines kids crashed into us. On purpose, I think."

Leo stopped in his tracks, holding Rabbit back. "What? Why?"

"Right before they hit us I heard Billy Dixon say, 'Now!'"

Leo and Rabbit held each other's stares. "You sure?" Leo said.

"Pretty sure. Yeah."

Leo whispered harshly. "Dixon."

"Coach," Rabbit said, shaking his head. "You can't tell. He hates me and my brother. Remember when he almost ran us over with his truck?" Rabbit's eyes pleaded. "You can't say I said anything."

"I have to," Leo said. "If his kid did this on purpose, and Dixon was in on it, they should be thrown out of the tournament. They don't deserve to be here."

"But Coach. He'll come after my family. He hates Mexicans."

"I'm not going to let him hurt you. Or your family. No way. But we can't let bullies and cheaters have their way." Leo shook his head defiantly. "We have to stand up for ourselves and our teammates." They watched Q-tip as he entered the first aid tent, cradling his left wrist.

Rabbit took a deep catching breath. He nodded okay.

The tournament director and Leo approached the Des Moines barracks. Leo knew himself too well to confront Dixon alone; his temper, unchaperoned—not a good idea.

It was 30 minutes until lights out and the team was playing poker. Dixon answered a knock on the door in a way that suggested he was expecting it.

"Mr. Dixon, can we have a word?" the director said.

"Yeah sure." He looked back inside. "You idiots keep it down."

Dixon led them away from the barracks out into the evening darkness.

"At least there's a breeze out here," Dixon said, his shirt sweat-soaked. He wore a sleeveless T-shirt that read Dixon Dodge on the front and We Will Never Steer You Wrong on the back. The shirt accentuated his huge stomach and arms. "I'm an AC man myself. Had a new unit put in my place back home. I said give me the big kahuna. Big enough to cool a Texas football stadium." Dixon laughed. "Got 48,000 BTUs. Forty-six-inch fan. Missing her tonight."

"Mr. Dixon," the director interrupted. "You're aware of the accident that happened earlier tonight?"

Dixon played dumb. "Accident?"

"The collision in the three-legged race."

"Oh. Yeah. I may have heard something about it. Tough break, no pun intended."

Leo grit his teeth.

The tournament director continued. "Two of your players were involved."

Dixon shrugged. "Easy to lose your balance in a race like that. You might want to reconsider having it."

The director bristled. "This is our fifth year. We've never had an issue."

"Your call," Dixon said, folding his arms above the ledge of his stomach.

Leo couldn't keep quiet any longer. "One of my guys says it wasn't an accident."

Dixon frowned. "Where would he get a crazy idea like that?"

"Right before the collision he heard one of your guys say, 'Now!'"

"Now?" Dixon asked. "What's that supposed to mean?"

Leo said, "Now as in 'go.' Like it was planned."

"Bullshit," Dixon said. His neck shook along with his head. "If he meant go he would have said go. Who heard this? I'm offended by the accusation."

Leo stared through the darkness at Dixon. "I bet you are. It doesn't matter who heard it."

"Was it the Tink boy? Or the wetback? Because that kid probably hardly speaks English."

"Don't call the young man a wetback." Leo took a step toward Dixon.

"And why not? That's sure enough what he is. No way his word is gonna trump an Iowa kid's on what was said."

"Can you really be that ignorant, Dixon? Both boys were born in Iowa. They're the same."

"Not the way most people see it, Coach. That wetback kid's word against my kid's word in a court of law, good luck with that." Dixon chuckled.

The tournament director spoke up. "We are not in a court of law here. It's my job to decide on any possible impropriety that could lead to disqualification."

The whites of Dixon's eyes suddenly shone. "Disqualification?

What are you talking about?"

The director explained that the tournament rules clearly stated that any behavior deemed dangerous or unsportsmanlike will lead to a team's disqualification.

There was just enough light to see a smug grin come to Dixon's face. "So *that's* it, huh, Coach? You know you can't beat me so you want me DQ'd."

Leo shook his head. "That's not it at all. I want to know if your players collided with my players on purpose. Or worse, whether you instructed them to do so."

Dixon lunged, grabbing for Leo. The tournament director did his best to get between them, but he was 15 years older and small-framed. Dixon's and Leo's shouts brought the Des Moines kids out of the barracks.

"Did you have anything to do with it?" Leo hollered, gripping Dixon's shirt.

"Hell no," Dixon yelled. The three men did an awkward dance in the dark, Leo's and Dixon's hands locked onto each other's shirt as the tournament director tried to pry them apart. "How is this not unsportsmanlike conduct?" Dixon huffed. "He won't let go."

Leo gave Dixon's shirt a final jerk before pushing away. The two men breathed heavily.

"Both of your teams will be disqualified if there is ANY MORE OF THIS SHIT!" The director's face was hot and flushed. He reined himself in, catching his breath. "Is that clear? Last warning. Both of you."

Leo said it was clear. As did Dixon.

The director was stern as stone. "Now, Mr. Dixon, did any of your players intentionally collide with the Dannaka boys in that race?"

"No sir," he said. "They most certainly did not."

"There was no plan that you or your players instigated?"

"No, there most certainly was not."

"You'll give me your word on that?"

"You have my word."

The director turned to Leo. "There isn't enough to go on here. But I'll be watching, as will the rest of my staff." He turned back to Dixon. "We will not tolerate any behavior that endangers our kids."

Dixon nodded politely. "Of course," he said. "There's no room for that."

Saturday

The sounds were gone now. The memories, though, were still audible: triples ringing off fences, tags slapping on runners, fastballs sizzling past batters. Jerome was capturing it all quickly, before it dispersed into the night sky.

What a Saturday of baseball it had been. Stadium light flooded down on the quiet bleachers, long emptied, except for Jerome. His solitary figure sat hunched over a yellow legal pad, perched on his knees. He was doing what made him happiest: losing himself in a story.

His pen scrawled across the second draft of *Jerome's Jottings*. No piece he wrote ever lacked for attention or professionalism, but what he was composing tonight stirred his soul. This column drew on nostalgia, resurrecting childhood passions about baseball at its best.

A stone pinned Jerome's first draft to the bleacher bench next to him. A mischievous breeze came up from time to time. Having had his pages scattered under the bleachers once was one time too many.

Intermittent walks along the field's perimeter kept Jerome's back and mind from growing stiff. He wrote from this spot because it was all still here, spectral, but palpable: a noon quarterfinal game and a 7:30 semifinal where evening light melted into darkness, leaving the game wrapped in an aura of stadium light.

The groundskeepers had finished preparing the field for tomorrow's championship game. One of them waved at Jerome and told him the lights were going off in 15 minutes. Jerome thanked him for the warning before slipping his pen behind his ear, stretching his legs, shoes resting on the forward bench. He read through the pages on his legal tablet.

SATURDAY

Thoughts preceding a championship game

By the time this article has gone to press and makes its way
into your hands, you will already know the outcome of the
Iowa Little League championship baseball game between the
12-year-olds of Dannaka and their cross-state rivals from Des
Moines. That conclusion will be, as the saying goes, old news.

But for me, as I write this, that game is some 14 hours off. I'm
sitting in the empty bleachers at Ames Municipal fields after a
jolting, exhausting Saturday of baseball. Currently, all that's
gathering here is the dew on the outfield grass—which glitters
under stadium light—and my thoughts. In the judgment of
this old newspaperman, with regard to a winner and loser of
tomorrow's championship game: Dannaka has already won.
Nothing about tomorrow's score could alter my thinking.

Permit me to rewind the day and explain. Dannaka won twice
today, in hard-fought fashion. First our boys beat Iowa City
5-3 in the quarterfinals. And then tonight under the lights, in
10 innings (games are scheduled for six), we nipped hometown
Ames 6-5 to advance to tomorrow's championship. That is a
first for our 12U AAAs—a remarkable victory for a town the
fraction of the size of the teams we're competing against.

But beyond the box scores, our boys have won in vastly
more significant ways. For instance, they've won by
developing into fine young men over the spring and summer.
They've learned the demands and rewards of hard work.
They've become tremendously skilled baseball players.
(Side note: It's a thrill for me to sit in the stands as our boys
uniquely warm up for a game, overhearing the astonished
comments of fans.) And they've overcome tough injuries to
key players. Baseball challenges you mightily, and at times
bests you. You can respond by making yourself better or
making excuses. This team doesn't make excuses. From my
vantage point, nowhere does youth shine as brightly as it does

361

on a sunlit baseball field.

These boys also won when their coaches opened up tryouts to Dannaka's nearby communities. New friendships were formed while the team became more diverse and talented. As Coach Leo Hamill told players and parents right from the beginning, "Dannaka is a great baseball town, but if you live in a bubble you're going to get popped."

Frankly, I can't say enough about our coaching staff. Tom Tink, the self-proclaimed "Pepperidge Farms man," is the epitome of honesty, sportsmanship and humility. He is constantly working behind the scenes, contributing in any way he can. It's hard to imagine a better role model for our boys than a man who says, "I don't believe in having a bad day."

As for Leo Hamill, Dannaka should count its blessings to have such a coach. He's a rare combination of Major League player and common sense guru. He once told me, "If a person isn't having fun playing baseball, somebody is doing something wrong." Think about the simple wisdom of that for a minute, and how often it's overlooked. He demands that players put their minds, bodies and souls into the game while constantly reminding them, "It's baseball. Not life or death."

That simple truth, in my opinion, leads to the biggest victory the boys walked away with this season: perspective. Perspective is a big word for anyone, not least of all a 12-year-old. Yet you'd be surprised, Leo says, how ready they are to grasp it.

If you followed the district or regional playoffs, or attended any of the state tournament games, chances are you noticed two jerseys hanging on the fence next to the Dannaka dugout— numbers 7 and 10. Those jerseys commemorate two high school players who Leo coached back in Naperville, Illinois. Tragically, the young men were caught in a storm that took their lives. Leo told me he often reminds his Dannaka team how lucky they are to be healthy and playing ball. There are many kids who don't have that same opportunity, so make the most of it and be grateful. But keep the game in perspective, he says.

Few 12-year-old baseball players are lucky enough to encounter coaches and lessons like these. Don't get me wrong, I'm not making these kids out to be saints or unbeatable. I wouldn't be surprised if the favored Des Moines team wins tomorrow. But my concluding thought before a championship game is that it doesn't matter. These boys will be victorious in life, which is the only game, in the end, that matters.

Jerome looked up from his pad, surprised to see Leo. "Oh, hey," Jerome said. "Didn't hear you there."

"Never interrupt a writer in mid-sentence." Leo nodded at the legal pad. "Something for the *Bugle*?"

"It is."

"A *Jerome's Jottings*?" Leo asked.

"Yes."

"I always look forward to them. I wish I could write like that."

"When we give something our heart, and supply sufficient effort, we become good at that thing."

Leo nodded, looking around the field. "Surprised the lights are still on. Drew me in like a moth."

"I think they're wrapping it up. Field looks immaculate for tomorrow."

As was his habit when thinking, Leo pulled off his cap and his hand combed through his hair. He looked at the circular-cut infield grass and the outfield striped with mower lines. "No prettier sight."

"Are you nervous?"

Leo looked at Jerome. "What do you think?"

"I think yes," Jerome said.

Leo inhaled the night air. "That's what makes you a good writer."

"How's that?" Jerome asked.

Leo doffed his cap before putting it back on. "Observant. And perceptive."

SUNDAY

The heat had broken. A patchy overnight rain had left hardly a trace on the ground but had transformed the air. Today's predicted high was 75 degrees, quite a relief from the nineties the boys endured on Friday and Saturday. The gusty winds weren't lost on Leo. He made sure the team's warmup included extra fly balls and pop-ups so the kids wouldn't be surprised by the wind's tricks on the baseball.

It was almost game time. Dannaka remained on the outfield grass after hitting wiffle balls. They went over the signs for the various plays they might deploy. The kids loved it when Leo flashed them signals for backdoor pickoffs, delayed steals, pitchouts, suicide squeeze bunts, first-and-third hijinks and more.

"Ten minutes," Leo hollered, going over his lineup card a final time. "Let's go bond with the baseball."

The boys let out a resounding hoot and hustled to the dugout. The stadium was jammed to capacity, with people standing, too. "Looks like we filled the joint," Pot Roast said. "How many, Math?"

Math looked around the ballpark, estimating people per row, rows per section and sections in the stadium. "Rough calculation, over 500," he said.

Earlier crowds had been sizable, but nothing like this. Many players and parents from eliminated teams attended, along with big turnouts from Des Moines and Dannaka.

The boys made a circle in the infield grass with a bucket of balls in the center. Bonding with the baseball began. They tossed balls from one hand to the other, focused on the red laces. In its own way, this calibrated the hand, the eye and the baseball. Quickly the maneuvers advanced to Harlem Globetrotters-esque displays of dexterity. Tosses behind the back, under a leg, plus solo and group juggling were a big crowd-pleaser.

Leo heard his name shouted out. Doc, standing by the out-of-play fence behind third base, waved him over with unusual urgency. Leo approached. "Heya Doc."

"Sorry to bother you. Have you turned in your lineup card yet?"

Leo pulled it out of his back pocket. "Just about to. What's up?"

Doc leaned closer. "Tom Tink says pencil in his boy. He'll be here. Says he can get you a few outs if you need 'em."

"His wrist is broken."

"Left wrist," Doc said. "His glove hand. It's casted up. Doctor Parten says he really can't hurt anything by pitching with his good arm, just can't do much with the other. Our catcher will have to roll the ball back to the mound. No rules against it. I checked, and talked to the tournament director, too. If you need a couple outs—and I bet you're low on arms after yesterday's extra innings—he might be just the thing, till a runner gets on base. Then you'll have to pull him."

Leo squatted, pulling a piece of grass to chew. "Or when he's due to bat."

"I suppose he could stand in there, hope for a walk. Then you'd pinch run him. One way to keep him in the game."

Nodding, Leo asked, "Do you know when he's due to get here?"

Doc said, "Best guess, right around first pitch. Tom called me before we left the house and said he was just back from the craft shop with a large sewing needle and heavy thread. Said something about his softball mitt—cutting the wrist strap, jerry-rigging some Velcro for the cast. Everyone on the field has to have a glove. Checked that rule, too."

"Hmm," Leo said. "The lineup card would look better with Q-tip's name in it. Possible sub. Why not? I'll mark him in." Leo took a couple quick steps toward the dugout.

"One more thing," Doc added.

"Yeah, sure," Leo said, in a hurry.

Doc waved him in. "I don't want to broadcast this." Leo came to the fence. "About today's game, and Dixon." Doc saw Leo's face tighten. "There's no telling what he might try. God knows, he's capable of anything and he wants that championship trophy in the worst way—if for no other reason than to shove it up our backsides for ousting him."

Leo looked off. "I'll keep my cool, Doc."

"Son," Doc said, waiting for Leo to make eye contact, "my father gave me a good piece of advice a long time ago. Now I'm passing it on. No matter what," he said, "don't get down in the mud with a pig. You both get dirty. And the pig actually likes it."

Leo cracked a half smile. He took a deep breath. Then he nodded. "Time for me to go fry up some bacon."

Doc clapped Leo on the back. "Attaboy."

Dixon, flanked by his captains Billy and shortstop Hud Doran, approached the umpire crew at home plate. Just then a collective cheer came from the Dannaka dugout. Q-tip had arrived, dressed to play, to the delight of his team. Tom Tink winced as the players mobbed his son.

"Careful. The arm," Tom warned. But the players couldn't help themselves. Leo chuckled at the reception.

"Coach," the head umpire barked at the Dannaka dugout. He tapped his watch. "Gotta get the show on the road."

Leo waved. "Okay. Rabbit, Bale and Q-tip, you're our captains." Each boy tossed an arm around the other and followed Leo out onto the field. "Tom," Leo said, turning to his assistant coach. "You too." Tom Tink straightened his hat, tucked in the front of his jersey and jogged to catch up.

Dixon's smirk widened as the Dannaka contingent approach home plate. "You got the whole town there, Coach?"

Leo addressed the head ump. "Sorry about the delay, Blue. A few last-minute adjustments."

Just then it dawned on Dixon. Q-tip was in uniform, apparently ready to play.

"What's he doing here?" Dixon demanded. "Hey ump. A kid can't play with a broken arm."

"Wrist," Q-tip corrected.

Leo spoke up. "No rule against it. We checked with the Little League rules committee and the tournament director.

The head umpire shrugged. "You got him on your lineup card?"

Leo handed his card to the ump. "Yep. One of my subs. Here."

"What kind of a name is *Q-tip*?" the ump asked.

"Take your cap off," Leo instructed the boy.

Q-tip did, revealing a shock of light blond hair topping off his long, thin frame.

"It's what they call me, sir."

Tearing the lineup card out of his book, Leo handed the original to the ump, one copy went to Dixon, one went to the PA announcer and the last copy stayed with Leo. After exchanging lineups and going over the ground rules, it was time for the coin flip.

"Des Moines, you're the higher seed so you get to call it," the ump said, pulling a 50-cent piece out of his pocket.

"My boy'll make the call." Dixon looked at Billy. "Heads," he commanded.

"Call 'er in the air." The ump's hand dipped down before launching upward; an audible ping sang out as the umpire's thumbnail sent the coin into the blue sky, sunlight paddling off each revolution.

"Heads," Billy Dixon said. All eyes traced the trajectory. The 50-cent piece hung in the air as if the baseball gods were manipulating its rotation. The coin landed in the batter's box with a soft thud. Heads it was. Thus beginning a ridiculous streak of good luck for the Des Moines squad.

"We're hitting first," Rabbit told the dugout. Putting their gloves aside, the top of the order made their way to the bat rack.

"Good afternoon, baseball fans." The PA announcer's voice swept through the stadium. "What a humdinger of a day we have for the 1990 12U AAA Iowa Little League championship!"

The crowd, awash in 75-degree sunlight, roared. "I know you're all anxious to get on with the game—especially you players—but first let me introduce our two outstanding teams, Des Moines Black and the Dannaka All-Stars."

A lone voice shouted out from the crowd. "Kick butt, Dannaka!" inciting a stadium-wide cheer. The underdogs had the crowd behind them.

The PA announcer interrupted. "Now, now. We want courtesy and sportsmanship to be our guiding principles, for players and fans alike." The crowd quieted. "All right, with no further ado, let me introduce you to our two best-in-class ball clubs." The teams came out and stood in front of their dugouts.

The announcer found his two lineup cards under a list of tournament sponsors. "First, our neighbors just to the south, the state's number one seed, Des Moines Black." A small contingent of the stadium shouted their support while the rest of the fans politely applauded. "Boys, when your name is announced, identify yourself by stepping forward and tipping your cap. Batting first, at second base, number 13, Teddy Tims. Batting second, in right field, number 2, Lucas McCann. Batting third, playing shortstop, number 20, Hud Doran. Batting fourth, playing first, number 18, Billy Dixon."

The boys continued to raise their caps to the crowd as the announcer eased through the Des Moines lineup. But when it came time for him to introduce the Dannaka players, he stalled. A shuffling of papers was amplified across the stadium, as well as some confused mumbling. Finally the announcer said, "Well … I guess this is it." He chuckled. "In my thirty years behind the mic," his voice rang out, "can't say I've ever seen a lineup card quite like this one." He cleared his throat. "From our neighbors to the southwest, the state's number three seed, the Dannaka All-Stars."

Most of the stadium jumped to their feet, erupting in support, the loudest cheers coming from the players of eliminated teams. Des Moines, not only stacked but arrogant, made it easy for teams to despise them. The announcer spoke through the cheering, slowly extinguishing it.

"Batting first, at second base, number 1 … Runt. Batting second, in left field, number 8 … Rabbit." The announcer continued, introducing Havoc, Rip, Money, Pot Roast, Math, Seeds, Walter, Gramps, Q-tip and Bale. He finished by adding, "And last, but not least, from Dannaka, their loyal mascot, Ike."

A cheer swelled. Many of those in the stands had seen Ike run the bases during opening ceremonies. A chant began. "We want Ike! We want Ike! We want Ike!"

Jess sat on the grassy berm behind third base with Ike securely leashed. But when the pup heard his name, he stood, alert, ears hinged upward, tail wagging. One of the nearby fans said to Jess, "They're asking for a curtain call."

"What?" Jess said.

"They want Ike to make an appearance on the field."

"No," she said. "Really?"

"Listen to the crowd," the fan said, joining the chorus calling for Ike.

Jess shrugged and stood. "You only live once," she said to herself as much as to anyone within earshot. She walked Ike down the berm, through the infield fence. The moment they stepped onto the field, the crowd exploded with applause. Ike, on leash, trotted high-tailed in a tight circle like he was showing at Westminster. Jess raised her Dannaka baseball cap to the crowd.

There was baseball to be played, and Jess knew it. She quickly headed off the field. Ike pulled the other way, wanting to join the boys in front of Dannaka's dugout. That drew a sympathetic aww from the crowd.

"Heya Jess," someone said as she and Ike came through the infield gate. Squinting into the sun, Jess lifted her hand.

"Who's there?" She could only see silhouettes.

"It's us," the voice said. "Nancy." There was a pause. "And Wade."

Jess yanked Ike to improve her vantage point. Sure enough, two rows behind third base sat Nancy and Wade. Jess did a poor job concealing her surprise. "Wow. Great you're here. Must have arrived early for those prime seats."

"You know Wade," Nancy said, patting him affectionately on the knee.

"Wade, how are you?" Jess asked.

Wade grinned. "Good." He glanced at Nancy. "Very good."

The three looked at each other. "Well okay," Jess said. "Nance, we need to catch up."

"It's been too long," they both said at the same time.

"I'll call ya," Nancy said. "Meantime, we'll be cheering hard for Truman. Or Runt, I guess."

Wade chimed in. "I'm sure it's a term of endearment."

Jess was just getting settled back on her seat cushion on the berm when the announcer's voice crackled: "Leading off for Dannaka, number 1, Runt." *Ohmygod,* Jess thought, hoping her butterflies were far worse than anything her son was feeling.

Runt took a few hard practice cuts and made the long walk to home plate. Ambient sounds were muffled as his heart pounded inside his chest. *Deep breaths,* he instructed himself. On the mound, rubbing the baseball, stood the Des Moines ace, Peter Novik. Or as he was better known, Peter Nohit. He had a lights-out arm and pitching guile to match. Runt spat. *He's coming with heaters.*

With one foot in the batter's box, Runt focused on Leo at third who flashed him the swing-away sign. Runt nodded, thinking about the scouting equation that Math had gone over with the team: *He's a 2xF-1C pitcher. Sit on the fastball, lay off the curve until deep in the count.*

Runt's second foot stepped into the batter's box. Muscle memory took over. His knuckles aligned atop the bat, his grip loosened slightly, his hands moved in tiny circles, ready to uncork.

"Play!" the ump bellowed, pointing to the pitcher.

Fastball's coming. Runt, balanced on the balls of his feet, shifted his weight slightly to favor his back foot. His front heel, just off the ground, would set his entire swing in motion: Heel drop triggers hip rotation triggers hands. That was the sequence to get the bat through the ball.

The first pitch of the championship game came at Runt. He was so convinced it would be a fastball, he didn't pick up the spin until it was too late. He had committed, then tried to check his swing, resulting in a pop-up so weakly struck, it rainbowed right back to the pitcher, which he caught with his bare hand just to make a point.

The Des Moines team broke into laughter, as did the crowd. Coach Dixon came out of the dugout and mockingly yelled for his outfielders to back up. That drew more laughter. Runt stood there so stunned by what had just happened, he didn't run out the pop-up. This offended every rule he and the team lived by. Runt dropped his bat and began to run when the ump said, "Hey kid. You're out."

The game of baseball rises and falls on momentum. There was something about Runt's bad start that went through the next two batters like a virus. It was the fastest three outs recorded on Dannaka all season.

Leo and Tom Tink jogged in from their coaching spots and rounded up the team before they went out to play defense. "Well that wasn't how we drew it up." Leo smiled, but he was the only one. "C'mon guys. Relax. Lotta game left. Runt, Rabbit, Havoc, what can you tell us?"

Runt spoke first. "He's not afraid to start you with a curve. Didn't identify. I messed up."

"Me too," Rabbit said. "My plan was to lay off the curve but it looked so juicy."

Havoc added. "I swung at his hot sauce but it wasn't in my Favorite Four. Didn't stick to my plan, either."

Leo tipped his cap back. "Guys. Don't dwell on it. But, but, but," he said with slow emphasis, "trust your plan in the batter's box. Okay? Just like you've been doing all season. Right now we are sitting on fastballs in your Favorite Four. Right?"

"Right," the boys replied weakly.

"Right?" Leo said with vigor.

"RIGHT!" they shouted back.

"Time to play Dannaka defense. We'll be back hitting in no time."

Walter, Dannaka's starting pitcher, was a natural side-armer. Despite being tall, his arms appeared too long for his body. As Leo watched him sling warmup pitches, he remembered nicknaming him after Walter Johnson, a dominant sidewinder from the early 1900s. Hopefully, Leo thought, the original Walter was up there on the big pitching mound in the sky, smiling down on them.

Apparently he wasn't. With two strikes on their leadoff hitter, Walter induced a routine ground ball to the right side of the diamond. Runt ranged over two steps, lowered his glove, but didn't get it all the way down. The ball squirted through his legs.

"No harm," Tom Tink shouted from the dugout. "Let's turn two."

Runt grit his teeth and pounded his mitt. Jess could see him knotting in anger. She burned inside, desperate to help. But there was nothing she could do except watch.

A fan behind her said, "How does anyone not make that play?"

Jess turned around, frosting him with a glare.

Leo clapped his hands from the front step of the dugout. "Okay boys. Let's get him an out."

In Little League baseball, a runner can't steal until the ball crosses home plate, making it a difficult play to pull off unless the pitch is wild. Walter was anything but wild. Nonetheless, the baserunner got in his head. With his focus slightly off, throwing one of his patented sidearmed curveballs, Walter's pitch stayed inside and grazed the batter's jersey. Now there were two on, no out for Des Moines.

The PA announcer's mic clicked on, squealing with feedback. "Batting third, number 20, Hud Doran." The Des Moines crowd jumped to their feet, sensing an early opportunity. Leo looked at Walter, who was staring a hole in the ground. "C'mon Walter. Go get him."

Walter had faced the Doran kid once before, in their pre-season scrimmage. He knew he'd be up there hacking, susceptible to a high fastball. Walter nodded to himself. He'd get him to chase.

The batter did not chase. He looked at four consecutive high fast-balls and took a free pass. Now the bases were juiced for the leading home run hitter of the tournament, Billy Dixon.

"Blue. Time." Leo said to the umpire.

The ump put up both hands. "Time!"

Leo walked slowly to the mound. The infielders started to move in, too. "No," Leo said calmly. "You guys know what to do. Force at any base. Let the ball tell you where to go." Leo met with Walter alone. "How you doing?" He put a hand on the pitcher's shoulder.

Walter pursed his lips. "In a jam, Coach."

Leo smiled. "Ever been in one of those before?"

"Yeah."

"How do you get out of them?"

"One good pitch at a time."

"That's all it takes, Walter. You just had a little bad luck working against you."

Walter nodded, finding a deep breath.

Coach Dixon hollered from the third base coaching box. "Hey Ump. We gonna drink tea or play baseball?"

The ump began his cursory stroll to the mound.

Leo put his other hand on Walter's other shoulder, squared the boy to him and looked him in the eye. "Walter, have fun. Do your best. Let the rest take care of itself. Got it?"

Walter cracked a smile. "Got it."

Leo jogged away from the mound, giving the ump an apprecia-tive nod.

Billy Dixon stood in the batter's box. The bases were loaded, his favorite sight.

"Blood in the water," Coach Dixon yelled to his son.

Spitting into his batting gloves, Billy let the bat handle settle into the crook of his fingers, swinging rhythmically, hips swaying, finding his groove. With each warmup cut, his smile became more prominent.

Walter came at him with a first-pitch curveball. Dixon was waiting for it like Monday's mail. He ripped a screamer to the gap between left and center. When the dust settled, Dixon was on third and Des Moines had plated three.

Walter tried to regroup. He got the next batter to hit a two-hopper to Money at short, but instead of taking the sure out at first he tried to cut down Billy at home. His throw pulled Pot Roast off the plate. Now four were in and a runner stood at first—with no outs. The Des Moines dugout and their fans were ecstatic.

What came next was a blur. A fielder's choice, a bloop single, another hit batter and the bases were loaded, again. Des Moines' number nine hitter, pitcher Peter Novik, stepped up to the plate. His teammates went nuts. Peter had struggled all year with the bat, but it didn't matter; he was on the team for his pitching arm.

Coach Dixon made no attempt to contain his excitement, either. Dannaka was on the ropes, big time. He cupped his hands around his mouth and shouted over the din. "Finish this."

It was a glorious, arcing grand slam. What baseball enthusiasts call a no-doubter. Peter trotted the bases and was mobbed in delirium at home plate. Des Moines was up 8-0. There was just one out. It was time for Leo to apply the only tourniquet he had for such situations.

The umpire granted Leo a timeout as he strode onto the field. "C'mon," he said to Tom Tink and the subs in the dugout. His arm pulled through air. "All of you. Out to the mound."

As Leo got to the pitcher, Walter reached out with the baseball, ready to hand it over. "You hang on to that," Leo said. "Everybody in," he called. Judging by his tone, it sounded like he was summoning them for a picnic. The team gathered on the mound. It was a sullen group. "I don't see a smile among you," Leo said.

"We're getting stomped," Money replied, spitting in the dirt.

Leo put his hands on his knees, bent forward, his eyes scanning the bunch. "I had this teammate in the minors. Everyone called him Brain. Which made no sense to me. I was new on the club and this guy seemed more likely to be called Air Head. Good guy, but really out there." Leo made a circling gesture with his finger near his ear.

"One day," Leo continued conversationally, "we got down big in the first inning. 10-zip. Nothing was going right. Maybe two or three balls were hit hard. The rest were dinks and dunks, errors, walks, he hit a few guys, you name it. The next thing I knew, Brain dropped his glove on the rubber, stepped off the mound and started rolling around on the infield grass. Looked like one of those hot dogs at a convenience store. I was playing third so I walked over to him. 'What's up, Brain?' I said. 'You hurt?' Brain told me he couldn't hear me from way up there so I got down on the grass, too. He said the secret to baseball when things are going bad is to roll in the grass. Grass fixes you. Grass is the life of baseball. When you roll in it, you come back to life."

Leo looked at the boys, who were pulled into the story. In the background Dixon was yelling for the ump to get the game going. "Guys," Leo said, "I'm not going to tell you that Brain had it wrong about grass being the remedy for a patch of bad luck. But what I think really happened when I got down and rolled with Brain was the muscles in my arms and shoulders loosened up. Just like Brain, I tucked my arms under me and rolled and I put them over my head and rolled some more. It felt great. I can only imagine what it did for Brain, whose pitching arm and back had to be tight and needed some adjustment. It also did something to my mind, and maybe that's where Brain got his nickname. The rolling reset my brain. When I got up, I wasn't pissed off any more. Might have been the grass. Might have been the motion. But I got up and felt like the score was nothing-nothing."

An impatient murmur was building in the crowd. It couldn't have been quieter in the circle on the mound. "Ready?" Leo said. The team nodded. "Gloves on the mound." A pile of gloves stacked up on the rubber. "Time to get rolling."

The crowd looked on, gobsmacked, as the Dannaka All-Stars and their two coaches rolled around on the grass. "Arms up high," Leo instructed as they rolled away from the mound. "Arms underneath," he said as they rolled back the other way. They bumped into each other. They inhaled the aroma of grass. Their bodies loosened. They began to laugh.

"What in tarnation is this all about, Coach?"

Leo opened his eyes to see the umpire above him, arms sternly crossed, blocking out the sun. "We're rolling," he said.

"You don't say," the ump replied. "Am I missing something here, or are we trying to play a state championship baseball game?"

Boos rained down from the Des Moines fan base. Coach Dixon ranted about delay of game.

"Okay boys," Leo called out. "Roll it in." Leo sat up. "Be with you in a sec, ump."

The team stood back at their positions, arms loose-hanging, light on the balls of their feet with two additions to the Dannaka uniform: Traces of grass stains on their pants. And smiles under their caps.

Walter quickly dispatched the next two batters: a weak pop-up to Runt and a backward K on a knee-buckling curve. Des Moines had sent 11 batters to the plate in their half of the first. The score was 8-0.

"Rip, Money, Pot Roast," Tom Tink yelled out the batting order. "Let's get the bats going."

Leo said, "Pull it in, guys." The group gathered on the dugout bench, looking to their coach for a spark. "What are the two kinds of energy in the world?" he asked.

"Positive and negative," the boys replied.

Leo nodded slowly. "These are the times," his finger pointing for emphasis, "these are the times that really challenge you to choose positive." All eyes were on Coach. "It's easy when you're up 8-zip. But to choose positive when you're down 8-zip, that's when you got it in here." Leo's finger touched his chest. "*This* is when you really learn what's possible when you choose positive. Are we together on this?"

All heads nodded yes.

"Hands in," Leo said.

The players' hands stacked up.

"Positive on three," Leo said. "One, Two, Three ..."

"POSITIVE!"

Rip drove the second pitch of his at-bat deep to center field. When the Des Moines pitcher saw it come off the bat, he dropped his head. He knew it was a home run. But replacing the muggy heat of the tournament's first two days was a blustery 75-degree afternoon. The wind blew in at a most inopportune time. The Des Moines center fielder, his back pressed to the fence, in the deepest dimension of the ballpark, leaped to make the catch. Almost the entire stadium of fans, standing, had watched the baseball's flight. En masse they went from their tiptoes to slumping back into their seats, capturing precisely how Dannaka was feeling.

"Way to give it a ride," Leo said as Rip curled off the base paths to head for the dugout. The boy didn't throw his helmet. His body stayed erect. He started clapping, laughing as he went.

"That baby's goin' out next time," Rip told his teammates, who greeted him with high-fives.

Money, the shortstop, and Pot Roast, the catcher, also scalded the baseball, but all it got them was a couple of loud outs.

Dannaka had their chatter back as they took the field for the bottom of the second. Walter was still on the hill. He was determined to hold the meat of the batting order in check. Des Moines' shortstop, who walked in the first, was late on a fastball but managed a seeing-eye-single between second and first.

That brought Billy Dixon, their cleanup batter, back to the plate. He was licking his chops after his three-RBI triple in the first inning. Walter knew Dixon would be taking a mighty hack, as did Pot Roast, who waggled four fingers, their sign for the slow, slow yakker. Sure enough, Dixon was way ahead of the off-speed curve, skying an easy pop fly over second base. Runt glided under it, taking a glance at Dixon, who stood at home plate pounding his bat into the ground. A barely visible smile came to Runt's face.

He lifted his glove to catch the ball. At the last second he raised his other hand, like the sun was in his eyes. When the baseball hit the dirt near second, Billy Dixon snapped into a sprint but it was too late.

Runt picked up the ball, stepped on second to force out the runner, then whistled a pea to first, doubling off Dixon by 10 feet.

The crowd roared as Billy Dixon got an earful from his dad, who had grabbed him by the jersey.

"C'mon Dad," his boy responded. "We're up by eight flippin' runs."

Walter went deep in the count with the next batter; he just couldn't get strike three past him. Finally the boy rapped a sharp single to center. The inning wasn't over yet.

Leo conferred with Tom Tink. "I don't think Walter has much left in the tank."

Tom agreed. "He's thrown a lot of pitches in the last two days."

Leo was out of mound visits; one more trip to the hill and Walter would be out of the game. Leo cupped his hands around his mouth. "Get this last out," he told his pitcher. "Then we'll switch it up."

Walter reached back and scraped out what remained of the velocity and courage inside him. He struck out Des Moines' number six hitter on three pitches.

Walter ran off the field, his teammates slapping him on the butt. "Way to get us out of it," Runt told him. Walter slapped Runt on the butt in return. "Sweet move on Dixon. Huge double play."

Math was the leadoff hitter to open the third inning. He gathered the boys together. "Guys, guys," he said excitedly. "I've been tracking this dude," he said of the Des Moines pitcher. "He's throwing us differently. He knows we eat fastballs for lunch. He's leaning hard on his curve. Go up there with a 2xC-1F plan. Sit big time on the deuce. Leave the first-strike fastball alone. I'm even laying off the second-strike fastball. Sound okay, Coach?"

Leo nodded. "Sounds solid, Math. Guys, believe in your plan at the plate. Don't stray."

The first pitch to Math was a get-me-over curve. And was Math ready for it. He ripped it down the line and it kicked around in the left field corner for a stand-up double.

Seeds hit two curves, but both went foul. He worked the count to 3-2. Now he had to swing at a fastball but was still looking for the deuce. He smacked a middle-high fastball deep to right, but the outfielder made a nice running catch.

Next up, Walter didn't chase fastballs, which were out of the strike zone. When he got the hanging curve he was looking for, he banged a single to left, but it was hit too sharply for Dannaka to score. Runners were on first and third, one out, with the top of the order coming up.

"Now batting, number 1, Runt," the PA announcer said, over the excited rumble of the crowd. The fans could feel a slight momentum shift as Dannaka was starting to hit the ball with authority.

Runt stepped into the box, his plan firmly in mind, looking for a hang-it-and-bang-it curve. Unexpectedly, Leo flashed him the safety squeeze bunt sign, sending a jolt through Runt. *Shit*, he thought. *The curveball sucks to bunt, unless I can get a low one.*

The first pitch was a borderline-high curve. "Steerike," the ump called, pumping his right fist.

Runt stepped out of the batter's box, reviewing his plan. *That pitch was begging to get popped up. You can't bunt the high stuff. Look low. C'mon fastball.*

Leo went through his signs, putting the safety squeeze back on. He took a step closer to the baserunner at third. "Still on," he whispered into the helmet ear hole.

The crowd was clapping for Runt as he stepped back in and tapped the plate. Jess pulled Ike onto her lap for support.

Another big curve floated in for strike two. Again, Runt laid off. It was a low-probability pitch for bunting.

"This Runt can't hit," Billy Dixon hollered from his position at first.

The Dannaka dugout jumped up in support. "C'mon Runt," they shouted. "RBI time!"

With two strikes, Runt almost fell over when he saw Leo flash the sign for the safety squeeze again. Bunting with two strikes is high-risk. If Runt didn't get the ball down in fair territory, he'd be out.

"You can do this," Leo said, clapping. "C'mon 1. Stick to your plan."

Runt took a deep breath followed by a few hefty practice swings to better disguise his real intention. *Look for something low. But if it's a big curve, adjust, stay on it and put it in play.*

The pitcher uncorked a fastball, coming in about knee high. To everyone's surprise, Runt squared around. He pushed a perfect bunt inside the third baseline where the catcher and the pitcher simultaneously converged on the ball. They looked at each other, no one called it, and Runt not only had Dannaka's first RBI, he had an infield hit.

"Somebody take charge!" Coach Dixon yelled from the dugout. "C'mon dimwits! Focus!"

The Des Moines pitcher was pissed. A two-strike bunt ruined his shutout. He stomped back onto the mound, glared at Runt on first and promptly airmailed his next pitch over the glove of the catcher, allowing the runners to advance to second and third. His next pitch was a hot one-hopper straight at him that he somehow speared, looked the runner back to third, and then took the sure out at first.

With two outs and both runners in scoring position, Havoc came up and drove a curveball to the gap for a double that plated two more. Suddenly it was 8-3. Much of the grating chatter from the Des Moines side had gone silent.

Rip stepped to the plate. In his last at-bat, the wind had pushed back a sure home run. Coach Dixon decided not to chance it. He signaled for Rip to be intentionally walked. Now he had a force out at any base but home to get out of the inning.

Money didn't stroll to the plate, he swaggered. He lived for this: runners on first and second, the pressure of two outs. He was sitting on a yakker and the curve came as expected. Money didn't miss it. He hit a rope down the third baseline, but the Des Moines infielder made an incredible diving effort. The ball popped out of his glove but rolled toward the bag. The third baseman lunged, picked it up and tagged the base just in front of the runner. Fans groaned and cheered, depending on their allegiances, but they all applauded the fabulous play.

It was another helping of hard luck for Dannaka, but the boys didn't hang their heads. In fact, Havoc, who was out at third, helped the Des Moines infielder to his feet and congratulated him on his highlight-reel play. The team knew they had just knocked around Des Moines's ace for three runs—and were inches away from adding more. Plus, Rip was pitching next inning.

Warming up, standing tall on the mound, Rip was throwing gas. He was ready to face the guys he'd played with last year, most of whom were in awe of him. They knew how dominant he could be, offensively and defensively. Coach Dixon tried to deflate his team's opinion of Rip.

"First, he ain't that good. And second, he's running on fumes 'cause he had to pitch extra innings last night to beat Ames." The Des Moines hitters were chalk-faced. "Just go out there and bust him wide open." The leadoff batter stood in the on-deck circle watching Rip's warmup pitches sizzle across the plate. He tried to spit but his mouth was cotton.

It was three up three down for Des Moines. Rip recorded two strikeouts and induced a harmless dribbler to first for an unassisted putout. Dannaka came racing into the dugout hungry to hit.

The PA system hummed stadium-wide as the announcer clicked on his microphone. Soft clouds pushed by persistent winds occasionally dimmed the sunlight on the field. "I want to take a moment to recognize two of our platinum sponsors who helped support this weekend's event. To the good folks from Ames Auto Body & Repair who like to say, we bend but don't break, and to Lenny's Landscaping who remind all of you, Lenny digs cool landscaping ideas, thank you." The crowd showed their appreciation for the sponsors' support as well as their slogans.

"All righty then," the announcer said. "Fans, hang on to your hats, and not just because it's breezy. We've got a lot of baseball left to play." He shuffled some papers. "Okay, leading off the top of the fourth, the Dannaka catcher, number 11, Pot Roast."

Earlier, while the announcer was busy talking about sponsors, Pot Roast, in the on-deck area, getting loose, squinted in concentration as the Des Moines pitcher warmed up. Pot Roast, like many catchers, was an astute observer of a pitcher's habits. He took one step backward toward his dugout and whispered over his shoulder. "Psst, hey guys. Guys! Listen up, but don't make it look like you're listening."

The team eased closer to the dugout fencing.

"Dingleberry out there is warming up with all curves. Nothing but curves. And he knows I'm watching. He's setting me up." Pot Roast snickered. "So I'm sitting on first-pitch fastball. And … I'm making a call: home run. Remember boys, you heard it here first." Pot Roast eased away from the dugout.

"Oh my golly!" The PA announcer blurted, forgetting he'd left his microphone on. The ball exploded off Pot Roast's bat. There wasn't enough wind in all of Ames to keep that first-pitch fastball in the park. As it went over the fence in left, the baseball was still climbing.

Pot Roast paused in the batter's box, looked at his boys jumping wildly in the dugout and gave them a wink. Then he trotted the bases, preparing for a mugging at home. Math followed with a sharp single to center and that brought Coach Dixon to the mound.

"We give you an 8-0 lead and what do you do with it?" His face was ugly red, his chins and jowls shook in anger. The pitcher dropped his head. "Give me that baseball. You're done." He grabbed the ball. "Idstrom!" he yelled at his left fielder. "Get in here."

The new pitcher promptly gave up a single. Dannaka had something cooking with runners on first and second, and Walter coming up. Feeling confident, Walter had stroked a single back in the third. This time, putting a good swing on the ball, he hit it sharply, but to exactly the wrong spot. Des Moines' third baseman scooped the one-hopper, stepped on the bag and winged it to second for a double play.

Coach Dixon was ecstatic, pulling his cap off, waving it, pumping his fist. "That's my team! That's how it's done! Whoo!"

That brought up the top of the order. Runt came to the plate. He and Math had conferred. They were mostly looking at a fastball pitcher. A 3xF-1C, which meant if he threw four pitches, three would probably be fastballs. Pitchers like this were the reason Leo spent so much time focusing the boys on hitting fastballs. Most big, successful 12-year-olds were too dependent on one pitch because it was enough to win in the younger ranks. But the Dannaka batters, thanks to their secret weapon Kojak, were ready for the heat.

The first fastball to Runt was high.

"Good discipline," Leo barked from third. He said no more. He didn't over-coach nor did he remind Runt what part of the strike zone to attack. Runt knew where his Favorite Four were located.

The second pitch was right where Runt wanted it, but he fouled it straight back. He cursed under his breath. That was his pitch.

"Two down," Leo shouted across the infield to the runner on first. "You're all wheels on contact."

The pitcher spun a curve, but Runt identified it early and was able to hold up as the ball dove into the dirt. The runner at first took a few hard steps, looking to advance, but the catcher made a nice block, keeping the ball in front.

Leo cupped his hands around his mouth. "Way to be ready," he yelled to his runner. "Look for those dirty balls, right?"

The next pitch was a fastball that Runt didn't miss. The right fielder, playing shallow on Coach Dixon's instructions, spun as Runt's line drive rocketed over his head.

Leo pinwheeled his arm. Walter rounded second, sprinting for third. Knowing it would take a perfect relay from right field to second to home, Leo sent Walter, who flew around third and dug for the plate.

When the cloud of dust settled, Walter was out. It was a bang-bang play that could have gone either way. *Where are the baseball gods?* Leo thought, watching Des Moines celebrate yet another miraculous exit from an inning. He laced his fingers together and let his palms come to rest on the top of his cap. *Deep breath.* He spat out a sunflower seed shell and watched it momentarily ride the wind, landing squarely on the white third baseline. A good omen.

Barn Burner

In a six-inning game, teams cross the halfway point of the contest in the fourth. The score was 8-4. The Dannaka All-Stars had cut Des Moines Black's lead in half. But the home team, Des Moines, still had their fourth inning at-bats to go. And the top of the order was coming up.

"Huge inning," Tom Tink said. The team had gathered around him, upon Tom's urging. He was quite excited. He was very proud of the way the team had responded to a crushing first inning. He was itching to fire the team up. "Remember guys," Tom said, scanning their eyes. "It's always darkest before it gets totally black."

The boys' brows furrowed, staring blankly: an expression often present when Tom unleashed a Tomifesto. Q-tip interrupted. "Dad, that's not how it goes."

"Yeah it is."

Q-tip continued. "It's always darkest before *the dawn*—that way it's positive."

Runt added. "Instead of a kick in the nut cup."

Tom's eyes brightened and his nostrils flared. "No no. Wait. Don't you get it? Darkest before it gets totally black. You know. As in Des Moines Black? As in we're totally going to get Black. You know, like win. Don't you see?" His eyes implored.

"Oh … YEAH," Money said with an exaggerated nod, hoping to encourage the group to follow suit so they could move on.

"OHHH," the team said as if a giant light bulb just went on in the dugout. "Totally get Black. Yeah."

"Good pep talk, Coach," Havoc said, hustling out of the dugout. Usually he was the last guy on the field.

Rip threw his warmup pitches, doing his best to disguise a sore elbow. The team needed him, here and now. He would push through.

Des Moines' leadoff batter sliced a single that dropped in front of Seeds in right field. It wasn't hit well but it found the grass. Had the ball been struck a little better it would have been an easy out.

Rip stepped off the mound, but instead of pounding his glove, his mind went to a positive place. *Lucky hit. We all get a few of those. Just bear down and get the next guy.*

Rip didn't waste any time on the next batter. Curveball, fastball, changeup and he had a strikeout for the inning's first out.

The next batter, shortstop Hud Doran, was a notoriously tough out. He worked the count full and then fouled off three two-strike pitches. Rip wiped his brow and peered in to his catcher for the sign. Pot Roast put down one finger and then pointed up with his thumb, the sign for high cheese. Rip shook him off. Pot Roast asked for the curve. Rip's arm was hurting too badly to snap off a good hook, so he shook him off again. They settled on a changeup.

Rip came aggressively out of his windup, striding hard off the pitching rubber, his body selling the notion that he was uncorking a fastball. The batter was fooled, swinging hard, well out in front of the off-speed pitch. Now there were two outs. But Rip wasn't out of the woods yet. With the leadoff batter still on first, Billy Dixon strolled to the plate.

The Des Moines fans jumped to their feet. Billy had an earlier three-run triple. They were hungry for more.

"Jack one, Billy," one of the moms yelled from the stands.

Billy, in exaggerated fashion, blew a kiss to the crowd, who ate it up. Then he dug in the batter's box, took a few practice swings, waggling his hips, finding a rhythm.

Rip's first pitch was a wild curveball that Pot Roast somehow snared, keeping the runner at first. Leo saw Rip wince and quickly called for timeout. Jogging to the mound, Leo put his hand on the boy's shoulder.

"I'm okay, Coach," Rip said before Leo could get a word in.

"Look at me," Leo said. "Rip."

The pitcher looked up at his coach.

"How bad is it?" Leo asked.

"I can get one last out. But no more curves."

"Pot Roast," Leo hollered to his catcher, signaling for him to join them on the mound. Pot Roast jogged out.

"C'mon Blue," Dixon complained from the coaching box at third. "Really? Another tea party?"

"Changeup, changeup, fastball," Leo said to the batterymates. "That work for you, Rip?" Rip nodded. "Pot Roast?"

"Yeah. Good call," the catcher replied.

"Finally," Dixon said, exasperated, as the catcher and pitcher settled in for the next pitch.

"Play!" the ump shouted, pointing to the mound.

Billy Dixon jumped on the first changeup he saw, which hung up in the strike zone. His line drive scorched over Money's head at short. With two outs, the runner on first was going on contact. Now Des Moines had guys on first and third.

Leo looked out to the mound at Rip. He was going to pull him.

Rip put up one finger. Most would think he meant "Give me one more batter, Coach." Unless you knew the Dannaka playbook.

Rip's one finger remained up until his catcher and first baseman saw it and confirmed it by nodding. "One more," Rip said to his infield, still holding up one finger. Now they were in on it, too.

Whether it was the countless times they had practiced this play or if the baseball gods had finally arrived in the Dannaka section of the stadium, who's to say. But the back-door pickoff worked to perfection. The Dannaka first baseman played in front of the bag, which Billy Dixon assumed was just stupid positioning with two outs. Rip purposely threw his fastball high and outside to the right-handed batter. Runt, playing a deep second base on the fringe of the outfield grass, snuck around the back of Billy Dixon, who took a big lead off first after the pitch crossed home plate. Pot Roast caught the pitchout and rifled a throw to first just as Runt arrived at the bag. Billy Dixon, looking at the first baseman in front of him, was flummoxed. Until

Runt slapped a tag on him and Dannaka was out of the inning.

Coach Dixon was frothing in the Des Moines dugout. He said he'd never seen a bigger bunch of losers in his life. They were handed this game on a silver platter, he said, and now they were taking a shit on it. He was especially hard on his boy, Billy. With every foul word out of the coach's mouth, the team's muscles tightened a notch.

"Rabbit, Havoc, Rip," Tom Tink yelled out the batting order. He added a little rhyme, "8-4, time to score."

"Actually, it's party time," Havoc said. The dugout was abuzz. The backdoor pickoff put a jolt in the team.

Rabbit turned a fastball around for a single that nearly took the pitcher's head off, known as a chuck and duck. Havoc banged a laser shot off the fence for a double. With runners on second and third, with most of the crowd on their feet, with everyone sensing that to blink was to risk missing something magical, Rip put the purest swing on a pitch, starting low, ending high, launching the ball over the center field fence.

"HOLY CRAPOLY!" Runt screamed, jumping into Math's arms. Bedlam broke out in the Dannaka dugout. Water bottles flew through the air. Sunflower seeds sprayed like champagne. A tangle of bodies spilled out of the narrow dugout door, running to mob Rip as he crossed home plate.

It was the loudest the stadium had been all afternoon. Cheers showered down on the diamond. Leo, standing in the third base coaching box, had the best vantage point in the park. The smile on Rip's face as he trotted toward third to make the turn for home was like none other. Pure baseball.

Des Moines turned a tough double play followed by a lineout to second to escape the inning, clinging to a one-run lead.

Leo asked Tom Tink for the third and last time. Tom was sure. Q-tip warmed up with no pain. He was good to pitch, cast and all. "You're in," Leo said. Q-tip didn't wait around for Coach to change his mind. His long legs strode straight for the pitching rubber.

"Pot Roast," Leo said. "Watch him. If you think he's hurting or something's not right, take a stroll to the mound. I'll come out and get him."

Pot Roast nodded, his mask tilted up.

"And hey, how are you doing back there?" Leo looked at his catcher. "Lots of innings squatting in the sun."

"Best seat in the house, Coach." Sweat streaked Pot Roast's face.

Leo shook his head and chuckled. "You are a dirtbag extraordinaire." For a catcher, there was no higher praise.

Bottom of the fifth. Dixon watched Q-tip throw his eight warm-up pitches. Every ball had to be rolled back to him at the mound. An incredulous undertone swelled from the crowd.

"This is wrong," one Des Moines fan shouted.

"A disgrace," shouted another.

A chorus of boos followed.

The PA announcer got on the air. "Folks. Now folks, please. I've got a note right here from the tournament director. Says there's nothing in the rules on how the catcher returns the baseball to the pitcher. Let's let the kids play baseball."

"This ain't baseball," a Des Moines parent blared.

"The rules say it is," the PA announcer said sharply. "And anyone who doesn't follow the code of conduct will be escorted from the stadium."

When Q-tip had had the bone set in his wrist, when he flashed on how he and Rabbit were purposely knocked off their feet, one thought dried his tears: *The next time I get a chance to pitch against Des Moines, I'm going to drill the first batter. Revenge pitch.*

Now he stood on the mound, in the championship game, a place he'd feared had been stolen from him. He gripped the baseball knowing he could throw it as hard as anyone his age in the state.

Pot Roast put down one finger, tapping the inside of his leg. Fastball inside.

Q-tip nodded, glaring in at a batter who looked like he'd rather be somewhere else.

After a big, easy windup, Q-tip pivoted his back foot on the rubber, lifted his front leg, coiled his body, rocked and drove his front leg toward the batter, his arm whipping over the top, releasing the ball out in front. The baseball was on the batter before he could react.

"STEErike!" the ump shouted. Q-Tip had decided to make his revenge pitch an unhittable fastball.

Strikeout swinging, routine 6-3 groundout, strikeout looking. The only thing that didn't go quickly in the last half of the fifth was the ball as it was rolled from home to the mound. All baseballs traveling the other direction had plenty of juice on them.

Down 8-7, top of the sixth, Dannaka had three outs remaining unless they tied the game and it went into extra innings. Leo called the team in. The boys made a circle, throwing their arms over each other's shoulders, swaying. "Well men," Leo started, "here we are." He smiled at the group. "Is this the best, or what?"

The guys hollered in agreement.

Leo tipped back the bill of his cap, nodding his head. "I'm glad I'm in this dugout right now and not that one." Leo pointed to the Des Moines side of the field. "We've outhit them by what, Bale?"

Bale looked at the book. "Twelve to eight. And we've gone yard two times. Should have been three."

Leo's eyes sparkled. "I would *not* want to be Des Moines right now. Know why?"

"Because Dannaka is coming," Money said.

Leo continued, call-and-response, like a Baptist minister. "Dannaka is coming."

The team cheered.

"I would *not* want to be Des Moines right now," Leo said mischievously. "Know why?"

"Because Dannaka is driving the bus," Q-tip said.

"Dannaka is driving the bus," Leo replied.

The team hooted.

"I would *not* want to be Des Moines right now. Know why?" Leo looked at the boys, rocking, locked together as a unit, bathing in baseball.

"Because the genie is out of the bottle," Runt exclaimed.

"The genie is out of the bottle!" Leo threw his hands above his head like he'd been touched by the spirit. The team hopped and hooted, tingling with positive vibes. They were ready for the top of the sixth.

"Ladies and gentlemen," the PA announcer said, "we got a barn burner going. As we head into our last inning, Dannaka comes to bat trailing 8-7." He announced the leadoff batter just as Seeds stepped to the plate with what looked like a giant chaw of tobacco in his cheek. He spat out a few sunflower seed shells and took three easy practice cuts.

"Stay hot," Leo said. Seeds nodded at his coach; he had a single his last time up. The pitcher got ahead with two quick strikes, but Seeds choked up, fought off several borderline-strike pitches until he finally got a high fastball that he squared-up and laced to center for a single. The Des Moines pitcher stomped off the mound. He had the leadoff batter in the final inning and he let him wriggle off the hook.

Walter was next. He got just enough of an inside curveball to drop a dead quail over the head of the third baseman. Dannaka had runners on first and second, no outs, with the top of the order coming up.

Runt drew a big cheer as he was announced. He was two-for-three on the day with a double and an RBI. He'd come a long way since opening the first inning with a weak pop-out and then an error through the wickets. Baseball rewards the resilient.

Runt looked at Leo. With runners on first and second, no outs, down by one, everyone knew what play was on. Leo flashed him the bunt sign. It was time to get those runners into scoring position.

Stay away from the high one, Runt thought as he squared early to bunt. The Des Moines team hollered BUNT! as the first baseman charged and the third baseman stayed back in case there was a play at his base.

The pitcher threw a high fastball hoping to induce a pop-up. Runt pulled the bat back for ball one.

Pivoting one foot out of the batter's box, Runt confirmed the bunt sign from Leo before stepping back in. Again, he squared, this time getting a pitch low and away, a perfect opportunity for a left-handed batter to push the ball down the third baseline.

It was a good bunt, but the pitcher made an outstanding play, charging, barehanding the ball and just nipping Runt at first. The Dannaka dugout emptied, storming Runt with high-fives. He had done his job. One baserunner now stood at second. And the tying run was 60 feet from home.

Rabbit took a deep breath, knocked the donut off his bat and strode for the batter's box. Beyond the intense pressure of the moment, he felt something more. He knew all eyes were on him. He wasn't just another white kid playing baseball. He and his twin brother had heard the names and the put-downs: *Hey Taco, why don't you play baseball in a sombrero? Do you know where your sister is, because my friends sure do.* Being the only Hispanics in a nearly all-white rural baseball district wasn't easy.

Choose positive, Rabbit thought as he looked at Seeds standing at third. *Just hit a fly ball deep enough and a run scores.*

Rabbit swung and missed badly at the first pitch, a curve.

"He's just a wetback," Billy Dixon said from his position at first.

The umpire flinched like he'd been stung by a bee. "Time!" he shouted, hopping out from behind the plate and pulling off his mask. "What did you just say?"

Billy Dixon looked the ump in the eye. "I said he's just a weak bat."

The umpire held the boy in his eyes. "That better have been what you said."

With the crowd noise, Leo couldn't hear the exchange from third base. He jogged in a few steps toward the umpire. "What's up, Blue?" he asked.

The umpire put his mask back on. "Just a misunderstanding."

Leo looked at Rabbit. "Stick to your plan. You got this."

Rabbit nodded, knowing a first-pitch curve was not what he wanted to be swinging at.

The pitcher tried two more curveballs, both in the same spot. Rabbit let them go for balls. Then the pitcher grooved a fastball and Rabbit smoked it. The center fielder streaked for the ball, reaching out, making a tough running grab. Seeds stayed on the bag at third until he saw the catch, then he tagged up and bolted for home. Making a mental mistake, the center fielder pivoted and attempted to throw the runner out at home. Seeds easily beat the throw, tying the score at 8-8. And the long throw to the plate let Walter tag up from second and gain third. Celebrations at home plate and in the stands erupted, but were cut short.

Coach Dixon sprang out of the dugout, volcanic. Despite the center fielder's fine running catch, despite the fact that 12-year-olds sometimes try to do too much on the baseball diamond, he began to scream at his outfielder. Dixon screamed and screamed and screamed, gesticulating wildly, spewing spittle, stamping his feet, hurling expletives, pounding his fist in his hand, stunning everyone stock-still as he raged on.

There was one in the stadium who had heard enough.

Ike bolted off Jess's lap. As he ran, the red leash by Jess's foot uncurled in a blur. She grabbed for the hand loop, only to get grass.

Racing down the grassy berm, Ike soon had his muzzle pushed against the infield fence, paws jabbing the steel wire. He let loose deep, guttural barks—like Jess had only heard from him once before. With unrelenting energy, barking and barking and barking and barking, not twenty feet from the screaming coach, Ike, it seemed, had lost his mind. Dixon, his voice finally stifled by the dog's cannon fire, looked over his shoulder. Ike delivered two more sharp barks. Then, quiet.

"Why doesn't somebody tell that thing to shut up," Dixon said, walking back toward his dugout.

"Why don't you shut up," a voice echoed out.

The crowd gasped, craning their necks, looking for the source of the rebuttal. Jess stood up, brushed grass off her shorts and walked down to the fence to get her exhausted pup. Whether they were recognizing her or the pup, it made little difference. The crowd joined together in applause.

"All right. Folks? All right. Please." The PA announcer tried to rein the game back in. "Never in my life," he muttered. "Let's get back to baseball." The crowd cheered.

With two outs, a runner on third and the game tied, Havoc adjusted his batting helmet. He looked at Leo coaching at third for the sign.

"Blue," Leo said. "Time?"

The umpire's body language said, are you kidding me? He removed his mask. "Make it quick, Coach." Then he issued timeout.

Havoc jogged out to confer with Leo.

"You ready for primetime?" Leo said.

"Always," Havoc replied.

"If you get on base, do your thing."

Havoc's eyes brightened. "For real, Coach?"

"You're on your own. Let it happen."

Havoc flashed a daring grin. "This is gonna be good."

Six pitches later, Havoc worked a walk. As he jogged to first, fully aware that the go-ahead run was on third, *and* that there were two outs, he shrugged. *No guts, no glory.* Havoc started sprinting 10 steps before reaching first and took a hard turn for second. He didn't slow down.

"He's going!" the Des Moines shortstop screamed out.

With the baseball back from the catcher, the pitcher was thinking about his next batter. When he heard the alarm shouted out, he looked up, saw Havoc turn and wheel toward second. He took the bait.

The pitcher ran toward Havoc, who slammed on the brakes and turned back toward first. The pitcher threw the ball to the first baseman. Havoc was caught in a pickle, exactly as planned. As he ran toward second, Havoc glanced to third, where Walter started to inch closer to home. The Dannaka Pickle Play was on. As soon as the ball gets released to second, the runner from third breaks for home.

When the ball was thrown to the second baseman everyone started screaming HOME! HOME! HOME! The second baseman momentarily took his eye off the ball. That's all it took. The baseball glanced off his glove and rolled into the outfield.

Walter slid across home scoring the go-ahead run. A huge roar went up from the crowd, which Havoc never heard. He was churning for third. The center fielder picked up the baseball and rifled it to the third baseman. He had Havoc dead to rights. Havoc's cleats slid to a stop. He headed back toward second. Once again, in a pickle.

Back and forth the ball went, Havoc went, the crowd's eyes went. Havoc was tiring as Des Moines executed perfectly, rotating in new players to bookend the pickle.

Finally Havoc went all or nothing for third base, faking outside and taking an inside route to the bag. With the ball in his glove, the Des Moines infielder got twisted up, swiping at Havoc.

Havoc went headfirst into the bag. There was a moment of suspended time.

"SAFE!" The ump's arms scissored. "You missed the tag."

"I got him!" the infielder insisted.

Dixon came running across the diamond. The infield ump who made the call crossed his arms. There was also an umpire behind home plate. "Ask for help," Dixon insisted. "Ask him what he saw." Dixon pointed to the home plate ump.

Leo had seen what happened. He had the perfect vantage point. The umpires quickly conferred and the home plate umpire would not overturn the ruling on the field. He didn't see anything definitive from where he was positioned. "Safe!" he shouted.

As the Dannaka team celebrated and Dixon ranted, Havoc caught his breath. Wiping the infield dirt off his jersey and pants, he confided in Leo.

"He got me coach," Havoc whispered.

"I know," Leo said. "I saw it."

They looked at one another.

"What should I do?" Havoc's face was tight, sweat streaming down. He wiped it with his jersey sleeve.

"What do you think you should do?" Leo asked.

"Tell."

Leo looked at him. "I'm proud of you." He put his hand on Havoc's shoulder and nodded. "Really proud."

Havoc went to the umpires and told the truth. He'd been tagged out by the Des Moines third baseman. Suddenly the home plate umpire put one hand on Havoc's back, and with the other, slashed down, signaling he was out. Confusion bordering on chaos ensued. The umpire wrote a note and gave it to Tom Tink, who raced it up the stadium steps to the PA announcer.

"Fans," the announcer's voice called out over the crowd. "Ladies and gentlemen. Please."

The crowd continued to buzz.

"I have a note here that explains everything, if you'll just give me your attention."

Silence ensued.

"Thank you," he said. "The Dannaka baserunner on third, despite being called safe, went to the umpires and told them he had been tagged. That's why he was ruled out. The boy stepped up and told the truth. Son, let me be the first to congratulate you." The announcer and the crowd began to applaud. One by one, they rose to their feet. "We have seen the definition of sportsmanship here today and have been reminded that it's never the wrong time to do the right thing."

Havoc got stormed by his teammates who, after leaving his hair and uniform rearranged, said that was the best display of base running he had put on all year.

Exhausted themselves, the crowd settled back in their seats as the team gathered around Leo before taking the field for the last half of the final inning. Leo could not have been prouder. "Hands in," he said. The team's hands stacked one upon the other. "Every Goliath," he said, "eventually meets their David." Leo's eyebrows raised as he cocked his head. "The time is now."

The boys ran to their positions, their feet hardly touching the ground. With the score 9-8, Dannaka was three outs away from a state championship.

In baseball, three outs can be an eternity.

THE DAZZLER

Q-tip had taken his warm-up pitches. He stood on the mound and adjusted the makeshift baseball glove on his cast. Tugging his cap, he peered in at Des Moines' eighth batter in the lineup, who dug in at the plate. *I got number eight and number nine. Then it gets tough with the top of the order.*

Pitchers quickly learn that it's a bad idea to look too far ahead of the guy you're facing. It's even worse to take a batter lightly. Q-tip's first pitch was ripped over the third baseman's head for a single.

Tom Tink looked at Leo in the dugout. "Did that just happen? That pitch was right down the middle."

Leo nodded. "We have to pull him. Can't roll the ball back now, they'll steal every base including home."

Tom was still processing what just happened.

"Who do you think," Leo said, going up the dugout steps. He asked the umpire for timeout. "Tom? Who would you throw next?"

Tom snapped out of it. "Runt."

Leo jogged out to the mound. Q-tip had the same baffled look on his face as his dad had back in the dugout.

"Dunno what happened, Coach."

Leo looked at him, patted him on the butt and put his hand out for the baseball. "They're a good team," Leo said. "That's all that happened." Q-tip slowly nodded. "Hey," Leo told the boy. "You got us to this point. With a broken wrist. Keep your head up. It's somebody else's turn now."

Leo turned to second base. "Runt," he said, waving him to the mound. Then he yelled to the dugout. "Gramps. You're at second."

Q-tip walked stiffly toward the dugout but the ovation showered on him slowed his gait and his breathing. He stood there for a second and sucked it in. Then he tipped his cap to the crowd and left the field feeling a lot better.

Runt, on the other hand, thought he might throw up. The walk from second base to the pitching rubber seemed like miles. Leo handed him the baseball. Runt looked up at him, his eyes pleading for sage advice.

"Ice cream for the whole team. Regardless." Leo gave him a firm slap on the butt and walked away.

Runt threw fastballs and curves for his warmup pitches. He didn't show the Dazzler. Pot Roast ran the last pitch back to the mound. "Why didn't you try the knuckleball? Too windy?"

Runt shook his head. "Nope. Wind helps. Let's keep it secret till we need it."

Jess couldn't watch. She got up to leave. Then she sat back down. Twice, she did that. Suddenly Nancy and Wade were at her side. "Need some company?" Nancy asked.

Jess grasped her friend's hand and all but pulled her to the ground. "Thank you," she said. "Yes. Thank you." Nancy and Wade sat on either side of her, making a Jess sandwich.

Runt got two strikes on Des Moines' number nine batter before he left a fastball up that was smashed down the first baseline. It's an impossibly long throw from the right field corner to third base, so when the runner took off from first, smartly, he never slowed at second. The throw from the outfield came in to second to keep the hitter at first. Des Moines, down by one run, had runners on first and third, no outs.

Coach Dixon stood at third base, feeling life come back into him. He'd been sulking since the inning began, but with the tying run right in front of him at third, he was restored. His leadoff hitter strolled to the plate. He'd been on base twice, an error to start the game and a single.

Dixon clapped and said to his batter, "You can hit this Runt."

Leo told the infield to play in. If there was a groundball, they'd cut off the runner at home.

Runt toed the rubber. *He just wants to hit a fly to the outfield. I need to get him under a curve. Pop him up. Keep that runner from tagging.* He looked in for the sign and nodded. He released a slow sweeping curveball and the batter couldn't resist. He took a big swing but hit it off the end of the bat.

The baseball skied toward Rip in center field. He stayed back on the ball, measuring it, positioning himself so when he caught it he would be coming forward, his momentum taking him toward home plate.

Rip caught the ball shoulder-high.

Dixon told his runner on third to tag up and go.

"FOUR! FOUR! FOUR!" the Dannaka infielders yelled.

Rip's momentum powered his body forward. After one fluid crow hop he released the ball with everything he had.

The baseball sailed over the cutoff man's head and beat the runner to the plate by two steps. Pot Roast hardly had to move. He stuck the tag on the sliding player as the umpire's fist swung down like a gavel. "YEROUTTATHERE!"

The crowd roared, on their feet. Pot Roast jumped up and down with the ball. The outfielders ran over to mug Rip.

"HEY, HEY, HEY!" Runt hollered at Pot Roast. "Guy on two! Watch him!"

The runner at second had snuck off the base, but Pot Roast marched at him, with the baseball cocked at his ear. The runner scurried back to the bag.

Runt called for timeout, and everything and everyone settled down. The Dannaka supporters were ecstatic. Not so much on the Des Moines side. "No outs, tying run on third," one player's dad said to another. "Why would he send him?"

"You really want me to answer that?" the second dad said.

"Yeah."

"Because our coach is a half-wit."

There were two outs and the tying run was still in scoring position. Runt took off his cap, wiped the sweat away and spat. *Be careful with this guy. Number two batter. No mistakes.*

Turned out, Runt was too careful. He walked him on four pitches, all of which were outside.

"You got this," Leo yelled from the dugout. "Force at any base but home." Des Moines's next batter stepped in, taking a few vicious practice cuts. "Challenge him," Leo continued. "Break out the Dazzler."

Runt's glove was up by his face as he looked over the webbing for the sign from his catcher. Turning the ball in his fingers, Runt got the knuckleball grip. Something didn't feel right so he waited for the fastball sign, found the two-seam grip and nodded. With good technique on the mound, including a high leg kick and a full stride to home, Runt's fastball was deceptively quick. His first pitch zipped in for strike one.

Let's see if he'll chase. Runt's second pitch was higher, out of the strike zone, but the batter took a big home run cut and missed. Runt was one strike away from game over, one hit away from game tied.

Runt spun the ball in his glove, his fingernails dug into the laces, finding the knuckleball grip. He nodded yes to the catcher's request for the Dazzler. Runt's windup was methodical, leg kick was high and ball release was pure.

The Dazzler came out of his hand with very little rotation. Perfect. It dipped right, then seemed to float on rippled water. The Des Moines batter was frozen, having never seen a ball behave like this. But every Dazzler has a mind of its own and this one decided to skid right until it ran into the arm of the mesmerized batter.

"Take your base!" the ump shouted.

Now the bases were loaded. If that weren't bad enough, Billy Dixon was making his way to the batter's box. Coach Dixon shouted, "Cue the funeral music."

Runt stalked off the mound, upset with himself. *You had him, and you hit him.* The umpire picked the baseball off the ground, got Runt's attention and tossed it to him. Runt looked at the ball and flipped it back to his catcher, asking for a new one. The ump dug out a different baseball, handing it to Pot Roast.

Jogging out with the baseball, Pot Roast stuck it in Runt's glove. "Forget about it." He tipped his mask up onto his helmet.

"I don't know, man," Runt said, rubbing the baseball.

"What do you mean you don't know?"

"Dixon. He's a prick. He's good. He's huge."

"Bigger strike zone," Pot Roast joked, spitting between the gap in his front teeth.

"I'm not kidding," Runt said, obviously intimidated.

Pot Roast's mouth fell open. "Runt, seriously? Don't you get it?"

Runt shook his head no.

"You're bigger than Billy Dixon. Everybody on this team knows you're bigger than Billy Dixon. Hell, I bet most of the fans sitting there waiting for us to stop gabbing know you're bigger than Billy Dixon."

Runt frowned. "Really?"

"Yeah, dummy. Really." Pot Roast pulled his mask down. "Cut him down to size."

Runt's first pitch of the sequence was the Dazzler. Billy Dixon swung so hard and missed so completely it looked like his arms might detach. Pot Roast crisply fired the ball back to the mound. The crowd was standing, loudly in support of Dannaka.

Work fast. Keep him off balance. Runt looked in, quickly okayed the sign and just as he started his windup, Dixon asked for, and was granted, timeout. He stepped out of the box. Squinting, he took a few herculean swings and stepped back in.

Runt's second pitch was a perfect curveball. It came out fast and straight, headed right down the middle of the plate, and then broke at the last minute.

"Ball," the umpire called. He held up one finger on either hand. The count was one and one.

How could he not swing at that? Runt snapped his glove on the ball thrown back by his catcher. *Stay positive.* He looked in for the sign. He shook off the fastball and okayed the changeup. *I'll make it look like the curve I just threw, but I'll throw it slower and for a strike. He'll be way in front.*

Again, Dixon asked for time, stepping out when he got it. He adjusted his batting gloves, looking out past Runt. Then dug back in, banging the outside corner of the plate with the tip of his bat.

Runt's mechanics perfectly hid the changeup. The tempo, the leg kick, the stride, the arm action, nothing was there to tip-off Dixon this pitch would be eight miles per hour slower. But Dixon waited on it. And waited. And then exploded.

The ball rang out as it jumped off the aluminum bat. A missile. It left the infield so fast there was hardly time for the third baseman to turn and track it. It was headed for the left field foul pole when it started to show a hook. Billy Dixon stood at home, leaning to the right, hoping to alter the ball's flight.

The baseball went over the fence on the wrong side of the foul pole, ripping into the trees. Certainly, a dramatic way to get strike two.

The umpire reached into his pouch for a new ball just as Runt asked for time. He signaled for Pot Roast to come out to the mound with the baseball. As his catcher arrived, Runt wiped the sweat off his face, looking down at the ground. "I want you to pretend I'm not saying anything important, okay? Don't react."

"Hey, just a long strike—"

Runt cut him off. "They're stealing signs."

Pot Roast's eyes grew big. "What?"

"Dixon keeps stepping out. Looking down to second. He knows what pitch is coming."

"No wonder," the catcher said.

Runt kept looking at the ground, talking quietly. He pulled Pot Roast in closer. "Put down one finger. Dixon will be expecting a fast-ball. I'm going to throw the Dazzler. Hold your glove in the strike zone. Don't move it. No matter how high or outside the pitch looks, don't move the glove. I want the ball to be perfectly framed so there's no doubt it's strike three."

Pot Roast locked eyes with Runt and nodded. "Don't move the glove."

Some games are earmarked by the baseball gods to be legendary. No one knows why. No one knows when. But they happen. And when you're lucky enough to play in one, or witness one, you don't have enough goosebumps to properly respond to the climactic moment.

One ball. Two strikes. Two outs. No place to put another baserunner. Dannaka ahead by one run. Des Moines is down to their last strike.

Runt, toeing the rubber, glove held nose-high, peering over the webbing, locks onto his target: the catcher's mitt. A single finger drops below it as Pot Roast gives the sign: fastball. Runt nods, his fingernails sinking deep into the laces of the baseball resting in his glove.

Dixon asks for timeout, sweeping at an imaginary bug by his face. Time is granted. Looking out beyond the pitching mound, Dixon sees one finger pressed against the dark uniform of his teammate on second. He steps back in the batter's box. A smile turns up the corners of his mouth.

A rumble from the crowd begins, distant, like an avalanche, getting louder, growing more urgent. "Runt. Runt. Runt. RUNT. RUNT! RUNT!"

Runt's body relaxes, feeling a pathway through the air to his target. He rocks back, his foot pivots on the rubber, his knee lifts high, his hands separate, his back foot pushes, his front foot reaches, his arm hurls forward and releases a baseball propelled by a dream so large, the ball floats and quivers and ignores the existence of gravity.

The Dazzler comes out of Runt's hand pushed by a gust of wind. Surreal, it has no spin. It moves through the air like a hummingbird: hovering, then darting right, hovering, then darting left. Halfway to home, the baseball's flight straightens, as if pulled by a tractor beam. Dixon is snake charmed, unable to move. The pitch is coming in high, at Dixon's chin, a foot above the strike zone. Nonetheless, Pot Roast keeps his catcher's mitt steady, in the middle of the strike zone. The umpire, seeing the ball coming directly at him, begins to duck, tucking his head behind his chest pad. Five feet before the ball arrives at home plate, it's as if gravity is turned back on. The baseball dives. Right into Pot Roast's glove.

The umpire, peeking over the catcher's shoulder, seeing the mitt hasn't moved from the middle of the strike zone, stands tall, turns sideways, and yanks his right arm across his body like he's starting a chain saw.

"STEEERIKE THREE!"

Sky high, the gloves of the Dannaka nine were launched. Pot Roast ran to Runt, picking him up in a giant hug. The players swarmed the mound, leaping on top of one another in a dogpile. Tom Tink, Bale and Q-tip came rushing out of the dugout to join the celebration as the stadium stood and cheered wildly.

Leo remained behind. He approached the two jerseys hanging on the fence. Placing his hands on them, he leaned in. "Jacob," he whispered, "Mikey, we did it. Thanks for being here today." Leo closed his eyes. He soaked it in. "There's a part of you in each of those boys, now and always."

"Coach!" A voice came from the field. "Get out here!"

Leo patted the jerseys, wiped his eyes and jogged out to join his team. The scrum hugged and hollered and held up one finger to the heavens. They were the best 12-year-old baseball team in Iowa.

Runt shouted over the din. "Handshakes. Line it up!" The team left a scattering of gloves and caps on the field and made a line at home plate. The Des Moines players came out of their dugout, red-eyed, sapped, and proceeded to shake hands. There wasn't much more said than "good game," but a few Des Moines players took a moment to congratulate Runt on his Dazzler, Rip on his throw from center field and Havoc for his honesty with the umps.

The crowd stood and cheered. They were worn out, too.

"Coach?" Q-tip asked. "Victory lap?" The Dannaka team looked excitedly at their coach.

"Give it a sec," Leo said, nodding at the Des Moines team, who hadn't finished making it back to their dugout. Leo walked toward the stands. "Line up at home," he said over his shoulder.

At the fence, Leo was inundated by congratulations, throngs of fans clapping, hugging, dancing. His eyes found Jess. He waved her down to the gate.

She and Ike pushed through the crowd. It was slow going, people celebrating, Ike wrapping his leash around legs. Leo lost sight of her. But then, Jess was at the gate.

The boys stood anxiously at home plate, itching for their victory lap.

With a four-foot fence separating them, Leo leaned over, pulled Jess to him, and gave her a long, happy kiss. The crowd applauded. "Couldn't have done it without you."

Jess smiled. "Nah. You just needed my kid."

Leo laughed. "Come here, Ike," he said. The pup strained toward the field as Leo bent down to unclip the leash. "Time for a victory lap."

EPILOGUE

A SIGN

Cleeve Klay was a third-generation sign painter. He still did some painting by hand, including the elegant lettering of the word *Eilleen's* on her bakery's storefront window, and the bold script on the front door of the *Dannaka Bugle*, but most of his work these days was done with lasers on giant automated machines. He did signs in vinyl, metal and plastic. Cleeve could router letters in wood, too, if the job called for it.

He met with Leo and Doc on the outskirts of town next to the city's landmark sign: Welcome to Dannaka. Home of the 1941, 1942 & 1943 State High School Baseball Champions—a sign Cleeve's father had built, lettered and painted back in the day.

Standing on the shoulder of the quiet road, Leo and Doc told Cleeve they were interested in engaging him to make a second sign, to stand beside the one they were looking at, one that proudly announced that Dannaka was now home to the 1990 12U AAA Little League State Champions, as well.

Cleeve scratched his gray goatee. He walked around the old sign, observing and photographing it from different angles. He said what if the new sign was actually an addition to the old one, matching its style and materials. It should complement what's already there, the sign painter said, and thereby make it more complete.

The three men folded their arms and imagined what that might look like. The sign painter's creative juices began flowing. He said the new sign could be round, painted white like a baseball with a hint of red laces to frame the lettering. Leo and Doc liked that thought. They agreed to come to his shop in a week to see some sketches.

Cleeve Klay didn't expect to see Leo enter his shop two days later with an idea about an entirely different sign, one that he wanted to keep secret from Doc. Leo showed Cleeve a piece of paper with a neatly drawn rendering. Leo said this second sign had been vetted and approved by the three members of the Dannaka city council. Cleeve put on his reading glasses, looking at it more closely. He wanted to be sure he understood what Leo was asking for. Two signs in all, Cleeve said. One like they had talked about earlier, and this new one, which should be kept secret. Leo said yep, that was it.

Cleeve told Leo a secret can't stay a secret in a small town for long, so he better get busy. They looked at a calendar as Cleeve chewed on the end of a pencil. Cleeve could have both signs ready by the Saturday before Labor Day. He wrote: 2:00 BASEBALL SIGNS in the space for that calendar day. Leo was instructed on what materials he needed to bring to facilitate the signs' debut, including four bottles of beer. One each for the three men to drink, and the last one to christen the modified sign for good luck, just as his father had done when the original was set in the ground.

Leo rose early on Saturday. He was excited on too many fronts to sleep. In three days, his first school year in a Dannaka classroom would begin. And today, he was going to surprise Doc.

Next to a long-handled spade and a pair of work gloves, Leo loaded 50-pound bags of QUIKRETE into the back of his pickup.

Then he stretched a garden hose from the front of his house to the street and filled five 10-gallon water jugs on loan from the football coach. With everything loaded into the truck bed, he drove out to the edge of town to meet Cleeve Klay, who was boring postholes with a power auger.

They leveled, plumbed and braced the posts, poured in the fast-setting cement and added water. Cleeve confirmed that the posts would be more than ready to be load-bearing when they returned to meet Doc at 2:00. He'd have both signs. He reminded Leo to bring beer, preferably Pabst Blue Ribbon.

With time to pass before 2:00, Leo stacked and restacked syllabus piles, ironed three dress shirts, washed and dried his breakfast dishes and swept the kitchen floor. He decided to go to the baseball fields for a run.

Acorns rattled off the sidewalk as Leo started up the tree-lined street. Squirrels were busy at work. The sky was so blue you'd think it was just repainted.

Leo's neighbor came around the front of his brick Colonial, dragging an extension cord from one hand. He had electric hedge trimmers in the other.

"Heya LeMar," Leo said, startling the man.

"Oh. Hey, Leo. Lost in my thoughts there for a moment."

"Might be the only way to get lost in Dannaka," Leo quipped.

"Say, congrats on taking state. You sure gave it to those Des Moinesers."

"I don't know about that, but we did manage to get one more across the plate."

Two houses down, Gibbs had a new fishing rod and reel. He was casting an orange rubber practice plug.

"How they biting?" Leo asked.

"Almost got me a squirrel," he said loudly, compensating for his poor hearing. "Hey Coach," he continued, "how does it feel to be the luckiest man in Iowa?"

"Not bad," he said.

"My nephew's boy was on that team you beat. Said they had you dead to rights."

LeMar pointed his hedge trimmer at his neighbor. "Leo, don't take any guff from that loud-mouth about luck. Gibbs," he shouted at his neighbor, "Leo's boys whipped 'em good. If you got such a sweet spot for Des Moines, why don't you up and move there?"

"Ah piffle," Gibbs said. "This neighborhood would go to ruin in a week." Then he turned his attention back to his spinning tackle, flipping a cast that tangled in his hedge. "Damn it all," he muttered. "Oh, by the way," he yelled at Leo. "They say they're going to get Dannaka but good next year."

Leo waved and smiled. "I look forward to it." He continued along the shady sidewalk, arms swinging loosely at his sides, his breathing unburdened. The street was quiet except for Leo's two neighbors arguing about the chance of rain for the coming holiday.

Jess stepped softly into her son's room. She clicked off the radio, which played low static. Truman had fallen asleep listening to a Cubs game. The channel came in on clear nights but the signal fell apart during the day.

Ike lifted his head and yawned from the foot of Truman's bed. Jess fought the urge to touch the back of her hand to her son's forehead. She hadn't been doing that lately.

"Go outside?" Jess whispered, tapping her hip. Ike cocked his head, processing her words. The pup stood, stretched and slipped quietly off the bed. "You're sure getting big," she said as they went down the hallway.

Outside in the crisp air, Ike did his business and then hunted the overgrown barn-side grass, nose to the ground. Rabbit scent, most likely. Jess sat on the front stoop, her palm resting flat on the sun-warmed wood next to her. "Hello step," she said. "We have a good day to surprise Doc. Leo's outdone himself." Jess smiled, unencumbered, basking in the Dannaka sunshine. She thought about Leo. And how at the end of some storms, there was a rainbow.

EPILOGUE

Nancy and Wade met at Eilleen's bakery. There was an open table outside and Wade saved it while Nancy went in for two coffees and two croissants. Nancy was the first to admit it. She was addicted to fresh, layered, flaky pastry.

They were more "friends" than "dating," but Nancy saw things in Wade that she could get used to. He was honest. He was considerate. He was a hard worker. He was most things men she had been with weren't. She had underestimated him from afar. The closer she got, the more she appreciated him.

What Wade most admired in Nancy was how she said what she was thinking. A man knew where he stood when he stood next to her. Smitten, Wade was cautious in every way, except matters of the heart.

Doc read the *Bugle*. His breakfast was mostly finished. He had scrambled two eggs and cooked in the last of their garden spinach. Summer was coming to a close. Last night, Margaret had baked a loaf of cinnamon swirl bread. He sipped his coffee with a piece of her dessert toast. If he found anything interesting to read, he'd slice off another.

Later that afternoon, they planned to meet north of town at the Welcome to Dannaka sign. It would be Leo, Cleeve Klay and himself—as far as Doc knew. They would fasten a new sign to the old one to commemorate the town's recent championship. Doc was looking forward to it. He'd always been proud that baseball was woven into the fabric of Dannaka.

Leo sat on the grass of the empty ballfield. T-shirt wet, he had run his laps. Often he chose this spot to stretch, appreciating the symmetry, how the first base bag aligned with the second base bag and then as his sightline continued away, his eyes were taken straight to the town's old silver water tower.

Leo imagined the water tower's stunning vantage point: overlooking the wind-stroked prairie, witnessing countless baseball games, hijinks in the schoolyard, mothers pushing strollers on Main Street, teenagers drinking beer, snowstorms covering dormant fields, funeral processions out to the cemetery. The old water tower had seen it all. Now there was talk of replacing it with something more modern. For the past two winters, during a stretch of below-freezing cold, the tower had frozen and Dannaka's citizens were asked to trickle open one household tap overnight.

"White, green, silver, blue," Leo said, his sightline tracing from the white infield bases to the green outfield to the silver water tower to the blue sky beyond. As he sat, his legs stretched in front of him, palms flat to the ground, Leo closed his eyes but he could still see the path. Fingers spread, Leo felt the grass spring up between them. For most of his twenty-nine years, Leo had lived on grass. The sun's energy was stored in every blade. He was part of it.

Doc's elbow angled out of his open truck window when he rolled in at 2:05. A suspicious look crossed his face. *What's Margaret doing here? And Jerome and Frank? And Jess and Truman and Ike?*

Leo approached the truck. "You look lost," he said.

Doc frowned. "I thought we were putting up a sign."

"We are," Leo told him.

"Must be a helluva big one, all the hands you've rounded up." Pulling onto the shoulder, Doc switched off the ignition and slid out of his truck. Surveying the surroundings, he put his hands on his hips. "What are those posts doing in the ground? Didn't we agree to just cap the original sign?"

Margaret spoke up. "Would you just get over here. Leo's got a surprise for you."

"Surprise," Doc grumbled, his hip biting as he walked down the ditch and up into the field where Dannaka's old sign had stood since his high school days.

Cleeve was leaning on his truck. "Put the little one up first?" he asked Leo.

"Yep," Leo said.

Jerome and Frank helped Cleeve get a sign out of the back of his pickup. It was wrapped in a blanket for transport. Jess pulled Ike out of the way; he was leashed to keep him from chasing after pheasants in the cornfield behind them.

"Who's got the lag screws and the ratchet?" Cleeve asked.

"Here." Truman held them up.

"What do you want me to do?" Doc asked.

"What you're good at," Margaret said, elbowing her husband. "Supervise."

With the pilot holes already drilled, and a few folks holding and a few folks fastening, it was only a matter of minutes until the sign shaped like the top half of a baseball sat affixed to the original Welcome to Dannaka sign.

Cleeve and Leo stood back and looked at their work. "This new sign, sitting flush like that," Cleeve explained, "will take the wind better." Everyone positioned themselves for a good view. The halved white baseball had red laces that arced around type that read:

Home of the Dannaka All-Stars
1990 12U AAA Little League State Champions

"Awe-some," Truman said, sidearming a rock across the highway.

"Very nice," Jess said.

"Doc?" Cleeve said, looking for his opinion.

"Perfect," Doc said, giving a thumbs up. He kicked an 8-by-8 post that stood in the ground next to him. "What's this all about?"

Cleeve said, "That's for a second sign. Something Leo cooked up."

With Frank and Jerome on one end and Cleeve and Leo on the other, they walked a larger sign in while Margaret kept a firm hold on Doc, who'd been made to turn his back to the activities.

"No peeking," Jerome instructed.

"The man has eyes in the back of his head," Frank quipped.

"Almost ready," Leo said, as they held the new sign in position. "Okay, you can turn around."

The oval sign was stained dark cherry with white painted lettering debossed into the wood. The words were enclosed in quotation marks.

"Truman," Leo said, "can you read that for Doc? In case he forgot his cheaters." But Doc needed no such assistance. He stood there, before the sign, looking at a quotation he often repeated, words his father had recited when Doc was a boy.

Truman read aloud. "If you're lucky enough to be in Dannaka, you're lucky enough."

Doc's lip trembled as Margaret took his hand.

"Well I'll be," Doc said quietly.

Leo took a step forward. "When Doc, Jerome and Frank came to Naperville where I was coaching, Doc did most of the talking."

Everyone laughed.

"He told me there was a job he wanted me to consider, in a town—'a fantastical place'—called Dannaka. I remember thinking, this Doc guy is nice enough, but boy does he spread it on thick when he talks about his town."

Truman leaned against his mother and watched as his coach spoke. Ike sat down.

"When Doc left, he gave me his business card. Told me to think his offer over. Said there was a school that could use a good teacher and a ballclub that could use a good coach. Gimme a call, he said.

"As you all know, I fell on some pretty hard times not long after that. Lost myself. Lost my way. One day I was flipping through an old scorebook, and what falls on the floor? Doc's business card. As chance would have it, I flipped it over. Handwritten on the back was a sentence. Eleven words. 'If you're lucky enough to be in Dannaka, you're lucky enough.'" Leo shook his head. "Those words were patient with me. It took me time to appreciate their truth."

Leo looked at Doc. "I thought we might share your words with the world, Doc. Tell visitors coming to town a special place awaits them. And remind the rest of us how lucky we are."

Just then, Ray Mattson and Edda, his wife of 57 years, drove up in their Buick. Ray stopped in the middle of the road, putting down the window.

"Any trouble here?" Ray asked.

Doc approached the car saying everything was fine. "How are you, Edda? Won't ask about Ray. He's always complaining."

Edda said she was good as can be.

Ray pointed with his pipe. "What are the boys handling there, Doc?"

"It's a sign."

"Well I can see that." Ray knocked the old tobacco out of the bowl. "Stand aside already so I can have a look."

The elderly couple took a moment, reading.

Edda giggled. "I like it."

Ray's eyes twinkled. "Sure enough."

"You coming uptown for the picnic Monday?" Doc asked.

"Wouldn't miss it," Edda said.

"Bringing your potato salad?" Doc's eyebrows raised hopefully.

Edda said she was.

"Ray, bring those dollars you got off me in horseshoes. I'll be taking them back."

"So you say."

"All right then," Doc said.

"All right then," Ray replied.

Tooting the horn twice, Ray took Edda's hand in his and eased his way toward town.

Leo walked over to Jess, Truman and Ike, who were backlit by the sun. "Maybe once we get that sign up," Leo said, "if we're really lucky, your mom will hit us grounders."

READERS' COMMENTS

Readers value what other readers have to say about a book—as do I. While *Runt* is still fresh in your mind, please go to **fivefriendsbooks.com** and share your thoughts on this novel in the Readers' Comments section. Thanks.

ACKNOWLEDGMENTS

Beginning with my wife, Kelly, I'd like to thank all the readers ~~that~~ who took on these pages before they went to print, making suggestions and catching typos like Willie Mays caught baseballs at the Polo Grounds. I'd also like to acknowledge all the kids I've coached over the years—including my two sons. It has been a delight to watch you grow into fine young men. You will be the next coaches. And you'll be great.